IN THE GARDEN OF STONE

In the
GARDEN
of
STONE

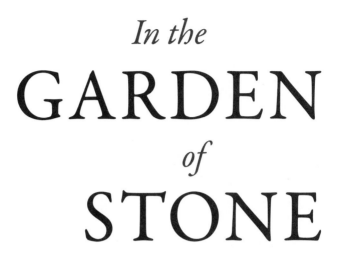

a novel by

SUSAN TEKULVE

HUB CITY PRESS
SPARTANBURG, SC

First printing, May 2013

Cover and book design: Emily Louise Smith
Proofreaders: Megan DeMoss, Emily Harbin,
Jill McBurney, and Lyn Riddle
Cover art from
    "American Moths," *Our Wonder World:*
    A Library of Knowledge. 1914. Picture
    Collection, The New York Public Library,
    Astor, Lenox and Tilden Foundations.
    "Fournier, after Émile T. Blanchard. Insectes:
    Hyménoptères, pl. 1," *Dictionnaire universel*
    d'histoire naturelle. 1841–49. Engraving. Picture
    Collection, The New York Public Library,
    Astor, Lenox and Tilden Foundations.
    Background ©iStockphoto.com / Andrea
    Gingerich

Although the town of War did exist, all characters
and events in this novel are entirely the inventions
of the author.

Library of Congress
Cataloging-in-Publication Data

Tekulve, Susan, 1967–
In the Garden of Stone / Susan Tekulve.
pages cm
ISBN 978-1-891885-21-1
(trade paper : alk. paper)
1. Appalachian Region—History—20th
    century—Fiction.
2. Mountain life—Virginia—Fiction.
3. Virginia, Southwest—20th century—
    Fiction.
4. Domestic fiction.
5. Historical fiction. gsafd
I. Title.
PS3620.E4385I5 2013
813'.6—dc23
2012043391

Support for the South Carolina
First Novel Prize is provided by
the Phifer Johnson Foundation
of Spartanburg, SC, and the
South Carolina Arts Commission.

186 W. Main Street
Spartanburg, SC 29306
864.577.9349
www.hubcity.org

For Mary Mulkey (1945–2005)
Whose quiet voice led me all the way through this tale

 PART ONE

❀ Emma, 1924

Washday

ON MONDAY, WASHDAY, the two boys standing outside the white frame house looked like wizened old men. They're old enough to stop speeding mine cars with wooden sprags, Emma thought. Old enough to chew their daddy's tobacco, they stood in the middle of the dirt road, their slate eyes searching for her inside her family's front window. The taller one had burned a black "Made in Poland" tattoo into his right forearm. The shorter one lacked a forefinger and thumb on his sooty left hand.

"Go stand in the window," Emma's mother said. "At least let them get a look at you."

"It's just a couple of spraggers," Emma said. "They should be at work."

"Maybe they're still in school." Her mother frowned, for a girl should be seen and not heard. But Emma was sixteen, old enough to work like a woman alongside her mother and speak her mind.

"They're too old for school," she said.

Turning away from the boys' longing eyes, Emma followed her mother out to the crumbling brick oven beside the rusted train tracks to boil water for the washing. It was late August, a cool morning. The red rising sun burned the dingy fog above the coal camp until the narrow sky turned indigo, the color of birdhouses behind the Poles' and Italians' houses down in the foreign place. Emma poured boiling water into the wooden tub as her mother tied ragweed into a handkerchief, dropped it down into the water, stirred in her father's and brothers' blackened work shirts. When her mother lifted them out with a broom handle, the shirts glowed white above the deep green water. Emma carried the wet bundles to the line strung between the sugar maple and hemlock. Warm and heavy in her arms, the clean clothes steamed and soaked the front of her dress.

She wished it was Wednesday, baking day, when the smell of bread filled the hollow, rising all the way up to the church cemetery on the ridge above the camp, and Emma's mother sent her down to the foreign place to help her Aunt Maria with the baking. When she was a little girl, Emma prayed for an older sister, and secretly she believed that her father's youngest sister was the answer to her impossible prayer. Maria kissed Emma on both cheeks, called her "Bella," making her feel shy and pretty. In her far-away accent, Maria gently bossed her around, teaching her how to stuff zucchini flowers with homemade ricotta and fry them in the skillet. In spring, Maria made rose hip pastries that tasted like perfume and melted against the tongue. In summer, Maria refused to make the heavenly pastries, claiming her hands were too hot for the delicate dough. Instead, she taught Emma to hunt for skullcap on the shale barrens beside the house, claiming the rugged landscape reminded her of Sicily. Believing the skullcap relieved nervousness and melancholy, she added it to the bread flour, extending it, making twelve loaves instead of ten.

Maria never wrote down any of her recipes. She measured out ingredients with a hand or fist. When she asked Emma to add flour, she said, "Quantobasta," as much as is enough.

"Enough for what?" Emma said.

"Enough for it to feel as it should."

"How much water then?"

"It is a dry day. Your flour may want more water."

Maria stuck a piece of paper into the wood oven, and when it came out the color of chestnuts, she put the bread in to bake. She drenched a slice from the first baked loaf with olive oil brought over by a brother who ran a longshore ship from the Bay of Naples, salted it, and gave it to Emma. The herbed bread sank like a stone in Emma's stomach, making her head spin, making her forget all hunger for days. Maria sold her bread to the single miners, made sure the newest schoolteacher got her share, gave away slices sprinkled with sugar to the Italian children who hung over her fence. Once a month, Maria sent Emma down to stop the train and trade bread for ice and lemons with the Norfolk and Western man.

"I'll give you the ice if you tell me your name," he'd said, the first time they met, and when she replied, "Tell me your name first," he'd teased, "My name's Caleb Sypher. I'll bet you loved ciphering in school. Matter of fact, I'll bet you're smart enough to be the schoolteacher down here." Emma had blushed, her sweaty hands melting the ice block down to half on the way back to her aunt's house. After the baking was done, Maria squeezed lemons over the ice and wild stevia, making lemonade that was cold, grassy, and sweet.

But it was still washday, and Emma's mother's face pinched over the dirty wash water cooling in the tub. Her slender, piano player fingers were chapped, red and knobby, her stiff thumbs turning inward with rheumatism. Emma had been wondering lately when her own hands would look this old. Her fingers had stiffened from the cold, and her back ached from carrying water-heavy wash to the line all morning. Her arms felt rubbery, and she shivered in her damp dress. Her mind had emptied from the long, quiet hours of washing, filling again with the single desire to keep the laundry clean until it was dry enough to take down from the line.

Her mother's mind darkened with the rinse water, and she told the story of her Aunt Maria's unfortunate past, calling her sister-in-law "the siren," because she'd once hennaed her hair and hung her nightgown on the line on a Friday night, luring a Sicilian miner to her bed. They ran off to Detroit the next morning to look for work in the Ford factory.

"She was never careful enough about her comportment with men," Emma's mother said. "She got into some kind of trouble up there and came home alone."

"Why?"

"They always come back. They have no family up there, and your family is your home, and if it's your home, even working in the camps is better than doing something anywhere else."

Now, Maria lived in her parents' house, renting rooms to single miners and caring for her aging father, a tiny man with hair shocked white from sunstroke. His birth certificate had been lost long ago, nobody knew how old he was, and he sat all day in a rocker on the front porch with a water glass of the dark, young wine he made in the shed. While the bread baked, Emma liked to sit next to him. Unsure of who Emma was, he called her Nina, held her hand as he talked in the old language of meeting Garibaldi, warning of dragons that lived beneath the Straits of Messina. When he tired of talking, he gently pinched one of Emma's arms, murmuring, "C'era una volta," until he fell asleep. Emma always thought he was saying, "I don't wanna," until Maria assured her that he meant, *once upon a time.*

Coal dust blew over the fence. A clothespin dropped from the line, and the water-heavy clothes sagged dangerously close to the earth.

"Can't keep anything clean here," her mother fussed.

The tightness in her mother's voice made Emma's stomach clench. The inevitable sadness of coal dust on clean laundry could send her mother to bed for days. Buried beneath a quilt scattered with books of saints and prayer cards, her mother took her own journey to a dangerous place in her mind, leaving Emma alone for days, the terrifying silence in the house echoing louder than a mine siren. Now Emma went inside for a slice of Maria's herbed bread, hoping it would raise her mother's spirits. Her mother refused to eat, calling it "demon bread." Quickly, Emma picked up two empty pails, followed the rusted train tracks beside the house, gravel tumbling beneath her feet as she headed toward the water pump in the middle of the camp.

At the culm bank, the two spraggers were stealing coal. The shorter one whistled low, murmured in harsh Polish, dipped his good hand into his pail. Before she could duck, a grease ball covered with coal dust slammed against her chest, leaving her breathless. She turned, running as a second grease ball smashed against her back, pushing her to her knees, her pails skidding across mud and slate. She stood, collected her pails and ran, chest and back aching from the grease bombs, balancing on the wooden planks leading through the muddy streets, slowing only when she no longer heard the boys' cruel laughter, their harsh, shushing language.

Reaching the mountain's flank, she found a ridge steep enough to lean against and rested. Her chest throbbed, and her back still ached, but she knew better than to go home to her mother empty-handed. The spraggers might not get their fill of stolen coal for hours, so she decided to fetch the priest's laundry while she waited. Raised a staunch Methodist, Emma's mother became a staunch Catholic when she married an Italian, and she often vied with the Polish and Italian wives for the privilege of taking in the priest's wash for free. Emma reasoned that the sight of the priest's coveted laundry would cheer her mother more than clean water from the pump.

The ridge's uphill path led through the church cemetery. Traveled only by widows and old miners, it smelled of laurel and decay, but it was safe. Sundays, when her father wasn't too tired for church, he walked this path with Emma and her mother, reciting names of shrubs and flowers that made them laugh—dog-hobble, toothwort, Dutchman's britches. In the middle of the graveyard, Emma rested beneath the old maple that grew into a hemlock. On one side of the entwined trees, blank plaques slid down the hillside, marking the graves of miners trapped and killed in a shaft fire, their anonymous bodies washed out of the mountain with fire hoses. Emma wandered down the other side of the slope, where tall tombstones were dug right out of a coal seam, etched with words in Italian, Polish, and Cyrillic. Here she found the small sarcophagus, the picture of a toddler brother who died in the pandemic before Emma was born, sealed beneath oval glass. They didn't have a photo of him when he died, so the women of the family had leaned his coffin against a coal seam, opened its lid and posed with his body. The brother's eyes were closed, one hand hanging from the open coffin, as though he'd fallen there exhausted by play. Emma's blond mother stood behind the coffin, flanked by her dark aunt and her grandmother, glaring straight ahead.

In early May, her living brothers, Michael, Carlo, and August, had followed the young priest from the white church through the cemetery, carrying the statue of the Virgin Mary on their backs. Wearing a thin, white robe, the priest swung a gold ball of incense from a chain while the statue teetered on their shoulders. Emma and her mother followed her brothers, singing, *Mary, full of grace. Purest of our race.* Spring frost thickened her breath as she circled the graves, her feet sinking through the soft snow, her heels hitting hard against the frozen coal seam.

Raised in a saint-haunted country, her father said the saints' stories were fairy tales for grandmothers and children. He believed only his own legends of how he came to America and met his American wife. On mornings that Emma fainted from the fast in church, he took her outside to sit on the steps, telling how he fell in love with her mother. Fresh from Palermo, he'd spoken no English, so the company put him in Emma's mother's second grade class with the eight-year-olds. Whenever his young classmates became unruly, Emma's mother would say, "Massimo, please stand," and her dark father would stand silently, in awe of her mother's blond hair and blue eyes, her proper manners and command of English, his height ending the unruliness of school children.

"She was a lady," he said. "She was so beautiful I could only look at her."

Her father always told Emma she favored her mother, but she knew better. Wide-shouldered and thick-waisted, she was built like a farmhand. Her face was round, even when she stood before the mirror beside the coal stove and sucked in her breath, searching for her mother's high cheekbones in her own face. She pulled her lank, brown hair into a braid that hung to her waist. She'd inherited only her mother's schoolteacher vocabulary and the habit of saying *going to* instead of *gonna*, which proved such a constant source of ridicule and amusement for her schoolmates that she stopped talking proper and dropped out to help her mother with the housework.

Down in the hollow, the last yellow squash of the season flashed among red and indigo birdhouses in the immigrant women's gardens. Emma climbed the stone steps bordered with rock lilies to the white church on the hill. The tepid holy water warmed her cold fingers as she blessed herself at the doorway. In the side aisle, the priest sat on the top rung of a stepladder, touching up the faded mural of Christ emerging from clouds, appearing to his apostles. The empty church smelled of candles, linseed oil, and the fainter scent of red wine and tobacco that always trailed the priest. Dressed in a pair of work boots and khakis, the blond priest called Emma by her full name, Mary Margaret, and praised her proper speech. As Emma approached, he smiled, wiped his hands with a turpentine-soaked rag and descended, motioning for her to follow him into the sacristy behind the altar.

In the sacristy, the chalice from Mass remained on the counter, a wine-spotted napkin slung over its mouth. Crumbs from the communion bread clung to the silver dish beside it. Emma wiped them from the silver dish with her sleeve. Glancing up at the framed picture of Mary sitting beneath the cross, holding her dead son in her arms, she remembered where she was. She blushed, setting down the sacred plate. The priest only laughed, nodding toward the picture.

"That was made by Michelangelo." He pronounced the name "Meek-el-angelo" because he'd once lived in Rome and could speak to the Italian miners in their own language. "Notice Mary's face. She still looks seventeen, too young to be holding a full-grown son in her arms. Now look at her hands. Those are the hands of a much older woman."

Emma thought of her mother's young, sorrowful face bent over the steaming tub of laundry, her old hands emerging from dark wash water.

"Is it a sin to grieve?"

The priest paused.

"Sorrow is essential to forgiveness," he said. "The soul must feel sorrow and detest the sin committed in order to reconcile with God."

"My mother never sins."

"Everybody sins. There are sins of omission. It may be something she hasn't done that is her sin."

Emma thought about her mother's chores, trying to recall something her mother hadn't done that could be her sin. She did laundry on Monday, ironing on Tuesday, baking on Wednesday, more washing on Thursday, cleaning on Friday and shopping on Saturday. Sundays, she knelt on the hard floor of this church, a rosary threaded through her chapped and twisted fingers.

She's done nothing wrong, Emma thought. She does everything. She works enough to wash away the sins of the world. "No," she shook her head firmly. "My mother never sins."

The priest stood warily, sorting through the vestments in his open closet, filling the pails with altar robes and cloths. Before closing the closet door, he pulled a tall, black book down from the shelf. At first, Emma thought he would give a sermon on how Christ died gladly for her sins, but when he opened the book rice paper fell from engravings of men carved in stone.

"Michelangelo believed the human form existed inside a block of marble, and that he was the only one who could release them," he said. "When he died, he left a series of men with one whole arm or a head emerging from blocks of marble, the rest of their bodies trapped inside the stone. They are called 'The Prisoners.'"

Named for the whole features that escaped from stone—Awakening Slave, Atlas Slave, Young Slave, Bearded Slave—they lined the hallway leading to the statue of David, a whole and perfect man. The priest closed the book and gave it to her. "You can take it with you," he said, tucking the book beneath her stack of laundry. "Let me know what you think."

Unsure of this man, his soft, clean hands, his book filled with men imprisoned in stone, Emma backed away. Walking out through the church, she passed the mural of Christ emerging from clouds. Standing over his apostles, he thrust his empty hands over their heads, as though proving nothing was up his sleeves. Outside, Emma walked down to the foreign place to show the book to her Aunt Maria, to ask if she ever heard of Michelangelo, to see if she knew of an Italian artist who could release the bodies of men from stone. Purple morning glory bloomed mysteriously on the right side of her aunt's pine porch. Goldenrod blazed across the shale barren to the left. The door to the house was open, revealing a darkened hallway filled with the grandfather's model sailboats and battleships, a statue of Mary standing behind a vase of roses.

Emma sat in the rocker outside the doorway, waiting for Maria to return, thinking how much she would like to hitch a ride with her longshoreman uncle, travel back to Naples, brave the dragons beneath the Straits of Messina, explore the wonders of Sicily.

The grandfather woke from his nap, walked outside, his faded eyes blinking against the late afternoon sun, his thin white hair flying. He touched Emma's shoulder gently with his bony hand.

"Ancora sa qui?"

Emma nodded, "Yes, I'm here again."

"She is gone."

Emma's stomach flipped with the terrifying thought that Maria had left for good, gone off to Detroit to find the man who abandoned her long ago.

"Dovè?"

The old man shrugged, looked over to the wash lines beside the house. "Today is washday. Maybe she goes to the pump."

In all these years, Emma had never imagined her once-beautiful aunt doing laundry, but men's briefs and work clothes and socks were draped over four militant rows of laundry lines, a single bed sheet snapped flat and pinned against the house. The sight of her aunt's loneliness filled Emma with such disappointment that she stood quickly, fled back to her mother's house.

At home, Emma's mother glanced over her dirty dress, the water pails filled with more laundry. She looked at the sun, measuring the time left before dusk.

"Those spraggers threw grease balls at me on my way to the pump," Emma explained feebly. "I went to fetch the priest's laundry. I know how hard climbing those steps to the church is for you."

Her mother nodded, took the laundry from the pails. "The men will be home soon. Wash your face before you go to the pump."

Standing at the end of the water line, Emma set the buckets at her feet. Recalling how her mother always claimed that many girls met their husbands at the water pump, she studied the worn faces of the women standing before her in line, the front of her own sodden dress. She couldn't imagine a man coming to this pump for anything but water. She looked for her aunt, thought of how Maria once hung her clean nightgown on the line, calling her lover to her on a Friday night. She couldn't remember a time when any part of her own clothing was clean or bright enough to call a man to her day or night.

When she got home, her father and brothers were already in the backyard, peeling off their dirty clothes outside the house. Standing naked in the back yard, they took turns hunching over the tin tub, their pale shoulders and tired arms polished by moonlight. Emma helped them wash their backs with torn pieces of old underwear, listening to them discuss a roof fall in their shaft. Though the fall happened over a week ago, her father's voice remained hoarse from calling out to her brothers, and the fear remained inside of them as they talked it out over their bath.

"I was walking like a duck as fast as I could to get out," Carlo said.

"The mountain was falling down behind me," August said.

As her father and brothers talked of the hazards inside the mine, Emma watched her mother's face, thinking of how her mother carried the mine inside of her all the time, always waiting for the siren to sound, for a son to come home too late, for that knock at the door in the middle of the night. When her brothers finished bathing, Emma hung their work clothes to dry behind the coal stove in the kitchen. Their trousers were heavy with dirt and water from kneeling in the mines all day, but they would wear them for several more days. Cleaning them before the next washday was pointless.

After the meal of pasta and butter, her father went back to the mine to work a night shift, and her mother climbed up to the garret to sleep in the wrought iron bed beside the empty cradle. Her three brothers slept crossways on the bed, pulled out in the middle of the kitchen. Lying on her bed tick beside the coal stove, surrounded by a curtain of black and sodden work clothes, Emma pulled out the priest's book of statues, split it open, studied the picture of David by the acetylene lamp. There dark, ropey veins were visible in his arms and legs, and his toes looked smudged. Only his pubic hair looked clean. In 1808, she read, the middle finger was stolen from his right hand, and a lesser-known artist was charged with replacing it. But the new finger was too large, distorted, and David would never be perfect again. Emma turned to the book's title page and read the inscription: For Edward Winnis, bought at the Catholic University of America, Washington, D.C., 1920.

Emma had bathed men since she was seven, scrubbed their naked, sooty flesh as she would their pants and shirts, but as she thought of the priest's eager face as he slid the book between folds of his laundry, his careful hands moving gently over the mural in the church, her stomach cramped. She recalled the Norfolk and Western man's gentle teasing, *I'll bet you loved ciphering in school*, and at the sound of her name used in the same sentence as the word *love*, a surprising heat bloomed between her legs, rising, spreading, until her whole body burned and ached pleasantly. Then she recalled her mother's story about her aunt's careless comportment with men. Terrified of becoming a siren, she slammed the book shut, slid it beneath her cot, turned down the lamp, promising herself that she would return it to the priest first thing in the morning.

A draft blew through the knotty pine wall, over her face and hands, and she breathed in the smell of mine water drying on her brothers' clothes. Waiting for sleep, she thought of men emerging from stone, and imagined being the nameless artist charged with replacing the missing finger of the most perfect man. She thought of her own father, handing him his dinner pail as he left for his night shift.

"What will you think about all night?" she'd asked.

"I don't think," he'd said. "If I let my mind wander, I'd lose an arm, or worse." Then her father rubbed her head, kissed her. "Every night, before I go down into the mine, I say a prayer."

The family's Christmas goose clucked softly behind the house. Her mother had nailed boards to its feet, making it swallow corn so that it would fatten, rubbing its throat until it swallowed. Emma remembered last Easter, when her father boiled and colored a dozen of its eggs, hid them out in the yard, inside the pots on the stove and in the empty cradle beside her parents' bed. When she'd found them all, her father told her to close her eyes, and he hid them all over again. Didn't he know she was too old for such games? she'd thought. Didn't he know that gathering the eggs felt like work? She didn't have the heart to tell him she was too old for this game, and they played until it was too dark to see the bright eggs.

"Emma?"

It was after midnight, and her mother wavered slowly in the dark kitchen, in her white linen night shift. For a moment, Emma mistook her for a curtain billowing in the window. She held her mother's arm, led her back up to the garret, helped her into bed. Her mother's faded blond hair was unbraided, tangled at the waist of her damp shift. The joints of her fingers were hot, knobbed, hard as ginger roots in Emma's palms. She turned her face to the wall, as though ashamed of her ugly hands, her failure to bear the violent tearing aches in her swollen joints and ligaments.

Emma went out to the brick oven, melted beeswax, and boiled the remaining wash water, carried the tub up to her mother's room. Kneeling beside her, she wrapped her mother's hands and feet in wool, poured melted wax over them, letting her sweat out pain. She winced as she touched her mother's hot, sore joints, feeling the phantom pains in her own fingers. Her mother called out, accusing her daughter of piercing her hands and feet with flaming arrows, but Emma continued to nurse her mother's failing body until she forgot her own.

Her mother's eyes fluttered shut. As Emma stood to leave, she grabbed Emma's forearm, pleading softly, "Stay here for a while. Please." She showed Emma how to scratch the soft skin above her wrist with a fingernail. "My mother used to do this when I couldn't sleep." Emma wanted to leave the drafty garret, the smell of her mother's night sweat, but she knew if she pulled away too soon her mother's eyes would fly open, and she'd have to stay even longer. She searched through the book-filled cradle still at the foot of the bed, looking for something to read. She found the *Dialogue* of Catherine of Siena, her Mother's favorite saint. She pulled out the *Dialogue*, opened it. Catherine's voice was immediate, comforting, a girl her age speaking of fountains: *It is just like a vessel that you fill at the fountain. If you take it out of the fountain to drink, the vessel is soon empty. But if you hold your vessel in the fountain while you drink, it will not get empty: indeed, it will always be full.* Her mother's eyes opened. She swatted the book out of her daughter's hands.

Emma continued scratching the underside of her mother's wrist, waiting for the last wakefulness to leave her mother's body. Yearning for sleep, she became uncertain if she was awake. She heard the train pulling itself through the hollow, heaving its weight through the mountain, its metal wheels grinding against metal tracks, its whistle sounding like an off-key church organ in the distance. As the train approached the house, she held her breath, waiting for it to pass. Suddenly, she heard a thundering crash, a rumble across the front porch, sudden footsteps, as though someone was running around outside to collect the laundry before the rains came. Lying back, Emma rested her head beside her mother's, on the pillow. Her mother's eyes began moving beneath their closed lids, her body sinking into sleep.

Relieved that her mother was finally asleep, and that one of her brothers thought to save the laundry from the rain, Emma went back to her cot. It must have been almost morning, because the stove was cold, but the shutterless window remained black. She burrowed toward the remaining warmth of her quilt, tried for a few hours of sleep before her mother came down to the kitchen to tell her to heat the stove and prepare for a day of ironing.

SHE WOKE AGAIN to the sound of shoveling outside on the porch, imagined the first snow fall, how she loved to run up the mountain with her youngest brother, Carlo, to play in the new snow before the coal dust settled over it. Rising from her cot, she stepped into the front room, found her brother lying precariously on the edge of the narrow bed, his corner of the blanket tied to the end so nobody could steal it. Anger pricked her temples as she imagined him sneaking outside without her in the middle of the night, to play in the immaculate snow beneath a moon blazing like sunlight.

Outside, the valley was train-haunted, snowless, and the blue air was thick with coal dust. Beside the house, a coal car had tumbled onto its side in the gravel, the coal spilling from it drifting over the yard and across the porch, rising over the windows of the house. Her father and two older brothers had shoveled the coal away from the door, and now they were digging out the coal that had drifted over the windows. They'd started a fire in the brick oven, and they stepped toward the flames every so often to warm their frozen hands. Though Emma couldn't see her, she heard her mother weeping in the shadows beyond the fire. Coal pricked her bare feet as she followed the eerie sound toward the brick oven, found her mother sitting cross-legged, rocking a dark bundle in her arms. The fallen wash line snaked through piles of coal all around her, half a shirtsleeve waving like a white flag from beneath one black heap.

Emma's eyes burned from the greasy dust. Her chest tightened beneath the weight of her mother's grieving, and her arms and legs shook with a raw, empty fatigue. Crushed by the thought of washing everything all over again, she picked through the first mound, unburying the waving shirt. A man walked toward her, tall and blond in the dim, blue light, and she recognized the Norfolk and Western man who sold her ice and lemons on baking day. Suddenly, Emma knew she'd give anything to be pulling soft loaves of warm bread from her Aunt Maria's oven, to be drinking lemonade cooled by the ice this railroad man brought to her all summer long.

The man squatted beside her, so close she could breathe his scent of sweet tobacco and clean sweat.

"Are you all right?" he asked, looking closer at her face until he recognized. "Why, it's the schoolteacher."

Emma nodded, her throat too dry to respond to his teasing.

"I'll tell you one thing," he said. "You all are sound sleepers. I waited a long time for somebody to answer me. I thought you all were dead in there."

Her foot throbbed, and she looked down, slowly noticing the cuts in the soles of her bare feet. She could take the pain in her body, but this man's kindness made her want to sit cross-legged on the ground and weep. She sat on a cleared patch of grass, but she wouldn't allow herself to cry in front of him. Following her glance, the man pulled a handkerchief from his pocket, set her foot on his knee. She stared at the white handkerchief, as though he'd just pulled a dove from his sleeve. As he began wiping the blood and grit from her foot, her body warmed and softened with the pleasure of his hands against her skin. She marveled at how well she already knew the back of his neck, his scent, the precise, lanky movements of his fingers. Then she looked down, noticed she was still in her nightclothes, remembering her Aunt Maria's nightgown and the illicit flight to Detroit. Emma shivered, knowing that only this thin piece of linen hung between this man and her naked flesh, and she couldn't help but think that she'd called him to her. She wondered, Is it the leaving or the return that will be my sin?

She pulled her foot away too quickly. He looked up, his blue eyes worried. "Am I hurting you?"

She looked down at her own blood on his handkerchief, embarrassed. "It was so clean."

He laughed, put her feet back into his lap, nearly lifting her off the ground. He pulled another white handkerchief from his pocket and went to work on her other foot. This time, she leaned into his hands, knowing that wherever this man took her would be worth the stain of leaving.

Honeymoon

IN SEPTEMBER, CALEB HAD NO MONEY for a honeymoon, so he gave his new wife, Emma, his cane fly rod and took her down to the Clinch River for a fishing lesson and a picnic. They entered the river beneath the "no scavenging" sign, where the cascades ran deep and swift around an old train trestle, reflecting the deep turquoise sky. Small rainbow trout chased each other around the deep pools, flashing silver in the sun; native trout hung below the cascades, steady against the strong current, still and gray as bedrock. Hundreds of blue butterflies clouded above the coneflowers and chicory that grew out of the limestone bank. On both sides of the river, old mountains folded softly into each other. Patched with swirls of yellow, rust, and green trees, they reminded Emma of the knitted afghan her mother spread across the foot of her childhood bed.

The night before, Emma's mother had sat at the foot of that bed, explaining what would happen on her wedding night. She opened the family medical counselor to the chapter on "Love and Marriage," called lovemaking "sexual congress" and warned Emma that feeding her new husband calves' feet jelly, dandelion, or too much salt would lead to reckless amatory feelings, causing irreparable mischief.

"Don't go with him if he makes you nervous," her mother concluded. "Marry him only if he loves you more."

Emma wasn't nervous around her tall, blond husband. She didn't know if he loved her more. He'd asked her to marry him that August, a week after the coal car tipped off its track beside her father's company house down in War. He'd sat beside her on her father's aluminum rocker out on her porch, offering her a house on forty-seven acres of Virginia mountain farmland on a ridge above a valley called God's Thumbprint. He'd married her at the courthouse in downtown Bluefield, because the Catholic priest in the coal camp wouldn't perform the ceremony. A longshoreman passing through the camp had put out word that Caleb had been married during the war to a girl from Naples, and that he'd stayed on in Italy to be with her after his tour of duty ended. He'd returned to the States alone a year ago, saying only that she was dead.

For their picnic, Caleb carried two Irish potatoes, a slab of bacon, and a short hunting knife in a pack on his back. He planned to catch and cook trout for her, but as long as he did not season them with too much salt, Emma didn't see cause for alarm. At twenty-six, his blond hair receded, and his shoulders stooped beneath his broadcloth shirt as he threaded the fishing hook through a grasshopper so skillfully that the grasshopper remained alive, grasping the line. I am married to this man, Emma thought. He is my husband. She was sixteen. She needed to hook these sudden facts into her mind.

Caleb stood, his long legs striding easily across a path of stones toward the middle of a rapid. He turned back, beckoning to her. She hopped across the stones and took his hand. This was the second time he'd touched her; the first time was a quick, public kiss on the cheek during the wedding ceremony. Standing in the middle of the stream, she liked the feel of his callused hand as he pulled her toward him, how he gripped her rib cage with both hands to steady her on the dry, flat rock beside him. When he let go, the absence of his touch was like a pain, and she became unsure of what to do with her own hands. She watched him cast the line to the far side of a cascade, allowing the grasshopper to float down to the pool at the end where the dark trout waited, rising to snap up real flies. Caleb gave her the fly rod, stood behind her, positioned her arm straight out before her, teaching her a roll cast. She leaned into his chest and cast out, but the line sank quickly beneath the tumbling water, and she reeled it back in.

"Try to get your hook to the other side of the cascades," he said. "Let it float down naturally with the rest of the flies."

His voice rolled like the surface of the mountains draped around them, mingling with the water's churning. The late morning sun warmed the back of her neck. She could have stood there all day, leaning against him, listening to his easy-going voice. She cast and recast until the hook reached the other side. She looked back at him, and he nodded, "That's better." The rod trembled and arched, and Caleb helped her slowly reel in a rainbow, kneeling beside the water to wait until the fish stilled. He lifted the fish, gently slipping the hook from its soft mouth, threading a slip of rope through its gills. He eased the fish back into the pool in the crevice beside them, securing the end of the rope beneath a heavy rock.

Emma gave Caleb the rod, and he walked over to the riverbank to cast out a few more times. She squatted on the rock, studying her fish. Its back was green with black spots, and its sides shimmered silver and rose. Its ghostly fins moved steadily beneath its body. It was so beautiful that Emma imagined it must be female. Another rainbow swam up beside her fish. Darker and greener, its sides were scarred white. It held itself beside Emma's captive fish, its gills moving as though it were talking, and Emma imagined it must be the mate. Icy water splashed over the rocks, soaking her boots, and she hopped from foot to foot until her frozen toes stung from the blood rushing back into them. She pulled her fish from the pool and went over to where Caleb was kneeling, cleaning and wrapping his three trout in water-soaked rhododendron leaves, slipping them into a woven creel. Emma looked down at her fish. It was dead. She shivered as Caleb wrapped it in the wet leaves, slipped it into the dark hole of the creel. She wished she'd let the fish go.

Caleb took off his wool sweater, gave it to her, and it smelled of his sweet tobacco as she pulled it over her head. He unjointed the fly rod, reeling the line through the guides. Hoisting the creel, he picked up the rod and headed along the uphill path toward the tree line.

"Let's walk for a while," he said. "I want to show you something."

The river path was steep, bordered by limestone bluffs and laurel. Pines grew sideways out of the rocks, bowing across the river, and the big native trout swam in the black pools beneath the cascades. Emma and Caleb climbed, stepping over roots and high blocks of limestone, until she tired and asked him to stop. Sitting on a fern-softened rock before a cave, she let the cave air breathe softly over her neck and shoulders. While Caleb jointed the fly rod and cast into the pool, she watched his long arms and graceful movements, deciding that he was handsome. The hiking had made her warm and drowsy, but she kept his sweater on, breathing his scent of tobacco and trout, wondering if he loved her, and why.

Emma was not beautiful. Once, she'd dared to ask her mother if she were pretty, and her mother replied, "Your hair is your one beauty. Don't ever cut it." Her father joked gently that she was built like a farmhand. Dark-skinned and broad shouldered, she'd carried two buckets of water from the coal camp pump for her mother every washday. She'd scrubbed floors and cooked for three brothers and her father since she was seven. Once, her father had come home with two coal pails full of blackberries he'd picked while out roaming the mountainside, giving the fruit to her mother before he went back to work a second shift in the mine. Emma knew that her mother was more nervous than angry with her father for taking an extra shift, that going back underground when he was already tired was dangerous. Her mother had turned away from her father, briskly ordering Emma to wash out the mason jars so they could can the fruit right away.

Her mother mashed the berries through the strainer. Her faded blond hair streaked gray at thirty-five, her stomach swelling softly with a fifth, unexpected child, she thumped through the sweltering kitchen that July day, her pale face pinched as she added sugar to the mashed fruit, filling the clear jars with black jam. Emma hated how readily her mother turned her father's sweet gift into a bitter chore. Looking at her own hands, raw and ugly with wash water inside the soapy mason jars, she swore she'd never marry. "You're too old to be pregnant," she'd snapped at her mother.

Now, Emma's own husband stood still and quiet beside the river, casting his line over and over into the stream. The fish were larger and wilder up here, fleshier than the little ones in his creel that would hardly make a decent supper. Then she noticed that Caleb was releasing these bigger catches.

"There's more meat on the ones you just let go," she said. "Why aren't you keeping them?"

"It's enough to know they are here," he said. "You can't cast toward an absence."

Emma had never met anyone who didn't eat the fish they caught. How is it enough just to watch a fish instead of eating it? she wondered. Before she could ask, Caleb unjointed the fly rod and began walking, no longer turning back to check on her. Following, she studied her husband's stooped posture, wishing this man were a little happier, more talkative, someone who didn't answer her questions with what her mother called "a fourth thought," forcing her to angle out the first three thoughts that came into his mind before he actually spoke. It worried her that there were still so many facts about his past that were absent from their conversations. The longshoreman had told the coal camp priest and her family that Caleb just appeared one day, walking over the mountain with a stack of books under one arm, a bundle of money tucked inside a guitar slung across his back. He put all the money down on a mountain farm outside of Bluefield, where he'd taken Emma to live after their wedding that morning. The longshoreman had heard that Caleb worked for some "strange" men while in Italy, that these men paid for his return to America and gave him the money that was in the guitar. Nobody knew where Caleb's people came from, or if he had any.

Unsure of what she believed, Emma thought of her dead trout in the woven creel at his side, remembered how deftly his hunting knife sliced through this fish, and for the first time she regretted her hasty marriage and flight from the coal camp. She imagined his Italian wife, slender and frail as the virgin saints, and wondered how she'd died. She considered following the stream back to the bottom, to the meadow filled with coneflowers and butterflies, hitching a ride back to her family's house, but she was too far into this to turn around. When the walking trail ended at a bare bluff, Caleb climbed the staggered outcropping of limestone. She pulled herself up by the limbs of rhododendrons, climbing until she reached the top, following Caleb along the ridge. Chilled by her own sweat, she looked down toward the stream, but no longer saw it. The soundless trees muted the water's comfortable tumbling.

Caleb hiked several feet ahead of her, his back straighter, more assured as he strode relentlessly across a dry meadow stabbed with dying firs, bare and white as bones rising into the blue sky. At the edge of the meadow, she caught up with him as he hacked through some blackberry bushes. She heard the water before she saw it. This new water poured from a great height, echoing against stone, slapping against more water. The blue butterflies reappeared, clouding above Caleb's head as he turned, his face kind and eager as he held the branches back so they wouldn't snag her. She stepped toward him, and he placed his hand against her back, guiding her eyes to the high ridge covered with fir and hemlock, the white water veiling the dark joints and faults in the cliff face, slapping on the surface of a deep pool. She breathed in the heady scent of fermented berries and limestone water. Caleb's hand pressed softly against her back, and as he leaned toward her, she could feel his mouth close to hers. She could breathe his light, sweet breath. Her heart fluttered recklessly. She wondered if she were heading toward the irreparable mischief that had trapped her mother in that sweltering July kitchen, canning jar after jar of blackberry jam.

Around the mountain pool, the butterflies flattened themselves against long, polished stones, drinking the water held in their dimpled surfaces. Emma took off her shoes and walked across the slippery rocks. Water sprayed her face and arms as she dodged the drinking butterflies and stood at the pool's edge, watching the giant trout swim around the pool. Dark blue and mottled, they skulled just below the surface, gulping up butterflies and water, their stomachs filling like empty buckets. She saw now why her husband had released them. She, too, was satisfied just to know that they were here.

When Emma looked back at Caleb, he had built a fire on a dry rock and placed the cast iron pan on the flames. He pulled the slab of bacon from his pack, sliced a piece into the cast iron pan. As it sizzled, he sliced the two potatoes into the pan and wrapped the trout in the remaining bacon. He fried the trout until their eyes turned blue and smoky, took the pan from the fire and placed it between them. He taught her how to pull the spine out of the fish by its head, all in one piece, and they ate the sweet meat with their fingers, from the cooling pan. After they finished eating, he pulled the slip of rope from the water, and in the dim light she imagined he was pulling a magnificent, shimmering trout out of the spring, one of the big, wild ones she'd been satisfied to admire just a little while ago. Her heart ached with confusion and disappointment. Then he set a green, glass bottle between his knees. He smiled at her, working the cork out of the bottle with his hunting knife.

"It's champagne." He poured some into a water glass. "I brought it back with me from Italy. I wanted it to be a surprise. Do you want to try some?"

The champagne flowed like liquid gold into the glass, so beautiful that even a child would be tempted to drink it.

"Oh, why not," she laughed, drinking. The champagne spread like sweet fire down her throat, around her breasts, under her arms and down through her ribs. When it reached her stomach, she felt sunshine, even though the sun had set and they were sitting beneath the darkening canopy.

"It's beautiful," she said, dipping her finger at the bottom of the glass.

"You're beautiful," he said, pouring more champagne for her.

She squirmed. My hair is my one beauty, she thought. I am built like a farmhand. She set the glass down between them. "Was she pretty?" she asked.

"Who?"

"Your first wife."

Caleb paused. "Men liked her. She was the kind of girl who could make you feel good about yourself. She made you want to tell her all your secrets."

"What happened to her?"

"She died of consumption."

Suddenly, Emma felt guilty, but now that she'd asked for his sad secret, she could do nothing but listen.

"It was so bad at the end, I couldn't watch," he said. "After she died, I stayed on for a while. The war was over, and most of my shipmates had gone home. The ones who stayed only wanted to find their way to the nearest bar, but I toured the churches. Each one was like a museum, filled with famous pictures of saints."

Emma recalled her mother's holy cards, the ones she brought out on nights when her father worked an extra shift. Her mother stayed up late, drinking tea or coffee in bed, reading the prayer cards to stay awake until he returned safely. Sifting through the pictures of saints, she recounted the lives of the young, female martyrs for Emma, praising their ethereal beauty, their vows of chastity, their painful austerities.

"Saint Rose of Lima rubbed her face with pepper to hide her beauty," her mother said. "When someone noticed the shapeliness of her fingers, she rubbed her hands with lime. The pain was so great she couldn't dress herself for a month."

When her mother reached the picture of Saint Teresa in Ecstasy, Emma studied the saint's schoolgirl face tilted upward, her eyes rolled back, mouth agape. An angel, more beautiful boy than vision, grasped a fold of her veil, poised his fire-tipped arrow above her heart. On the back of the holy card, Emma read about Teresa's spiritual marriage with Christ, the angels piercing her heart, and how the sweetness of her excessive pain surpassed all desire to be rid of it.

"That one was always having ecstasies," her mother said.

"What is an ecstasy?" Emma asked.

Her mother quickly slipped the card to the bottom of the stack. "Our bodies are like overcoats for the soul," she said. "Until you are married, you must never let a man touch or kiss you anywhere but on the cheek or the hand. If you find yourself alone with a man, pretend that you are with Jesus."

Caleb's fire was dying, but she could feel him beside her, see the shape of his long and elegant fingers laced across his chest as he looked up through the canopy of trees into the clear night sky. Alone with him, she had to remind herself that he was a regular man, not Jesus, and that she could allow him to touch her anywhere he wanted. She imagined him unraveling her chestnut hair from its long braid, finger combing it down to her waist. She felt a pleasing ache travel down through her chest and stomach, and she wondered if this was the beginning of a pain that could be so sweet she'd never want it to end.

"I wish I could have seen some of those churches with you," she said, quietly.

Caleb turned toward her, his voice sharp. "If I stepped into a church right now, the walls would come crumbling down around me."

Emma flinched at his gruffness, chastening herself for making him the object of her vain and childish desires, for disregarding her mother's most obvious lesson, that a man's brief sweetness would lead only to endless chores, and a whole lot of bitterness. She recalled Caleb's cold kiss at their courthouse wedding, how afterwards he'd walked her down to the Norfolk and Western station to show her where he worked. Standing in the railroad hub, they looked up a steep street shadowed by East River Mountain. Caleb pointed to a white, stone bank tower that looked like a church steeple, saying, "That's Italian stonework. It looks just like some of the buildings you see in Italy."

Emma waited quietly in the dying firelight, certain now that Caleb's mind was far away from her, in some Italian hill town, where she imagined all the women were fine-boned and wore red silk scarves and walked gracefully up steep streets lined with buildings so beautiful they resembled churches. She began to envy Caleb's first wife, the lovely one who suffered the austerities of illness, died and still lingered in Caleb's memory. Emma looked down at her own callused hands and thick waist, feeling disconnected, unworthy, plain as a brown overcoat heaped on the ground beside her husband.

"I wouldn't mind going back to Pompeii." Caleb's voice was gentle again. "After I'd seen enough churches, I bought a ticket to the ruins. The day I went, a farmer was burning trash on the hillside, and I could hardly see where I was going through all the ashes in the air."

Emma didn't think she'd like Pompeii. Trudging over tumbled stones through hot, cindered air wouldn't be much different from walking through a coal camp in the height of summer. As he told of walking the loose cobblestoned streets lined with ancient, caved-in houses, she felt lost and sweaty. But she held her tongue, grateful that he was talking again.

"I hired an old Neapolitan guide," Caleb said. "He took me to the house where no women were allowed to go and led me down a hallway lined with square rooms, each one fitted with a single, stone bed. Above the doorways were frescoes covered with white cloths. The old man started lifting them one by one so that I could see. The first was of a naked woman perched on a man's chest." He described the faded frescoes of bare, plump women of pleasure, making love in various positions. One lay on her side with a man curled behind her, tracing her spine; another crouched before a man with her hand on his head, as though giving him a blessing. "The guide said that the girls working in the brothel would howl like wolves out their windows at night to generate business from the streets. He said he knew a real woman he could call for me."

"What did you say?"

"I told him to go away."

"Why would you want to be alone in an old house full of dirty pictures?" Emma asked.

Caleb laughed. "They were erotic, but not dirty." He paused. "They looked playful, maybe a little instructive. I guess they made me feel lonely, and the old man's ugly talk only made it worse."

Emma's heart clenched as she thought of her husband, standing alone and lonely in some crumbling, stone house with a dirty old man. She spoke quietly, hoping he wouldn't hear the longing in her voice, her own sad certainty that he would never love her as much as his first wife. "You must miss her very much," she said.

"The last fresco was the most faded, but I could make out a woman sitting on the end of a dark couch, a man beside her," Caleb continued. "The woman was beautiful. The man was lean, dark as the earth. The two of them sat with their heads bent together, smiling, like they were telling each other secrets. I tried to recall my wife's voice, but I couldn't hear it. I couldn't remember her face or body, or how it felt to love her. She was gone completely, and I couldn't feel anything. That's when I saw that the man and woman in that ancient, scratched-up painting were more alive than I was. That's when I knew I needed to leave Italy. I took a job working for some men in Naples. They paid for my passage back to the States."

Emma remembered the longshoreman's tale of the "strange" men Caleb had worked for in Italy, the banjo filled with money. "What did you do for those men?"

"It was a long time ago," he said. "It doesn't matter at all because we'll never have to worry about it again."

Caleb stood abruptly and walked down to clean the pan in the spring beside the waterfall, leaving Emma to ponder the meaning of his story. Had he told it to instruct her in the details of love-making? Was he testing her to see if she could handle the sad and sordid parts of his past? She recalled the yoke over her shoulder that held buckets of water she'd carried from the coal camp pump every laundry day since she was seven. She'd been raised to carry heavy things. She could bear the weight of her husband's history, if he'd allow it.

Watching him stoop over the pool of water, washing the cast iron pan, she wanted to lie beside him, her face in his hands, listening to all his secrets. She pulled his sweater over her head, then her dress, lying back to feel the last of the day's heat rising from the stone. Caleb turned from the river, his eyes wary at the sight of her bare skin. He walked over and sat beside her, and she rolled toward him, but the glass of champagne remained between them. He held her back, his hands finding a purchase on her rib cage, as though his hands were memorizing her body.

"It's okay," she said. "I'm built like a farmhand."

Caleb turned away and stood, taking off his shirt and trousers. The moon shone through the canopy, lighting the woods and water as he walked to the edge of the pool. Wading in, he floated on his back, his hands treading the dark water's surface, turning green, then white, then transparent. He flipped over and swam to the waterfall, toward the black joints and faults in the limestone on either side of the high cliff. When he ducked under the water, Emma held her breath. After he disappeared, she walked cautiously over the slippery black rocks toward the spring. She watched the giant trout circle slowly, their hooked mouths gulping as they surfaced to snap up a blue moth and sink again. Emma recalled the touch of Caleb's hand as he pulled her to him, the feel of his solid chest against her back. She recalled her mother's advice, *Don't go with him if he makes you nervous.* She liked the tingling nervousness her new husband had sent through her body. She would follow it.

The champagne thickened at the back of her throat, and her

chest tightened with panic as she waded into the icy water. She
breast stroked toward the waterfall, ducking under the veil and
into a slender crevice that led to a cave. Too big to squeeze between the rocks, she dove deeply and opened her eyes, seeing
only blackness, and crawled forward until her lungs burned. She
broke through the surface, and breathed. In the air-filled chamber, moonlight poured through a primitive hole that pierced the
cave's ceiling, casting a blue hue over the stalagmites that rose in
clusters from the cave floor.

Caleb swam out to her, wrapping his arm beneath both her
arms, pushing his hip against her back, pulling her to the side.
Her whole body shook as she pulled herself out of the pool and
collapsed, allowing him to lay her across a flat stone, covering
her with his own body until her breathing slowed, and his heat
warmed her.

She awoke in his arms, still wondering why he'd married her,
and if he could love her as much, if not more, than his first wife.
"Why me?" she asked.

"Holding onto Anna Maria was like holding onto a stream of
water," he said.

Satisfied with his answer, Emma kissed him deeply, surprised
by her own boldness. He startled, then kissed her back until she
felt lightheaded. She turned her face away and opened herself to
him. He ran a finger along her collarbone and slowly down her
sternum, resting his palm softly across her abdomen. He wrapped
one arm beneath her, using his own body to cushion her back
against their hard, makeshift bed.

The waterfall echoed outside the cave, and the cave pool lapped
and shimmered against the stones around them. He looked into
her eyes, and when she flinched from the brief, necessary pain, he
pulled away. She closed her eyes, pulled him closer and held on,
rising to him. For a moment, her mind detached from her body,

mingling images of his frail first wife and the virgin saints with the buxom women forged on the ancient brothel walls, leaving her with one final question: Am I the water or am I the stone? She opened her eyes. The cave had darkened, but she could feel his eyes still upon her face, his hands firmly grasping her back. I am here with him now, she thought. He's not casting toward any absence.

When it was over, she stood, dove into the spring and swam out of the cave, letting him follow her this time. On the outside, it was nearly daylight, and the morning sun shivered down through the maple and hemlocks. A shaft of light frosted a spider spinning its web on a fallen pine. They dressed each other, repacking the knife, skillet, and water glasses. They walked down the mountain and out of the forest.

※ Emma, 1937

Italian Villas and Their Gardens

IN LATE MAY, CALEB CAME HOME from his railroad job in mid-morning, his truck bed heaped with stones. He swerved the old black Ford off the gravel driveway and drove down the loamy slope of land behind his house, parking beside the boundary wall brushed smooth by overhanging pine and hemlock. Emma was kneeling in the kitchen garden beside the back porch. She stood, brushing a cluster of lavender, releasing its soapy scent, feeling both the pleasure and uneasiness of seeing her husband home from work in the middle of his shift.

She walked down the hill and stood beside Caleb's truck. He leaned over the bed, picked up a small stone streaked with ore and garnet. He chiseled it apart with his thumbnail, explaining that stones were like wood, with sap inside them that needed drying so they could not be snapped by a freeze. He tossed the pretty, cracked stone back into the heap and picked up a slab of dull, gray limestone, running his hand over its flat surface.

"This is the kind we need," he said. "We need the dry ones that still have their faces."

"What do we need them for?" Emma asked.

"We're building an Italian garden," he said.

Emma looked back up the slope, surveying the lavender and sage swaying in the mountain breeze. Yellow blossoms tasseled her squash and tomato plants. Above the neat vegetable furrows, damasks and Scottish roses bloomed deep red against the white chest of drawers they used for bee boxes, climbing the lattices entwined with grapevines. Squirrels had carried her spring bulbs over the boundary wall last fall and winter so that her orange lilies now blazed like rogue fires across the ridge above the house. Seeing nothing she wasn't pleased by already, Emma rested her hands on her hips.

"We've already got a garden," she said.

"This is going to be something else, a real old-country garden with a pond stream and a fountainhead," he said. "It'll be like the ones Italian cardinals built during the Renaissance, when they were hiding out from the pope."

Emma considered saying something smart, like, "Since when did you start hiding from the pope?" Then she remembered the harder question she needed to ask. "Why aren't you at the railroad?"

"They cut my salary by fifty percent today," he said. "Can't bring home a decent paycheck anymore. Might as well quit, see if I can make this land work for us. It will help."

"How will making our garden Italian help?" Emma wondered.

Caleb pointed to where he would build the pond stream and fountain in the middle of the slope, beneath the rose garden, explaining how he'd terrace both sides of the streambed, tucking fiddlehead ferns between the stones. "You'll see," he said.

Emma didn't see yet. She watched his pointing and plotting, growing worried, wondering if he'd already quit his job at the train station, and whether his quitting would put them off their land. They still owned forty-seven acres, part of it upland laid down by soft bluegrass, loamy enough for a good garden patch and orchard. The rest was mountain land too steep and cold for cultivating anything but rye, and even if they could grow an abundant crop, no one wanted to buy it. They still needed his wage work to pay taxes on their land, cash money for the mortgage on the two-story house they'd built upon it.

"Too many things now that call for cash money," she said.

He turned away and started unloading the stones he'd collected from nearby roads, hills, and summits, separating the small ones from the big ones, creating two piles three feet away from where he planned to build the cascade. He went to work, digging into the topsoil, then deeper, running a plumb line up the hill. He used whatever stone he lifted, dropping the small stones between the large ones. At first, the stream bed looked off kilter, but Emma kept her own counsel. She knew from her father, who'd been a stonemason in Sicily before coming over on the boat, that only a fool criticized half-finished stonework. After Caleb built the first two feet, he stepped back and paced, tore down his work, and started over. Soon, the stones and colors began working themselves out beneath her husband's swift, expert hands.

Emma watched him work, knowing she would have to wait out his mood, which was black and remote, his withdrawal into his still-invisible garden so deep that even if she'd tried to speak, he would not hear her. She could feel herself withering beneath his hard silence while the railroad that had cut him back thrived, boring more tunnels, adding double track, sending empty cars into West Virginia to bring back coal. All through the Depression, whenever coal demand fell, the company cut worker salaries ten percent, then ten percent more. A lot of men got angry and quit, and they hadn't worked for seven years. Caleb had stayed on with the company, unsurprised by the cutbacks, bearing it all quietly until that morning. Now, an angry vein pulsed just below his blond, receded hair line. Fine worry lines etched the corners of his blue eyes. He needs this muscle work, Emma thought. She should let him lift and drop stones in the garden until his anger sank into sinew, and he was ready to talk.

Emma joined him, fetching and carrying the stones that he dropped into the sides of the stream bed. She mixed mud and sand for him to mortar. By the time they finished the stream bed, the mountain's shadow wrapped around them like a dark arm, casting them into silvery dusk while the pale evening sun held itself above the black pines beyond the boundary wall. Caleb took out his railroad watch, winding it absentmindedly. He planned on giving it to their son, Dean, on his twelfth birthday in early August. Emma knew by his watch winding that her husband was wondering where their son had gone.

"He's down at the Chapel place," she said.

"Dr. Chapel's a busy man," Caleb said. "You shouldn't let Dean go down there every day."

"He's learning a lot about horses," she said.

"He should be learning how to work here at home. He should know how to make something of this land."

"Horse doctoring is a kind of work that even you don't know."

"Let's hope that's all he's learning down there."

Emma flushed, irritated by Caleb's slighting comment. Dean had been roaming down to the veterinarian's stables since he was six, and Emma had never seen the harm in letting him go. Despite rumors that the vet was a drinking man, Emma had seen him only sober, and he never drank when the moon was full and his services were most needed. Lately, Dr. Chapel stayed so busy healing sick farm animals through the valley that he'd grown accustomed to Dean's help with his own horses, which seemed to multiply more quickly than the chickens and rabbits the farmers gave him as payment. Whenever another local farmer gave up and joined the Conservation Corps, he took his horse to Dr. Chapel for some small ailment, and left it.

The vet kept all the left-behind horses, an odd local mixture of Tamoleons, Yoricks, and Packalets, many of them too old to work, some half wild, all of them requiring time and upkeep. Dr. Chapel jokingly called his stable "my glue factory," teaching Dean how to care for the old and sick ones, letting him work the younger ones that were still able. He gave Emma as much horse compost as she needed for her garden, and she let him pasture his healthy horses on her mountain land. This arrangement had happened so easily and slowly over time that Emma had hardly thought about it. Only now did she realize that she'd never mentioned it to Caleb.

Emma walked to the top of the slope to get a better view of the Chapel place, to see if Dean was on his way home. Her hands and knees ached from a whole day of carrying stones for her husband. She sat on the clover path beside the kitchen garden and picked up some gravel. The sun-warmed gravel eased the stiffness in her hands as she scattered it beneath her circle of herbs. Looking over her budding garden and the growing pond stream, she felt uneasy, though she had no reason to be afraid. It was just a feeling, as when she looked at a still-cloudless sky and knew rain was coming, or the way she'd predicted she'd have a son long before he was born.

She looked beyond the boundary wall, down to where the Confederate and pandemic graves leaned in the shady hollow between their property and Dr. Chapel's land. The vet's house and stables sat above the creek that shimmered like broken glass through bent arms of sourwood, the understory thickened by ivy. The woods were still safe, she reminded herself. Her son took the old paths unknown to transients and strangers that wandered through the valley. The vet worked for himself, and had no shortage of sick animals. The Chapel place seemed immune to hunger and the depraved economy, his barn a sanctuary of healing horses.

Caleb walked up the slope and sat beside her on the clover, crossing his long legs at the ankles. He looked at the empty stream bed as if already he could see water rushing down, settling in the fishpond. Feeling her husband's body calm beside her, Emma asked if he'd already quit his job at the railroad.

Caleb shook his head, no, and took her hands, kneading her sore joints that were red, twisting slightly inward. He stood, lifting her with him, putting his arm around her waist. He led her through the roses until they reached the bee boxes. As he opened a drawer, Emma held out her hands to him, trying not to wince as he placed a honeybee on each swollen joint. After each bee stung her, he pinched it between his thumb and forefinger, flicking it to the ground. He finished the apitherapy by kissing each sting, working the healing bee venom into her arthritic joints.

Down the hill, the vet rode a sorrel with a flax mane and tail out of the woods. He'd put Emma's son up on the horse with him, and he was bringing him back up the hill. A widower, the vet was forty-eight, but he looked closer to sixty. His hair was shock white, his face was red, and his nose was webbed with veins. A drinker's nose. His blue eyes were kind and knowing as he lifted Dean off the horse.

"I believe I've got something that belongs to you," he said. "I found him in my barn." He patted the horse, then winked at Emma. "When I got home from my rounds and found Queenie's stall already cleaned, I thought the angels had gone and played tricks on me again."

As he nodded at the vet, Caleb's smile was a twitch, a gesture he reserved for those people he endured for Emma's sake. The vet nodded back, straddled his horse and looked down at Caleb. "Your son's doing a fine job. He's a fast and strong worker. Can't find anybody else to do the work he does in the time he takes to do it."

As the vet rode off, Dean ran to the stream bed and balanced on its edge. His eyes were brown, like Emma's, but his skin was as fair as his father's, nearly glowing in the sudden moonlight. The rocks shifted gently beneath Dean's feet, and a few tumbled out of the new stream wall. Emma shooed him down.

"Why did you put a pile of rocks in the middle of Mother's garden?" Dean asked.

"I'm building a waterfall," Caleb said. "This part here will be the reflection pool at the bottom. We can put fish in it."

Emma held her breath, willing her son to see what she could not envision herself.

"Big ones?" Dean asked.

"Big as your arm."

The boy laughed, skipping stones into the empty pond. Caleb paced the ground around the basin, his eyes searching the dark grass. Suddenly, he dropped to his knees, feeling around the grass as if he'd lost something. Still kneeling, he presented Emma with a four-leafed clover, his apology for being moody and silent all day. She accepted the clover, knowing she would have forgiven him even if all he'd given her was a blade of grass.

THAT NIGHT, AFTER A SUPPER of sausage and Irish potatoes, Caleb cleared the kitchen table and opened a book he'd bought from a roving agent. Called *Italian Villas and Their Gardens,* its pages detailed the most beautiful gardens of Italy. He explained how he was using the book to plan their garden's stonework, its rushing and motionless water, the laurel hedge that would wind tightly into a maze leading out to the woods. Caleb turned the book's pages, reading aloud passages about the three factors in Italian garden compositions—stone, water, and perennial verdure.

"What's a perennial verdure?" Dean asked, yawning and leaning against his father.

"Plants that stay green through all the seasons."

"What will we do with my flowers?" Emma asked. "What about my vegetable patch?"

"We'll move your flowers to the terraces and set your vegetables out on the sunny side of the house," Caleb said.

Caleb paged through the faded photographs of pleasure gardens built by the Renaissance cardinals.

"What kind of priest would spend so much money on a garden?" Emma said.

"The kind that believed that a garden's beauty could restore the soul better than any church."

He showed her a picture of the Villa d'Este, a garden made entirely of fountains, describing how water dripped down hillside balusters into mossy conchs and the mouths of stone serpents, how streams flowed through tubes beneath other fountains to produce organ notes and bird trill. In one reflection pool, two dragons rose, spraying water that cracked and clapped in the air like the sound of wind. The pictures in the book were as faded as memory, but Caleb described each detail of this remembered garden as if he were still inside of it. The faraway wonders he'd seen thrilled and terrified Emma. She suppressed the urge to call him home.

"Parts of our land looks a little like Italy," he said. "Our back slope seems a haunt for any goddess."

"Can we afford to keep a goddess on our land?" Emma asked, instantly hating the tightness in her own voice.

"We don't need to go out and buy a bunch of statues," he said. "Our garden will be laid out and planted on the same principles as an Italian garden, but suited to our land."

He turned to a more humble garden, the Villa Lante. "Now this is a garden we could live in. Look."

Caleb guided her eyes along its path, through the labyrinth hedge at the bottom, the single cascade running through the middle, the plane trees on either side of the water source, a natural spring gushing from the surrounding wooded hills into a pool called "The Deluge," two stone dolphins arching in the water. "See how it's part of the house and the woods?"

Dean had fallen asleep where he sat at the table. Caleb settled the boy on the bench and kept talking, his hands reaching across the tabletop, lightly touching Emma's hands when they landed, rising again, and she felt her mind slowly bending to his strange and baffling ideas, trying to turn them familiar and close. As he described the cascade's water circling around stalagmites pulled from the Cimini Mountains, she began to hear the sound of nearby waterfalls they climbed in summer. When he told of spring brides having their pictures taken in the flower garden that surrounded the fountain, Emma felt bridal again.

Her husband's blue eyes had softened, and his hands moved beautifully over the book. He kept his voice low so that he wouldn't wake their son, and Emma leaned in to hear him. Drawing closer, she felt his familiar heat, his long legs folded around her legs, lightly grazing her knees. The word *home* came to her again, more urgently this time. Her body soon followed her yielding thoughts. Her muscles ached pleasantly, and a languid desire awoke, tugging inside her tired body. Caleb glanced up from the pictures, his distant eyes slowly noticing her, and she knew he'd come back from the remembered Italian garden. He saw her real and sitting at the table before him. He sighed softly, his signal for wanting her. He lifted Dean in his arms, and Emma followed him as he carried the boy upstairs.

At the top of the staircase, they parted quietly. Caleb carried the boy to his room in the back corner of the house, and Emma went the other way, into the bedroom she'd papered with pink and white magnolia blooms swirling against navy. Caleb had brought home surplus government cotton, replacing the straw in their mattress with fresh, clean cotton, saying, "We're on the up and up now. Let's christen this new mattress."

Emma undressed, lifting her white night shift off the peg in the corner, then hanging it back up. She climbed into the bed and waited the aching minutes for her husband to come to her. Caleb moved silently into the room, and she helped him off with his shirt, kissing his sunburned arms and pale chest, exploring the dark and light places on his body. They sank into each other, giving the soft mattress another christening.

Afterwards, as Caleb slept with one hand resting on her hip, Emma stayed awake, feeling unaccountably restless. She slipped out from beneath his fingers, leaving the warm curve of his body. Her hip aching dully where his hand had rested, she put on her night shift and haunted her own house. She walked through the parlor rimmed with a high plate rail that held the fine china Caleb brought home to her from the auction in town, the year she was too pregnant and tired to go with him. The living room was filled with rigid cherry furniture, two marble end tables bordering the couch, Dean's copy of *Treasure Island* on one, the Bible on the other. A book of sheet music sat open on the walnut piano's stand, split open to the "Celeste Aida," the song Caleb had been teaching her to play lately. Caleb's beautiful gifts, his insistence on teaching her how to play the piano and to cook fine meals they lingered over for hours on Sundays, thrilled and unnerved Emma. Raised in a lean home, she couldn't quite shake the uneasiness her husband's extravagant ways stirred in her. Once, when she asked why he bought so many things they didn't truly need, he replied, "I buy them so we'll have more than what we have."

In their urgency, she and Caleb had left the gardening book open on the kitchen table. Emma sat in Caleb's place beneath the railroad calendar, studying the faded pictures of Italian villas and gardens, slowly translating the language of stone, water, and green as she would a foreign language. She wanted to understand why her husband had begun speaking it. At sixteen, still newly wed to Caleb, she'd pictured his late wife, imagining a slender, black-eyed Italian girl with almond skin, feeling her own wide-shouldered body hulking and awkward in comparison. Now that she was twenty-nine and a mother, she thought of the first wife as just a pretty little girl who'd died too young.

So it wasn't thoughts of the dead that filled Emma with a chill wakefulness that night. Her dread stemmed from memories of her own family still living back in the coal camp. She recalled the last time she'd gone back to War, to show her parents her new son. Her mother's dull, blond hair was woven into tight Victorian braids, her schoolteacher's back even stiffer with rheumatism. She spent most of her days in bed with the shades drawn, gold pills and prayer cards pooling together in the empty groove where Emma's father hardly ever slept. Dean was only three months old then, but her mother toggled him in the crook of her arm like a country ham, handing him back too soon. "You take him before he pitches a western on me," she'd said.

"He's a good baby," Emma said. "He hardly ever cries."

"What's he got to cry about? You spoil him so. He'll end up just like your husband, always living above himself."

"Caleb is a good husband."

"You haven't been married long enough to know what a good husband is."

"He built me a house," Emma said. "He gave me this son."

"You fell in love too easily."

"What's wrong with loving easily?" Wanting to prove her mother wrong, Emma listed her husband's assets to her mother, his forty-seven acres of land, the two-story farmhouse, his steady job with the railroad. "I'm not going to shut myself up in a room and hide away from happiness like you do."

Her mother sighed. "You know nothing," she said. "Sorrow is a privilege. It's how we earn our truths. You haven't even begun to earn them."

A draft blew through the wide crack beneath the window, fluttering the pages of the gardening book. Before Caleb, Emma had never met a man who bought books and read them to her. He was the only man she'd ever known who used the words *soul* and *beauty*. He was the only man to make her a bed out of cotton.

He is the only man, she thought, laughing softly at herself, flushing with the memory of his hands upon her skin on their high, soft mattress. Emma may not have earned any sorrowful knowledge, but she knew the truth. She'd married a good man, and she aimed to keep him. If building an Italian garden in their backyard helped her husband go to work at the railroad, if it would help bring him home to her every night, then she would dig, lift, and furrow the flesh-warm earth of early summer with her own hands. She returned to the bedroom and curled into the curve of Caleb's chest. She'd forgotten to pull the window shade, but she didn't rise to close it. In the morning, the open window would be like another one of Caleb's gifts, the wallpaper magnolias framing the real magnolia blooming just outside.

THE ITALIAN GARDEN HELPED. Caleb went back to the railroad. Every day before first light, he drove down the hill in his truck and went to work. Every night, he returned with some small present. He trapped rabbits, picked wild asparagus and strawberries in the fields along the road he took home. He bartered with the other railroad men for rare ingredients from distant places, a jar of olives, a pint of figs. Sundays, his only full day off from the railroad, he cooked up everything he'd traded for, picked, or killed, filling their plates with rabbit braised with honey and vinegar, covered with wild onions and figs.

The Sunday morning after Caleb brought home the load of stones and built the pond stream, he announced that they needed river rocks to fill the stream bed, so they drove down to the river for a day. The current was swift, chilled by the last spring snow melted off the summit. Emma kept Dean close to the bank, walking barefoot through the icy water, digging up fresh water mussel shells while Caleb waded up to his chest near the deeper eddies, his head disappearing as he reached down to find rocks tumbled by the water, polished into perfectly rounded yellow and black stones.

When he'd gathered enough river rocks, Caleb took out his fishing pole and baited Dean's hook for him, teaching the boy how to cast toward the shadowy places where the brown trout hung, untangling Dean's line when he caught it in the overhanging willows. He threw back the bluegill, waiting out native trout that jumped and turned, flashing silver above the cascades. The chill water made Emma's joints ache and her heart pound. While her son and husband fished, Emma warmed herself by walking the laurel path along the river. Reaching the downhill stream that crossed over the trail, she rock-hopped to the middle and sat on a large stone. Eyes closed, her mind swirling with the current, she startled at the splash of water next to her.

Looking toward the plopping sound, she saw a short, dark figure hulking over the stream and thought it was a bear. The bear stood, transfiguring into a man, a dusky-skinned stranger fishing in a pair of black wingtips and shiny gray pants that were too short for him. He baited his hook with canned corn, and had a string of fish the size of bluegill. A knife flashed in his left hand as he gutted the tiny fish into the river. Emma studied the man's wrong clothing, his knife slicing through the wrong fish. Nobody from around here fished in wingtips. Nobody ate bluegill if they could help it.

The man's eyes were bright red, and he blinked as if they were filled with coal dust. The knife was a stag-handled Bowie, just like the one Caleb had brought home from the war. Her husband kept his own Bowie knife above the fireplace mantel along with the Civil War swords he'd bought at auction. The man followed her steady glance and lowered the knife. His round, dusky face reminded Emma of the portraits of distant relatives pictured on grave markers in the immigrant cemetery back in the coal camp, the ones drafted into the war, their bodies returned by freight train. She wondered if this strange man standing before her had fought in a war, or if his mean looks had come from battling more recent hungers.

She nodded at the bluegill lying on the river grass. "Not much meat on those."

"I fry them like potatoes and eat them." He spoke in a Sicilian dialect different from her father's, yet familiar. He handed her a string of skinny fish. "Here, take. Ti aiuto. I am helping you."

She felt a pang of homesickness as she heard his Italian. She softened her voice, speaking back to him in his own language. "Nothing wrong with working for your food, but those fish aren't yours to sell."

"I am helping you," the man said in English. "I work for you like a job."

"We work our own land," she said. "We can give you something to eat, but we don't have any jobs for you. We do for ourselves."

"Look," the man said. "Can you do this?" The man picked up the smallest bluegill and made a swift, invisible slit in the belly, flipping the fish heart on the stone beside her. He pointed the knife's blade to the heart, showing her how it kept beating outside of its body. He looked pleased with himself, his expression almost childlike, as if he'd just performed a parlor trick, but Emma's heart began to pulse lopsidedly. She tried to measure the distance she'd walked away from her husband and son. How long had she been walking? A half hour? An hour? She stood, brushing the dried river silt from her feet and dress. The man laughed without mirth, flicked the heart into the river with the tip of his knife. She walked away, turning back once, but the man was already oblivious to her, cleaning the rest of his catch.

On the subject of tramps, Emma and her husband remained divided. Caleb believed in feeding transients and strangers, claiming that a hungry man was more likely to fall to mean and peculiar temptations. Caleb stacked a rock cairn on the boundary wall, signaling the tramps that hopped the trains in the valley that they were welcome to come up to the house for food, sometimes work. Growing up in the coal camp, Emma had lived through winters eating only beans, spending coal-poor summers plucking dandelion greens and wild herbs for salads. The hunger had not made any of the men in her family mean or as peculiar as the Italian tramp by the river. Even in the leanest times, her brothers smoked sausages with their Polish and Hungarian neighbors. Her father simmered cheap cuts of meat with carrots, celery, and onions until their bones nearly dissolved. He urged Emma to dig the marrow out of the soft bones with tiny spoons he'd brought over from Sicily, sharing this delicacy with her, his only daughter. The day she married, her father had given her the tiny marrow spoons along with the rest of his own mother's wedding silver.

"When you got something, someone always wants it," he said. "You don't show off what you got, not even your happiness. If you are happy, you go into your room and lock the door. You jump up and down where nobody gonna see your happiness. If you hide all your shiny things, ain't nobody gonna take them away."

Right after she married, Emma had placed all the silver in her trousseau, the heart pine chest of gowns and bridal linens her Aunt Maria had sewn for her. Years later, as the Depression grew deeper, she'd begun hiding the silverware in the female places of the house, the drawers of her vanity, inside the mattress of the cotton bed. The wedding silver was the only secret she'd kept from her husband through thirteen years of marriage, but it had made her feel safe. Now, she had a second secret, a decidedly unsafe one. If she told Caleb about the Italian tramp by the river, he'd probably invite the man home to eat with them, and Emma didn't want a man with red, swollen eyes and a mean knife in her house. She didn't tell Caleb about the tramp while they were still at the river, or while they filled the garden's stream bed with the small river stones. She kept the knife incident to herself while Caleb cooked a supper of trout fried with bacon, cornbread slathered with sweet cream butter and honey. When she finally got around to telling Caleb about meeting the man who'd cut out the bluegill's beating heart, she thought he might be angry that she had kept it a secret for so long, but Caleb listened, his eyes unsurprised. In all the years she'd known him, she'd never once seen him look surprised.

"He probably is a soldier, or at least he used to be one," he said. "I see them selling apples on the street corners in town."

He walked over to the fireplace, where he kept his collection of cavalry swords and sabers. He thought them very beautiful. She wished he'd take them out of the house before Dean got a hold of one and lopped off a toe or finger, or worse. Caleb took down a 42-inch saber and called Dean over. The boy ran to him, his eyes magnetized by the blade.

"They called this one the 'wrist breaker,'" Caleb said, holding the straight blade down for Dean to see it. "The blade doesn't have much of a curve, so you ended up hurting yourself more than the person you were striking, usually breaking your own wrist."

He took down a cavalry sword and showed Dean the curved and etched blade. "This one belonged to a horse soldier," he said.

"If you didn't learn how to use it right, you ended up riding a lot of lop-eared horses." He pulled a thin, worn handkerchief out of his pocket and tossed it into the air, holding the slender blade beneath it. The handkerchief floated down, splitting delicately as it hit the blade, landing like two halves of a horse's silky ear on the floor. He leaned the two swords in the corner of the fireplace and took down the Bowie knife. "The man who first used this kind died at the Alamo," he said. "Legend holds that he killed three assassins with it. The first man was almost decapitated, the second was disemboweled, the third had his skull split open."

He let Dean hold the knife, and the boy parried and backslashed the air before him. Emma's chest tightened. She stepped forward, speaking quietly so that her son wouldn't hear the tremble in her voice. "Where I come from, boys are never taught to play with knives."

"I want to make a point," Caleb said. "If you'll just let me finish." He took the knife back from Dean. "We don't use this knife for those peculiar purposes anymore. You can use it for hunting or camping. You can use it as a machete in deep brush or to chop wood. You can use it for protection, but only if you're in a pinch. A man can be shot and beaten, but he'll still win a fight with this knife."

He handed the knife to Emma. "Your mother may need to protect herself while I'm at work," he said to Dean. "She needs a good lieutenant to help her while I'm gone. Can you be a good lieutenant for her?" He looked above their son's head and into Emma's eyes. "Hide it anywhere you want. Just be sure you can get to it."

She carried the blade upstairs to the brass bed in the magnolia-papered room and slid the knife beneath the mattress. She lay on the bed and put her arm across her eyes. When Caleb came into the room, she kept her eyes closed and didn't move toward him. She imagined feeling the knife through the layers of cotton, wedged between them. All night, she lay very still, feeling unsafe.

THE NEXT MORNING, some time before dawn, a thief crept onto their property and stole the copper wiring from beneath Caleb's truck. Emma told Dean to run down to the Chapel place to see if he could borrow a horse, but Caleb stopped him, claiming he didn't mind walking the eight miles over the mountain to get to the train station. He said he would stay in town all week. He needed to work extra shifts to make up for his lost income, and he couldn't walk back up the mountain in the dark.

With Caleb gone, Emma became wary of her own house. The rooms he left behind seemed crowded with rigid furniture, filled with a heavy silence that hung over her head like the coal dust over the camp where she'd grown up. The silence made her miss her family. She missed her father simmering some kind of meat on the coal stove. She even missed her mother a little, though she did not miss the endless housework, the washing and ironing, the church work that required her mother to bathe the bodies of the dead and keep them in the front room of their double-frame house until the coal company priest was ready to say the funeral Mass. Always, in her memory, there was a coffin in the corner of their parlor whenever anybody in their church or neighborhood died. The smell of alcohol and creosote her mother used to bathe the lifeless body lingered in the house long after the coffin was taken away, and buried in the cemetery.

Mostly, she missed her brothers sitting at the kitchen table during these wakes, telling ghost stories. Short and dusky, their shoulders stooped from working in the mines, they hunched around the table, dipping cookies made of honey and almonds into sweet, young wine. The oldest, August, would begin with a story of the albino woman, a wild-eyed forgotten creature who roamed the woods around the coal camp cemetery.

"She wears a wedding dress, has pink eyes and long white hair with black showing in it," he'd say.

"She carries a small poodle," added Michael, the middle brother.

"No, it's a pet squirrel," Carlo, the youngest, would say.

"She's harmless," her father would say softly, trying not to laugh.

"She has killed!" All three brothers would yell together, breaking into laughter, patting each other on the back, pouring more wine.

Emma had always felt protected by their husky laughter, their lively eating and drinking in the room beside the wakes, their ghost stories that sounded like jokes. She liked the fact that they'd remained "the boys" long after they'd become full-grown men who worked long, dark hours inside the mine. She could not go home to anyone in her family, and yet the big house without Caleb in it felt empty and cold, even though it was nearly midsummer. Nights, a frozen wakefulness settled over her skin, sinking slowly through her bones, stiffening her joints, especially her hands. She started taking Dean with her to sleep in the Cold Potato, the cedar-shingled cabin where she and Caleb had lived when they first married. A single room furnished with a bed and a woodstove, the Cold Potato was never cold, and they'd never stored a single potato there. Named after an old song they sang while building the big house, it warmed easily when she stoked the woodstove, filling Emma with a newlywed feeling, reminding her of a time when they didn't rely on Caleb's wage work for a living.

Days, she filled her slack time by building up the terraces on either side of the stream bed, hunting fiddlehead ferns in the woods, tucking them between the stones of the pond stream.

Every day at dusk she walked down to the Chapel place to collect Dean. She told herself he could no longer safely walk alone in the woods, though she supposed she'd grown a little lonely, and she craved Dr. Chapel's conversation. She ignored the paths newly blazed by the Conservation Corps, marked by stone cairns that looked like topsy-turvy towers. She followed one of the old trails, Elizabeth's Path, a rhododendron tunnel the vet's late wife used to walk alongside the creek below the Chapel place.

Inside the barn, Emma found the vet standing outside a stall that held the sorrel that he'd ridden up the hill the night she and Caleb started building the waterfall. As he schooled Dean about the different breeds, his face looked bright red and vein-runneled against his beautiful white hair. His hands were slightly palsied, but still strong.

"Now, your Tamoleons are docile and easily kept in order," the vet said. A black horse swung her head over the gate of the next stall, nudging the vet's hand. "This one is said to have sprung from Yorick, the bitter foe of the Indians. She's small, but fiery. She'd make an excellent saddle horse for you."

Emma stepped into the warm barn and kissed Dean on top of his head. The boy allowed the kiss and ducked away, heading toward the black horse that stomped and rocked in her stall, demanding his attention. Emma admired her son as he sponged down the legs and belly of the fierce, hot horse, letting her sip from a bucket of ice water infused with mint. When Dean had caught pneumonia as a baby, Dr. Chapel, not the town physician, had shown her how to mix butterfly weed with a little whiskey to clear her son's lungs and bring down his fever. She thought again of how dear the vet had become to her, how different he was from her mother or even Caleb, how his own knowledge of sorrow had made him into a healer—knowing, steady, and kind. She greeted him as she always did, so that he would not startle or become embarrassed.

"I came to check on my boy, make sure he wasn't bothering you," she said.

The vet smiled, gruffly warming to her, replying with his usual, "The boy never bothers me." Then, he added, "He's generally a good judge of a horse. He has them well used."

"He's got a lot of horse in him," Emma agreed. She saw no point in hiding her pride around the vet.

Dr. Chapel turned to Dean. "Could you go out and drive in the rest of my glue factory?" Dean smiled, and Emma understood that the two had a conspiracy. The vet never asked a question he didn't know her answer to, but he always asked anyway, out of respect.

"How old is Dean now?"

"He's got a birthday coming up in August. He'll be twelve."

"That's old enough. I've been thinking about hiring him to work for me, all day for the rest of the summer, maybe after school next fall."

"He already works for you."

"I want to pay him a little something. The boy needs to learn how to handle money, especially now that he's planning to go to college. He wants to be a veterinarian."

Emma nodded. Her son was growing up. When Dean was seven, he'd created his own growth chart, claiming he would be 5' 9" tall when he was a man, and that he wouldn't stop growing until he reached this height. Now that he'd set his mind on becoming a horse doctor, Emma supposed he was already charting out veterinary schools on a map he'd secreted somewhere in his room. "As long as he keeps in school," she said.

The vet fed the Yorick a flake of hay, his head tilted so that she knew he was still listening.

"Do you think it's wrong to tend something on your land that you can't eat or put in a tincture?" she asked.

The vet looked directly into her eyes. "Nothing grows in vain, even if you can't see its uses." He gestured over the high stall doors. The horses had turned to look out their windows, and all she could see were their rumps. Their beautiful tails swishing back and forth felt comforting, and she felt relief once she understood that their beauty and comfort was in itself useful.

"Just what are you and Caleb setting out in your garden this year?"

"Caleb wants to build an old-country garden, like the ones in Italy."

The vet laughed. "My Elizabeth talked me into taking one of those steamers back to the other side for our honeymoon. We saw a lot of those old gardens in France and Italy."

"Caleb says ours will be the kind we can live in. He says it will help, but I'm not sure yet how this will be so."

"The oldest gardens butted up against the farms and orchards so the people could live off them," the vet said. "The newer ones were meant just to look at. They were filled with a bunch of broken statues. Some of them put me in mind of a battlefield with all those statues of men with their arms and legs cut off."

"That's the part that bothers me. I don't want strangers coming by and seeing our garden, thinking we have more than what we have."

"Some gardens are there to look into, and others to look out of. You'll just want to be sure that you make one to look out of."

Dean came back with the horses. He smiled at the news of his summer job and begged to spend the night in Dr. Chapel's barn, and Emma allowed it. As she retraced her walk along Elizabeth's Path, Emma considered the vet's advice. His pasture was laid down with rich meadow grass that you wouldn't notice until you stepped on it. The paths surrounding his land were sheltered by silvery blue laurel and rhododendrons, branched so tightly seeing inside of them was impossible. Emma felt a tremendous sense of relief that the vet had understood Caleb's garden designs. She decided to tell Caleb that they should leave their laurel and rhododendrons alone instead of scything them down into a low, vulnerable hedge.

When she reached the guesthouse, she unlaced Caleb's boots and kicked them off, falling across the bed. She picked up the Italian gardening book, letting the names of the villas—Belrespiro, Lante, Medici—roll off her tongue, each one sounding like something Caleb might cook on a Sunday, some beautiful, hearty dish that would fill her so completely she wouldn't have to eat for the rest of the day. The ancient villa names conjured the old argument she had with her mother, who read only the Bible and prayer cards and took no pleasure in food. Once, the only time her parents had come up for a visit, Emma had made a pound cake, its shell heavy and golden, its center filled with wild blackberries and red currants.

"This cake calls for twelve egg yolks and a pound of butter," Emma had said, proud of having a dozen fresh eggs and a pound of butter.

"What did you do with the egg whites?" Her mother lifted her slice of cake, as if looking for the egg whites beneath. Emma stared at her slice of cake, too ashamed to say that she'd thrown away the whites.

"I composted the rose garden with the shells," she said feebly.

Her mother picked up her fork, stabbing the cake. "That man will be the end of you." She ate bite after bite, her face pinched, as if eating the cake were a tasteless task she must complete. When she finished, she told Emma to wrap up the rest of the cake, claiming she would take it home to the boys, "so that nothing else would go to waste."

The memory of her mother sitting at her dining room table,

eating the beautiful cake without pleasure, sent Emma running outside and down the back slope in the middle of the night, in her nightgown. She stared at the still-empty pond stream, trying to imagine water cascading down the stream bed, gathering in the basin. Crickets churned loudly in the woods, predicting a hot summer. Crows clambered over the dry stones, pecking for bugs and seeds. Looking into the empty stream bed her husband had made from faceless stones, she became furious all over again at her mother's blank face and mean comments. She promised herself that she would never allow her own body to slowly petrify with rheumatism. She would not allow her mind to grow rigid with religion or any other sorrowful knowledge.

"He is my beginning," she said aloud, scattering the crows. "If he is my end, so be it."

Her head foggy with sleep and bitter arguments, she hadn't noticed the mist rising from the creek, or that it was morning. She heard gravel churning beneath boots, saw the tall, lean body shrouded by mist as he climbed toward her on the driveway. She ran to meet her husband. He didn't ask why she was standing in the middle of the yard before daylight, or why the door to the guesthouse stood wide open while the door to the big house remained locked. He carried a bundle of copper wire in one hand, a large gilded frame in the other. She gave him a long deep kiss. The copper wires snaked wildly in his hand. The gilded frame dropped to the ground.

THAT NIGHT, AFTER CALEB REPLACED the copper wiring beneath the truck, he came into the kitchen, carrying a leather pouch. He loosened the pouch neck and poured kernels into her hand. They rolled in her palm like brown pearls.

"It's popcorn," he said.

Slowly, without much planning, they had a little homecoming party. Emma lit the stove and popped the corn while Caleb went out to the smokehouse to sift salt from the meat box, bringing it back to pour over the popcorn. They took down the china from the plate rail, and Emma took her wedding silver out of hiding. They ate the popcorn from the good china bowls, spooning it into their mouths with the wedding silver. Afterwards, Caleb brought inside the gilded frame he'd carried home with him that morning. It was filled with a dark oil painting of a sad-eyed Christ perched on a high, rocky summit, overlooking the Garden of Gethsemane. He said he'd picked up the painting while searching for the copper wiring in the town wreckage yards. In the parlor he put the frame in the easel backwards and glued an entire deck of cards to the painting's back. Using the tableau, he taught Dean a version of play poker, throwing darts at the cards to see who could get a pair, three of a kind, a full house.

After Dean went to bed, Caleb came to Emma in the magnolia-papered room, carrying the gardening book. His eyes were tired and distant, his back and shoulders stiff to her touch.

"They went for the jobs of my crew this week," he said. "They hired a bunch of unskilled laborers to replace my men."

"Why would they do that?"

"So they can pay them piece rate. Hiring a man who doesn't know what he's doing costs less money."

"Isn't that dangerous?"

"Fights are breaking out now that more men are losing work." He paused. "I've started taking one of my swords with me. I put it under the front seat of my truck, just for protection."

Emma's heart pounded, and a panic fluttered in her throat. "Quit and stay home," she said. "We can rent out garden patches to some of the men who still have their jobs, pay for the land taxes that way."

"It won't help," Caleb said. "With the piece rate salaries, the workers don't know who'll have money from month to month."

"We could sell the orchard and pay off the whole mortgage at once—"

"I'd rather have it timbered than sell it."

"What will we do?"

Caleb opened the gardening book to the picture of the Villa Lante, his favorite, showing Emma a picture of water pouring out of an enormous stone fountainhead at the top. Part monster, part woman, the creature's hair was carved into writhing snakes. Water poured out of its mouth and down the stream bed, circling stalagmites pulled out of nearby mountains.

"What is it?" Emma asked.

"It's a gorgon."

"It's ugly."

"It's generally thought to be good luck and protection."

"From what?"

Caleb's eyes were tired. He flicked the monster's head. "It's what we need."

"Can you make it?"

He nodded. "I know where I can find the marble. I'll need some cash money to buy it."

He looked down at the mattress, and Emma flushed, embarrassed by the discovery that he'd known all along where she'd secreted her silver. She knelt on the floor and reached beneath the mattress for the Bowie knife he'd given her. She slit the mattress, pulling out the dainty marrow spoons her father had given her on her wedding day.

"You can get a lot of money for those," she said, aching with unaccountable sadness over the lost spoons, the memory of her father saving the soft marrow for only her to eat. She wanted to hide the spoons and the happy memory of her father where nobody, not even her husband, could take them away. She felt tricked, as if the whole night, the popcorn and the poker games, were a pretense for getting her to give up her beloved wedding silver. Why couldn't he sell this ugly Bowie knife, or one of his treasured swords? They still had more than what they had, but at what cost?

Caleb set the spoons aside, without even a nod or a thank you. He slid the knife back beneath the mattress. When he reached for her, she no longer loved him as keenly as she had before. His soft kisses felt faithless, his breath rank with desire. As his body heaved upon her, she turned her face away from his mouth. His sweat pooled across her sternum, between her hips, but she felt cold. The cotton mattress was flat as stone beneath her, the knife running like a sharp ledge beneath it. She waited until she could no longer feel him inside her. Then she pushed him off. As she pulled her nightgown on, her groin and knees and toes cramped. Her stomach ached from eating only popcorn for supper. Cotton, she thought. Popcorn and poker. For the first time, Emma began to understand her mother's bitter assessment of marriage. Perhaps she had fallen too easily for her husband's soft favors.

THE NEXT DAY CALEB CAME HOME with a slab of marble in the truck bed. It was the color of dirty snow, but Caleb claimed it was similar to the stone mined from a quarry in Carrara, Italy, where Michelangelo had gotten the marble for The David. He wrapped a rope across his chest and around the stone, carrying it up to the barn. Inside, shafts of dusty sunlight poured between the barn's wide planks. Mourning doves roosted in the rafters, the straw from their nests falling like golden strands of hair to the dirt floor. Caleb had made a table from a door and two trestles. He'd cut off a pair of his own trousers, stuffing them with old rags to make a cushion for the stone. He set the stone upon the makeshift cushion and began knocking the rough outline of the fountainhead with a point chisel and hammer. His lean forearms flexed powerfully with a strength she'd never seen before. Marble dust showered from the block, flying above their heads. Emma stood behind him, suspecting him of destroying the expensive stone, of squandering the fine silver that she'd kept safely hidden for so long.

"What are you doing?"

Caleb paused. "I'm taking away what shouldn't be there."

He opened a toolbox, showed her a set of chisels, a rifling rasp and a fine emery cloth. "I apprenticed myself to a stonemason in Italy so that I could earn my passage back home," he said. He held up the rasp. "The mason gave me these tools before I left. Some of the best stonecutters in southwest Virginia have tried to buy them off me, but I won't sell."

When he finished the muscle work, Caleb dug a fine curve into the roughed-out form, sanding the powdery cut with the rasp. He dipped an emery cloth into a bucket of water, wet sanding the curve in the stone. He paused, taking her hand, running her fingers across the underside of her own arm, then running them across the sanded stone.

"Soft as your wrist," he said.

Emma's arm tingled from his touch, but she pulled away. "When will it be done?"

Caleb took up the emery cloth and started sanding. "We've got to stop talking now. It will only slow me down."

JUNE PASSED. When he wasn't at the train station, Caleb worked on the fountainhead in the barn. He wouldn't let Emma watch his progress, so she lingered below the barn, working in the garden.

After the Cherokee roses bloomed, she went into the woods and dug up a few, transplanting them on the highest terrace with the Scottish roses and damasks. Because Caleb was so obsessed with the fountainhead, she got her way with the labyrinth. He left the laurel alone, allowing her to make a softer maze of black basil and rosemary hidden by the great rhododendrons that surrounded their house and garden.

By July, she and Caleb no longer slept together on the cotton bed in the big house. He worked all night long on the fountainhead, taking catnaps on a straw bed tick in the barn. He no longer discussed the railroad with her, claiming that he didn't want to bring his job into their home. He didn't want to argue over whether they should sell off parts of their land. He still took her up to the bee boxes for her daily apitherapy. Nights, when Caleb worked out in the barn, Emma slept alone in the little guesthouse. She ached for the pleasing sting his touch and kisses stirred within her.

She blamed his distance on the railroad and the garden. Mostly, she blamed herself for telling her husband to stay with the train company. Wishing she'd told him to quit the railroad the day he came home with the first load of stones and started the Italian garden, she began thinking up different ways to make cash money so that she could bring him home for good. She filled her slack time by making beautiful things to sell to the home extension agents— bridal wreaths woven out of bird nests, roses carved out of soft wood. She wove baskets from reeds, filling them with grapes to sell at the street markets or to the train passengers stopping at the station.

One Sunday in early August, she went out to the arbor to pick grapes. The vines were thick as her forearm, knobby and twisted. They'd braided themselves thickly along the arbor above her head, heavy with fruit. The grapes' flesh was liquid beneath the dark purple skins, and the bees circled dizzily around them. The warm air smelled like church wine, closing around her like a mouth. Emma nearly ran from vine to vine, picking and filling the basket. As she stood eating from a cluster, two of Dr. Chapel's rogue horses wandered up to the stone boundary wall to watch her, and she walked over to feed them grapes. As they nibbled delicately from her outstretched palm she looked up to the ridge where the orange lilies should have been blooming. The slope had been scalped, and it unfolded like a mangy, brown coat all the way down to the woods. Beneath the canopy, the tramp walked through the pandemic cemetery with bundles of orange lilies perched on both his shoulders, flickering as he walked through the trees.

She ran after him, too furious to be afraid. She came up on him as he rattled his knife inside the collapsed ends of the oldest tombs, scaring off the snakes before he dug flowers off the graves. As she came closer, Emma's stomach ached from all the grapes she'd eaten. Her face, arms and hands itched from the juice. Her sunburned skin chilled suddenly in the shade.

"Those aren't yours," she said, nodding at the lilies.

"Oh, I did not know they belonged to you." The man's red eyes flamed with infection and madness, and there was a mean puncture wound on his left forearm that he seemed not to notice. He dropped the flowers at her feet and kicked the washed-out end of a grave. "These souls have escaped with the rains," he said. "Do you not have doubts about where your own soul will rest?" His mad eyes roved over her face. "You are a lady," he said, and before she could step back he touched a blunt finger to her grape-stained mouth. "Lipstick."

Jolted by his too-familiar touch, Emma ran, her hip bumping the basket. By the time she reached the house, the grapes had burst open, and there were bees drowning in the liquid sweetness. She went into the big house and up to the magnolia room, taking the Bowie knife from beneath the mattress. She carried it in its leather sheath down to the Chapel place, becalming herself by practicing the line she would give the vet when she arrived: "I've come to see a man about a horse."

By the time she reached the barn, she stood trembling before the vet, cold sweating in her stained dress. Dr. Chapel pulled a milking stool over beside him and motioned for her to sit. He turned to Dean. "It's getting dark. Why don't you go drive in the horses."

When the boy was out of hearing distance, the vet looked slowly over her stained dress, her hair unwound from its braid. Emma lifted her hand to tuck in a loose strand of hair. Glimpsing her grape-stained fingers, she put her hand back down.

"I must look a mess," she apologized.

The vet's face softened. "Most of the people I see all day have horse on them."

"That's why I've come down." She was afraid that telling the joke would lead to crying, so she said simply. "I want to buy one of your horses." She took the Bowie knife out and set it across her lap. "Caleb gave me this knife to have in the house when he's gone, for protection," she said. "I don't need it."

"What do you need?"

"I need *him* in the house," she said. "He needs to be at home, where he can stay safe, away from that job. I only want to take care of him. I don't know how to do that anymore." She placed the knife back into its sheaf and passed it to Dr. Chapel. "He could use a horse to make our land work for us so that he wouldn't have to go to that job. I can trade you, a horse for this knife. It's foreign made. I think it's worth something."

The vet put the knife back into Emma's lap. "You keep your knife," he said. "You can have the horse. I'll bring it by whenever you need it."

Emma smiled, so relieved she could barely speak. "Tomorrow," she said. "It's Dean's birthday. We'd all be pleased if you could stay for supper."

They agreed that Dr. Chapel would ride the black Yorick up to the house the next morning so that she would be hitched and waiting beside the pond stream when Caleb and Dean awoke.

As she reached the bottom of the slope, Emma saw Caleb walking along the highest terrace, a giant bundle of burlap strapped to his back. She watched as he attached the covered fountainhead to the natural spring they used as the water source. The sun was setting behind it, so she couldn't see the fountain's face as Caleb removed the burlap and finished running the pipe from the pond to the water source. Soon, Emma heard water slapping and circling stone. She walked slowly up the hill, savoring the cool spray on her face as she reached the stream bed and dipped her hand in the reflection pool. Lifting her eyes, she saw water rushing downward, channeling around stalagmites Caleb had pulled out of a nearby cave and placed in the stream bed. The fountain niche was adorned so finely with a mosaic of gold and black river rocks that at first she thought she was seeing real sunflowers. Caleb lit the candles he'd placed inside the clam shells on the ground around the fountainhead, staging it. He stepped back. This wasn't a fountain. It was a whole show. Emma caught her breath as she watched it.

In the flickering light, the gorgon was terrifyingly beautiful, with long, ropey hair snaking around its face, back holes for eyes, water pouring from its mouth. Caleb motioned for her to sit on the edge of the basin. She dipped her feet in the cool, swirling water. He held a lantern over the water, pointing to a pair of goldfish big as full-sized carp, slowly circling the basin. A mountain breeze blew over the boundary wall, and Emma shivered. The fountain water sounded like wind and trilling birds, and the white moon ran behind the black silhouettes of mountains. Frogs creaked desperately from overhanging pines.

"What are those frogs doing up there?" she asked.

"I think it's just one frog," he said. "He's calling out to the female."

"He sounds hard up."

"Maybe he is."

Emma nodded toward the gorgon. "Tell me again how that awful goddess is going to protect us."

Caleb wrapped his work shirt around her shoulders.

"One look from her can turn a person's enemies into stone," he said, explaining that blood taken from the right side of her head could bring back the dead, blood from the left was instant poison. As Caleb talked, the frog's call grew louder, shrill and sorrowful, muting her husband's voice. Emma couldn't help but think of her mother's unhappy voice. She argued with it. Happiness is a woman's privilege, she thought. *Happiness* is the truth we need to earn.

Emma took Caleb into the simple guesthouse adorned only with their newlywed bed and woodstove, its windows lit by the running moon as it dodged in and out of softly swaying pines. She told him how she worried while he was away, how she sometimes felt like he never really came home from work. She talked about the horse Dr. Chapel was giving them, the plans she'd made so that he could quit his job and stay home and make their land work for them. When she finished talking, Caleb looked at her unsurprised. "When I'm at work, all I think about is coming home."

Finally, just before they slept, the female frog answered the male. Her call was soft and steady, a simple release.

EMMA AWOKE AT DAWN. Caleb was gone, and there was no warmth in the mattress where he'd fallen asleep beside her the night before. She rolled over onto the gardening book, finding the note sticking out from between its pages, *Gone to check on some things at work. I know a man who lives by the tracks who sells sausage. I'll buy some for Dean's birthday supper, and I'll scare up a bottle of wine. We'll have us a real party when I get back.* She put her good blue dress back on and rushed outside to see if Dr. Chapel was on his way with the horse. A storm had blown through before dawn, chilling the air over night. Now it was autumn. The sky shimmered blue between mountains draped with orange, yellow, and red leaves. The rain had beaten all the jasmine from the vines, and the blossoms had tumbled into the pond stream. The two goldfish circled beneath the debris, rising to feed upon it. Emma went into the big house to find something to strain the pond.

Passing the parlor, she looked above the fireplace mantel, studying Caleb's sword collection. She'd returned the Bowie knife to the mantel, but the space below it, where the "wrist breaker" had hung, was empty. A dim panic rose in her throat. She took down the Bowie knife, the one a man could kill with even after he'd been shot and beaten. She wished he'd taken it with him. She heard Caleb's Ford churning up gravel, and she looked out the window. Dr. Chapel sat in the driver's seat of Caleb's truck while Dean sat in the bed, blinking and trembling like a colt unaccustomed to sunlight. It was odd seeing her son and the vet without horses. She wondered numbly where the Yorick was, and why Caleb wasn't driving the Ford.

As she walked outside to greet them, Dr. Chapel unfolded himself from the truck and took her hand. He'd never touched her before. His rough hand holding her hand felt so strange that at first she resisted. He spoke to her slowly, gently. She heard the words *accident* and *down by the railroad.* As he coaxed her over to the truck, she understood how he was able to move so many massive, stubborn animals.

A canvas tarp lay across a low heap in the truck bed, and for a moment Emma thought the vet had brought more stones for the garden. Dr. Chapel rested both his palsied hands on the tarp until they stilled. His sad, ruined face softened, turning almost boyish as he looked down at his fingers. He pulled down the canvas, unveiling a man lying on his back, an old fedora placed across the left side of his face.

"They found him on the tracks this way," the vet said. "Someone shot him in the head. I put one of my hats on him so that you wouldn't have to see where the bullet went through."

Emma lifted the hat and looked without recognition into the face, the mouth surprised into a perfect "Oh," all its teeth broken. The left cheekbone was crushed, the left eye swollen shut. In all the years she'd known him, Caleb had never looked surprised. This stunned and broken face did not belong to her husband. This was not him.

"What was he doing at the station this morning?" the vet asked.

"He was picking up sausage, I think."

The vet pulled a package from the seat, and Emma stared at the white butcher's paper bloodied at its creases.

"He was gunned down by a tramp on the tracks." The vet pulled Caleb's railroad watch, stopped at 6:19. "The police think that this was the time of the shooting. They think his watch broke when he fell on it. Could be why it didn't get stolen."

The sight of the watch twirling on its chain wrung blood and air out of Emma's head and lungs. The earth turned black, and she fell to the ground.

Dr. Chapel put his hand under her arm, asking her to come into the house, but she shook him off, refusing his offer to help her up. The vet nodded and took his hand away. He asked Dean to help him carry Caleb's body into the kitchen. Unready to start bathing her husband's body, Emma lingered in the garden, seeing it through her mother's disenchanted eyes. On the highest terrace, the rain-torn roses were mildewed, their red blooms faded against reptilian vines. The fiddlehead fern around the stream looked like weeds overgrowing an old, battered feeding trough. The fallen jasmine had clogged the basin's drain completely, water sluicing over its sides, soaking the grass and clover beneath her.

Though she was sitting, Emma still felt herself falling, only now it was more like sinking. Strangely calm, she became concerned by the blooms clogging the pond stream's drain, the water miring the garden. She spied the Bowie knife lying in the grass where she must have dropped it. She stood and picked it up. Wading into the fountain, Emma could feel chill water rising through the hem and waist of her dress, her body sinking deeper. She began to stab at the drain with the knife, digging and releasing it from the debris. She was making headway when suddenly she felt a firm hand taking the knife away, a thin arm hooking beneath her arms, pulling her out of the basin and up to a dryer part of the slope. "Mother, what are you doing?" The horror on her son's face woke her from the dreamlike task of saving the garden from flooding. As Dr. Chapel wrapped a blanket around her, the smell of alcohol and creosote enveloped her so strongly she gagged, nearly choking.

She threw off the blanket, but she remained sitting beside the vet. He stood, one hand hooked behind his neck as he surveyed the ridge above the house scalped of its lilies, the lavender and thyme pounded by the night's rain. He knelt over a few remaining ferns on the terrace, brushing the torn fronds with the fronts and backs of his fingers. "So many flowers," he said, but all Emma could see was stone. Rain had pummeled random stones from the stream walls, tumbling more stones from the terraces. Among the ragged roses and grapevines at the top of the garden, the gorgon's face stared down, its gaze stiffening Emma quickly and symmetrically—both hands, both hips, both feet—until the last of her body turned to stone.

🌼 Bambino, 1937

La Mèrica

HE CROUCHED BESIDE a pile of rocks at the mountain's summit, flipped a stone over and found the snails clumped together like a black fist. The snails pushed their horns out, felt the night breeze, burrowed back under. He shook them into the burlap bag he carried slung over his shoulder. He turned each stone, poking around them with his finger. He carried a Bowie knife, but he didn't use it. The blade would cut too many of the snails in half. It was 3 a.m. in early July. A rainstorm had blown through, shredding the night sky, leaving pale threads of clouds across the moon. It was raining still, lightly seeping into his clothes—a thin suit and a pair of dress shoes given to him at the church down in the train town at the bottom of the mountain. The new shoes leaked and pinched his feet. He kept gathering. If he collected two or three pounds of snails before dawn, he would have enough for a stew that night.

His name was Bambino, and he lived near the spine of East River Mountain, in a plywood hunting shelter abandoned by one of the rich men who owned land in the hills and valleys surrounding Wilderness Road. He slept on a car seat ripped out of a

Ford Model B, beneath the shelter's only window. He started his workday in the middle of the night, gathering snails by moonlight and starlight. Later, in daylight, he would remain in darkness and damp, obscuring himself within leaf cover from the rich landowners who cursed him for trampling the grasses meant for their cows and horses. The creeks and rivers, he believed, belonged to no one. Their banks shifted continually, crossing boundary lines. He caught fish in the currents, gigged frogs in still pools at night. He was always hungry, and when he became too hungry he could not see through his eyes. He could see well on this night. He would take everything he could find.

He rolled the upturned stones back over, fitting their damp undersides back into the earth. He stood, ambling silently down an Indian game trail that hadn't been blazed for many years. He dodged fallen pinecones that rested like empty hand grenades among the light brown pine needles. The spiders had worked all night, weaving webs that floated like tiny, silken clouds inside laurel and rhododendron branches. The fine webs veiled his face and arms as he passed through them, cooling his skin. Kneeling beneath a laurel bush, he poked at mounds of turned-up earth, searching for shiny tracks leading to tiny holes. The snails had come out, and the frail moon had made them fat. He admired the snails, how they ducked their heads under when the wind blew, or curled up tightly during a downpour of rain, hidden and safe. Near the creek bed, he knelt and looked down in wonderment at five pairs of snails in the act of mating, sticking to each other above the ground. He pulled two apart and studied them, trying to figure the male from the female, mother from father. He couldn't tell them apart, but he didn't mind. He'd found ten snails. Knowing he would eat that night would make the day easier.

The trail thickened with briars and meandered. He stepped through the thickets, lifting each limb, oblivious to the pricks that tore his calloused fingers as he searched the thorns for baby snails that hung from the tips. Small and newly hatched, the snails' skin was so fine he could see right through it. He shook them into his hand, popped a few in his mouth. He sucked them out of their shells, and the meat melted across his tongue, sweeter than the mating snails because they'd had no time to eat any grass.

When the red sun burned a hole through the morning fog over the mountain, and the snails went into hiding for the day, Bambino walked over to a clearing owned by a rich man who didn't curse him for picking greens on his land. He walked into the meadow, digging up borage, dandelion, tansy, wild thyme. He put the plants in a second burlap bag and kept company with a feral dog that slinked behind him in the high grasses. Still young, its matted fur swirled with gray tufts, and its bones poked through its haunches. He called the dog Briciola, little crumb, and spoke to it as if it were a small child. "You are afraid of something," he said. "You want my protection." He tossed some wild onions aside, and the dog pounced on the greens, devouring them. He sang to the dog, humming a tarantella that his mother taught him when he was a boy in Sicily: *Cicerenella, the gardener's daughter, sprayed her garden with wine and with water, watered it well, tho she hadn't a pail, ah!* He sang, thankful for the moonstruck snails and the warming sun, the woods that had given him good wages that morning.

He'd worked a wage job in a city once. When he'd arrived in La Mèrica, he'd lived in the river bottoms in Cincinnati, working in the baseball factory. For eight hours a day, he hunched over rubber corks, sewing cowhide strips over them with red, waxed string. The factory room was dark and made of concrete, with a single window. In summer, the river dredged up offal from all the slaughterhouses, snapping power lines that fell and sparked the greasy surface. The heat made him slow. The smell of the slaughterhouses and hot, gritty air creeping in the factory window burned his eyes sharply, as if someone had stuck one hundred needles into them. When he could not see through his eyes, his mind could not make his hands sew quickly enough. He was almost relieved when the boss accused him of having trachoma, and fired him. He'd hopped trains down into these mountains to look for labor outside.

Here, he'd found clean water and shady meadows rich with borage whose leaves he steeped into a soothing wash for his eyes. His sight got better, and he found his wages in the woods and pastures. If he collected enough greens to make one hundred bundles, he could sell them that day to the middleman down by the train station for three cents apiece. He could count to fifty, and he knew what a half dollar looked like. Beyond the number fifty, he became confused. He imagined returning that night with too many coins to count. Maybe, if he earned enough this summer, he would learn how to count higher, how to add and subtract. He would learn to understand money, to buy and sell things for a profit. Like buying shoes for a half dollar and selling them for a dollar. How much had his own shoes cost? Their soles were slick, and they made him slip and fall. He only wore them when he walked to town so that the rich women who lived there would not lower their eyes and turn away when they saw him in the streets.

The scent of rain-soaked honeysuckle wafted over him, perfuming the air. Down the hill from where he stood, honeysuckle vines blanketed a low, stone wall so thickly that it was hard to tell where the field ended and the stones began. Inside the wall, a lemon tree grew in a garden that looked like the grove in his village outside Palermo, where the streets were lined by lemon trees, their full limbs hanging over stone walls, dropping fruit on the pavement. For a moment, Bambino blinked, moving closer, unsure if he were seeing a lemon tree in this Virginia valley. A woman knelt on a terrace below the tree, scattering gravel around the base of a rosemary bush that had grown so large it looked prehistoric. He'd seen the woman once before, down by the river. Her face was round, and her eyes were dark as an Arab's. She'd looked familiar, like the Madonna his mother had worshipped in the church in the piazza. A boy with brown hair and pale skin flung open the garden gate and ran up to the woman. He carried a pail of water and a basket of eggs. The boy dropped twelve eggs into the water, watching all but one sink to the bottom. The boy glanced back at his mother, but she'd already turned back to her work. He balanced a single sinking egg on the boundary wall, on the shady spot where the rich man left food for hoboes who wandered through on their way to hop a train. The boy threw the floating egg over the wall. He carried the rest of the eggs into the house.

The boy reminded Bambino of his older brother, Rosario. Fair-skinned and blue-eyed, Rosario had been his mother's favorite because of his Norman looks. She'd given Rosario the heels of her bread—when she had bread—and called him The Baron. Bambino's father was always away or in jail, so there was no money or food. Rosario and Bambino had roamed, stealing the lemons that fell onto the road outside the groves. They climbed the mountains together, gathering the eggs of finches and robins. Their mother wore black wool, even in summer, and she stayed inside the stone house, as if *in consolo*, though her husband was still alive. She cooked everything her sons brought home, her wrists wrapped with rags so that she wouldn't sweat into what she cooked. *If you drop a piece of bread, you pick it up and kiss it,* she'd say. She would have beaten both her sons if they'd thrown anything away, especially a good egg that sank, even a rotten one that floated on water.

Walking down the path along the boundary wall, Bambino kept outside the honeysuckle, inside the understory, behind the dark green ferns that bounced in the morning breeze. Looking into the garden that was like the groves in Sicily, he felt spectral, his mind filled with the memory of the lemon trees in his village. The woman in the garden stood, straight as a sundial, in a white cotton dress. The limbs of the lemon tree arched toward her, as if reaching toward her light. The giant rosemary spiraled and crawled, prostrate at her feet. Bambino imagined crossing the boundary wall, kneeling before this woman, touching the hem of her dress. When he'd seen her by the river earlier that summer, he'd asked her for a job on her property. She'd stood firm, but fear flashed in her eyes before she'd lowered them, turning away. Now, as she tended the rich man's garden, she wore the same white dress, her hair woven in a braid that reached her waist. She was a lady. He kept hidden inside the understory, so close to the garden that he could have reached out and touched her, but he couldn't bear it if she turned away from him again. He reached out, snatched the good egg from the wall, wrapped it in wet fern leaves and placed it in the burlap bag, inside a nest of the picked greens.

"If anyone say bad words about the Madonna, I kill him," he muttered aloud.

He walked on to the cemetery, to the section where the old graves were low, cool, and friendly. The bottoms had crumbled out of a few sarcophagi and washed down the slope; dark ferns and yellow lilies sprang wildly from their sepulchral openings. Bambino rattled his knife in the open ends of graves to startle away any snakes. He worked the knife swiftly, cutting the plants in the graveyard, reciting the names and curative powers for each green he dropped into his bag: dandelion leaves, drenched with olive oil, relieved the symptoms of gout; belladonna could be made into a tea that relieved hunger; artemisia could be put in your shoes while traveling, affording protection against weariness, wild beasts, and sunstroke.

Working among the graves, he kept company with the black and tan cats that slipped between the crumbling tombstones, some sunning themselves in patches of sunlight. He would not go under the hallowed ground. In Sicily, when Bambino was twelve or thirteen, Rosario had fallen in with some *tomboroli*, grave robbers who plundered the necropolis outside the village. Bambino went out with his brother only once. As Rosario led him down a dry country road that smelled of sheep, he'd said, "Everybody out here has a grave in their backyard." Rosario explained that most of the country people owned a private collection of artifacts, amphoras, oil lamps, and jewels hidden in secret drawers, back panels of wardrobes. "If we don't dig up the graves, they will." When the boys reached an open field, they climbed up to a tomb cut into a gentle hillside. Descending the crumbling stairs inside the tomb, Rosario said, "The dead don't mind if we are here."

But Bambino had minded the dead. The chamber they'd entered belonged to a woman who was buried with needles and thimbles. The ceiling became lower as he crawled toward the back wall lined by a smooth, stone, funereal bier. The walls buzzed, as if angry spirits lived inside of them, and Bambino worried that the dead woman's angry soul would enter him, driving him mad. He had to remind himself that his brother working beside him was alive, human, doing the same job. Near the back of the chamber, the ceiling became too low to crawl under. The walls buzzed even louder. He looked up, saw a net of black gnats crawling over him. He backed slowly out of the tomb, climbed over to an empty, shallow grave that had once held the funerary urns of the rich woman's servants. When Rosario emerged from the rich woman's tomb, his pale skin looked even more delicate, nearly transparent in the sunlight. Bambino told him that he would not go under with him again, that they didn't have any business inside the graves. Rosario had shrugged, "You like the light, I like the dark."

After that, the boys had separated, Rosario going under the dark graves, Bambino climbing higher into the mountains, picking borage and wild fennel under the scorching sun. Each morning before they left to their separate laboring, Rosario always called out, "In bocca al lupo," *into the wolf's mouth,* because it was unlucky to wish someone good luck, and Bambino always replied, "Crepi il lupo," *I hope the wolf will die.*

The train town's clock pounded the silent air, hammering twelve times. It was full daylight. The air beneath the canopy heated up, and the cemetery began to smell of decay. The cat that sunned itself on the tombstone woke and slipped away. His bag full of greens, Bambino stood and followed the main road that led into town, picking chicory from the roadside ditches. He stopped on the hill overlooking the passenger station, coal wharf, and yard. Black tracks ran east and west through the yard, slicing the station and the whole town in half. Beyond the coal wharf, a passenger train sat empty.

The middleman worked a half mile west of the train yard, at a produce stand on the road that ran alongside the tracks. The middleman was tall and wiry, the skin on his neck scorched black by the sun. He led Bambino to the back of the produce stand and sat behind a plank table propped up by two barrels. Bambino walked over to a third barrel filled with clean water. He took out the fern-wrapped egg and placed it in his pocket. He poured the greens into the tub, soaking the dust and worms out of them. He sorted the chicory from the borage and dandelion, wrapping them into bundles, tying the bundles with a single stem. When Bambino finished, the middleman counted them up, took his cut of twenty bundles. He put the rest in a basket. He slapped Bambino on the back, and told Bambino to follow him into the stand that smelled like overripe melons, its bins half-filled with plums, tomatoes, and squash. Fresh sausage links hung from hooks nailed along the wall behind another plank table topped with a jar of pickled eggs and a cash box. As the man opened the cash box, he said, "What was your name again?"

"I am called Bambino."

"Bambino?" The man laughed. "No, tell me your real name."

"My mother, she was so tired when I was born, she ran out of boy names, so she give me this one."

"You're no child now. You're not even young. How old are you?"

"I have forty-two years, maybe forty-three."

"Let's be real men now," he said. "Let's start by giving you a real man's name. From now on, I'm going to call you 'Bam.'"

"How do you say it?"

The man shaped his forefinger and thumb like a gun, pulled an invisible trigger. "You say it like this," he said. "Bam." The man pulled a quarter out of the cash box and tried to hand it to Bambino.

"It isn't enough."

"Take it or leave it," the man said.

Bambino looked at the pickled eggs on the table, the fresh sausage strung from the hooks on the wall. His sight had grown dim, and his head ached from hunger, but he would not take the coin.

"You are a funny old boy, but you're still spry," the middleman said. "Look. Plenty of real work can be found down here. Now that freight service is falling off, the railroad's using angelinas like you to do the section work. I might could get you hired on as a gandy dancer for a while."

"The railroad would hire me to dance?"

"You wouldn't be dancing. You'd be straightening sections of track that the trains pound out of alignment. They like to call you Italian snipes gandy dancers because you all sing and do a little jig while you work."

"I can do this dancing work."

The man glanced out the open door, his sharp eyes cutting toward the west yard, where a tall, blond trainman was coming out of the empty passenger train. "Go on, now. It's too damn hot to be standing around in here. Come back tomorrow morning, and I'll see what I can do."

Bambino tied the empty burlap bag around his waist and swung the one full of snails over his shoulder. It took him four hours to walk up the mountain, and when he reached the shelter he saw that it had been used for target practice by some hunters, maybe forty rounds shot into its walls. The single window was shattered. Outside the shelter, he soaked the snails in water and bran to sweeten them. He went over to his fire pit beneath a stand of pines and struck some flint together, trying to spark a fire. The wood he'd collected was still wet from the night's rainstorm, and blue tendrils of smoke rose from the wood. He gave up on the fire and ate the snails raw so that he would not grow too hungry and lose his sight. The snails tasted faintly of dirt and creek water, still bitter from eating the grasses.

When he finished the snails, he broke the egg and ate the yolk. He soaked a rag in the egg whites and covered his sore eyes with the compress as he lay on the car's front seat inside the shelter. When the compress dried, he could see the bullet holes in the wall before him. They looked like bright coins, silvery in the moonlight. Now that he had a job, he would buy a hammer and nails to build a shelter for his wood, eat macaroni and sausage that he cooked over a blazing fire. He might buy a new pair of shoes, the kind that didn't slip. He imagined buying four pairs of shoes, selling three pairs for a profit. He counted the bright holes in the wall until he reached fifty. He lost count, and dozed, dreaming of eggs sinking into a pail of water, lemon groves in Sicily, the Indian figs growing around his mother's stone house, sheltering the white walls from the relentless Sicilian sun. In his dream, his mother hummed another tarantella, *Figliola, mother, virgin, fountain, climb the mountain, enter the garden, go across waters, make this young girl happy, heal her. The moon is white and you are dark.*

THE NEXT MORNING, Bambino walked down to the train station in darkness and stood outside the train office with four other men—one Southern Italian and three Sicilians. They waited for work beside a sign that said: MEN WANTED FOR TRACK WORK ROCK BALLAST STRAIGHT TIME RAIN OR SHINE PAID WEEKLY. The stenographers at the baseball factory had taught Bambino to read a little in English. He recognized the letter *w* in *work*, the letter *p* in *paid*. The tall, blond trainman who'd come out of the passenger car the day before came out of the train office, accompanied by two Slovak guards who carried rifles. He introduced himself as the foreman and led the crew a mile west of the station, where the track curved around the mountain. The foreman spoke Italian as well as any native, with a Northern accent. He explained to the crew that the tracks were held in place by wooden ties and the crushed rock ballast beneath them. He said that each pass of a train around the curve shifted the tracks, and that such shifts accumulated with time and the train's heavy repetition, causing derailment.

"It's your job to pry the tracks back into place." He dug the iron bar into the ballast, showing them how to force its tip into the rocks beneath the track, push the rail toward the inside of the curve. "You won't see any movement in the track for a while."

The work was like dancing. The men stood shoulder-to-shoulder, facing the rail and the caller, the Southern Italian from Abruzzi who was named Felice. The rest of the crew—short, dusky men with round faces and curly black hair—tapped their lining bars against the rails in perfect time to the caller's two-line, four-beat chant, *Big cat, little cat, teenyiny kitten. Big cat.* When Felice reached "big cat," the men angled their bars under the rail, and gave it a hard pull. All morning, they tapped the tracks with their poles and lifted. As the foreman promised, they saw no big shift in the rail. The foreman stood back, aloof and unreachable, a solid black figure cut out of the soft gray mist. The three Sicilians and the caller from Abruzzi had worked on the foreman's crew before. They gently teased the foreman, calling him "Garibaldi" because he was tall, and his blond hair turned ginger in the sun. The Slovak soldiers sat on an outcropping of high rocks among the weedy banks of the rail bed, their rifles resting across their laps. They scanned the ridge above the rail bed, their sharp gray eyes trained on the deep green and blue summer woods where invisible cicadas churned, interrupted only by staccato chirps of crickets. The tracks disappeared around the bend, into the morning fog, and the mountain loomed over them, dark and moody inside the gray haze. The other men on the crew worked beside Bambino, swirling like black flames in the cool mist.

The red sun rose over the mountain and burned through the fog. When the men tired from the work and heat, the caller changed his chant to uplift their minds and bodies, *Susie, Susie, don't you know, I can make your belly grow.* They began prying the rail with a one-handed flourish, stepping out and twirling back on beats one, two, and four, pulling with two arms on the third beat. Bambino was afraid to work with one arm; he still wore the stiff, slippery shoes, and the ballast rocks shaled out from beneath his shoes as he pried and lifted the rail. He watched the younger men work with abandoned energy. He listened to the tapping of the gandy poles, the iron rail ringing, wondering why the armed soldiers were here, and if they would shoot at him if he stepped out of time, or made a mistake. He thought of Rosario saying, "In bocca al lupo." He couldn't believe his luck. The men beside him worked together, in silent agreement that they would not speak of the *miseria* that only the Sicilian-born would know—the lost and dying children, the wives and mothers they'd abandoned on the island. With these men, Bambino didn't need to discuss his bandit father's permanent jail time, his brother's grave-robbing, his own descent into the Ohio River bottoms to sew baseballs in blinding heat and slaughterhouse stench. Why speak of such *miseria*? You had to look forward. If the head turns back, the body turns with it. His arms and legs ached pleasantly from the track work, and his mind filled with thoughts of having money for bread, eggs, and macaroni, good shoes. If he kept this job, he might even save enough to send to his mother.

When the fog burned off completely, and the sun burned white in the deep, blue sky, the foreman released the crew for supper. Felice and the other crew members—whose names were Ciolino, Gaspare, and Vincenzo—lived in a camp made up of three bunk cars and a kitchen car. They bought eggs and milk from the middleman, and they cooked frittatas over an open fire. The foreman sat by the fire with the crew, spearing chunks of bread and sausage onto a skewer, grilling the bread over the open flames, giving slices to the crew members and the soldiers. The Slovak soldiers sat off to the side, eating the bread smothered with soft white cheese, speaking to each other in their low, ringing language. Bambino sat alone, slinging rocks into the side of a bunk car. The foreman walked over and gave a piece of grilled bread to Bambino, who tried the bread on his remaining teeth. The bread crumbled, most of it falling out of his mouth. He gave up on eating and listened to the crew members quiz the foreman about Garibaldi, creating a call and response that seemed as familiar to them as the gandy chants.

"What did they call him?" the men asked.

"The Blond Bomber," the foreman answered.

"Why is he the hero of all Italians?"

"He defeated the Bourbons and unified Italy."

"What did he do while in exile on Staten Island?"

"He made candles."

The candle-making fact struck all the men as funny, and they broke out laughing.

"Who is in charge of Italy now?" Bambino asked.

The men stopped laughing. They turned and stared at him. "Where have you been?"

"I leave the paese in 1913," Bambino said. "Since then, I am living in La Mèrica, first above the Ohio River, and now here."

A low plane buzzed overhead, and everyone looked up.

"Mussolini," the foreman said. "He is in charge of Italy now."

"Who is this Mussolini?"

The caller from Abruzzi spoke first. "In Italy, he is like a god," he said. "I remember seeing him, one day, in the field outside my village. He was watching military maneuvers. Two nuns, their long black veils flying behind them, carried out a basket of peaches to give to him."

"He is like a peasant," Vincenzo said. "He speaks like a peasant, and the peasants come running to him. They lift their babies up for him to kiss."

"He's no god, and he's no peasant," the foreman said. "He's a very dangerous man. He's about to lead Italy into another war for no good reason."

The foreman stood abruptly, ending any further discussion. Bambino wondered if the foreman was angry with him for asking who Mussolini was. As the foreman went into the passenger car, Bambino wondered aloud if the foreman was a *galantuomo* or a *don*. The crew assured him that the foreman lived on his own land, but that he did not profit off the work of other men.

"He brought his wife up from a coal field, and they have a young son who is beautiful as a banner in a breeze," Vincenzo said. "He is a civilized man, good as bread."

The foreman returned with a pitcher of warm milk, a small porcelain bowl, and an Italian *moka*, filled with coffee. Each man held out an empty cup, and the foreman poured warm milk and coffee into their outstretched cups. He dipped a tiny silver spoon into a porcelain bowl. He held out a heap of sugar on the spoon. He sprinkled the sugar over each cup of coffee, and the men solemnly watched it fall, settle, and reform in their cups. When foreman reached Bambino, he handed him an empty cup, pouring milk and coffee into it. He held out the sugar spoon, pouring the crystals over the top. Bambino stared at the man's fingers, slender as a woman's, but longer and thickly calloused. Bambino watched the coffee, amazed by the black beverage mixing with milk, turning the color of a monk's robe. A creamy head formed on top of the coffee, holding the sugar briefly until it sank, slowly settling and reforming inside the beautiful brown coffee. The rest of the crew drank Italian style, tossing it back with two short sips. Bambino stared in wonderment into his cup, the cream on top holding the sugar crystals, the sugar sinking and settling.

"Prendi il caffè con panna e sugo?" the foreman asked.

"Mai," Bambino mumbled.

"You never drink coffee with cream and sugar?"

"No, I never drink coffee like this in La Mèrica. I never see coffee like this since I am in Sicily."

The foreman neither smiled nor laughed. He filled the rest of Bambino's cup, motioned for him to soak his bread in the coffee. "Here, eat your bread like this," he said. "The coffee will soften it."

The strong, sweet coffee and bread worked on Bambino like an opiate, making him so homesick that his eyes watered. While the rest of the crew rolled tobacco into papers and smoked, Bambino stole glances at the foreman, the fine blond hair that curled over his receding hairline, his piercing blue eyes. The foreman tossed his coffee back like the Italians, but he didn't smoke with them. He looked off toward the curve of track where the crew had lifted and straightened all morning, winding his railroad watch absentmindedly.

If he is not a *galantuomo* or a *don*, then who is he? Bambino wondered.

"You don't like to smoke?" he asked.

"I used to when I was in the army over in Italy, but I quit," the foreman said.

"Those soldiers over there." Bambino pointed to the Slovaks. "Will they shoot us if we make a mistake?"

"They are here for your protection."

"From what are they protecting us?"

The foreman looked into the wooded ridges, the sun rolling over the summit. He looked back at his railroad watch. He stood. The crew followed him back to the section of the track where they'd been working all morning, and, as the foreman promised, they saw a little progress. The track had budged an inch. The sun beat down, silencing the cicadas that had churned all morning. In the distance, Bambino saw a train car that he hadn't seen that morning. Hulked beside the retired passenger car, this new car was rigged with iron-plate siding, its side slit in places.

"What is that?" Bambino asked.

"The Death Special," Vincenzo said. "See those holes in the side? The Baldwin-Felts men used to put machine guns in those holes and drive the car through the coal camps. During the mining wars, they made lace out of the tent colonies outside the camps."

"They made lace out of women and children too," Felice added.

"That car is retired," the foreman said, though he told Felice to stop calling the rhythmic chants. "This isn't a dance we're doing out here," he added quietly in English, and Bambino thought he heard him say, "We are in another kind of war now."

When a freight train returned, the crew stepped away from the bed and watched it rush by, closing their eyes to the dust and smoke that blew off its coal cars. When the men stepped back up to the rail, Bambino stood back, feeling his skin prickling as he watched the train brake at the station, waiting to be emptied and graded. The Slovak guards stood now, searching the ridges, their guns following their eyes. They made Bambino even more nervous. He felt certain now that one of them would shoot him if he stepped out of line or made a mistake. He wondered what the American foreman had been doing in the military, living in Italy when there was no war. In Sicily, nobody joined the army willingly. The military didn't pay, so if you went into the army, your family starved. Bambino had hidden from them in a barn, but the guards had found him. They put him on a train in Palermo, in a wooden boxcar that swayed and shook as if it might split in two. The train arrived at the barracks in the Cefaltic Military district while it was still night, and they took him inside to shave his head. They gave him a hat and two wooden slats to keep the corners of the hat stiff. They gave him a bed with a sheet, pillow, and mattress. Unused to sleeping on anything but straw, he stayed awake on the too-soft mattress until the officers came in at daylight.

They drilled him for weeks, teaching him how to salute with one hand stretched toward the eyes, thumb tight against his hand, fingertips touching just under the cap. They taught him to look only forward, cautioning him that if his eyes shifted, his head would follow. Finally, the officers got down to teaching the real work of killing men. They started with empty hand grenades without fuses, kept in wooden crates, like apples. The first time, Bambino was so frightened he threw the bomb before pulling the pin. When he was no longer afraid of grenades, they put him in target practice. They stood him at the end of a dry field and taught him how to aim a rifle at six men made out of wood, telling him to always shoot first, ask questions later. He fired, nicking the dummies. One splinter of wood meant one man down.

For two years, that was military life: throwing empty hand grenades, shooting the wooden men, asking no questions. He got out before the war started. Released with an honorable discharge in Germini, he returned to Palermo and found his mother and brother. Rosario laughed at him when Bambino cried at seeing him alive, and not in prison for grave robbing. "They couldn't put me in jail." Rosario had said. "They couldn't afford to feed me."

The railroad work began to feel like an unending military drill. He could feel a fight coming in the air. The Slovak soldiers stood with their legs braced, their eyes scanning the forest. The crew had stopped dancing and singing. They began jacking up the track in low spots, pushing the ballast under the raised ties with the square ends of their poles. They leaned shoulder-to-shoulder in this never-ending task. They stopped to replace a rotten tie. Felice pulled the spike from the tie. Then Gaspare and Vincenzo loosened the tie with a pair of tongs, carrying the rotten wood away from the railroad bed while Bambino and Ciolino cleaned out the bed.

As the new tie was put in place, and Felice began driving the spike in with a hammer, a stone flew out of the understory. Bambino heard the hissing sound of voices, "wage-cutters, dagoes, guineas" as more rocks and stones flew out of the woods. A gunshot rang out, then another, and Bambino realized the soldiers were not shooting at him, but into the forest. A rock hit him on his lower back, another on the back of his right knee, knocking him off balance. His right foot slipped between rail and ballast. As he fell, his ankle flipped between the iron and stone, and he could hear a ripping of muscles, like a root being torn out of the earth. When the pain started, it clasped his ankle like a metal band, tightening, rising through his leg. Blood rushed out of his head until all he heard and felt was a white raging pain.

He lay on the grass, staring at the sky, listening to the final round of gunshots, waiting for the stones to stop flying. He sat up, staring at his ankle that swelled, growing purple. The foreman knelt before him, pushing the sole of his bare foot, turning it in a careful circle, asking him if and where it hurt. He set the foot back on the ground.

"It's not broken," he announced.

"Are you a doctor?"

The foreman shook his head. "The doctor won't come," he said. "The company won't pay for him to fix this."

"The man who gave me the job said I worked for the company." The foreman shook his head. "You're not on the payroll."

"They lied?" Bambino said.

The foreman nodded. "These days, I don't know too many people who have a healthy respect for the truth." He grasped Bambino's forearms, pulling him gently to his feet. "Can you walk?"

Bambino stood and, miraculously, the ankle held. He could walk as long as he kept his feet and head forward. If he turned his foot to either side, a pain rifled through him. The foreman watched him walk and nodded. He gave Bambino a cup like the one that had held the sweet coffee. "Here. Drink this. It will fix you right up." Bambino tipped the cup, expecting more of the sweet coffee. He nearly gagged on a sour concoction that smelled of the moscadella grown in the vineyards back in his village. "It's sour wine and honey." The foreman urged him to keep drinking. "I make the wine from my own grapes. And I robbed my own bees for the honey. Drink up. It's good for whatever ails you, and it won't give you a headache the morning after." He gave Bambino the green, unlabeled bottle. He looked back toward the track, and Bambino followed his gaze to the slippery dress shoe still wedged between rail and ballast. The shoe stood as if an invisible man were still wearing it. "The men who threw those stones at you used to work on this crew until the company let them go," the foreman said. "They think you took their jobs. They'll be back. Next time, they'll bring more than stones to aim at you." He pulled a silver coin out of his pocket and placed it in Bambino's palm. "It's not safe to bring you back tomorrow. Buy yourself a decent pair of shoes. Walk as far away from here as you can."

The foreman wrapped Bambino's ankle with strips of his own shirt. Then he moved on to the Slovak soldier who'd been nicked in the head by a stone. While the foreman dressed the soldier's wound, Bambino slipped into the woods and searched for the soldier's rifle, finding it where he'd fallen. He took it to the general store, planning to sell it. He passed a row of leather boots and stopped, thinking, What do shoes mean now that I have no job to go to? He kept the rifle. He bought a lantern, a silver serving fork, and a ball of twine.

Days passed as he lay inside the hunter's shelter, holding his swollen ankle over the edge of the car seat. He tried propping his right foot at different angles at the edge of the seat, but each time the foot touched down, a pain shot through him. He dozed, his sleep nearly malarial, his body pinned to the car seat by heat and thirst. Only his foot remained suspended over air. He dreamed of drinking cup after cup of sweet coffee, sugar floating above its foam like ice crystals. He dreamed of Rosario bringing snow and sugar cane home from the Madonie Mountains, mixing it with juice from lemons and bitter oranges he'd found on the ground outside the grove. When Bambino awoke, his mouth was dry and sour, and his eyes were so gritty in their sockets that he could not see well through them. The bottle of sour wine and honey sat beside him. He soaked a rag with the wine, letting the gall scour the gritty blindness from his eyes.

It was still July. Though he couldn't see very well, he could hear the thrumming of frogs, deep and loud, like bulls in a distant pasture. When his eyes cleared, he saw that his ankle was no longer purple, but it still throbbed and swelled, and the shiny shoe would not fit. Barefoot, he went outside and searched the woods for a long stick. He went back into the shelter and tied the silver fork to the end of the pole with the twine, fashioning a makeshift trident. The white moon shone through the bullet holes the hunters had shot into the plywood walls of the shelter; the holes looked like stars in a black night sky. He went outside and gathered the brass bullet casings lying in the dirt, planning to sell them to the middleman or maybe to the blacksmith. He recalled the name the middleman had given him down by the railroad tracks. In the military, the officers had called him many names—bandit, green-flicker, dirt-eater—but none of these names had seemed as savage as the words hurled with rocks and sticks by the American railroad men who thought he'd taken their jobs. He repeated the words, "Wage-cutter, dago, and guinea," angering himself all over. He cocked the invisible trigger and practiced the razored-down name the middleman had given him, his real man's name, saying it aloud, "Bam."

The only escape from being hunted was to keep hunting. Carrying the makeshift trident, the lantern, and an empty burlap sack, he walked down the game trail with his eyes forward, mincing his steps so that he would not turn his ankle. The mountain had become older since he'd last walked down it. Brittle spider webs broke across his face, and the stones on the path were fossilized by moonlight. He turned one over and saw a clump of snails, their skin dry and white as the peel of an onion. He flipped the stone back over and kept walking. His right toe hit a fossilized root, and a pain rifled through his ankle. The pain enraged him so much that he yelled out, but his voice was muted by the droning of frogs in the still pool of the river, their voices joined with the high trilling of tree frogs in the limbs that loomed over the creek.

When he reached the water, he climbed down four crumbling stone steps and sat beside a pool rimmed by tall grasses rising from the water that lapped languidly against the sandy shore. The smell of sulfur wafted over him. It was the stench of malaria, the smell of children dying. He took out the lantern and waded into the water, patrolling the grasses. The water warmed and soothed his aching ankle. Silver moonlight broke over the surface, sinking and settling around the rocks. He recalled the sugar crystals settling around the beautiful coffee, and he felt calm. He shined the lantern on the grasses. The beam hit two yellow eyes, blinding them for a moment. He stabbed toward the eyes, pulled up the fat frog. The frog's eyes were full of fear as he dropped it, wriggling, into the burlap bag. He gigged frogs all night until the sack was filled. He looked inside. In the lantern light, he saw the bulging eyes of the frogs, their yellow throats and swollen stomachs. They looked like starving, malarial children he'd grown up with, their hunger more frightening than any form of violence. He thought of the rich railroad man who would not hire him back, afraid of risking more violence. This man, who could afford to give away bread and sweet coffee, should have to look into these violently hungry eyes.

He went back up to the shelter and cleaned the frogs, snipping them cleanly between femur and pelvis, pulling off the skin from the hips down. He threw the frog legs on the fire and ate them. He steeped his last bundle of borage, cleansing his eyes until his sight returned. He walked down to the meadow to look for more healing greens. The morning sun burnished the field, its heat already moving in waves. A few green comfrey leaves coiled among the high, golden weeds. He knelt, working his knife into the ground, digging up the stem and roots of the healing plant.

Behind him, the high, dry weeds shook and parted. He looked back and saw a dog that was not Briciola. Still as stone, this dog had the head of a wolf, the body of a stout hound, and for moment Bambino thought he was seeing a Cerberus. Its slate eyes were watchful as Bambino walked by, and he felt a sliver of ice slip behind his heart, pins pricking his skin. The dog let him pass, and for a moment Bambino felt relieved. Maybe he would be lucky. *In bocca al lupo,* he thought. The dog began to growl, and Bambino saw that it had only one head, not three heads like the fabled Cerberus. It stood guard over nothing but a sun-scorched clearing, bracing its powerful legs, readying itself for an attack. In an instant, Bambino's fear hardened into rage at being watched and hunted. As the dog charged him, golden fur rippled within the black fur of its muscular forelegs, its back paws clawing up earth and dry oats, sending a shower of golden chaff over its back and hind legs. The dog lunged, its body full of power, hunger, and rage as it knocked Bambino to the ground, straddling his shoulders with its forelegs. Bambino gave it his left arm to save his eyes, feeling the first punctures of the dog's teeth, the tearing of his flesh, his own energy and rage draining as the dog held him down and pulled his arm back and forth. His right hand still had feeling, and it still held the knife. He slashed blindly at the dog's mouth and throat until it released him. The animal lay on the ground, bleeding and panting. *Crepi il lupo,* he thought, willing the dog to die. He knelt, found a stone, and smashed it down on the dog's head.

He stumbled up to the hunter's shelter and found the rifle. He walked down to an old tree stand and climbed into it, rifle slung

over his back. Sun and rain had dissolved the stand's leafy camouflage; strips of dried leaves hung like long, gray cobwebs from
around the platform, dissolving at his touch. The tree stand's platform overlooked the clearing. He sat, sentinel, looking for more
mad dogs, but all he could see were mangy sheep grazing around
outcroppings of stones. Two skinny horses hunched in the shade
at the side of the pasture, swishing their tails against flies, pawing
the dust. The flies bit them beneath their tails, and they ran wildly,
bucking. The goats stared at the wild horses, forgetting to eat.
Below the fallow land, lilies escaped the rich man's garden. They
ran like bright flames through the old cemetery, sparking between
the tombstones.

The sun scythed over the tree stand. When it struck, sweat
poured out of him, cooling him like soaking rain, a relief from the
sun that shimmered over the scorched and golden grasses below.
He was no longer afraid of mad dogs hiding in the meadow. He
was more frightened of the men who had crouched in the woods
beside the rail bed the day before, hurling their rocks, starting
incomprehensible wars, equipping their train cars with machine
guns that made lace out of women and children. He felt tired, so
tired that the shady graveyard began to look like a good place for
a long sleep. He climbed down from the tree stand and headed
for the cemetery. He lay down beneath a braided limb of a sassafras tree, in the soft shade grasses between a headstone and a
footstone, setting his rifle next to him.

Dozing, he saw again the Cerberus charging him, and he
wondered if he were lying at the gates of hell or heaven. He had
doubts about where his own soul would rest. He dreamed of Rosario coming home from digging up graves in the malarial plains
below the slope of Etna. His white skin had turned yellow, and he
shivered inside his shirt. The doctor said that Rosario suffered
from the *febbre intermittente*, an intermittent case of malaria that

could be treated with sulfates and eucalyptus decoctions, but Bambino knew that the fever was caused by all the souls Rosario had robbed. The dead were living inside of his brother, shaking his body and soul.

Rosario would not take the sulfates or the eucalyptus medicine, and the fever took his brain. He stopped shaving, and his blond whiskers glistened in the sun, turning his features boyish. He sat for hours on a bench in the piazza, hands flat against the bench, waiting for the morning Mass to end, and for their mother to come out of the church. On the feast of Saint Rosalia, Bambino's mother went to the early and late Masses, so Bambino went with Rosario to wait in the piazza. Rosario slouched on the bench, his unshaven face intent, his eyes clear and wide. He seemed impossibly weak and cold, lost.

"Late Mass ends at twelve-thirty," Bambino offered. "We could go in and pray with Mother."

"There's something else I'd like to do."

They walked down the sloping streets, down past the lemon groves. Rosario pulled two lemons from a limb hanging over the wall and put them in his pocket. When they reached the shore, the tide was coming in, and the waves crashed over the lava rocks, pulling away. The brothers knew the rhythm of the waves: ten minutes in, twenty minutes out. They had time to crawl out onto the black rocks and sit on a dry, flat stone just above the rising waves. Rosario peeled the lemons. They were hopelessly sour. Bambino spat his out, tossing flesh and rind into the sea. Rosario continued eating the lemon, oblivious.

"We live so close to the sea," he said. "Why don't we ever swim in it?"

"Because it could kill us."

Rosario looked to his left, where the broom grew sideways from the black cliffs, its yellow, star-like blossoms reaching into the obsidian, churning it slowly to soil. He looked right, toward a crescent spit of sand that led back into town. He turned to Bambino, saying, "It's you who are dead, brother."

When Rosario jumped, the water splashed up cold, but the salt breeze was warm. Bambino dove in after him, but the tide was moving out swiftly, carrying his brother away until he could no longer see him. Knowing the tide's relentless rhythm, *ten minutes in, twenty minutes out,* Bambino swam towards shore. Two anchovy fishermen, casting their lines off the deserted boardwalk outside the ancient city walls, fished Bambino out. He looked back one more time, but his brother was gone. As he climbed the steep and narrow street, the rough stones of the low houses were blindingly white in the sun, and the Indian figs rose like green, prickly bars over the windowless windows. He reached the Piazza del Duomo and saw his mother standing in front of the church, the rosary wrapped around her fingers, her knuckles whitened by the tight grasp of the rosewood beads.

When he told her what had happened to Rosario, she didn't cry, and she didn't look at him. Instead, she pulled up the bottom of her black dress and ripped the hem open. Hundreds of lire notes fell from her skirt, settling like pale leaves around her feet. She raised her dry, melancholy eyes to him. "This money belonged to your brother. Take it and go to La Mèrica," she'd said. "You're getting old. Soon, the fever will ruin you too."

The Norman towers of the church loomed over the piazza that was nearly empty, except for the old men in black suits who gathered at the corners, the women in black hunching in the dark doorways of their low houses. For the first time, Bambino noticed that only the old and dying remained here. He gathered the money at his mother's feet, bought passage on a steamer heading from Palermo to La Mèrica the next day.

Wind blew through the sassafras tree, and a few dry leaves dropped over Bambino. Climbing out of his heavy dream, he felt fevered, and filled with a vague dread. *Why am I still in this world?* he thought. *To eat, to work, to earn wages.* He wondered if the souls of the dead had entered him while he slept. He reasoned: *If the dead are already inside of me, then they won't mind if I take from them.* He rose and pried an iron crucifix off a tombstone, dropped it in his burlap bag. He would try to sell it along with the bullet casings. He began cutting the yellow lilies with orange stars in their centers that ran away from the rich man's garden. He would make them into bouquets, sell them on the street corners of town to the rich ladies waiting for their husbands to come home from their wage jobs.

As he walked through the graves, he chanted a half-remembered poem Rosario often recited before his favorite tarantella: *My grandfather was a peasant who gathered hunger in his hands but knocked not at the palace door.* He reached the stone boundary wall. The honeysuckle had wilted, its blossoms tumbling across the graves, but there was a sweeter, headier scent coming from the garden. Deep red roses towered over the stone wall, tangling with vines of moscadella. Fermenting in the sun, the grapes smelled like the wine the foreman had given him the day before. His eyes watered, and they felt gritty despite the soothing medicine. He worried he would lose his sight. He closed his eyes, rubbing the grit out of them. When he opened his eyes again the Madonna stood before him, her white dress stained a deep red, those Arab eyes flashing at him. She didn't turn away this time. "Those aren't yours," she said, nodding at the flowers.

"Mi dispiace," he said. "I do not think they belong to you."

He dropped the flowers at her feet, thinking, *If you are real, and you are the Madonna, why don't you give me a job?* He reached out and touched a single finger to her lips stained the same deep red as her apron. Her warm breath shocked him. He spoke the first English words that came into his head, "Lady," he said. "Lipstick."

He left her standing there, the cut flowers flaming around her feet. Ducking into the woods, he walked down the hill, reaching the train station at dusk. He began to collect the coal tossed off the locomotive, planning to sell it too, buy a train ticket to the next town with the money he made. He picked in the far part of the train yard where the stationmaster did not patrol with his lantern. He kept his own lantern off, picking by moonlight until his eyes were gritty with the dust, and the morning fog began to roll down the mountain, hanging low over the tracks. The trees beside the rails rose black against the white fog, their black leaves bouncing over a halted freight car. Crickets rang beneath the fog, reminding him of the *cianciadedda*, small tinkling bells that rang on the horse carts in his village. The bells dragged themselves over the tracks that vanished into the fog in the distance, backlit by the rising sun.

Near the vanishing point, a black figure appeared. Tall and rigid, the figure walked towards him, in the middle of the tracks. Fog at its back, the figure remained faceless, moving toward him like a fever dream. Bambino staggered backward, his ankle and arm throbbing, his mind fogged by hunger and headache. He craved something sour. He thought of Rosario's fevered cravings for lemons the day he gave himself up to the sea, his mother's dry eyes as she handed him the money his brother had plundered from the dead. Bambino wondered if the figure walking toward him were one of the souls from the cemetery above the rich man's garden, come down to hound him for taking the crucifix and the flowers from the graves. Then he heard the crunch of gravel, the stomping of wood ties beneath its feet, and he knew the shadow was a real man, maybe another bandit come to take his coal away, or one of the jobless, ready to throw more stones. The man stopped at twenty feet, reached toward his waist.

Bambino felt sure he'd been seen. It was too late to hide or flee. He slipped the sling of the rifle off his shoulder, opening the breech. There were still two bullets in the magazine. He bolted the breech shut, locked it down. He aimed like he was taught in the military, shooting first, without questioning. The stock kicked his right shoulder as the first bullet hit the man's waist, and the man twisted forward. The second bullet splintered the head, and the man was down. Bambino stood, weary from the work of killing. He gathered the brass casings, which were still hot in his hand. He walked down the track and knelt beside the crumpled figure, saw the railroad watch, its crystal spiderwebbed by the first bullet.

He pulled the man off the tracks, cradling the head in his hands. As he adjusted the body in the grasses beside the rail bed, he dared not look down at the ruined face. He looked away, toward the light behind the vanishing point. The light was growing brighter, and the fog hung like a curtain catching on fire. His sore eyes burned in his head like two torches. His tear ducts had scarred over a long time ago, but his languid heart thumped against his rib cage. The pounding sound marched into his head as he saw the full bottle of wine, the sausage wrapped in butcher's paper, the hands covering both, as if to protect them. Slender and calloused, these hands had served him sweet coffee and given him a whole silver piece for half a day's work.

Bambino sat back on his haunches, holding the wine bottle in one hand, the white butcher's package in the other. Alive, this man would have given away the wine and sausage to anyone who'd asked for them. Dead, he wouldn't mind if Bambino took these things from him. He folded the hands across the man's still chest, winding the railroad watch's chain through the fingers. Against the man's long, elegant fingers, his own calloused fingers were torn and frostbitten, permanently scorched by the sun, savaged. How had such a civilized man ever lived? he thought. He tucked the wine and sausage safely under the man's hands. He would not take from him.

The freight train came alive and rocked forward. Steam rose

from it, swirling into the fog. Soon, a new crew of Italians would arrive and stand in their places on the track. More jobless men would sneak out of the woods, hurling stones, or worse. He felt the fever of an oncoming war. He would get out before it ruined him. The train heaved forward, and Bambino ran alongside it. He caught the hand grab of an empty boxcar, hoisting himself up. The train worked up speed, losing itself in the morning mist.

PART TWO

❀ Dean, 1939

The Nipper

DEAN HAD BEEN LIVING with his grandparents and uncles in War for two years when his Grandmother Palmisano decided it was time for him to get a job in the mines. Though Dean was fourteen, too young to work underground, his grandmother paid the foreman twenty-five cents for an age blank, passed Dean off as a small sixteen year old so that he could be the nipper. This was in late February, still winter in the coal camp, and the road leading from his grandparents' frame house to the mine stretched before Dean like a white lake. Because he was small for his age, Dean's Grandpa Palmisano and Uncle Carlo had to carry him through the high, spring snow on his first day of work. When his grandfather tired, his uncle lifted him onto his shoulders. In the pre-dawn darkness, Dean felt his uncle's stout chest heaving beneath his calves, his hobnail boots slicing right through the snow, his heels thumping hard against the frozen earth. Uncle Carlo's tobacco breath floated upward, clouding the gray icy air. This manly smell comforted Dean as they approached the black breaker hulking over the colliery.

At the bathhouse, his grandfather and uncle stripped off their street clothes, placed them in metal baskets, and pulled them up to the ceiling, where they hung limply from hooks among hundreds of empty white shirts. After dressing, Carlo went down to the stables to currycomb his mule and check the fit of her harness, while Grandpa Palmisano took Dean to the gangway and showed him the heavy, wooden door built across the tunnel opening.

"Inside the door, a giant fan pulls fresh air into the mine," his grandfather explained. When the door was closed, the air hit it, turning back into the underground tunnels and chambers where the miners worked, keeping deadly gasses from building in pockets, pushing out the black damp. For the next twelve hours, Dean needed to keep the door shut so that the good air remained inside, opening it only to let full cars out into the coal yard and empty ones back in.

Grandpa Palmisano showed Dean how to handle the door when a mine car approached, how to pour water over the carbide to light his lamp. Then, suddenly, he blew out the flame, showing Dean just how dark it could get beneath the earth, telling him how this solitary job as the nipper would breed the courage he'd need to become a miner some day. The flint snapped again, and his grandfather's face reappeared in the blue lamp light, warning Dean that he must never fall asleep.

"How do I stay awake?" Dean asked.

"Play with the rats." His grandfather turned, walking down the gangway to the mine trip car. His lamplight fluttered like a yellow bird, casting shadows against the tunnel walls. "Share your lunch with them. Keep them close, and they will tell you when the roof is working."

When the mine trip car disappeared around the first bend of the tunnel, Dean shut the door and sat on his bench beside a pile of shale, putting his carbide lamp beside him. In the sudden, heavy silence, he wondered, How does a roof work? But he heard only an occasional pickaxe from a nearby chamber, a rat scuttling across the floor. It stood on its hind legs in front of Dean, and begged like a squirrel.

"You ain't no squirrel," Dean said, tossing a piece of shale at it. The rat whipped its naked tail at Dean's lunch pail, knocked off the lid. Dean pulled his lunch closer, checked on his ham biscuits and beans while the rat slipped back into a hole in the wall, its fat belly and fur dragging across the dirt floor. Dean hated rats. Playing with a rat, he thought, would betray the memory of his father, a railroad man who'd called coal operators "sewer rats" and never worked in the mines. Once, an army of real rats infested an abandoned dairy below the mountain farmhouse where Dean and his parents had lived. For a month, Dean's father came home after a day of building up railroad beds for the train company and sat in the open kitchen window, shooting off the rats as they marched up the sloping ridge below their house, the same ridge tramps wandered over, glassy-eyed from whatever they drank from their paper sacks, asking his father for money, sometimes work.

"You're like tramp bait," Dean's mother had told his father, claiming a tramp could find his father among a crowd of one hundred. Though his father rarely had cash money or work to give, he always offered each tramp a boiled egg, or some rhubarb jam on biscuits. Dean's mother worried over his father's habit of feeding the tramps, but his father claimed they were harmless, just hungry. The day after the tramp shot his father dead by the train tracks, hopped back onto the train, and was never seen again, Dean's mother climbed into her big brass bed, pulled her ivory wedding ring quilt up to her chin. Dry eyed, neither awake nor dreaming, she stayed in the bed with her angry, grieving face turned to the wall while Grandmother Palmisano explained that she was taking Dean back with her to the coal camp in War, West Virginia. She would send his mother to the home for rheumatics until she could get herself straight.

Now, as he sat in the mine gangway, Dean pondered how he

should play with the rats and stay awake so that he could keep his job and earn enough money to get out of the camp, rescue his mother from the home for rheumatics. Trying to think up a rat game, he looked around the chamber, found an empty powder tin and baited a piece of wire with a slice of ham biscuit. Placing the wired ham biscuit inside the tin, he set the trap on the floor across the coal car track, laying a sheet of paper over the tin's opening, holding the other end of the wire that would slam the heavy powder lid over the rat.

A rat crawled out of its hole, sniffed the air around Dean's trap, slipped inside. Dean pulled the wire, slamming the lid over the tin, running to clasp the lid in place. Holding the jerking can in his arms, Dean listened to the angry keen of the rat, unsure of what to do now that he'd caught it. His carbide lamp flickered weakly. He was afraid that if he set the angry rat free, it would turn on him and bite. This ain't play, Dean thought. Truth was, the only game Dean wanted to play was poker.

THE PREVIOUS SUNDAY, Grandpa Palmisano took him to eat supper at the boarding house that his mother's favorite aunt, Maria, ran for single miners. Short and plump, Maria smelled of dirty dishwater and the cigars she smoked when she sat in her aluminum rocker on the front porch every day. All through the meal, she'd stood at the head of a long picnic table in the dining room, between the pictures of a crucified Jesus and Henry Ford that hung on the wall behind her bench. Serving macaroni and tomato sauce from a bone china bowl, she passed around tough bread seasoned with the bitter herbs she found in the woods, ordering all the men to eat with a "Prego. Prego." When the pasta bowl was empty, the men moved outside to gamble on the back porch. Hands wrapped around water glasses filled with young wine, they bet each other on who could eat the hottest pepper each had grown that summer. They bet on hand after hand of stud poker, five card or seven. They bet on who could tell the dirtiest joke.

While the men gambled on the porch, Dean helped Maria clear and wash the dishes. Despite his great aunt's dishwater smell and frightening table manners, Dean understood why his mother loved her. Maria wore a faded yellow, silk dress beneath her stained apron, and gold, hoop earrings. Her round face remained smooth, her brown eyes wide and innocent, even though Dean's mother said Maria had a sordid past, a story the older family members whispered, and never told completely. At fifteen, she'd run away from the American man her father betrothed her to, an old miner she couldn't love. She'd taken off with a young Sicilian miner who left her for dead in Detroit, and Lord knows what kind of trouble she got into before she appeared back in the camp and took over the boarding house from her parents. That was a long time ago. Maria's siren beauty and flight to Detroit had become only one of his mother's bedtime stories. Now, Maria kept a deck of playing cards in her apron pocket. After she wiped down the picnic table, she dealt a hand of poker to anyone who'd sit across the picnic table from her. Too young to play cards with the men on the porch, Dean gladly accepted the cards that his aunt dealt swiftly and deftly with her fortune-teller hands.

"What do you wanna play poker for?" his aunt asked.

"Money," he said. "You can make hundreds of dollars if you're good at it."

"You gonna buy a mule like your Uncle Carlo?"

"I got other plans," he said.

"Good," she said. "Mules are more expensive than men and twice as hard to keep. Now Carlo, he is a little pazzo about his mule." She circled her finger near her head and rolled her eyes.

"That mule gives him three broken ribs, but he treats her like a sweetheart."

Dean laughed. "He calls her Peaches."

Maria studied him, her brown eyes teasing. "You got a sweetheart? You find a pretty girl down here?"

Dean considered the girl he'd seen on his first morning in the camp. Tall and willowy, she'd stood perfectly still on the wooden plank before his grandparents' house, as his grandfather and uncle were leaving for the mines. Wearing muddy hobnail boots and a flour sack dress, her thick blond hair sprang from its braid, haloing her round face in the dim morning light. Her blue eyes were long-lashed, wary, as she stood frozen, looking only at Dean, and Dean felt an empty longing that was stronger than homesickness, the urge to wash the mud from her boots, to gather her wild hair up in his hands, brushing and taming it with his fingers.

He wanted to ask her name, but Uncle Carlo shooed her away. "Vai. Vai. Didn't your mama teach you to wait inside until the miners are all gone to work?"

The girl sprang away, disappearing into a laurel thicket beside the house. Wait! Dean wanted to call after her. You got to tell me your name. You got to let me wash your shoes. His uncle spat his whole plug of tobacco on the path where the girl had stood.

"Now we're not gonna go to work today."

"Why not?"

"Can't. It's bad luck to see a woman on your way to the mine. A roof will fall."

Dean had found a pretty girl all right, but she was spookier than the mine rats, trickier than his great Aunt Maria, who slapped and swished the cards on the damp picnic table before him, dealing him another hand.

"Forget I ever told you about my plan," Dean said.

Maria looked steadily at him. "Those men on the porch aren't real poker players. They are gamblers."

"What's the difference?"

"A gambler bets a hundred dollars on what he has in his hand. A poker player bets on what he thinks the other players have."

"How do you know so much about gamblers and poker?"

"I was married to a gambler who worked as a sweeper in the Ford plant," she said. "I became a poker player to get back home after he left me in Detroit."

"I'm sorry." Dean waited, hoping she'd give him the parts of the story that his mother had never told him, but Maria only patted his hand. "It was long ago. C'era una volta."

Dean didn't want a mule or a girlfriend. One could kick you in the ribs, the other in the heart and head. He figured both could maim you somehow in the end. He wanted the cash money to buy a train ticket out of this deep hollow, where the sun shone for only three hours a day. He would go back to his family's farmhouse, wake his mother from her deep, grieving melancholy. He'd help her plant a garden and buy a horse, become the gentleman farmer his father had always planned to be when he quit the railroad.

"What did the blind man say when he passed the fish market?" Uncle Carlo yelled out on the porch, his voice thick with young wine.

"Cosa?" the rest of the men called back.

"Morning, ladies."

From the kitchen table, Dean heard laughter, winning coins pouring into his uncle's leather pouch. Only gambling would occur down here in the camp, but Dean would approach his plan like a poker player, telling no one, watching and waiting to see what the men around him did before he played his own hand.

THE POWDER CAN JERKED in Dean's arms. His fingers had fallen asleep from holding down the lid, and he couldn't remember why he decided to catch the rat in the first place. He knew only that a rat was too dumb to play poker. Even if it had the brains for a hand of five card draw, this one would probably cheat. When a coal cart rumbled to the door, Dean clenched his rat trap shut with his left hand and opened the mine door with his right to let his Uncle Carlo drive his mule through. Standing on the front car bumper, his braided whip curling from his belt, Carlo guided his mule by voice, speaking softly, "Vai" and "Va bene," until the mule stepped into the gangway. Dean closed the door, holding tightly to the tin can.

"What have you got in the can?" his uncle asked.

Dean shrugged, feeling foolish, and the can nearly jerked out of his arms. "A rat," he said.

Carlo looked from the can to Dean's face, but he didn't laugh. "Why did you put a rat in the can?"

Dean flushed. "Grandpa Palmisano told me to play with the rats so I could pass the time and stay awake. I caught this one, but now I can't figure out how to let it go without getting bit."

Carlo dismounted his coal car, squeezed past his thick mule. He placed one hand on the lid of the can, the other on the bottom. Setting the can down on the other side of the track, he backed away. The angry rat burst from the can, screeching and lurching toward his uncle. Carlo cracked his black whip above the rat's head, and the rat scuttled behind the pile of shale.

"A mule would make a better pet," Carlo said, pulling sugar cubes out of his pocket, offering them to his mule on his flattened palm. "My Peaches knows her way through these tunnels without looking. If I get lost, I just unharness her and follow her to the surface."

"Is she blind?"

"No. During the strike a year ago, all the mules were brought up to the surface. They trembled in the sunlight, but not one of them was blind. Peaches was hard to get out of the pasture and back into the mine. I think she has been a little bit angry about it ever since."

Carlo pulled two boiled eggs, two sausages, and two fried apple pies from his pocket, feeding one of the eggs, a sausage, and a pie to his mule, eating the rest after his mule was fed. "You want to hear another secret?"

Dean nodded.

"It's Peaches' birthday today. That is why I give her the pie with her sandwich."

"How do you know it's her birthday?"

"Because it is my birthday, and I bought her on this day four years ago. Now, we are like *gemelli*," he paused, searching for the word in English. "We are...like twins."

"Well, happy birthday to you both, I guess."

Dean studied his uncle's mule. Her long ears were filed down by the low mine ceilings, her wiry coat singed from her back during a long-ago mine fire. When Dean moved a little closer, Peaches tried to nibble Dean's flannel shirt right off his back. He suspected that the mule was even older than his uncle, who at twenty-five was the best and oldest mule driver in the mine. Still, the mule was short, stocky and dark, like his uncle; she favored Carlo the way a pampered dog will come to look like its faithful owner.

"What time is it?" Dean asked.

Carlo shrugged. "The foreman took my watch away when I became a driver so that I would think only about the number of cars."

"How do you know when to quit?"

"All I need to know is that I have six more chambers to get to before I can go home. I stay until the work is done."

"Aren't you ever afraid of being alone after the other men leave?"

Carlo laughed. "You are just a boy, but you talk like a very old man. Peaches takes me through tunnels where the foreman never goes. It is better than sitting all day in the gangway, or hunching over like a monkey in a hole. For me, the work is freedom. It is like paradise."

Carlo stood, brushed his lunch crumbs from his coveralls, squeezed past his mule. When his mule refused to budge, Carlo cracked his whip in the air above her head, coaxing, "andiamo," and the cart moved slowly toward the end of the tunnel, toward white sunlight. Sitting back on his bench, Dean imagined Carlo twisting and turning through miles of the deepest mine tunnels, oblivious to time, as carefree and graceful as a boy on a holiday sleigh ride. Dean envied his young uncle's freedom, his courage. Most of all, he envied Carlo's lunch, which was packed by Aunt Maria, who treated Carlo like her own son.

The scent of fried apple pie lingered in the gangway. Dean's stomach tugged with hunger until he remembered his own lunch, packed by his grandmother, a tall, blond woman who had come down from Ohio to teach in the company school and stayed after she married Dean's Italian grandfather. She made Dean sleep on the cot behind the coal stove in her kitchen, his mother's cramped childhood bed. His grandmother's country ham tasted like sweat and salt, and the dry biscuit crumbled when he lifted the sandwich to his mouth.

The dark gangway smelled like the inside of Dean's mother's oven, and he longed to be in his mother's kitchen on a Sunday morning when, off from the railroad, his father always planned supper while his mother was still washing the breakfast dishes. The yellow kitchen was warm and narrow, but Dean lingered at the round trundle table, watching his father cook with his mother. Hands moist with dishwater, his mother peeled potatoes and carrots while his father dredged strips of wild rabbit in flour and mustard, wrapping the winter vegetables and rabbit inside a buttery pie crust. His father gently touched the small of his mother's back when he reached around her for the salt and pepper; she arched her spine absentmindedly to let his arm pass. Now, as he sat in the cold gangway, looking down at the loveless, watery beans in his lunch, Dean thought of his father's cooking as a graceful dance by a man who never grew old or bitter enough to hate food and his own family.

Dean forced a biscuit down, and it sat like a stone in his stomach, cramping his left side. He set his carbide lamp on the floor and lay down on his bench, kneading the cramp with his left hand. When the cramp loosened, he grew dangerously sleepy. He stood, taking a deck of cards from his coverall pocket. Though she hadn't packed a lunch for him, his Aunt Maria had given him a deck of cards before he left her boarding house last Sunday, teaching him a makeshift game—a cross between five card draw, solitaire, and a carnival penny toss—that would amuse and keep him awake while he waited and worked the heavy gangway door all day.

Kneeling, Dean dealt the cards face up on the dirt floor, seven cards to a row, until he'd dealt out the whole deck. He dug five small pieces of coal from the wall with his thumbnail and tossed them one by one at the cards before him. Leaning over, he read the cards where the coal chips landed by the blue lamplight. During the first few hands, the coal chips landed on a pair of jacks, a three-of-a-kind and a flush. When he heard a car rumbling toward the door, he picked up the cards and opened the door. Closing the door after the car passed, he reshuffled the cards, dealt another hand on the floor, tossing the coal chips towards the cards that lay beyond him in the darkness.

Time passed. Thinking only of card playing, he was no longer bored or lonely or afraid. Just as he started to believe that he might just master the darkness and solitude, he dealt a hand, tossed the coal, and walked over to the cards, slowly reading the ten, jack, king, queen and ace of spades, each lying beneath a coal chip. Heart pounding, Dean recalled sitting across the picnic table from his Aunt Maria, her dark hands folded around his hand, warning. *There's always a chance of a royal flush. It only happens once, if it happens at all. One day, if you get one, you'll wish you'd been playing for cash money.* Stomach sinking, Dean knew he'd gotten his only royal flush, that he'd spent it on the floor of a mine, in his own penniless company.

"What are you doing?" His grandfather stood over him, looking puzzled at the scattered cards on the mine floor. Dean followed his grandfather's gaze to the gangway door, which must have swung open sometime between the last coal car and his discovery of the royal flush. His grandfather's worried eyes weren't blaming. Still, the shame and fear washed over Dean so suddenly that his skin burned with it.

"Where's Carlo?" his grandfather asked.

"I saw him a little while ago at lunch time."

"It's six o'clock. All the other drivers have gone home."

Dean's hand moved to his left forearm, toward the promise of his father's watch. He found only his naked, bony wrist. He looked toward the drift mouth, at the dark hole where daylight had flickered across the melting patches of snow the last time he'd looked. His grandfather turned, stooped and weary this time, heading back down the gangway. When Dean asked if the other miners would help search, his grandfather explained that you got paid for removing coal from the mines, not the pieces of another man's crushed and buried body.

"This is the bad work," his grandfather said. "Go home and tell your grandmother that I'll be late."

Dean ignored his grandfather's command, following him, and his grandfather didn't resist. Down and deeper into the drift mine, the tunnel narrowed, and they passed abandoned coal seams, some dry, some sinking beneath a foot of water, all of them cut between stripped timbers that squeezed beneath the mine roof. Dean's stomach clenched from the narrow tunnels, from the thought that he and his grandfather were completely alone, and Carlo could be miles away, trapped beneath a roof fall, passed out from invisible gas that could have crept through the tunnels while Dean was playing cards in the gangway. As they approached the deepest level of the mine, where the mules were kept in stables, a stream of rats rushed past them, heading up and out of the mine.

At the stable door, Dean heard his uncle singing, *Happy birthday to me. Happy birthday to you.* Inside, the stable was cut out of stone, and it smelled of old manure, straw, and his Aunt Maria's fried apple pie. Carlo sat western style on Peaches in front of the other twenty mules that were already put up in their stone stalls, their rope halters hanging from pegs nailed into the mine ribs. Carlo wore a pointed birthday hat on his head; another sat between his mule's ears. Dean nearly cried with relief to see his crazy, living uncle, still in one piece, singing a drunken birthday song, his terrible voice chasing the rats from the stables. Moving closer, he saw that his uncle was not drunk. Carlo's eyes were glassy, but no bottle was in sight. The other pit mules swayed and stamped in their stalls, kicking up lime and straw with their hooves. Their eyes wild, they strained their thick necks toward the open doorway, knocking over their feedboxes. Peaches stamped her hooves, looking ready to kick three more of Carlo's ribs and charge out after the rats, but Carlo hung on, finishing his strange serenade, *Happy birthday dear me and Peaches. Happy birthday to me and you.* His grandfather shook his head slowly, saying, "It is the gas."

Dean's grandfather began releasing the twenty mules from their stalls first, telling Dean that mules were more expensive to replace than men, and that the loss of them would cost all the other miners in the camp several months' worth of food and supplies at the company store. He said the mules had a good instinct for direction and survival; they would find their way to the top, alerting the other miners that a disaster had struck inside. After Dean and his grandfather released ten of the mules, Uncle Carlo passed out, his body sliding off his mule, but Dean's grandfather caught Carlo before the frantic animal could stomp him into the ground. He lay Carlo on a mine plank, forming a makeshift litter that the mule could drag out of the mine behind her. Then he tied his handkerchief over Dean's nose and mouth, motioning for Dean to hand him the rope halter hanging on the peg beside him. As his grandfather began to lash the end of the plank to the mule's belly, the mule swayed violently, squeezing him into the wall. His grandfather stumbled, hitting his head on a coal seam, the breeze of his falling body snuffing out the carbide lamp.

Alone, in the complete darkness that was supposed to make him adult and brave, Dean wanted to flee, following the rats toward the surface. Though he couldn't see them, he felt the rats climbing over the still bodies of his grandfather and uncle. He recalled standing at the head of his father's casket, feeling his father's weight shift as he helped lift the coffin into the black wagon, knowing his father's face was directly beneath his fingertips. The truth of his father's death settled over him like the mountain's deadly weight, pushing down, squeezing the breath out of him. He knew that if his father were alive, he would tell Dean that manhood wasn't about cutting your losses, planning your own elaborate escapes.

Reaching down, Dean found his grandfather and pulled him on top of his uncle on the plank, stacking the men as though readying them for a long, upward sleigh ride. Guided by touch and sound, he let the other pit mules out of their stalls one at a time, allowing them to lead the way toward the surface. He stroked Carlo's mule on her flank, becalming her enough to remove her harness. He released the last ten mules and followed them up through the tunnel, toward open air and safety, steadying the plank that held his uncle and grandfather.

The bodies of the two fallen men seemed heavier than the mule that stood above him, pulling the makeshift litter as Dean pushed from behind. The boy and the mule stumbled up the grade, level to level, slipping six inches for every foot they climbed. He spoke to the mule and to himself to bolster his courage.

"Pick up your feet," he said. "No time to be a weakling."

They struggled against the litter, churning coal and slate beneath their feet. The floor trembled beneath the weight of the mules running ahead of them, bending the mine timbers, working the roof. Icy water dripped faster from the shifting stones above Dean's head, splattering across his face, chilling him, though he was hot and gritty with coal dust, sticky with mule sweat. The bodies of his uncle and grandfather teetered across the plank, and Dean wondered if they were still alive. He began imagining the mule dropping the litter, letting it fall back, pinning him beneath wood and the men he hoped to save. The mule's haunches quivered, and Dean fought the trembling fatigue that threatened to drain his own body of strength before they made it to the top.

"They're still alive," he assured the mule. "I know what I'm doing."

When he reached the drift mouth, Dean was met by a group of the single Italian miners who'd played cards on his Aunt Maria's porch last Sunday. After listening for Dean's grandfather's and uncle's breathing, the miners loaded the two unconscious men into a horse-drawn wagon and took them back to Aunt Maria's boarding house. Later, the mine inspector would say that the stable air was impure enough to make a grown man fall, but it had not been as deadly as the black damp. Now, at this odd hour, the breaker whistle blew, and the streets jammed with miners' wives spilling from tarpaper shacks, walking toward the colliery, their faces tilted shyly toward disaster. Dean already knew the crisis had been averted, that he had in fact saved twenty-one pit mules that were worth twice as much as his uncle and grandfather in the eyes of the foreman, but he walked unnoticed against the steady stream of women, away from the colliery, dodging dirty, melted piles of snow along the road that had stretched out before him that morning, white and pristine in the blue, dawning light.

Following the train track down to his Aunt Maria's house, he saw an Italian boy sitting on the rickety back steps of a tarpaper shack. The boy was wrapping string around a rubber ball, covering it with black electrical tape. He threw the makeshift baseball against an empty coal car, running to field it. When the baseball landed at Dean's feet, he paused, staring hard into the boy's familiar face, but he couldn't recognize him. Dean stepped over the ball and handed the boy his deck of cards. He kept walking until the breaker whistle sounded, like a tired voice in the distance.

❀ Dean, 1940

Graybeard

"WHERE DOES MY HELP come from?" Dean wondered as he stood at the trailhead beneath Graybeard Mountain, staring at a poplar growing out of a giant limestone bluff. The tree's mossy roots twisted around the stone, silvery green in autumn morning light. Crickets churned steadily within the blue rhododendrons clambering along the old trail that followed the creek up the ridge.

Easy to see why the coal company priest had asked Dean to tame this portion of wilderness into a prayer path for the Ladies Hiking and Bible Club, a group organized by the wife of the coal company's superintendent who lived in a three-story Victorian, in one of the free cities above the mining camp.

Father Edward, the priest Dean worked for, had explained yesterday that the superintendent's wife wanted one mile of the old wilderness trail relocated and reblazed into a path for hiking and contemplation. He'd drawn Dean a simple map, marking the points of each prayer station: the boulder, the old reservoir, the trestle road, and a view of Long Meadow. At each station, psalms were already etched into a plaque, the name of the superintendent's wife, Mrs. St. John, scrawled in big letters beneath the psalms because she'd donated the path. The priest explained that this woman would pay well for someone to clear part of the old trestle road and bushwhack through the rhododendron that had grown over the path leading to Long Meadow.

"Give her a good ridge, a vista over the meadow," Father Edward said.

"It's all wilderness up there," Dean said. "A lot of steeps, no switchbacks. Nobody goes up there but bears and hunters."

"You don't have to do this." The priest spoke in his even-tempered voice, the one he used in the confessional. His blue eyes had darkened in his pale, soft face. Sweat beaded beneath his blond hairline, as it often did after he'd spent a whole morning in the rectory parlor with the superintendent's wife. Dean had felt a little sorry for him. He liked pleasing the priest. He also liked working for the clean, white church that stood on the hillside overlooking the drab coal camp.

"Somebody's bound to do it," he said. "Might as well be me."

Now that he was up on Graybeard, the prayer path job seemed like a bad idea. He was fifteen, and the scythe he'd carried up here already felt heavy and awkward against his shoulder. He could have used some help with the muscle work, but he felt too guilty to ask any of his Italian relatives who lived and worked down in the coal camp. They would not want anything about this mountain changed or relocated. Though the cartographers and coal companies had given this mountain an official name, Dean's Grandpa Palmisano and uncles always called it Graybeard because they relied on the gray clouds bearding the summit to predict when the rain channeled down the ridges, making monkey holes—mine chambers where the water flooded knee-deep, their unstable roofs seeping. His Aunt Maria, whose boarding house sat above the creek, used the mountain to divine when she needed to stoke her fire high so that the mud chinks would not run from her stone chimney in a flood or downpour.

Dean stepped onto the path's beginning, a steep scramble cobbled unevenly with roots and rocks. It followed a good creek with giant, mossy stones tumbling down its stream bed. All Dean needed to do here was clear the deadfall clutter from the creek bed and make sure the lady hikers could find the high, dry stones good for rock hopping across the water. As he cleared the deadfalls, acorns plopped in the water around him, bouncing off the river rocks like yellow and brown marbles. He stopped to read the psalm posted where the first prayer station would be. It reminded him of the old songs his Uncle Carlo sang and played on his guitar. If you took out the word *God* from any one of the psalms, Dean decided, you could make a pretty lyric about heaven, love gone wrong, love gone right, work, rambling, or murder.

"Joleen, I long for you as a deer longs for flowing streams," Dean sang aloud, then stopped, wondering if he should use Bible verses for love and murder ballads. He decided he would check with Father about this later. Right now, he was completely alone, nobody around to hear him, at least not any humans. Far-off branches broke beneath the feet of moving animals, mostly squirrels, maybe a deer. He'd seen bear scat along the trail. Their heavy musk wafted past him a few times. He decided to keep singing. "My soul longs for you, Oh Joleen," he sang louder, warning off any unseen bears.

After clearing the first station, Dean bushwhacked over to the reservoir, to a second station, a gazebo overlooking the old water source. He scattered pine straw around the berm circling the marshy water. When he reached the gazebo, he stopped to rest. The gazebo smelled of new-cut wood; its floor was already painted with a labyrinth. Beside the maze, nailed to a signpost, were the words from Psalm 32, "I will instruct you and teach you in the way you should go; I will counsel you with my eye upon you."

Dean had trouble using these lines in a song. The only woman's name he could rhyme with "go" was "Flo." That wasn't musical. The gazebo reminded him too much of the vesper garden of the rectory, where the priest sometimes tutored him in the catechism within its tight maze of rare white lilies. Lately, the priest had been trying to teach Dean how to focus on a single flower and bring himself to a low, contemplative place inside of himself, where all pain and sins were diminished. The priest's contemplation lessons never took. Dean could bring himself low, but his thoughts continued to plummet into the memory of his father getting shot on the railroad tracks three years ago, his grieving mother's body crippling with the onset of rheumatism that was taking her symmetrically—both hands, both knees, both feet until, during her bad spells, she spent days in her rocker or lying in bed, petrified by pain.

Standing somewhere between the old reservoir and the trestle road, Dean felt lost in the memory of his mother as he'd last seen her, before his Grandma Palmisano put her in the home for rheumatics and took him down here to live in the camp. Sitting in a rocker, his mother had stared through hands gnarled as tiny oak branches, as if trying to remember her own body. Dean didn't think the sight of those painful hands would ever diminish. He looked up at Graybeard, still lush and wild, just a few leaves turning red and yellow, fluttering inside the green foliage. He reminded himself that if he could finish the prayer path, he would earn good money, enough to pay the back taxes on his family's land and bring his mother home, where he could take better care of her.

To his right, the old wilderness trail doglegged. Dean took out the priest's map, turning it around in his hands until a wind caught and tumbled it up the ridge. He stepped onto the dogleg, following the fluttering map up the old trail, along the creek. When the trail began to look like a bear path, the map disappeared. Dean looked around, saw only large, mossy stones tumbled down the creek bed, water pouring around them. He'd lost the prayer path. The wrong turn felt provident. Dean decided to bushwhack farther up the ridge and take a peek at the waterfall, see what the Ladies Hiking and Bible Club would be missing by staying down on the trestle road. He stopped every few hundred feet to stack stone upon stone, leaving rock cairns, marking his way. As he climbed higher, the winds untwisted the low thoughts he'd been having while on the prayer path. Happily lost, he yelled, "Aye, Aye Mateys" and "Yo ho ho," somehow feeling that the buccaneer language he'd learned from reading *Treasure Island*, the last book his father had given him, was more suited to these outlaw heights. "By thunder, get to work you swabs," he hollered down at the colliery, feeling instantly guilty for calling his grandfather and uncles, who were all at work inside the mine, "swabs."

Carlo had recovered from the mine accident, but his grandmother no longer allowed him to call her Grandmother. She let him live with her, but her refusal to look at or speak to him made him feel put out. So he stayed outside, roaming the woods surrounding the camp, avoiding the miners on their way to work. One day, Dean wandered up to the white church on the hill. Sitting with Father Edward in the parlor, he told of the accident he'd caused, and of the shame that weighed on him because he'd almost killed his uncle. The priest studied the picture of *The Last Supper* that hung on the wall above his couch, saying, "Do you know what this picture means?" When Dean shook his head, Father Edward said, "It's possible to forgive anything."

The next day, Dean started working for the priest and learning how to contemplate. Whenever Dean felt guilt over his losses, the priest said, he should try to get low and empty himself. But the guilt always built back up again.

He looked down at his grandmother's house. "Get to work, you broomstick rider!" he yelled.

He reached the waterfall. It wasn't much, just a low bluff, but the cascade rushing over the stones sounded like the time he and his parents had fished the Clinch River together, the summer before his father died. His father had baited Dean's hook with grasshoppers, teaching him to cast toward the shadowy places where the brown trout hung above the gold river rocks, while his mother waded out to the train trestle with her fly rod, her long brown braid dipping into the swirling water, her skirt hitched and knotted above her dark calves.

The memory of his mother standing strong against the current, his father's lean arms wrapped around him as they cast, made Dean thirsty, reminding him of his purpose for being on Graybeard. He knelt, cupped his hands, and drank from the tiny plunge pool, filling his canteen. He turned back, running and sliding down to the dogleg, finding the trestle road. Plenty of sunlight was left, but the road was on the dusky side of the mountain, shaded by tangled rhododendron. As he slashed the rhododendrons into an arch over the path, his kidneys began to ache. He drained his canteen. Too late, his lips and tongue had parched. Sitting in the shade grass beneath a tree, he closed his eyes. His kidneys pounded more fiercely, his skin chilling and fevering. He thought back to the water he'd drunk near the sluggish waterfall, recalling the flecks of ore glittering it. Slag water, he thought, just as the girl appeared.

He'd seen her before, down in the camp, on the first morning his Uncle Carlo tried to take him into the mine. Now she was up on Graybeard, standing before him again, still wearing the same muddy hobnail boots and flour sack dress she'd worn the last time she'd crossed his path. Her blond hair had unwoven completely from its braid, and her pale face had grown thinner, taking on a gray tinge. She'd outgrown her dress. The fabric strained across her chest and stomach. Her slender wrists, poking out from her too-short sleeves, were heartbreakingly beautiful. He wanted to keep her near, if only until his kidneys stopped pounding. He tossed his lunch to her, a pack filled with food from the rectory kitchen—two apples, half of a roast chicken, buttery pastries stuffed with apples and black currants. She fell upon the pack, sitting where she'd stood in the middle of the path.

She didn't startle as Dean moved closer and sat beside her. She gave a good piece of her back to him, hoarding the two winter apples, eating their flesh, seeds, and cores. She moved on to the roast chicken, tearing the fat and meat from the bones with her hands. When she got to the pastries, she unwound the crust off the croissants, spooning out the apple and currant filling with her fingers. While she ate, Dean feasted his eyes on her, the silken hair on her arms, her ankles dainty in those men's boots.

The girl finished and leaned against the tree, folding her arms across her swollen stomach. "Yo ho ho," she said, laughing so wildly that Dean couldn't help but laugh too. His throat was still parched, his head spinning with fever. The sound that came out was a croak. The girl sprang to her feet, eyeing him. He didn't blame her. How had such an old, frightening sound come from a boy his age? He tried again, keeping his voice low and human, as when he spoke to a deer.

"What's your name?" he asked. "Is it Lily? You're good looking enough to want a name like that."

She blinked, and Dean saw the bewildered look of the foreigners when they arrived in camp with the coal agents who met them at Ellis Island, luring them down into the mines with the promise of work, a steady paycheck. His Grandpa Palmisano had told him that when he first arrived, some American miners taught him dirty words to use on the boss so that he'd get put in the bad spots in the mine. After hearing that story, Dean tried to learn the languages of the foreigners, practicing a few of their words so that he could be friendly with them.

"Parli Italiano?" he tried, though from the looks of her she was not Italian. "Hablo Espagnol?" When he ran out of romance languages, he tried Czech, Hungarian, Polish. "Czy Polski?" The girl nodded. He didn't know any more Polish, except "pivo" and "kielbasa," so he tried those words out on her. She laughed, eyeing the pack between them.

"I don't have any beer or sausage in there," Dean said. "You sure can eat. I've eaten with a whole table full of miners down at my aunt's house. Those men ain't got nothing on you." As he spoke, a plan began forming in his head. He'd wasted a better part of the day bushwhacking up the wilderness trail, pretending to be a pirate. He still felt a little weak in the kidneys, and his mind blurred with fever and fatigue. "I'll bet you can work like a man. Do you want to help me? I could use a little help clearing the rest of this path."

He went over to the tree where he'd leaned the shoulder scythe. He pointed to the arches he'd already formed and pointed to the blade, making a swinging motion with his arms. "We can take turns. One of us can cut, and the other can clear. I could pay you well, throw in another meal or two, maybe a little pivo and kielbasa."

Carefully, he held out the scythe. She grabbed its handle and waded into a tangle of rhododendron. She swung the scythe easily, her arms flexing with remembered movement. "Looks like you know what you're doing," Dean said. "Why don't you cut first." They started working, Lily wielding the scythe while Dean gathered the fallen branches into heaps. As they moved down the path, he taught her all the phrases he could remember from *Treasure Island*—*grog*, *pieces of eight*, and *mutiny*. He told her about the book's young hero, Jim Hawkins, and his meeting with Long John Silver, the fierce but respectable one-legged pirate. She seemed to enjoy it when Dean gave orders and talked to her as if he were a pirate. "You're able to hear, I reckon'. Leastways your ears is big enough," he said. "You'll berth forward, and you'll live hard, and you'll speak soft, and you'll keep sober, till I give the word: and you may lay to that, my girly." She laughed, unguarded now. Her pale skin had turned rosy from the labor. Her eyes took in everything.

After so much silence, he was glad to be talking to another human, even if he had to speak in seafaring language to this girl. She was foreign, probably a runaway, but as he looked at those blue eyes and blond hair he longed to be landlocked with her. If he took this girl home with him, he could bring his mother out of the home for rheumatics. He suspected the girl would be happy to have a job nursing his mother, helping him with chores on the farm. She worked so easily, and she'd be lively company for his mother. He imagined his mother saying, "She's a real work-horse," voicing her highest compliment for anyone. He saw the two women sitting together at his mother's kitchen table, hands wrapped around tea cups, talking in English and Polish, because surely his mother would want to learn this girl's language—once she started speaking again.

At twilight they finished reblazing the trestle road section of the prayer path and fired the heaps of cut branches.

"I guess you stay somewhere around here," Dean said. "I'll bet you've been living in one of those old hunting shelters over in Pot Cove. Those will keep out some of the critters, but be careful. Don't go walking around up there at night." He picked up his axe, but the girl stood staring at him, her face looking pale against the fires that smoldered around them. Her eyes flashed with terror as he threw sand over the last of the fires and slung the pack over his back. "I've got to take this pack with me. A bear could smell the food that was in it and come looking. You can live with the bears, but they need to stay wild. Don't give them any excuse to come near."

Dean considered taking the runaway girl down to his aunt's house. Maria had a soft spot for runaways, especially for foreign girls whose families married them off to older miners. Maria took these child brides in when they were distressed by the discovery of their husbands' advanced ages. If she thought they were in danger in their own homes, she used the trainmen to smuggle messages to their families back on the other side. Once, Maria smuggled in a letter from Dean's mother, a single sentence sent from the home for rheumatics that read, "Get me out of here or I will die." After he was paid for the prayer path job, Dean would let the girl choose. She could go with him when he went to get his mother out of that terrible home for rheumatics, or she could take her pay back to wherever she came from. Until then, he would keep the girl away from the camp, even if he had to hide her from his well-meaning aunt.

"Go on," Dean said. "I'll be back in the morning with some grog and sausage."

Dean turned, feeling the girl's eyes upon him as he walked away. She didn't need to speak to tell him how she felt about his leaving. He could feel the pull of her, as if their bodies had joined while working side by side all day, but he kept walking. He had a half hour to get down the mountain before black dark.

DEAN'S KIDNEYS POUNDED HARDER as he walked into town and passed his grandmother's frame house. Her parade quilt hung over the porch rail, set out for some autumn saint's feast day. A candle flickered in her bedroom window. At this hour,

Dean knew, she'd be propped up in bed, drinking tea and coffee as she waited for Dean's grandfather to come home from a late shift. Her prayer cards spilling across her quilt, she'd be reading the *Dialogue* by Saint Catherine, her favorite saint, the one who kissed lepers and stared into the eyes of repentant thieves while they were beheaded.

"The reason Catherine is so misunderstood is that very few people can understand the tradition of self naughting," his grandmother once told him. "To make oneself zero is much different from spending your entire life reacting to circumstances, without moving toward a goal. It's this refusal to *become* that is a very grave sin, especially for women. Your mother, for instance, was prone to belittling herself. Her biggest problem is that she fell in love too easily, settling with that shiftless railroad man and living above her means. That's why she's so sick now. Her suffering is God's punishment."

Dean looked up at the white church on the hill. The priest had taken him in at a time when his own grandmother had all but put him out. This meant something. Still, he wasn't sure Father Edward would understand why he now planned to take in a half-wild, half-clothed girl he'd found in the woods. Dean wasn't even sure why he wanted her so. Knowing only that he was too tired to climb the rectory stairs and explain the girl to the priest, he stepped off the plank road and walked the other way, taking the trail above the creek that led to his aunt's boarding house down in the foreign place.

Ahead, he saw a black shadow beside the creek, stooped like a small black bear. Dean clapped his hands. "Go on," he shouted. "Git." The form stood, transfiguring into a skinny little boy standing in front of him with his pants down. He'd been relieving himself beside the creek, near the remains of an outhouse that had tumbled into the stream during the last downpour. Dean thought about telling him to go deeper into the woods the next time, away from the water source, but the boy looked at him steadily, his eyes hollow, his head probably ringing with too much hunger to listen to anything Dean would say to him. He pulled up his pants and darted back into the woods.

Aunt Maria's two-story saltbox squatted above a mine shaft, pieces of wood nailed over its outside seams to keep out the cold and rain. Maria rented to single miners, mostly Italian ones, even when they were injured or unemployed. Whenever the earth above the mine shifted and parts of her house sank with the cave-in, the grateful miners pulled the sunken parts out, repairing and relocating them on more solid ground. As Dean approached the boarding house, he heard the crows cawing through the woods, his aunt's cow murmuring on the foothills behind the house. Maria sat in her rocker on the front porch beside a basket of chestnuts, smoking her cigar. She'd pulled her hennaed hair back in a bright yellow scarf. Her hooped earrings trembled as she scored the chestnuts. Trumpet vine twisted along her porch railings, and the hydrangeas bloomed pale blue in the dusky light.

"You hungry?" his aunt called out.

Dean smiled at her familiar greeting, but his kidneys pounded with each step, his head swimming with fever.

"I could use a glass of water," he said. "My kidneys have been talking to me all day. Feels like someone's been kicking them."

His aunt stood, barely taller than the porch rail, and he followed her into the kitchen filled with a picnic table. Behind the coal stove was a shelf lined with tincture bottles. Dean sat at the table while Maria pulled down a brown bottle and dosed him with sulfas.

"When did this start?" she asked.

"While I was up on Graybeard."

"What were you doing up there?"

"Working for Father Edward."

"What kind of work does the little priest have you doing for him up on the mountain?

"I'm clearing a path for the superintendent's wife." Dean explained the prayer path, describing each one of its stations, reciting the psalms that would be etched on the plaques at each one. "I'm not sure if the prayer path will be of use to anyone around here," he said. "Seems like the money would be better spent on some outhouses."

"Do you think that the rich woman will want to put her name on outhouses?"

"I guess not. But Father Edward thinks that if we build her a path with her name on it, she might be willing to pay for a few outhouses."

Maria folded her brown hands on the table before her, "What are you gonna do?"

"I guess I'll clear the path. I can make good money at it." He paused, unsure if he should give away the rest of his plan. "Did my mother ever do anything really wrong when she was younger?"

"What kind of wrong thing?"

"Grandma says Mother's sickness is a punishment from God, for loving my father too much."

"I do not like that," Maria said, slapping her blunt hand on the table. "I do not like the way your grandma talks. She is like the horses with the blinds on their eyes." She put her hands on either side of her face.

"Blinders," Dean said. "Horses wear blinders."

"Your mother is not being corrected." Her voice softened. "She is repairing. When you get older, you will see that all of us spend our lives repairing ourselves, and sometimes others. We spend our days swinging from tree to tree, hoping we don't fall and need as many repairs." His aunt slapped her hand on the table again. "Your grandma talks just like the little priest. I don't like that."

When Maria wasn't calling Father Edward "the little priest," she called him a company man, a man who thought only about making wrongdoings look right for the company. Though she never gave the details, his aunt hinted that her war with the priest was old and deep, rooted in the time she'd tried to run away from the camp. Father Edward never spoke badly about Maria, except to remark upon her absence from Mass. Even then, all he ever said was, "I think we both know that your aunt has some problems with authority."

Now his aunt moved expertly around the kitchen, making him drink eight mason jars of boiled well water to wash down the sulfas. She put him to bed in the room behind the kitchen, the one his Uncle Carlo slept in when he wasn't out timbering. Despite Carlo's recovery from the accident, the coal company refused to hire him back, claiming that the gas had made him feebleminded, a liability. Both Father Edward and Maria had reassured Dean that he hadn't poisoned his uncle's mind with methane gas, that Carlo had always been a bit *touched*. Carlo affectionately called Dean "the murderer," but he bore no real grudge against him. When he wasn't out timbering, he played guitar on the porch, teaching Dean driving breakdowns and ballads by ear. Hearing of Dean's interest in music, Father Edward had given Dean one of his old guitars and had begun teaching him notation. Both men encouraged him to make up his own lyrics.

Outside, the yellow moon hung over the black mountain, shredded by rain clouds. Dean had felt the heaviness in the air all day; he was relieved to hear the clean rain sweeping through the valley. As he lay in the warm darkness of his aunt's back room, he hoped the girl was safely sleeping inside the hunter's shelter by now, or, if she was out haunting the mountainside, that her footsteps were sure and soundless. Dean opened the window and pulled his guitar out from under the bed, draped it over his left knee, fingers lightly touching first string and twelfth fret, sending a bell tone out toward the mountain.

"Come kiss me. Come kiss me. Oh, come kiss me, my darlin' Lily," he sang.

"Who is this Lily?" His aunt stood before the open window.

"Nobody," he said. "It's just a name that rhymes with the other words I need for this lyric."

"You need to rest." Maria shut the window and locked his guitar in its case, pushing it back beneath the bed. She told him to lie down. She sat beside him, putting a cool cloth on his warm forehead, rubbing his temples with her blunt fingers. He fell asleep to the sound of rain knocking acorns out of the trees, acorns battering the eaves of his aunt's house, crows calling through the rain. A few acorns pounded against the window, startling Dean from sleep. He fell back into a light doze, wondering how the rain could pitch acorns directly at the windows.

HE SLEPT FOR THREE DAYS. On the fourth morning the kidney pain had gone, but the memory of the girl, Lily, made Dean ache to get back on Graybeard. When the church bell chimed on the hill, he went to Maria's kitchen and filled his pack with more apples, another half of a roasted chicken, a rope of sausage, and more pastries from the bread basket. He went outside and pulled a bottle of Carlo's young wine from beneath the shed, planning on surprising Lily with "grog." Up on Graybeard, Dean walked straight to the trestle road, but all he saw were the remains of the rhododendron fires. He hung the pack in the tree above the spot where the girl had eaten three days before, hoping she was out there watching him, waiting for a signal that she could safely come out. He swept the ash heaps from the trestle road, listening for a branch breaking underfoot on the ridge, a stone kicked along the path.

Finished with the rhododendron tunnel, he walked over to Pot Cove and looked into the empty wooden shelter. Its air smelled of damp and woods, old camp smells. Nobody but hunters had slept in here for years. He looked up a barren oak, saw a dented pail hanging from a limb, memorializing the railroad men who died in train wrecks back before the train stopped running up here. He imagined his blond, willowy father perched on one of the railroad beds he used to build, his dinner pail at his side, eating the meal his mother had packed for him: water on the bottom, beans in the middle, a slice of chess pie on top. He stumbled away from the empty shelter and rusted pail, feeling dimly chastened by the empty signs this mountain had given him.

Down at the reservoir, he sat on the puncheon bench beside the meditation pond. It looked smaller that afternoon, green and still, its surface clotted with red sourwood leaves. He skimmed the leaves off the water with his scythe, and waited. As the late morning sun dappled the pine path, Dean gave up and ate the lunch in the gazebo, leaving sausage and wine in his pack in case the girl showed. He walked over the trestle road to Long Meadow and began clearing gravel from around the final prayer station, a field of coneflowers, Solomon's seal, Jack-in-the-pulpit.

Dean did not want to consider the lilies, as the plaque beside this last station suggested. The meadow was hot and buggy beneath the mid-afternoon sun. Gnats flew into his eyes, and the monarchs swarmed, feeding on milkweed. A few flew straight at him, slapping his hands with their wings as he worked. He tried a little pirate language, hoping the girl would come running out of the forest, laughing.

"But wait, the air be without breath up here," he yelled, but the girl did not come. He felt foolish for planning an escape with a runaway girl he hardly knew.

On his way back down to the camp, Dean stepped carefully. He was tired, his sight dimmed by his darkening thoughts. Falling was easier when you felt this way. He'd begun to remember why he thought this whole prayer path was a bad idea, especially its beginning, where one wrong step between tree root and jutting rock would snap anyone's ankle. More red sourwood leaves had dropped here, nearly covering the trail before him, ending at the first prayer station, the limestone bluff with the oak growing out of it.

Here the leaves seeped into the ground beside the limestone bluff. A fermented smell mingled with the cool breeze blowing out from the narrow space beneath the boulder. The air was muskier than damp leaves, though not as strong as a bear, and it carried a low moan. Dean looked under and saw the girl wedged beneath the stone. Her white dress looked rusty. Through the thin cloth, he could see her stomach, still swollen as when he'd last seen her, but her arms and face looked even thinner. Her head was gashed, her big eyes haunted by pure melancholy.

"Lily?" he said.

He spoke low so that he would not startle her, so that she would not hear the terror in his own voice. The girl wedged herself deeper beneath the stone.

"I ate my lunch a while ago, when you didn't show," he said. "But I saved you some grog and some kielbasa." He set the wine and sausage on the ground, but the girl turned her head away, and he heard a retching sound. Dean pulled the food and drink away from her, straining to find the words in Polish, then in English, that would draw her out from under the stone. Finally, he settled on the only language that had made sense to them both.

"Yo ho ho," he said.

The girl smiled weakly and lifted her head, bumping it on the low stone. Dean hooked his arm beneath her, pulling her out. As he carried her, he saw that that her skirt was soaked with dried blood. He searched her body for claw marks, found her arms and legs covered by raised bruises. Deep purple in the middle, green around the edges, they looked meaner than any mark a wild animal would make.

❀

AUNT MARIA STOOD as she saw him heading toward her porch with the girl in his arms.

"What did you do to her?" Maria took the girl from him and turned to go into the house.

"Nothing." Dean spoke to her back. "I found her like this, up on Graybeard. She don't speak English. I don't know her name. I've been calling her Lily. She likes to be called that. I think she's a Pole."

Maria put the girl on the kitchen table and instructed Dean to cover her with a blanket. A Polish neighbor was summoned, and after a brief discussion Maria informed Dean that the girl's name was Magda, not Lily. She was thirteen, but she'd been married off to a forty-year-old miner when she'd arrived in the camp last spring, and the man had beaten her whenever she tried to lock him out of the bedroom. She'd been living in the woods all spring and summer, eating mushrooms, an occasional loaf of bread smuggled to her by a sympathetic miner's wife. For some reason, she'd tried to come into town a few nights before, and the husband had gotten to her.

The girl complained of stomach pains, nausea, breathlessness. She calmed beneath Maria's touch and allowed Maria to pull her arms away from her stomach, down to her sides. Maria plied the girl's abdomen with her fingers, then walked over to the coal stove. She boiled a glass of wine steeped in garlic, adding three hot embers. She lifted the girl's head and coaxed her into drinking it. When the girl's eyes closed, Maria turned to Dean.

"It is the bad mother," she said, explaining that the girl was suffering from a pregnancy that was taking a dangerous course.

Maria dressed the girl's head wound with spider webs and gave her another warm drink made from juniper, honey, and one of the tinctures she hid behind the other brown bottles on her kitchen shelf. She asked Dean to put the girl in Carlo's bed, ordering

Dean to soak strips of old bed sheets in water and comfrey in the kitchen and bring them back to her. When he went into Carlo's room, the girl was lying still on a mattress that was wrapped with layers of sheets.

Dean knelt beside her, lightly touching the silken hair on her bruised arms, straightening the sheet she'd kicked off, pulling it back over her bare feet. The full moon glowed bright outside the window above the bed, and as he reached to close the curtain he recalled the acorns bouncing against the pane while he had lain in here, recovering from his own ailments. He imagined the girl following him into town, trying to find him, the husband finding her first. The close air of the room smelled of earth and blood and roots. Dean bent beneath wave after wave of his own lonely nausea. When his aunt bustled into the room, he looked up. He saw in the window's reflection how he must have appeared to her—guilty and prayerful, hunched over his own disfigured heart.

"Little priest." Maria tsked beneath her breath.

She may as well have said "murderer."

DEAN SLEPT ON THE PORCH all night, afraid to go back inside. When he woke the next morning, the girl had disappeared. He looked around, but the only trace of her he found was a bundle of blood-soaked sheets and the empty tincture bottle behind the fallen privy. He walked slowly up to the rectory and out to the vesper garden, near the place where the priest had tried to teach him contemplation. He fell to his knees, pawing the ground for a single flower to focus on, hoping to diminish some of the pain he'd caused over the last two days. The beds were wintered in, composted with leaves. Pale bed sheets billowed along the wash line, purifying in wind and sunlight, and for a moment, Dean remembered his mother telling how she'd taken in laundry for the priest when she was a girl. He imagined his young mother standing beside the line, her arms tanned beautifully from a morning of hanging clean sheets.

The priest parted the sheets and stepped through, wearing his gardening clothes—khakis with his white shirt, his sleeves rolled up. His face had reddened in the sun, but he didn't look ruddy from the outdoor work. He smelled like his rectory, of stale holy water, old books, harsh soap.

"She's alive," Father said. "Though what your aunt did last night was officious. She could have hurt that girl more than helping her."

"Where is she?"

"With her husband."

"He beats her. He's worse than an animal."

"He is a foreman for the company. I married them in this church. That was her grandmother your aunt spoke to last night. She said the men in the family could lose their jobs if she doesn't go back to her husband. Her whole family could be put out." Father placed his hand on Dean's shoulder. "We may not agree with our families, but we must love them and forgive what they do."

A breeze blew into the garden, turning up a sheet. The girl that was his mother was gone now, and so, with her, the rest of his family. "Father, can I ask you something?" he said. The priest nodded. "Did my mother ever do anything bad when she was young?"

"Like what?"

"My grandmother thinks my mother's sickness is a punishment from God."

"Not all suffering is given as punishment," the priest said. "Sometimes, it's given for correction."

The priest reached into his pocket and pulled out his money clip, snapped around a stack of ones. "I walked the prayer path with Mrs. St. John this morning," Father Edward said. "It seems I've been corrected. She thinks the path is too steep, and the psalms are too long. I'll fix the psalms, of course." He paused, holding onto the money. "I was hoping you might consider helping me grade the path into a gentler slope."

Dean looked at the folded bills. It was real money, not company scrip. He didn't reach for it. Dean thought of his mother sitting still in that rocker, staring through her twisted hands. She'd loved his father well, and he died. Then her body failed, and her son left. She didn't need more punishment than that. She didn't need any correcting.

"I've done enough fixing up there," he said. "You don't have to pay me for it if it's not what you want."

The priest put all the money in Dean's hand, folding Dean's fingers over it. "You're right. You earned every bit of this. I'll fix the path. It will be a way that I may correct myself."

Dean stood and took the priest's measure. Father Edward wasn't openly bad, like Magda's husband, but he could bully with words smart and sacred, twisting them until all wrongs looked right for the sake of the coal company, this church. Dean wasn't sure if he was the worst kind of man; he knew only that he would not be brought any lower by the priest. He put the money into his pocket. He didn't stay long enough to hear if Father Edward was calling after him, and he didn't want to know what he was being called by his relatives back in the camp. Little priest, murderer, company man—these names all meant the same thing to him now. He didn't want to be called by any of them.

By noon, he stood on Graybeard's summit, his guitar strapped to his back, his money clipped inside the guitar. He sat on one of the high rocks snaked by petrified roots. He looked back over the coal town that smoked like a charred fire pit in the middle of the deep, green valley. Dean walked over to the other side, where spruce and fir grew as if out of the air, bristling into the deep blue sky. He could see all the way to the mountains where he'd lived with his parents. The distant mountains echoed pale blue beyond these close, black mountains, kettling the pretty white train town where his father had worked. He recalled that Graybeard was called something different by the land families that lived on this other side, something gentler, more welcoming. He clambered down, trying to remember the name of the ridge he was descending, Horse Barn, Garden, Rich, or maybe just Home.

❀ Sadie, 1942

The Passage

THE SPRING AFTER HER OLDER DAUGHTER DIED, Jane Musick took her younger daughter, Sadie, up to Wilderness Road and told her it was time to learn how to stay alive in the woods. Jane began her lesson at the old game trail marked by an oak growing sideways to a scarred bend, curving up, its top branches rising into the sky. Sadie was thirteen, old enough to guess the tree had been struck by lightning, but its shape called to mind a swaybacked horse with a long nose. She mounted the tree's back, sitting sidesaddle, listening to her mother explain that the bent oak was a language tree, meant to guide passing travelers toward water, game, safety.

"Some old Cherokee tied it down when it was a sapling," Jane said, rubbing her hands over the scarred bend of the tree. "He cut its nose open with a sharp stone and packed it with moss to leave a message for other travelers."

Sadie watched her mother, finding her suddenly old at forty-three. Blue veins rose across the backs of Jane's hands, tangling. Her bony fingers moved knowingly over the tree bark. Frightened by Jane's sudden aging, Sadie thought up ways to keep her mother talking. She patted the language tree she sat upon.

"What's this one saying?" she asked.

Jane looked down the slope toward a stream glimmering through a winter pasture. She squinted up to a rock ledge running along the mountain's spine. "It's pointing to that creek, maybe over to those caves on the ridge."

"Are all these trees talking?"

Jane nodded. "If we knew their language, they could tell us some good stories."

An axe felled a tree in the distance, and Sadie jumped.

Jane laughed softly, her dark eyes humorless. "This one's too bent to be of use to any logger." She swatted Sadie down from the tree. "Go on. You're old enough to know what you can and can't taste. It's time for you to become a woman. That means learning how to take care of yourself out in the woods."

It was late April, the season of sudden rains and paths shifted by thaw, faded bloodroot pushing up through mats of decayed leaves. A time of yearning for all that was new and green. They set out toward the creek, Jane aiming to teach Sadie the names and uses of wild herbs. She jumped off the trail, digging her hands deep into the earth, gathering the healing plants into her game pocket, a sack of burlap the size of a country ham that bulged beneath her loose cotton dress. She walked swiftly, ignoring the "No Trespassing" sign posted by the Syphers, the family that owned the pretty brick farmhouse at the top of Wilderness Road, the horse and milk cow nibbling reeds along the pasture fence, their sides the color of maple syrup in morning sunlight. Jane had skipped making breakfast to get an early start, and Sadie was so hungry she wanted to run into the pasture, dive beneath the cow, milk it straight into her mouth.

She turned back to her mother, saw Jane's white silhouette headed away from the pasture, dissolving into a laurel hell. She ran after her mother, fearing how, suddenly, Jane could be lost to the silent language of trees, wandering as she had all winter after her sister, Grace, died of cancer, and Sadie's father buried Grace in a plot in West Virginia, a full day's drive from Bluefield. An Irishman who climbed for the timber company, Sadie's father had explained that having Grace buried in a remote place was a kindness; if he'd buried her closer to home, Jane would visit the cemetery every day, growing feebleminded with grief.

After the funeral, her father fed her mother sleeping pills, claiming he was doing her another kindness, that he didn't want his wife to wake too soon to her misery. He went off timbering, and the pills dwindled by the end of the first week he was gone. Jane awoke fiercely, demanding to know how to get to Grace's grave. Sadie dimly remembered the trip down to the coal town so deep in the mountain that darkness fell at midday, her father driving slowly, jabbing the brakes with every switchback, while her mother slept in the back seat. He didn't tell Sadie where they were going, or how they could get back to visit Grace. When Jane questioned Sadie about where Grace's body was, Sadie felt buried beneath all she could not tell her mother.

All winter, Jane had roamed the woods, searching for her older daughter's grave, leaving Sadie alone in the cabin. The cabin's walls were made of pine and plywood, its metal roof dented by hard rains. Winds whistled through the chimney and through the stone fireplace that had not been lit since her father had left. The warped pine shelves in the tiny kitchen held the last jars of backyard apples they'd canned the fall before Grace had gotten sick. Their lids had rusted shut, and Sadie could not open them.

While her mother was gone, Sadie burrowed in her parents' bed, her stomach clenching with hunger and the fear that her mother might never come back, counting the apple slices glowing like bloated fingers in the glass jars. She staunched thirst by sucking on river rocks, a survival technique Grace once taught her while they were out exploring the woods together. She was sleepy, but she couldn't sleep for fear of missing her mother's homecoming. She staved off lonely memories of Grace's coffin in the corner of the cabin by reading the four tin mugs hung from hooks beside the fireplace mantel, each one etched with the same phrase: "Today I drink, for tomorrow I may go without."

When the first bloodroot pushed through decayed leaves, her mother returned and opened every window of the cabin. She twisted lids off jars of apples, stirring them into cinnamon in a kettle above a fire blazing in the fireplace. Murmuring unwritten recipes to herself, Jane spread the hot apples between layers of molasses cake. Her frigid fingers dug into Sadie's shoulders as she pulled her upright in the bed.

"Taste this," her mother said. "I think I've found it. I think I've found the right one."

Sadie obeyed, letting her mother spoon apple cake into her mouth. The cooked apples were too soft, neither tart nor sweet, and they burned the inside of her mouth until it peeled. Beyond hunger, aching to fall back into her mother's warm bed and sleep, Sadie kept eating, knowing she must finish every last bite of the comfortless apples. It was the only way to stop her mother's frantic stirring in the kitchen.

Now, on the path off Wilderness Road, Sadie's mother began to look younger the deeper she moved into the spring woods. Her hair woven into a loose braid that hung to her waist, she walked on slender girl's legs through hemlock and locust, the scent of lavender trailing her. Sadie caught up with her in the middle of an old lumber road softened by new dandelions. Kneeling in a patch of sunlight, Jane brushed the stems with the fronts and backs of her fingertips.

"You can eat every part of these, raw in salads, boiled tender to release the tang," she said. "You can dry and roast them to stretch your coffee until it's time to hunt chicory."

Jane placed a dandelion stem on Sadie's tongue. It tasted peppery and alive. Giddy from eating living plants, Sadie ran around, plucking dandelions for her mother, brushing the stems with the fronts and backs of her own fingertips, wondering what it would feel like to be a dandelion beneath her mother's hands. She stole glances at Jane's renewed beauty, the high cheekbones carved by last winter's grief, her slender fingers brushing nimbly over dandelions. When they'd picked enough for a salad, her mother stood and tucked the game pouch under her dress. She headed for the creek, explaining that the woods were so abundant that they needn't remain hungry for very long, even in the far, silent places. Purslane and mustard could be eaten raw. Nettles could be boiled gently into tea. Rosehips could be nibbled to attract a man. A decoction of sage and juniper could stop a new mother's milk from flowing. Lavender dispelled guilt and melancholy.

A wild turkey called in the distance, its voice scraping like the chalkboard Grace had used to teach Sadie the alphabet in winter, when the snow was too high to walk down the mountain to the town school. Two years older than Sadie, Grace had brought the chalkboard home from the Syphers' house, where she worked as the hired girl for Miss Emma, a young widow who'd returned to this homeplace in the valley the year before and now lived alone with her sixteen-year-old son, Dean. Grace loved telling Sadie about the Syphers' farmhouse. Swathed in hemlock, it had a fireplace *and* a furnace, a parlor with a plate rail running close to the ceiling where Emma sat china bordered with delicate silver pinecones and needles. It was a source of wonderment to both girls that nobody ever ate from these plates. Once, Grace had told of dusting them. When she turned one over, she'd seen that it had a name, "Sierra Pines."

"Miss Emma likes me because I'm the only one who appreciates her fine china," Grace said. "Her husband brought it home to her when she was pregnant with Dean, and she couldn't travel with him to town as much. Dean says they can get a lot of money out of those plates. He'd take them all and turn them into cash if Miss Emma would let him. He hates them, but I love them."

Sadie listened to a cascade rushing beneath laurel vines, longing for Grace's voice. She looked up at the black pitch pine bristling along the bare ridge, missing Grace's fairy tale stories about the Syphers' house, warmed by a fireplace and a furnace, Miss Emma's Sierra Pines plates, so fine that nobody ate off them. She watched her mother pick up a dead trail running down a ridge, her braid weaving with mist tendrils rising from the stream. Jane had never appreciated Grace's stories. She'd accused Grace of selling herself into child slavery, of having no pride, of beggary. Jane ate and drank out of the same tin mug that hung beside the stone fireplace.

Feet hidden by a layer of fallen leaves, Jane seemed to glide through chill air, reading the silent trees until reaching the stream that ran high and swift from the rain, still clear enough for Sadie to see the gem-flecked stones on the bottom. Despite the candle ice dripping from the far banks, her mother tied up her dress and waded in, feeling among the nooks of the stream bank, showing Sadie how to catch a fish by forming a cave with two hands, cupped motionless.

"There's trout all up and under these rocks," she said. "Close your hands quick enough, and you'll catch one."

Sadie kept close to the bank, walking barefoot through the frigid water, digging up freshwater clam shells with her toes, setting them on the bank grass. She picked up the water-polished stones, slipping them into her own dress pockets. Her mother caught a brown trout, a beauty. "Come here and smell this," she said. "It's so fresh it don't even smell like a fish." Sadie waded out to her mother and sniffed the fish, breathed in its smell of river water mingling with her mother's lavender scent. Jane turned away, leaning down to the stream. Her mother kissed the fish on the head before releasing it. Or had Sadie imagined this kiss? The fish slipped like an eel beneath the water's surface, Sadie chasing after it until it disappeared completely. Jane laughed, pointing down river, toward a shady place where trout boiled just beneath the water's surface.

"Some feeders are over there," she said. "Go and see if you can catch one for supper."

Up to her waist now, Sadie admired the colors of the river stones—gold, pink, black—finding each one prettier than the next. She recalled Grace, the beautiful one, inheritor of their mother's Cherokee good looks—dusky skin, raven hair, full lips. In awe of her sister's dark beauty and bold ways, she'd followed Grace everywhere, the two roaming the woods for hours, finding pretty things. Once, the two sisters spent a whole summer down at this creek, collecting the colorful river rocks, Grace teasing Sadie for wanting to ask permission from the Syphers to take the stones off their property.

"If you don't see anybody out here with a gun pointed at your head, it's not stealing," Grace had said. "Don't be such a chicken."

"I am not a chicken," Sadie had yelled, but her sister had only laughed, wading into a deeper eddy, gathering prettier and prettier stones.

They'd built their mother a birdbath out of the river rocks, but the stones had too much water in them, and they'd frozen and cracked with the first cold snap. By spring, the birdbath was a chalky heap in their mother's garden. Now, Sadie filled her right pocket with the small rocks, filling the left to balance out the weight. She reached down for one last stone and saw a girl's face beneath the water's surface, her eyes large and startled, hair springing from her braid. The current knocked her over, took her swiftly. She tumbled downstream in the icy water, her body weighted by stones. She sank, letting the water push and pull her, feeling a dire urge to sleep. What a relief it would be to sleep at the bottom of this river, never again rising to thoughts of her sister buried alone beneath a hidden patch of earth. I am not a chicken, Sadie thought as she sank deeper. I am not afraid of this. But her body rose unwillingly toward the pale watery sky, and the grasses reached softly to her from the bank. Sadie clutched a bundle of river oats, pulled herself out. Her heart hurt from the icy water, thrashing inside her chest. She lay on the bank, closing her eyes. Waiting for her heartbeat to slow, she felt two strong hands upon her, water forming a suction between wet fabric and wet skin as the rough hands peeled off her dress. Sadie's frozen flesh prickled and burned as her mother rubbed blood back into her arms and legs, but she didn't cry out for Jane to stop. It had been a long time since anyone had touched her. She closed her eyes and leaned into her mother's rough hands as they urged the warm blood back through her, stilling her frantic heart.

Jane stopped, sitting wearily back on her heels. She stared down at Sadie, the fear in her eyes fading into long distance, gone to wherever Grace must be. Lying back on the grass, Sadie listened to her mother twist water from the dress, her stomach sinking with each stone falling back into the water. She felt ashamed for nearly drowning herself, guilty for causing her mother more worry. She wanted to say she was sorry, but her mother had turned away already, her broad back like a closed door Sadie wanted to throw herself against.

The sky had become the color of lye soap. It made Sadie feel unbearably raw and naked, and she longed for her dress, no matter how sodden. It had been her mother's last gift, the way Sadie found out about Grace's illness. Instead of letting out the hems of their old dresses that fall, Jane had ordered two new ones from the seamstress downtown—one satin and organza swing dress good for parties, one cotton shirt dress, good for school. Grace had taken the swing dress, and Jane had let her keep it.

"She's been wearing pants under her skirts all year," Sadie had tattled. "She don't even like dresses anymore."

"Your sister needs to be the prettiest girl at the party this year," Jane had said.

What party? Sadie wondered until she saw the sickness in her sister's eyes, and knew to stop sassing her mother.

Jane threw the ruined dress onto the grass beside Sadie. "You keep putting rocks in your pockets and walking into rivers, it will be the end of you."

Sadie recalled Grace lying in the coffin wearing the satin party dress, their father leaning over the edge, fussing endlessly with the carnation he'd pinned to her collar. Sadie wished she'd given that dress to her sister freely, without betrayal or argument.

"No matter," Jane said. "Going to rain. We'll shelter in those caves."

Sadie looked up to the thunderheads above the mountains, feeling the first rain feathering her face. She put on the wet dress. It felt heavier than it had with all the rocks in its pockets. She shivered beneath its weight, still feeling unaccountably exposed. She wondered if she would catch pneumonia from the damp fabric.

This dress will be the end of me, she thought to tell her mother, but Jane was already climbing the next slope. When the downpour hit, she became less surefooted with each new torrent. She moved off the trail, circling, white limbs criss-crossing her path, green undergrowth tangling her feet. She started in one direction, changed her line, starting the other way.

"Mama, are we lost?"

"You don't ever get lost from what you do," Jane said. "You get lost from what you've left undone."

Pondering what she might have left undone, Sadie thought of

her father's abrupt leaving. The day before he went off, he'd taken her out walking behind their cabin, stopping at the old oak at the edge of their allotment. He taught her how to climb the tree when she was lost in order to find a safe, open valley. He'd scaled the trunk, showing her how to find branches big enough to support, small enough to hold. A toppled poplar once crushed his left arm, and he'd set it himself because he'd been too far out to find a doctor. He balanced high above her in the tree, his broken arm hanging bent and useless. His pale Irish skin blended with the winter sky, and Sadie felt him already disappearing. She caught herself memorizing his poorly set arm, two of his fingers lost to frostbite. Her father looked down, caught her staring.

"I'm sorry, Sis," he said, shaking his head. "There is not a thing in this world that I can give your mother to make her happy now. That woman could make an art form out of grief." His voice wavered, as if asking Sadie's permission to leave. Her stomach clenched, and she wanted to say, "You make *me* happy. Please. Stay here for me." Feeling neither artful nor womanly, she kept quiet as he climbed down and went inside to pack his belongings.

Sadie would finish this path. It was the only thing she knew how to get done, and keep from getting lost. Stumbling behind her mother, she tried to remember a time when her family had been happy enough to have a party, before her mother took up the art of grieving. Jane had always said she could never live with their father year-round; that's why he took up timbering, so he could spend long months away. But Sadie secretly liked it when her father stayed home in winter. He'd been the first to call her "Sis," claiming her real name sounded like something you'd call a horse. He roasted potatoes in a tin drum outside while Grace and Sadie tobogganed down the slope beside the house, sister stacked upon sister on the long sled. At the bottom of the hill, her father would be there with his old Ford, hitching the sled onto the car and pulling them up and around the road leading to the house again, as many times as they wanted. That was great fun. That was a party.

Her mother's uphill path had become steeper, narrowing. Jane and Sadie climbed along a ledge bordered by limestone softened by wet moss. They reached two giant boulders and walked between them. Inside the passageway, the stones buzzed, as if filled with thousands of angry bees. Rain dripped from the walls and through a ceiling made of windfall branches that sheltered them from the narrow sky. Her mother's pace quickened with the humming until they reached a shallow cave that smelled of musk, its clay floor dimpled as if by tiny feet. Jane stopped beside a petrified pool the size of a bear wallow.

"Bears could be in here," Sadie said.

"Not this time of year," Jane said. "Loggers probably scared them off anyway."

Jane pulled a dry match and cedar bark from her game pouch, struck the two together. Lowering the sparked cedar into the dry pool, she breathed softly over it, feeding it dry lichen, grasses, an abandoned bird's nest she pulled from her game pouch. When the flames bloomed, she ordered Sadie to take off her wet dress. She swept the flames gently aside and told Sadie to lie where the fire had been.

The ground was warm and friendly. Sadie closed her eyes and listened to the rainfall just outside the cave's mouth, muting the terrifying buzz inside the stone. Dozing, she thought of all the caves she and Grace had explored, searching for treasure that the Cherokee had left behind during the Removal. The caves had been plundered, but Grace always found deep chambers colored by symbols along the walls, filled with objects broken or lost. Once, they'd discovered a chain of diamonds carved into a cave wall. They'd traced the chain with their fingers until reaching a deeply carved "V" that resembled a cloven hoof.

"Is that the devil's foot?" Sadie asked.

"It's a door to the other side," Grace said.

"What's the other side?"

"It's where the Indians buried women and babies who died in childbirth. They put a 'V' over the stone to mark the place so they wouldn't forget where they were. They brought their living daughters back up here to visit right before they married. They thought that if the girls touched the 'V' they wouldn't die when they were having their own babies."

Sadie imagined her sure-footed sister running lightly up the ridge to touch the "V" so she wouldn't die, wondering why her mother hadn't taken them both to these caves before it was too late, before Grace could only lie in their mother's bed, her once-slender arms and legs swollen, the skin stretched so tightly over her hands and feet that Sadie feared they would split open if she touched them. At the very end, Grace's lungs had filled with fluid, and she gasped whenever she tried to speak, but her dark eyes locked onto Sadie, never leaving her sister's face. Sadie went to her, kneeling beside the bed. Though Jane had told her that Grace could no longer speak, Sadie heard Grace whisper, "Sis."

"Can you see it yet?" Sadie asked. "Can you see the other side?"

"Not yet."

When Grace's eyes shut, Sadie's whole body ached, and she couldn't breathe. She sat on the floor, curling into a tight ball, uncurling, curling up again. She prayed and chanted into the silent air of the room to any god that would listen, "Take her. Take her. Take her to the other side," until she felt her sister gone, and Jane assured her that the body twitching on the bed was not her sister anymore, only muscles remembering movement.

Jane's fire cracked and hissed. Sadie opened her eyes and saw her mother hunched over the dying light in a low corner of the inside chamber. Above Jane's head, five red hands were seared into the cave wall, some with fingers missing. Sadie thought they must be the handprints of girls hoisted up at arm's length to reach a woman's height. As she crawled toward the hands, the rock hummed louder, as if women and babies were behind the stone, trapped between this world and the next, murmuring in some forgotten language. Wondering if Grace were on the other side of the wall, Sadie stood, reached shyly toward the hands.

"Go on," Jane said. "You're meant to touch them. This is a holy place, no place to be timid. No such thing as timid and holy."

Sadie placed her hand over the last hand, the perfect one with all its fingers. She pushed and pushed, trying to open the door and pass through, the buzzing so close that she nearly thought herself inside the stone. When the buzzing stopped, Sadie looked up and saw a net of gnats vibrating across the crumbling ceiling. She looked down and saw her hand still pressed against the red, stone hand. All around her, the chamber was empty.

Sadie backed out to the cave's mouth and sat on the ledge beside her mother, who was staring out at the black cliffs shiny with rain and evening sun. As she followed Jane's gaze, Sadie saw what amazed her mother. Hundreds of birds were filling the canyon. Brown swallows swooped, turning on thermals, diving toward invisible insects. A white dove floated down into the feathery trees, its wings flashing white against the black cliffs. Her mother turned and blinked, as if adjusting her eyes to light after too much darkness.

"Your skin's so pale, like your father's," Jane said. "I can almost see through you."

Sadie winced at the word *you*, feeling unnamed now that Grace and her father were gone. Who would she be now that she was no longer called "Sis"?

"You think he'll ever come back and finish what's left undone between you?"

Jane shook her head. "I was never any good at marriage, so I just quit after Grace left us."

Sadie considered her mother's choice of the word *left*. It gave her the picture of Grace on a long road, walking away. It sparked the dim and unreal hope that her sister might somehow return.

"Grace once told me the Indians buried their dead inside these caves so that the living could come back to visit them," she said.

"The dead have no business in here," Jane said.

"Then who made the hands?"

"Shaman artists. They put them here for the living, to help them remember. The dead are all outside."

"Even Grace?" Before Jane could answer, a pigeon flew at them, so close she could hear wing and bone snap, and feel her own dead heart flutter and spark. She ducked, fearing the bird's beak would blind her forever. The pigeon landed one ledge below. Stepping sideways, hesitant, it looked down at the bare trees twisting above the green undergrowth. Watching the bird, Sadie felt the dark wing of her mother's grief lift, and in that moment she knew her sister was out there roaming along some otherworldly ledge or river, not buried beneath earth and stone. Sadie sat beside her mother, breathing easy, feeling found.

The swallows thinned out, and the doves darkened into bats.

"It's over now," Jane said.

"Can we come back here?"

"We only needed to do this once," Jane said, adding that they needed to get home to close the windows before dark so the bats wouldn't fly in, drawn to their house lights.

On their way back, they took a shortcut along the highway, following the drainage ditches. Occasional headlights swept over the gravel, lighting a stream of debris cast from passing cars. They made their way through crushed beer cans, a sodden diaper, torn bed linens. Another car passed, and Sadie saw a slender, white rectangle lying on the ground. She thought it was a patch of dirty melted snow until her mother picked it up.

"Come help me," Jane said. Another car passed, its headlights revealing her mother holding a mattress, more bloated than the soiled diaper beside it.

"Why do we need that?"

"You're too old to be sleeping in my bed now," Jane said. "Go on. Take an end."

Sadie took the end, feeling its weight awkward and wrong. Her mother walked ahead, pulling faster than Sadie could move up the steep road. She stumbled on gravel and leaves, slipping six inches for every foot they climbed, but they made it to the cabin. Inside, her mother pushed the mattress into the corner farthest from the fireplace, covering it with oilcloth and a rough, brown blanket.

Jane sat beside the hearth and started a fire, not even using the bed. Sadie's mind stoked with anger and resentment as she stared at the bed's sheets forming empty tunnels she still longed to burrow within. Sadie sniffed the air, dreading the scent of canned apples and cinnamon, warily awaiting her mother's stirring at the fire, blasts of wind coming from every open window. Instead, the warm room smelled of lavender. Her mother's wild hair hung loose around her shoulders, two thick gray strands framing her face. She looked old again, but softer, almost holy, and Sadie knew that Jane had told the truth: the day's rough passage had made Sadie too old to sleep beside her mother ever again. Sadie read the mugs above her mother's bent head. She would never go without. Now that she knew how to get what she needed, she would take what she could get.

Wrapping herself in the blanket, she carefully adjusted her back to the dimpled mattress that smelled of ditch water and exhaust. She breathed again, catching the smell of talcum powder deep inside the mattress, the ghost scent of all the newly-grown women who must have lain on it before her, surviving its hardness. Sadie folded her hands beneath her face and closed her eyes, drifting into the temporary shelter of sleep.

🌺 Sadie, 1942

Beauty: A Winter's Tale

SADIE AWOKE TO HER MOTHER stoking the fire in the stone hearth. She held a finger out from beneath her blanket, testing the air and wind speed inside the cabin. Now that it was September, her mother had started leaving the screen-less windows open all night, believing the first fall chill was healthier than summer air. All the windows were open, but the room was full of warm smells, wood smoke, and the rosemary growing out in the kitchen garden. Jane's game pouch wriggled wildly on her bed, covering something the size of a country ham or a small turkey. Sadie hoped for a turkey, recalling the last Thanksgiving meal her parents had prepared together for Sadie and her older sister, Grace. Her sister had been dead ten months. Her father, who'd gone off timbering after the funeral, had written home the week before to ask for a divorce so that he could marry a coal operator's widow from Roanoke. In his letter home, her father claimed that he still loved them both, but that he no longer wanted to live poor, or stricken. He just wanted a moneyed woman to take care of him.

The pouch moved again in all different directions, and Sadie recalled the two young mourning doves her father once knocked out of the old oak at the edge of their property while he was trimming it. He'd brought the birds home still alive, poured them out of his game bag onto the hearth. They stumbled, dazed and crawling like rats around the stones. Jane had wanted to kill and dress them with honey and vinegar, but Grace had seen wild doves flying in the woods, and she cried until their father brought in an apple box lined with ferns and moss. He said his daughters could put them out in his garden shed and try to keep them alive. Together, Sadie and Grace fed them milk-soaked bread until one day the birds simply disappeared, though Grace assured Sadie that she'd seen them fly away. "We forgot to name them," she'd said. "That was our mistake. You've got to name something if you want it to stay."

Jane picked up the squirming bundle from the bed. A head ringed by dark, red curls popped out. Sadie saw that it was a child, a boy big enough to walk. He might have been old enough to talk, too, but he wasn't talking, at least not in any language Sadie recognized. He was crying, his face deeply red. Her mother wrapped the quilt tighter around the boy, swaying him. The ends of her black hair ebbed and flowed at her waist, two thick gray stripes of it framing her high cheekbones as she looked down at the child in her arms. Sadie wished fiercely that her mother had brought home a turkey. If it were a turkey, she could wring its neck, pluck its feathers, stuff it with sage and wild garlic, cook it in a pot over a high, steady fire. Instead, her mother had brought home this screaming stranger, allowing it to sleep beside her on the high, full bed, where Sadie no longer was allowed to sleep.

"Come and meet your new brother," Jane said.

"Where did you get him?"

"Over at the McCauley place." Jane smelled the child's head. "If I could bottle the smell of this baby, I'd make millions."

"He looks too old to be pitching a western like that," Sadie said. "Why can't he walk and talk yet?"

"He's a late-life child. The mother didn't want anything to do with him. I said I'd raise him." Jane swayed back and forth like a pendulum, twirling with the baby to becalm him. "Just hold him and sway until he stops fussing. Like this. I call it the baby dance."

Jane put the child into Sadie's arms. He felt too large even to be a toddler, closer to five or six years, his overgrown toenails scraping her bare knees. He grew heavier, and Sadie wondered how long she would need to hold him. Afraid of displeasing her mother, she swayed the child until he stopped crying and looked up, gazing calmly at her. Jane turned back to the hearth to heat a kettle of water. Four tin mugs stared out at Sadie from the mantel above her mother's head, etched with the familiar words, "Today I drink, for tomorrow I may go without." Sadie drank in the smell of the child's head, trying to understand why someone would pay for a bottle of his scent. Salty with sweat, the boy did smell better than the soggy canned apples her mother had fed her all winter. The puncheon floor splintered her bare feet, but she kept swaying and spinning slowly, the boy heavy and warm in her arms. When the water heated, Jane took the child back. Sadie felt light and empty handed, surprised by her own womanly ache to hold the child again.

"Come here, little man," Jane said, unwrapping the child. "You're the man of this house now, the only man."

The boy howled and reached for Sadie.

"Hush now. You're too pretty to be angry," Jane soothed, pouring pitcher after pitcher of warm water over his back. "Pretty children don't need to pitch fits to get what they want."

As the child stilled beneath the pouring water, Sadie looked at her mother in wonder. She thought of her sister, Grace, the pretty raven-haired one, crying herself ugly with tear-streaks, fussing to get her way and keep their mother from killing those doves. She studied the boy now that he was calm. His hair was long, curly, shot through with every hue of redwood—mahogany, rosewood, bird's-eye maple. His skin was as pale as skim milk, unmarred by birthmarks or moles. His eyes were large and brown. Doe-eyes, her father had called them. Whenever Grace was in trouble with Jane for something, trying to cover up some trespass, their father said she looked like a deer caught in the headlights. It was the doe eyes, so much like her sister's, that made Sadie decide to name the boy. She searched her mind for boys' names to give him.

She came up with the first name of Michael, testing it to make sure it could not be rhymed with bad words, school-children taunts. Before she'd dropped out of the seventh grade to help minister to her sister's illness, her own name had been rhymed with "Shady Lady" by her classmates. As the schoolchildren chanted, *Sadie, Sadie, Shady Lady*, the taunts had felt unfair and dimly true, as if they were hinting at some flaw hidden deep within her. She wanted a name immune to cruelty and ridicule. Michael could be rhymed with *bicycle*, and it could be shortened to Mike or Mickey, but that was the worst that could happen. Next, Sadie considered Autumn as a middle name because that was when her mother had found him, but that was a girl's name, so she pushed it back to August. His last name, McCauley, was easy. That's where he'd been found. By the time her mother finished bathing the boy and dried him in the quilt, Sadie had made up his whole name. She leaned over the boy, testing it out on him, "Michael August McCauley."

"What's that?"

"His name," Sadie said. "I came up with Michael because it can't be rhymed with bad words. August and McCauley because that's the season and place you found him."

"But it's September."

"I thought about that. September isn't a real name, and Autumn belongs to a girl, so I pushed it back a little to August."

Her mother nodded. "It's a strong name." She gently trimmed the boy's water-softened nails with her teeth, so as not to scare him with a knife. Sadie smiled, pleased.

IN THE GARDEN OF STONE

"What now, Miss Priss?" Jane said. "You're awfully full of yourself."

Sadie didn't mind her mother's name calling. "Miss Priss" rhymed with "Sis," her old nickname, the one her father had given her, the one she'd lost after her sister was gone, and her father was gone, and nobody was left to use her name except her mother, who had not called her anything at all for the last six months. Jane toggled the boy in the crook of her arm, the look on her still-pretty face savage and holy. Sadie was too pleased to stop smiling, so she covered her mouth with her hand. She who had never been called pretty, whose pale skin freckled thickly from the sun, whose hair was reddish brown and frizzy, had not needed to pitch a single fit to get what she wanted.

THE NEXT DAY, JANE CAME HOME with a black swivel chair, a barber's kit, and a paper bag of pastel butter mints. Jane bolted the chair to the floor of the kitchen and unzipped the barber's kit, laying it out beside the sink. She poured the mints into her good buttermilk pitcher, the one with the Dutch windmill painted on the side.

"Now that I've got an extra mouth to feed, I needed to figure out a career," she announced. "I'm going to open a beauty parlor."

"But you don't even cut your own hair," Sadie said.

"Don't need to," Jane said. "It's the married women that lose their looks young. I can help them keep themselves up a little while longer."

Jane went out to the old shed room and came back with the family's Bible. Bound in white leather, it nearly covered the top of her mother's pastry table when Jane opened it to Psalms 34 and 35. She blew across the frail pages. Dust rose and swirled, making Sadie sneeze. She turned to the color picture of Samson in the treadmill before the cover page. Samson was already shorn and in chains, his muscular right thigh exposed all the way up to his loincloth. Sadie had never known her mother to read the Bible. She'd never seen her mother pray, not even during Grace's illness.

"What's that for?"

"We've got some good little Christian people around here," Jane said. "This Bible will attract the kind of clients I want."

"What kind do you want?"

"I'll settle for the kind that wash their hair and faces. I can work with that."

Her mother unrolled a movie poster that pictured a girl in a blue dress wearing a pair of glittery, red shoes, facing a road and a crystal castle in the distance. Sadie had seen one like it in the marquee of the Colonial Theater, the last time Jane had taken Grace and Sadie to a movie, which turned out to be *The Wizard of Oz*. Sadie had not liked the movie at all; it had given her nightmares about flying monkeys for months. Jane had not liked Judy Garland, whom Jane had read about in one of the Hollywood gossip magazines Grace had begged for after seeing the movie. Judy Garland, she discovered, was really a grown woman who chain-smoked, flirted, and swore like a sailor every time the camera was off, though neither the smoking nor cursing was what Jane minded.

"Something's wrong with her," Jane said. "What kind of grown woman makes herself up like a little girl to get a job?"

Grace, of course, had loved the movie and made Sadie play-act it in the woods every day until she could no longer play. Always, Grace was Dorothy, the corn-fed farm girl with the red shoes, while Sadie had to take turns at being the tin man, the scarecrow, the lion.

"What's that for?" Sadie asked, looking at the movie poster.

"It will help business," Jane said. "My beauty parlor is going to be called 'The Yellow Brick Road.'"

"How is that going to help?"

"We're not going to get much street traffic out here," Jane said. "So I have to play up the journey part of getting here. A woman will walk the extra miles if she thinks she can get something back that she's lost. She'll do almost anything to get back something that's been lost or taken from her, especially if it's her beauty, even if she's never had it to begin with. Remember that. It's a woman's biggest weakness."

The boy, Michael, had not talked yet, but he could walk. He was a climber, too. While Jane and Sadie discussed the business of beauty, he'd scaled the kitchen cabinets and eaten the whole pitcher of butter mints. A wet rainbow of sugar had dried on his cheeks, chalking up his newly-washed hair. Sadie held her breath, angry with him for eating the mints she'd wanted to taste. She winced, too, as she awaited the beating he would get.

Jane laughed and gave the boy a dill pickle to chew on. "He's a buster," she said. "You'll have to help me with him, keep him out of the way until I can build up a list of regular clients."

"What about school?"

Her mother shook her head, "You're old enough to stay home and help out some around here." Sadie's stomach fell at the thought of not going back to school, especially in the depths of winter, when darkness covered the valley at two o'clock in the afternoon. Other than the Bible, no books were in the cabin, not a pen or a piece of paper to amuse herself or the boy with. Sadie must have said this aloud because Jane replied, "Plenty of pretty amusements right here in these home mountains." Jane swirled the barber's chair, patting its seat. "Step right up, girly. Let me play with that rat's nest of yours. You'll be my first customer."

Sadie climbed into the chair, and her mother grabbed the back of her hair into a ponytail, cutting it off at the base. "You're lucky to have all that natural curl from your father," Jane said.

"Do you realize they didn't even have perms when I was growing up? Beauty shops did Marcel waves, with irons heated on a gas burner at their stations, and the first perm that came out was a spiral perm: their hair was wrapped around thin metal tubes and then curling rods were slipped over them. They turned on the electricity, and you looked like something from outer space while you were getting your perm."

Sadie shivered, feeling an alien breeze at the base of her neck, listening to the close, friendly sound of her once-quiet and remote mother. Her mother's hands, moving expertly in her hair, sent a gentle pleasure through Sadie, giving her the hope of having beauty, something she'd never considered for herself before.

"I don't know what they did in setting hair," Jane went on. "They didn't have rollers for a long time. I think they used pin curls to set 'em with a lot of sticky waves. I think I was sixteen when I got my first spiral perm, and then they came out with 'the realistic,' or what they called the 'cold wave,' which was without electricity. They didn't take too well in my hair. They weren't very curly, and they would drop out in a couple of weeks."

Sadie lost herself in the feel of her mother's hands on her head and neck, wondering if her mother had really ever had a perm, or if she was just practicing her beauty shop banter. Before now, her mother had worn her father's flannel shirts and work boots; the closest she'd ever come to perfume was tucking a tuft of lavender in the front of her shirt.

Jane had stopped talking. She stood before Sadie, tussling the girl's new bangs, brushing the cut hair from her collarbone.

"There now," Jane said. "All that long hair was making you look old. You've got beautiful cheekbones, beautiful eyes. This short cut just makes your features pop right out like a movie star's. In fact, I owe you an apology for never seeing how pretty you are. I guess I just never saw it before." Jane lifted her hands. "Now wait a minute." She disappeared into the shed room. While she was gone, Sadie shivered again, feeling delicate and fluttery, almost embarrassed. Part of her wanted to hide from her mother's sudden noticing, before her mother had time to forget about her again. Being suddenly pretty felt odd, a little unsafe. Grace was pretty, and look what happened to her. The other part of Sadie couldn't wait to see how the new cut made her eyes and cheekbones pop out like a movie star's.

Jane came back with a towel and a hand mirror. When she held up the mirror, the first thing Sadie felt was absence: the lack of her mother's hands in her hair, the missing of her sister's quick fingers French braiding it, her father's work-roughened thumb no longer flipping her ponytail as he passed by on his way out the door. The short cut was stylish, exactly like pictures she'd seen in all the movie magazines, but her fine hair had curled up too tightly, and her face looked pale and puffy in the small mirror. The only features that popped were her freckles, which she'd always hated, spending hours rubbing lemons over them so they'd disappear. Her mother's narrow kitchen had begun smelling of vinegar, from where Michael had gnawed a dill pickle down to a core. He'd climbed into Jane's bed and had fallen asleep, his small body curled into a perfect "C." Looking at his long, beautiful hair, still intact, Sadie ached with envy.

Careful now, she thought. A woman's weakness is to long after what she's lost.

She remembered last winter's grief over her sister, felt its heaviness hovering just above her head, a black storm cloud about to split open. She would not give in to this new rush of loss over something she'd never had to begin with.

HER MOTHER WAS RIGHT about one thing; the September woods provided plenty of pretty amusements. While her mother drummed up business, Sadie entertained her brother by keeping him outside, following the only rule that Jane sternly enforced. "Don't let anybody see you or the boy," she'd said.

"Why?"

"Because if anyone sees you with him, the *away* people might come up here looking. They might see one candle too many."

"Who are the *away* people, and why would they be looking for candles?"

"People who would come and take away Michael," Jane said. "They would think the candles are signs of devil worship, human sacrifice. This boy is high born. They'd use any excuse to take him away."

So Sadie kept Michael out of sight, which was easy to do if she took the old, lower paths. Michael could walk the gentle grades, and the woods were thickened by rhododendron tunnels, oak and hickory leaves. The paths were unmarked, forgotten by most of the locals, but Jane had taught them to Grace and Sadie. The lower paths afforded plenty of vistas over the sparsely populated cove. Walking inside of them, Sadie could remain hidden from anyone.

Mornings, Sadie walked Michael all the way around Harmony Path and down to Lake Elizabeth, which was really a pond owned by the country vet. The rising sun lit the yellow leaves of trees on the ridge above the lake, their reflection flaming across the water's still surface. Sadie named the two swans patrolling the rim of the lake Elizabeth I and Elizabeth II. The swans glided regally toward them, but up close they presented their clown faces to the children, snatching up pea gravel from the berm, and when they found nothing of interest they snaked their long, white necks beneath the surface toward the minnows and tadpoles, flipping their bottoms into the air like upturned canoes. Up for air, they snorted like hogs, which made Michael laugh, delighted and amazed that such ugly noises had come from such beautiful creatures. He was an easy child with a deep belly laugh. He liked to be held, and though he was too big for it, Sadie sometimes held him in her lap in the shade where the wood ducks gathered. Showing off for the few females, the bright males looked unreal as they twitched their orange and blue tail feathers, pecked each other with red beaks and puffed out their snowy breasts. When Michael wandered toward the lake to chase the ducks, Sadie had only to murmur, "Danger." Though he still hadn't spoken a single word, Michael understood her and backed away from the water's edge.

By late morning, when the swans folded their silky necks back on their wings and fell asleep, Michael and Sadie got hungry. They sauntered over to the old orchard behind the Sypher place to wait for Dean to come outside. Sadie had memorized his habits, such as how at this time of day he collected the fallen winter apples from beneath their trees, carried them to the boundary wall, dumping the bruised fruit over for the half-wild horses that the vet grazed on their mountain land. After Sadie and Michael had eaten their fill of deadfall fruit, they lingered. Sadie let Michael nap in her lap, curling his coppery hair around her fingers. Even when her own legs fell asleep beneath his sturdy body, she shifted his weight just slightly to ease the pins and needles, but not so much that she would wake him. That way, she could stay a while longer, watching Dean work his horse in the pasture.

Sometimes, Dean stared straight into the woods, as if he could see Sadie and Michael, but he never came back to the wall or tried to frighten them away. Grace once told her that he was the kind of boy who talked best to cows, deer, horses, and bears. Sadie looked down at Michael, who tugged his ear in his sleep, curling like a bear in her lap. She wanted to follow Dean inside the Sypher house, see if he could get Michael talking. Grace had described the inside of the house in great detail; rare heart pine framed every door and window. She had described a heart pine window seat before the front bay window, and a heart pine bookcase filled with books that Grace had been allowed to bring home to read.

Sadie imagined herself sitting on that window seat, reading *Wuthering Heights* as Dean talked with Michael in whatever animal language they both knew. She felt a low buzz course through her body, as if she were getting one of those old electric perms. Then she remembered her lost hair, the remote cabin she came from. Would people living in such a beautiful house have anything to do with a shorn, low-born girl? They might have been interested in Michael, with his crown of coppery curls. Maybe they would be *too* interested. If they knew about him, maybe they'd come asking questions about candles and take him away. She woke Michael and backed into the woods, pulling him behind her.

By dusk, they headed home to sit on the back porch while Jane finished her last client. This was the blue hour, when the deer were moving, and Sadie taught Michael how to sit so still that he wouldn't startle the doe who came through every evening, followed by two tiny fawns, one all brown, the other dappled by tufts of powdery white fur. The mother deer clipped through the yard, chewing through everything green on the ground. If Michael made a noise, the deer looked up, staring at the children, so close that Sadie could see the veins inside her long ears that stood straight up, wavering like antennae. As the doe moved on, her fawns lingered, not knowing yet to be wary. When they all finally disappeared, Sadie let out her long-held breath. "She's a nosy one," Sadie said, excited every time the deer came to visit. "They all think we're pretty interesting."

Though the road leading to her mother's beauty parlor was not yellow or brick, just a bunch of unpaved switchbacks, the women did follow it. Jane's clientele list filled up quickly, mostly with the wives of railroad men. Jane promised the bookish ones "a thinking-woman's haircut." She styled the aging ladies' hair into a cut she called "the classic." She stressed the importance of working with what they already had to make themselves attractive. All the women left wearing the same cut, a cross between a Marcel wave and a helmet shellacked by hairspray. They all seemed pleased to have found what they thought they'd lost, full of praise for Jane's high cheekbones, her magic hands.

Word of Jane's magic touch spread beyond the female population to the trainmen, who came at night for a shave and a haircut after their second shifts ended, sometimes after dark. Whenever the trainmen arrived, Sadie would have to wake Michael and take him back to the shed room and wait for her mother to finish with the men. She didn't mind. It was fun to sleep on the bed her mother kept beneath the overhang, especially on warm nights when the black bear sauntered out of the woods and climbed the green apple tree out in the yard. Holding onto the trunk with one paw, he edged out onto the sturdier limbs, grabbing at the green apples with the other paw, cramming the fruit into his mouth. Once, he balanced on the bird feeder on all four paws, reaching into the wooden house to scoop out the birdseed. The bear was better than a tightrope performer, or a comic acrobat. Sadie had to keep herself from applauding, which would have interrupted her mother's appointments with the trainmen. When the men emerged, they all looked a bit like Samson in the treadmill. Shorn and well muscled, they stood unmoving in front of the house, staring back at Jane's closed front door, as if invisibly chained forever to her stone porch steps.

RAIN FELL HEAVILY the day the old couple drove up together in the '41 Packard, so Sadie and Michael had to stay inside during their appointment. The woman was pleasantly plump, wearing a flowered dress and a straw hat with plastic cherries on the wide brim. She wore thick, red lipstick and pulled her dyed, blond hair into a high ponytail like a girl. She reminded Sadie of the wood ducks down on Lake Elizabeth, all puffed up and feathered by so many bright colors she looked unreal. She called her husband "My Charles" in a foreign accent that made Sadie think she was calling the man beside her "Ma Challs." The man wore a gray car coat and dapper fedora, but his face was ravaged and thin. Beneath his sweet cologne, Sadie could smell his sickness. He smelled like Grace had smelled near the end, his breath coming up from stomach and kidneys too devoured by cancer to hold anything, his skin musky as a tree limb rotting from within. He didn't have much hair to cut, just a silvery rim of fuzz over both ears, but the woman said, "We have heard of your magic hands. Ma Challs would like a shave and a haircut."

The man shook the woman's hand off his arm and took the porch steps on his own. "Show me my way to your magic chair," he said. He looked down, surprised by Michael, who was standing inside the doorway, holding onto one of Sadie's legs with both his arms. "Well, that's the prettiest child I've ever seen. No, really. Sometimes you have to tell a mother her child is pretty even when it's ugly, but I really mean it about this one. She is the prettiest." Then he looked over Sadie's face, his eyes lowering to her stomach softly swollen from eating so many winter apples. "And this must be the little mother."

It wasn't a question, and Jane didn't answer it or correct him. She hushed Sadie with a glance, as if to say, "What does it matter?" But Sadie flushed deeply. She was reminded of the taunting voices of her schoolmates, "Sadie, Sadie, Shady Lady," and felt her innocence pierced unfairly by a dark arrow of shame. Jane ushered the man to the swivel chair in the kitchen. Then she told Sadie to take the lady back to the shed room and shut the door.

Outside, the woods were gray with rain. Soft drops fluttered the apple tree leaves and bounced the apples, which had started to turn brown, softening on the bottoms. The bear wouldn't come down into the yard this early, and the rain and the woman's talking would, in any case, have kept him away.

"Call me Miss Lucy," she said, as she looked down at the quilt on the cot in the shed room. She took out an embroidered handkerchief, spread it over the quilt and sat on it, folding her skirt upon itself, as if trying to keep the fine fabric from touching any part of the quilt. Sadie flushed. Batting puffed out where the quilt had been torn at a few seams, but it was perfectly clean; Sadie had taken it out that morning and beaten it with a wooden spoon, letting it purify in the wind. Miss Lucy began talking, oblivious. She'd been raised in the Mississippi Delta, but My Charles was a native Virginian, she said. As her dying husband got a shave and a cut in the next room, she told Sadie a love story.

"Do you want to hear about how I fell in love with My Charles?" She went on, not waiting for Sadie's answer. "It involves a bird. I had brought a pretty canary with me when my parents moved up here to Virginia from the Delta. It was a rare, beautiful bird, foreign to these parts, and we kept him out on the sun porch all summer, and sometimes we put him out on warm days in winter. One day, just as winter was coming, we forgot and left the bird outside on the porch all night. The first snow came that night and blew the porch door open. When I awoke the next morning, I found my bird lying there, all stiff looking, but I couldn't get my hands through the cage door to get to the bird. My Charles happened to be walking by, and I called to him for help. He came running, and he got his hand right into that cage, even though his hands were much bigger than mine."

Miss Lucy looked down at her gnarled hands, as if remembering when they were dainty. Her eyes darted over the rest of the shed room—the chinked walls, the Dutch windmill pitcher Jane had refilled with butter mints. Sadie held the pitcher out to Miss Lucy, offering her a mint, which she considered dainty. Miss Lucy shook her head furiously. She patted her hips, "Oh, no, darlin'. I never eat sweets." Sadie put the pitcher down, looking into the mints, amazed and dimly hurt, growing more suspicious of this woman. She didn't believe her. What kind of person never ate sweets? The back of her throat thickened and her stomach ached. Michael snaked his hand into the windmill pitcher, and Sadie saw how grubby his fingers were. She slapped his hand, and he looked at her in wonderment. She'd never slapped him before. She felt ashamed of her own meanness, unaccountably angry with Miss Lucy for bringing this ugliness out of her, for making her see how grubby her brother's hands were, for making her slap him. The whole shed room began to feel dark and cramped and grubby. It smelled like damp.

"Well, even though My Charles' hands were much bigger than mine, he got them into the cage and pulled that bird right out," Miss Lucy said. "He wrapped it in his own handkerchief, saying, 'Why, Miss Lucy, I do believe your bird is dead.' I just cried and cried until he bent over my canary, saying, 'Well, maybe she is just frozen.' He pushed on that bird's little heart with those big old thumbs of his. That's when I fell in love with him—when he tried to bring my bird back to life. Can you imagine?"

Miss Lucy laughed, but Sadie imagined the old man in the kitchen as a young man, placing his handsome hands over the tiny bird's chest, trying to bring life back into it. For some reason, this image didn't strike her as unrealistic or funny.

"The bird died anyway, but My Charles carried it out in the backyard for me. He buried it in his clean, white handkerchief, beneath our magnolia, which my daddy had brought up from the Florida Panhandle because they are very rare, impossible to find up here. I married him the day after. He has been my husband for fifty years, a good husband, and I wanted to bring him to see Miss Jane for one last, good haircut."

Miss Lucy stopped talking. She looked down at Michael. The boy had moved away from Sadie and curled up on the very edge of the cot. "I suppose this child's father is alive and well. A big, healthy girl like you is probably married to some strapping boy working down at the quarry or in one of the mines." She spoke to Michael. "Is your daddy at work? Is he bringing home the bacon while your mama takes good care of you and the little one that's on the way?" She cut her eyes sharply at Sadie's stomach, and Sadie's hand rose up to her innocent abdomen. She felt flushed and winded, as if the woman had gut-punched her.

"He don't talk," she said, suddenly loving the boy's quietness. It wasn't such an unpleasing trait.

"Oh, bless 'im," Miss Lucy said. Sadie knew what this phrase really meant; it was the term her mother reserved for her most difficult clients, the kind who would never be pleased by the looks Jane had to work with. "Oh, bless her," Jane would say after one of these unpleasant appointments. Then she charged the difficult client an extra ten percent with hopes she wouldn't come back.

Miss Lucy's eyes alighted on the Bible. She opened it to Psalm 86, "The afflicted soul longs for a token."

"Shall we pray for this poor child?" This woman's nosy presence was not a pleasant token, not like when the gentle doe brought her lovely fawns to Sadie's window. Miss Lucy's offer of prayer seemed more like a dark and ugly taunt. *Sadie, Sadie, Shady Lady.* Perhaps Sadie was still ashamed and angry with her mother for making this woman believe she was Michael's child mother, someone to be pitied and judged. Maybe she was just restless, aggrieved by the loss of a whole day spent inside while it rained, unable to see the swans or the deer. This woman's voice, as it sailed out the windows and deep into the woods, had clearly scared away the acrobatic bear. Sadie opened her eyes wide and said sweetly, "My mother never prays."

Miss Lucy drew back, the plastic cherries on her hat trembling. Sadie had begun to hate those fake cherries. She wanted to chew them up and spit them back at this woman with her too-young ponytail, her mean lips flaking with red lipstick. She wanted this woman gone, never coming back, so she added, "Mother does light candles all around the cabin sometimes. Maybe she practices some other kind of religion."

Miss Lucy stood quickly, backing away from Sadie just as My Charles walked into the shed room. Shorn and grinning widely, he did not look like Samson, but Sadie could see how handsome he must have been long ago, how his offer to resuscitate a tiny canary would have charmed any woman into falling in love with him. He held both of Jane's hands in his own, giving the backs of each one a gentlemanly kiss, patting them. "Take care of these magic hands," he said. The couple left the back way, Miss Lucy brisk and quiet as she guided her husband's happy, rickety steps around the cabin to their fancy car. As they drove away, Jane sat on the bed beside Michael, stroking his long hair and soft face. Her own face looked pale and drawn, her eyes deepened by the dark circles beneath, as if she'd given part of her youth to that old man.

"I don't ever want to do that again," Jane said.

Sadie felt a pang of guilt as she looked into her mother's tired face. "I don't either."

They fell asleep on the porch, lying on either side of Michael. The boy twisted in his sleep, flinging an arm over Jane, a leg over Sadie, his sleeping body warming them both as the chill night breeze blew through all the open windows.

BUSINESS SLACKED OFF in the weeks that followed. Jane blamed the coming winter weather, the snow clouds pouring over the mountain and into the valley like skimmed milk. Sadie was sure it was because Miss Lucy had told about the candles, invoking all forms of devilment in the minds of anyone who would listen. Still, nobody came up to the cabin to take Michael away. This got Sadie thinking about why nobody had ever come to question Jane about her new child. She began to wonder about the place Jane had found him, whether he'd been given or taken by her mother.

One snowless morning, Sadie bundled Michael in her own warmest sweater and took him out walking on the higher paths. They circled Horseshoe Loop until reaching the path to Rattlesnake Summit. No snakes were up there, just rugged rocks streaked with ore and garnet, and a clear view over the McCauley place. Sourwood burned bright red behind the empty corncrib and barn, and the house's windows were dark and sightless. The fallow field was colored only by yellow and orange fallen leaves that swirled around the rusted sorghum mill. Nobody had lived there for years, at least five, maybe ten, judging from the thickness of the rust on the farming equipment.

She shook Michael gently. "Where did she find you?" The boy's eyes widened. Looking deep into them, Sadie saw Grace's eyes. They were Jane's eyes, too. But his ethereal face was not shaped like anyone's in the family, not even her father's. "Where did you come from?" The boy stared beyond the abandoned homestead, off into the mountains rising on the other side of the valley. He mumbled something, his unused voice creaky as the dying, old man's voice had been, muffled by the sweaters she'd pulled partly over his mouth to keep him warm. Unsure if the boy had said "her" or "here," Sadie tried to get him to speak again, but he wouldn't. Then she just stopped trying. She stood quietly, looking over the mountains ridged like the bare backs of women shivering in the winter breeze. Michael could have sprung out of that earth and stone. He could have come from a real woman. She thought of how My Charles had called her Little Mother, and how he hadn't sounded mean or shady, only kind. Even Miss Lucy, however unkindly, was only pointing out what now seemed just obvious—Sadie's own shift from younger sister to Little Mother. Nothing about mothering this pretty, lost child was ugly or shameful. Who else was there to do it? Sadie would never know for certain where he'd come from because Jane would never tell the truth, and the McCauleys were all gone. Only beauty was here. It spoke to her. That was enough. She no longer needed anyone to explain it.

🌼 Sadie, 1945

The Stranger Room

SADIE MET DEAN SYPHER the summer the mines closed, and the operators who'd bought up farms in the valley below Wilderness Road left behind their houses filled with furniture, their barns locked up with the livestock still inside. When Dean wasn't managing his mother's property, he worked for the veterinarian who lived down the hill from the Sypher house, going out at night on large farm animal emergencies, looking after the abandoned animals. At sixteen, Sadie worked as a hired girl for Dean's widowed mother, Emma, cleaning and cooking in exchange for piano lessons. She thought the worst veterinary cases were the horses. Unable to afford the feed, the operators set free their thoroughbreds before leaving. Arabians roamed, half feral with hunger, nuzzling bitter acorns dwindling in the woods at the edge of the sloping pasture, some of them dying, some never born.

Inside the parlor, Sadie stood beside the piano, staring through the bay window that overlooked the woods behind the house, waiting for the horses to appear. Emma sat on the piano bench, her hands twisted like ginger roots in her lap.

"You've got true instinct," Emma said. "If you would

concentrate and practice, you could be good enough to play in church."

After a month of piano lessons, Sadie could play only one hymn, "Adore and Be Still," but Emma kept encouraging. Sadie never mentioned that she had no practice piano in her mother's cabin over on Dump Hill. Jane Musick's kitchen was filled with the single barber's chair she used to cut hair for the railroad wives of Bluefield. The boxy bedrooms of the cabin remained embittered by the smell of permanent solution that made Sadie wish she could live year round in the Sypher house. Cooled by mountain air in summer, heated by a coal furnace in winter, the house was filled with everything Emma had made before her rheumatism set in— hand-painted tablecloths, lamps woven out of reeds.

On the early June morning that Sadie stared out the window and waited for the horses to come out of the forest, Emma's hands began paining her so much that she gave up the piano lessons. She allowed Sadie to snap a music roll into the player piano, letting her peddle out old show tunes: "Oh Promise Me," "Canadian Sunset." While Miss Emma swayed beside her on the piano bench, Sadie stared out the bay window again. All around the house, spring had come quickly; for the last several weeks she imagined she saw the trees greening, a sight that made Sadie's whole body ache with unnatural stillness.

When Emma tired of the songs, Sadie helped her to bed and ran down the hill to feed the horses. At the bottom of the slope, in the remains of the old orchard, she gathered fallen green apples in a laundry tub and carried them to the fence at the edge of the woods. A black and a bay appeared under the leaf cover, but they shied away from her hands outstretched to stroke their knotted manes, retreating slowly into the forest. She dumped the fruit over the fence, turned, and walked slowly back up to the hill to look for Dean.

She found him inside the barn, kneeling beside a chicken coop, staring at his latest veterinary project. After the last farm animal emergency, Dr. Chapel allowed Dean to bring home some abandoned chickens, and Dean had made a project of nursing the pecked chicks before trying to put them back in with the healthy ones. The project had gone badly. The dead chicks were all lying in the dirt, pocked and bloodied, while Dean paged through his father's old Boy Scout Handbook, searching for the section on animal husbandry.

Sadie doubted that Dean had ever been a scout. When he was twelve, his father was gunned down by a tramp while working at the Norfolk and Western station in Bluefield, and Dean had dropped out of school to go live with relatives in West Virginia. He'd come back a few years ago, and he took over his family's farm. When World War II came on, the draft board deferred him from the service because he had a weak heart. Twenty now, Dean was short and barrel-chested, and he didn't look like a man with a weak heart. He was not handsome, but his face had a power— high and broad cheekbones, a nose broken twice by a fall from a horse, brown eyes so solemn that Sadie could never imagine him young.

As Dean scanned the pages of the Boy Scout Handbook, Sadie felt sorry for him, knowing he wouldn't find a section on resurrecting dead chickens. She placed her hand above his shoulder, close as a touch, not touching. "I'm sorry," she said.

Dean looked up warily. She dropped her hand, willing him to read her mind, *You know me*, until his gaze softened into recognition.

"A cow's about to give birth up at the old McCauley place," he said. "I need to go up there and wait for the signs. You can come if you want."

She nodded, but he'd already turned and walked out the door.

Framed by evening sun, he stood at the pasture fence, calling and running a thistle along the wire mesh until a white speckled quarter horse came running, bumping her head against his chest as he rubbed her throat and crest. Though Dean had found the horse half starved in the forest, he praised her high withers and long cannon, noting her resemblance to an Indian pony.

"I think she might have some Barb blood in her," he said. "I named her Cherokee."

Dean went back into the barn and returned with a saddle. The horse nickered softly as Dean slipped the halter on and tugged her ear. He saddled the horse and lifted Sadie into it, tucking her feet inside the stirrups. She teetered from the fourteen-hand height as Dean led her out of the pasture and toward an old game trail. He walked ahead, talking over his shoulder while the horse snaked her head at laurel branches, snatching up deadfalls until she choked.

Dean looked back. "She's an easy seat, but this time of day everything around her looks like a smorgasbord," he said. "Hold the reins close to your stomach and pull the next time she goes for something."

The horse's gait was sloped and broken, but Sadie held on until the reins blistered her fingers. When the horse stopped straying, Sadie looked up. The night was spectral. Along the path, white pines were moon-bleached, arching like frozen fountains from craggy limestone bluffs. Dean was different in the woods, less wary than when he was around the house and barn. He carried a lantern, training it beneath the great rhododendrons, explaining how the locals preferred Dr. Chapel to the young town vet who kept nine-to-five hours and transferred his emergency calls to another vet all the way in Princeton.

"Dr. Chapel works by the moon," Dean said. "He plans his social life accordingly." When the moon was thin, Dean explained,

Dr. Chapel went down to the Open Bar to drink Old Crow until reaching oblivion. When the moon was full, he'd wait at home for the phone calls. Dean talked and talked, and the horse felt steady beneath her, relaxed and supple now, traveling strongly. Sadie listened to the woods, to the horse's tail swishing like silk over silk, to Dean telling of how they were on a game trail blazed by Cherokees one hundred years ago as they crossed the mountains into the valley to hunt deer, elk, bison.

"They camped and hunted in the cove for weeks, sometimes months at a time," he said. "They were just passing through. They never lived here."

When they reached the wild white roses spilling over the path, Dean helped Sadie dismount and urged her to smell their apple scent, explaining that the wild rose bloomed for only four days out of the year. He helped her mount the horse again, reaching back to break off a branch of blossoms, handing it to her.

"Sub rosa," he said. "It means that anything that happens under these roses stays beneath these roses."

He pointed to the full moon that shimmered like a white coin, holding itself above the pine tops. "It's definitely a calving night," he said. "That moon's pulling the water in their bodies like it pulls the water in the sea."

They reached an abandoned house sitting above a creek bed. The back of the house was a chinked log cabin, but a room made of sawmill lumber had been added on the front porch. Dean helped Sadie dismount and carried the saddle and horse blanket over to the front room. It was empty, except for a bare bed tick pushed up against the wall beneath a small, wavy window. No door led from the new room into the old house.

"This is the stranger room," Dean said. "Travelers could spend the night here without having access to the main house or the family inside. We'll shelter here later on."

He folded the blanket on the bed tick, placing the wild rose branch on the windowsill above it. They went back outside. Beyond the smoke house, Dr. Chapel stood outside the barn, dressed in a tweed cap and Wellingtons. His thick hair was shock white, his nose webbed with slender veins, but his blue eyes were good-humored as he looked Sadie over.

"Nothing a gal likes more than seeing a cow give birth on a Friday night," he said.

"She's interested in the cycle of life," Dean replied.

Dr. Chapel laughed, nodding over to the calving pasture, toward a black cow standing among a herd of brown ones beside a pine windbreak. "That one's done this twelve other times," he said. "Just make sure you keep the calf from cold stressing." He looked Sadie over one more time. "Well, I'll leave you to it."

After the vet left, Sadie asked what signs they were waiting for.

"She'll pull away from the herd, or we'll see a wet spot on the ground beneath her," he said.

"Is he coming back?"

"Who?"

"Dr. Chapel."

"It's a full moon. He's probably tending cows all over the valley. He might even be helping a mountain woman or two give birth."

Sadie studied Dean and wondered if he was teasing. He was still new to her; she'd yet to hear him laugh. When a slow smile blossomed over his face, she breathed easy again. "Come on," he said, picking up his lamp. "It'll be a while still. I want to walk and tell you everything about this place."

He led her down the hill to a white, clapboard church, its tin roof streaked with rust. Inside, an angel carved from a piece of petrified driftwood knelt at the back, holding an empty pewter plate. They sat side by side in the last pew.

"Who were they?"

"Primitive Methodists," Dean said. "They were strict. If you belonged to them you didn't play cards, you didn't dance, you didn't work on Sundays. You didn't do anything, not even your sewing. You got your food ready on Saturdays, and you rested on Sundays." He paused, resting his hand gently on the bare pew between them. "They're all gone."

"Where'd they go?"

"Home. Back to wherever they came from. They were just passing through."

"Like the Cherokee?" Sadie teased, wondering if anyone beside the Sypher family truly belonged to this valley.

"They were always different. In all the other churches, the men sat separate from the women. In here, a woman could sit next to a man."

Sadie felt his hand on the pew beside her, and just as Sadie began wondering if she should take it, Dean stood. They wandered out into the cemetery, through a path of gravestones that leaned into a leaf-covered slope. They passed into a clearing, where the grave markers were large and uncarved. At the very edge of the cemetery, Dean stopped in front of three white crosses planted above a bed of lavender, sage, and rosemary. A pale white ribbon tied to a cypress swept down and along the ground, hedging in the herbs and three small plaques nailed to the footstones.

"These are the saddest ones." Dean sat in the grass, holding the lamp near the three plaques, allowing her to read: Infant, December 19, 1918; Infant, February 18, 1916; Otis, February 27–September 5, 1917. "I always wonder how the mother got through this."

Sadie shook her head, recalling the old photograph her mother kept in a pine chest in her bedroom. It was of Sadie's older sister, Grace, toddling beside a pram that Sadie must have been in, an unseen infant. Jane knelt on the grass beside Grace, her dark eyes gazing softly at the older daughter, a stray curl of raven hair blowing across her unlined forehead. The photo was the only evidence of the lost sister and father that Jane had kept. Sadie took it out and studied it often, knowing by her mother's sultry looks that the photo had been taken by her father, a man still besotted by wife and children. She guessed it was this memory that had kept her own mother going.

Dean stood, swinging the lantern below another rhododendron. "Can you see it?"

Sadie shook her head.

"It's a spider's eye," he said. "My dad taught me how to find them like this."

Sadie strained to see the spider's eye, but all she could see was dew glistening in the grass. Dean walked deeper into the cemetery, training the lantern beneath shrubs, pointing at glistenings he called the spider's eye. Sadie hated spiders. Once, she'd killed a bunch of spiders that were living beneath her bed. When Jane found out, she asked Sadie how she'd like them dressed, saying, "Don't ever kill anything unless you intend to eat it." As Sadie followed Dean, she hoped he wouldn't kill any spiders or tell her that they would be eating them. She nodded "yes" every time he spotted one, because she liked how he leaned close to show her the glistening in the grass, the promise of his hand hovering above the small of her back.

When they reached the wooded edge of the cemetery, she saw a drop of blue larger than any spider. The blue drop moved slowly out into the open until she saw the swish of a white tail. The buck stared at Sadie and Dean, scraping its cheek against a headstone. He stamped his hoof, huffing like a small dog.

"A doe bed must be around here," Dean said. "He's out laying scrapes, patrolling."

"Will he come up on us?" Sadie asked.

"No, he's just a homebody," Dean said. "He's just telling us he's the boss on guard. He's doing his best John Wayne swagger to scare us off the premises." Dean spoke to the deer in a human voice. "Okay, Duke. We're not going to hurt your lady friend. We're just passing through."

An even bigger buck appeared, standing guard at a distance. Behind him, a doe sat in the grass, her delicate legs folded beneath her as she nibbled at the foliage. Dean swung the lantern, and both deer looked up, mildly staring back at them.

"Is she having her fawn?"

Dean shook his head. "It's too early for that. Right now, she's choosing her mate. She's a quiet one. My guess is she'll slip away from that old harem master and visit with Duke here. At least, that's what he's hoping. Until then everybody stays calm, fat, and happy."

The lantern smoked, and Dean turned it down. They sat on one of the low footstones, letting their eyes adjust to the darkness. Sadie felt Dean beside her, very close again, his hands milky in the moonlight, turning beautifully as he talked. She'd never been so close to a man, and she breathed deeply, catching his scent of horse and sweet hay, the sun's heat still in his hair. She waited for him to lay one of his hands beside her again, for his fingers to graze her hand as it rested on the stone between them. She wondered if he was waiting for her to give a sign, for her to do the choosing.

Sadie longed for an older sister's counsel, someone who would speak plainly about the unspoken language between men and women. When it was time for her to learn how to become a woman, her mother had taken her out into the forest to learn the names and secret uses of herbs. Rosemary and sage could evoke a man's desire; lavender could help her to remain chaste, "if that's what you want," Jane had said, adding that a woman could drink a decoction of juniper laced with turpentine to induce early labor "when nature failed to take its course." None of her mother's lessons explained what to do with this man sitting beside her, talking and talking, his hands moving around her, never landing.

Dean stood. "We'd better get back."

Sadie followed him, confused by how close they'd been, dimly disappointed, certain that whatever might have happened between them had passed. When they reached the pasture, the cow had pulled away from the herd. Dean ran to the struggling animal, Sadie trailing behind. The cow let out a low, defeated moan, and Dean spoke softly into her ear.

"Hey there, Delilah," he said. "Shh, everything will be all right."

He led the cow to a narrow corridor of aluminum piping that ran along the pasture fence, shoving a bar down behind her, feeling her haunches for broken bones. He rolled up his sleeve and stuck his arm inside, feeling for the calf. He motioned for Sadie to roll up her sleeve and stand beside him.

"I need your help," he said. "The umbilical cord's around the calf's neck, and I can't get my fingers under it. Your fingers are smaller than mine."

She nodded, and Dean grabbed her hand, pulling her whole arm into a sticky warmth so spacious she felt she could have crawled inside. She reached toward the calf, feeling the cord like a wet rope around calf's neck. She slipped two fingers beneath, loosening it. Dean felt again, nodded, "That's good." He tied a rope around the calf's hooves, and they pulled together, the air filling with watery sounds, the mother's legs buckling as the calf landed on the soft grass, its wet fur bluish in the moonlight.

Sadie stared at the still calf, shivering as the birth blood cooled on her bare arms. She stopped breathing as Dean pulled off the placenta and flung it aside. Reaching down, he massaged the calf's heart, pressing and circling with his thumbs until the mother heaved and righted herself. She licked the calf until it lived.

Sadie's mind darkened from not breathing, and her body

swayed. Dean caught her in his arms and led her down through a laurel hell, guiding her into the creek. Standing with her in the shallows, he washed the blood off her arm, his hands moving over her skin firmly, gently, until he reached her shoulder, his thumb grazing the side of her breast. He stopped and looked into her eyes, his glance pulling all the blood through her body, and she wondered if the moon had begun working on her too. He let go, took off his shirt, and began washing himself. When he finished, he slung his shirt over his shoulder. They walked back to the stranger room.

Inside, the air was colder than the outside, the walls and window bare except for the branch of wild roses arching on the sill. "Come here," Dean said, unbuttoning her blouse and arranging it with his own shirt across the bed tick, urging her to sit down, pulling the musty horse blanket over them both. They sat side-by-side, closer than they had in the church and cemetery. They kissed until she felt slightly nauseous, and he pushed her down firmly, moving her around the bed tick until he seemed satisfied with the way their hips joined. Her skin thrilled beneath his rough hands, her arms and legs weakening from the strange heat sparking in her stomach, traveling lower, until she felt an ache so pleasing it softened her mind, and she could only marvel at being there with him, chosen.

A pinecone dropped on the roof, startling them both. Dean stopped, looked down at her. "You can't ever tell about this," he said.

He was above her still, but as he started moving again, he looked beyond, his eyes flinty, full of sadness and rage, and she knew that that he was no longer aware of her beneath him. Feeling him drift away, her mind and senses sharpened painfully to the stark room and the forest around it. She smelled the river they'd bathed in, the fainter scent of the blood they'd washed themselves of. She heard the wind rush through the pines like water. Her back ached, and she could feel the wooden floor through the bed tick, but she kept still, knowing that once started, even the loneliest of tasks must be finished. She closed her eyes, reciting the names of the loving herbs. Rosemary, sage, jasmine.

When it was over, Dean stood and paced the room, the bed tick already lacking his heat and weight.

"I know of some herbs—" she began to say, but he hushed her by giving her the branch of wild roses from the windowsill.

"This can't happen again," he said.

She looked down at the branch, its blooms closing in the darkness. She added to her list of loving herbs, *sub rosa*.

WHEN SHE GOT HOME, Sadie found her mother sitting cross-legged in the flowerbed outside the cabin, hedging a bed of irises with empty beer bottles. Jane's black hair was woven into two loose braids, her strong arms deeply tanned from a morning of gardening. Her prized irises were deep purple, bearded, mail ordered from a catalogue, but they seemed wilder than the flowers she'd transplanted from the woods. The iris stems bullied the coneflowers and lilies, but her mother never thinned them. All the flowers surrounded the rose of Sharon that Sadie's father had planted to honor his lost daughter before he left, and Jane spent whole days moving and transplanting flowers around it according to some internal landscape unknown to Sadie.

Jane didn't look up as her daughter approached.

"I went on a large farm animal emergency with Dr. Chapel and Dean Sypher," Sadie said. "We helped a cow give birth. It happened near dawn. That's why I was out all night."

She retold the story, beginning with Dean's failed chicken project and the cow birth, leaving out the part about the stranger room, ending with a list of the rescued animals Dean kept in his barn, the ones he'd shown her in the forest.

"He's got an Indian pony named Cherokee, and he's made friends with a deer he named Duke because his hero is John Wayne."

Jane glanced sharply at Sadie's waist. "That boy sure likes strays."

"Oh, he's got a heart like the world," Sadie said.

"If it's like this world, are you sure you want it?"

"He's a good man. He doesn't do a thing unless his mother tells him to."

"That's the worst kind of man."

"What does that mean?"

"Emma Sypher is a high and mighty one. She's got her eagle-eye on everything." Jane paused, considering the dirt beneath her fingernails. "Sometimes, the worst thing you can do is give someone what they want."

Sadie waited, wishing her mother had given her a curfew and had whipped her for breaking it. Instead, Jane gave her this puzzling admonition that would linger in her mind longer than any punishment. She recalled Dean's stern words before leaving the stranger room. *This can't happen again.*

"He wasn't offering anything," she snapped as she turned and went inside the cabin.

Now that she'd been with a man, her room felt crowded by everything a girl leaves behind when she's not returning. Ragged china dolls lay side-by-side across her pillows; talcum spilled over its box on the vanity, dusting her silver brush and comb set. Above the bed hung a picture of Sadie taken by a traveling photographer a year ago, the kind touched up by a paint brush so that her skin looked as rosy as one of the china dolls. The photographer had posed Sadie on a milking stool dressed in a gown she'd borrowed from Miss Emma, her long braid slung over her shoulder like a bullwhip.

Jane came to the doorway. She'd changed into a white nurse's dress and her unwoven hair swayed at her waist. She'd been a nurse during the Great War, and she'd kept her uniform, once confiding that she liked the way men still turned their heads when she walked by in that dress. Whenever she wore it, she didn't come home until the next morning.

"I'm not telling you how to marry," Jane said. "I never married well, so I quit. I'm only saying we have to be careful about the way we treat men. We have the power to make or break them."

"Who said anything about marrying?" Sadie said, but Jane was already gone.

After Jane's truck pulled away, Sadie went to her mother's room and flung herself across the bed. A rain-scented breeze fluttered through the window screen, and Sadie rose to stand beside the pine chest that held the picture of her mother and sister beside the pram. She knelt, lifted the hope chest lid. It resisted. She tugged again, sinking with feelings of betrayal and embarrassment, as if her mother had known she'd come looking for the photograph that day, and she'd locked it away.

The clock chimed suppertime. Sadie's stomach cramped with an emptiness greater than hunger as she imagined the Sypher family sitting down to eat on their screened-in porch off the kitchen. Everybody had his or her own silver napkin ring. Dean's was big and heavy; Emma's was smaller, with little beads around it. A few weeks before, Emma had caught Sadie polishing and admiring it. Emma gave it to her, saying, "Every girl should have her own napkin ring." After that, she allowed Sadie to set a place for herself after she served. She gave her two linen napkins a week, which Sadie never dirtied. She rolled them back into her silver ring at the end of each meal, placing them on the side table beside the silver oil lamp. Sitting in her mother's room, she watched waves of clouds pour like milk over the next ridge. She longed unbearably for that silver napkin ring, for her place at the table on the Sypher family's airy back porch.

By BLACKBERRY SEASON, it stopped raining. Storm clouds hovered above the valley, their dusty tendrils never reaching the ground. Streams dried up, ponds stagnated. Poisonous plants rooted in the dry pastures surrounding the abandoned farmhouses, their fence posts stacked in the center, clumps of rusty barbed wire scattered like tumbleweeds around them. Jane sent Sadie out with two empty buckets to pick berries, but the wild blackberries remained small and bitter from drought, and Sadie wandered for hours with half empty buckets. Afraid to go home without the berries, she walked over to the Sypher place on her days off.

Sadie still kept house for Emma. During her bad spells, Emma sat for hours, staring through her cupped hands in her lap. Some days, she lay awake in bed, drinking coffee and hot tea. She talked hoarsely, continuously, as if her talk was the only thing keeping her mind from leaving her slowly petrifying body.

On one of those drought days when Emma was too ill even for much talking, she asked Sadie to read to her from the love letters her husband had written from town, the summer before he died, when he'd begun working extra shifts at the railroad to save enough money to make the farm self sufficient. His love letters always began with the same salutation, *Darling Mine, My Love Divine.*

Received your letter today. Sadie read. *You write a good letter—when you write one. Work went fairly smoothly today. No fights among the other men anyway. They wanted me to do a little work Sunday, but I told them I'd rather not if he didn't mind. The weather has been inclement, so I'm sitting in the station, looking out at a moving storm. From my window, filled every minute or so with a lightning flash, I can see the beginning of the rain unrolling from the clouds. Before I finish this letter the first raindrops will begin bursting against my window. I used to like the rain, especially at night. I always loved watching the heat lightning in the summer. Stars would be out, but off in the distance, above some other valley.*

"You would have liked him," Emma said. "He was tall and kind of silent. He smiled slowly when he smiled."

"Why weren't you writing him back?"

"We'd had some unpleasantness between us," Emma said. "We were in the depths of the Depression, but Caleb still had his job with the railroad. They were beginning to cut salaries. A lot of people were mad, and they quit their jobs and didn't work for five years, and I remember telling him, 'I don't care what they cut it to. Stay there because look what's happening all over.'

"The morning he died, I had been making plans so that he could quit his job and come back to breed horses and homestead. He went into town before I awoke, to buy something nice for Dean's birthday supper. He chose sausage, I think."

"Dean's father died on his birthday?"

Emma nodded. "That's when they found him lying by the train tracks and brought him home."

"How did you get through it?"

Emma kept talking, oblivious to Sadie's question. "Sometimes, I don't think I ever really knew him. He belonged to that damn railroad. He was a staunch Mason. Now why do you think he joined a group of men who keep secrets they won't even tell their own wives and children?"

Wanting to cheer Emma, Sadie spent the rest of the morning fixing her hair and applying her makeup. She rolled the wheels beneath Emma's rocker and pushed her over to the dining room table near the picture window that overlooked the farm. As she ministered to Emma, she romanced herself into feeling more like a devoted daughter than a hired girl. Emma had given her the spare room in the basement, a space wide enough for a chest of drawers and a wooden peg on the wall for her dress, a slender cot to sleep on when it was too late to walk back over the mountain to her mother's place.

Sadie's room was near the backdoor, beside the room with the claw-footed tub Dean used when he came in from working. Dean hardly ever used it. He stayed outside for days, as if keeping himself away from her. When he wasn't helping some animal give birth, he spent his time mending pasture fences around the valley, disposing of the rusty barbed wire, dropping the old posts, stretching new woven steel between them. For the whole month of June, Sadie trained herself to avoid Dean, as he avoided her. She hardly knew him, she reasoned. He could be the worst kind of man, loyal only to his mother. She forced herself to quit wanting him. Still, whenever he came inside, she could feel where he was in the house, even when she couldn't see him. When she heard him moving in the next room, her whole body ached for him, wanting.

They kept living. The less she saw of Dean, the more Sadie's role in the Sypher house filled out. She overcame her fear of Dean's outlaw horse, Cherokee, who sometimes broke out of the barn and wandered down the hill to stand at the dining room window. The horse was just paying a visit, but she spooked Emma, who ordered Dean to hobble the horse to keep her from wandering. Straps joined by a short chain were put around her forefeet so that she could only hop, but when Dean tried to leave the hobbles off, she broke out again. When Dean could not be found, Sadie walked the horse back up the hill, coaxing her back into her empty stall. She filled the water bucket and gave her a flake of hay. She never hobbled her. She sat on a chair beside the stall, smelling the sweet hay, the horse breathing softly on her face.

One night in early July, Dean came inside while Sadie was using the tub, steeping herself in lavender water. She felt raw, exhausted from not wanting him. Just what was so wrong about getting what you wanted? As he stopped before the open door, she left herself uncovered, gave him a tired smile, a little wave. They ended up at the cemetery below the Methodist church, beside the three white crosses marking the baby graves. This time, Dean told her to train the lantern on him as he stood among the crosses, his arms outstretched. Sadie heard a flurry of wing snap as yellow, orange, and tiger-striped moths flew into the light. He stood haloed by moths that pulsed like slips of paper along his shoulders and arms. He lifted each one on his finger, naming them for her.

"Royal moth," he said. "Tiger, hawk, sphinx." He lifted a drab gray moth. "This one here's a run-of-the-mill moth."

A luna moth appeared, large and green and delicate above the grave. Suddenly, the moth flew toward the white cross, bashing its fat rat body against it. Sadie felt betrayed by its up-close ugliness, emptied, and she begged Dean to turn off the light and release the moth into darkness. Her heart thrashed terribly. Dean calmed her with stories about luna moths, explaining how they emerged for only one week a year. They hid in hickory and walnuts until their wings filled out, and they could fly.

"The adults don't have any mouths," he said. "They eat nothing. They live solely to mate."

A strange heat bloomed inside of Sadie, drawing her closer to him, almost unwillingly. As she reached to touch the drab moth that clung to his shoulder, he clasped her hand, leading her up to the stranger room. This time, she took her pleasure quickly, before his mind could turn away, before he could forbid her to tell anyone of their lovemaking, or say that he never wanted to see her again. Outside, the mongrel horse bumped against the porch rail, stamping her back hooves. Unhobbled, she did not wander, and Sadie knew why the horse remained helplessly close, so bound to Dean that she would stampede inside the room if only he would call to her.

Another pinecone fell across the roof. This time, Sadie imagined gunshot, Dean's father falling along the train tracks. She felt Dean's mind start roaming, searching for the father who taught him how to spot spiders and name all the moths, a man so terrestrial that the earth must have heaved and scattered for his son when he died. Before Dean could leave her completely, Sadie began talking him back to her.

"Am I one of your strays?" she asked.

Dean looked down, his eyes clear and unsurprised. "You aren't so to me."

After that, Dean took her out on all his nightly farm animal emergencies. Each time they ushered in new life—the barn cat's litter of kittens, a semi-wild horse's foal in the forest—they ended up back in the stranger room, her body soft against his. She liked being that soft and sturdy place beneath him.

In AUGUST, ON HER BIRTHDAY, rain began again, and Sadie went back to her mother's house. She wanted to be with someone who would remember her birthday, but she didn't mention it to Dean or Emma, afraid of stirring the sadness that birthdays always brought to the Sypher house. Sadie's mother had not watered during the dry spell, and the drought had claimed everything but the iris stems and the spindly rose of Sharon. It had downpoured for three straight days, and the rose of Sharon blooms spooned rain that the hard, cracked earth would not take. Her mother's cabin seemed adrift in the muddy water ponding all around it.

Inside, Sadie's room smelled of olives. Because Sadie loved them, Jane gave her a bottle of green olives every year on her birthday, warning Sadie not to eat them all at once. Sadie kept the bottle on her windowsill, and Jane allowed her to eat one olive every five minutes. That morning, as Sadie sat in her small room with the door cracked, waiting for Jane to call out, "It's time for another olive," she imagined Dean's father landlocked at the train station, writing love letters and watching the moving storm, wanting to get back to his family.

Sadie fished out seventeen olives, one for every year of her life. Feeling too old for this ritual, she ate the olives all at once, her lips burning from the salt. Outside, the muddy rain circled the hills of parched earth, making her feel thirsty, swollen. She wore one of Dean's soft shirts because her own shirts had begun to strain around her middle. She'd filled out from all the good meals at the Sypher house, and lately she'd taken to eating a whole loaf of bread in one sitting. Suddenly, she felt too warm, dizzy, and her arms and legs shook from a deep exhaustion she'd never felt before. She touched the swell of her lower abdomen, certain that she'd inherited her sister's illness. The smell of olives closed around her. She heard the glass jar breaking against the floor.

When Sadie came to, Jane was smoothing a cloth soaked in lavender water across her daughter's forehead. Beneath her mother's touch, Sadie ached for a time when she was younger, fevered with flu, when illness still inspired her mother's tenderness.

"How far gone are you?" Jane asked.

"It might have happened in June, or maybe July," Sadie said. "Dean and I celebrated too much whenever we saved a calf." Sadie followed her mother's glance toward her stomach. "I guess you already knew that."

Her mother nodded. "I could see it in your eyes. You were losing your waist," she said. "Do you love him?"

Sadie nodded, unsure how to answer this unexpected question. "At first, he seemed so sad. I felt sorry for him."

Jane paused. "Sadness isn't love. Not all men need saving."

"Dean doesn't need saving," Sadie said. "He's the kind of man who'd give you the shirt off his back."

"I know his kind. It's probably not his shirt to give."

Sadie looked down at the broadcloth shirt she wore, knowing it had belonged to Dean's father. Jane looked down with her.

"You're carrying low," Jane said. "It will be a girl. Soon, she'll be wrapping herself all the way around your middle, like her fingers are reaching for her toes. Before you know it, she'll be robbing the breath out of you."

Her mother stood, her heels clicking briskly as she went down the hall to the kitchen. She returned with a cup of tea and put it on the bedside table. It smelled of earth and juniper and something more tonic than permanent solution. Sadie studied the photograph of herself on the milking stool, deciding she looked young and foolish, her features unreal beneath the gaudy paint. She now saw Dean through her mother's eyes, a boy dressed up in his dead father's shirt. Sadie knew that their lovemaking had been reckless, maybe even dangerous, especially if he became the kind of man who would up and leave without any notice. But he'd taken her back to the stranger room with him. Even his most transient affections in that borrowed room were sweeter than her mother's bitter herbs, this sad promise of tea laced with turpentine.

Sadie pushed the tea away, spilling it across the bedside table. "I think you're the robber."

Her mother stood, her hands steady as a painter's as she reached for Sadie's portrait. She turned her daughter's face to the wall.

SADIE FOLLOWED THE LOW CREEK bordering the old game trail, looking for Dean. The rain had stopped, and the afternoon sky's frail light filtered through poplar and pine. Midges flew into her eyes, and the wood fern and nettle had overgrown the trail so completely she had to trust her memory of the path. The cemetery looked different in daylight, the headstones blackened by mold, the deer vanished. The rain had rotted the droughted roots of an oak, and it had fallen down the ridge, its root ball reaching up like a gnarled hand from the sooty mud.

Dean stood at the edge of the cemetery that overlooked the valley, staring beyond the fallen trees. She could hear no wind or crickets. In the distance, a horse whinnied, searing the afternoon's silence. She followed the sound and Dean's glance to where the speckled white horse stood, her forelocks spread, her head extended, a loop of old barbed wire fencing around her throat. Her breath labored, she lay in the mud, and stood up again, twisting the barbs deeper into her neck. It was the worst sight, that white horse bleeding and falling in the black mud. Dean stood, his face unreadable, his dark eyes trained on the horse. High and mighty, Sadie thought, hating him for standing by, for cruelly doing nothing. She wanted to hit him; she wanted to bury her face in his chest so that she wouldn't have to look at the horse dying terribly in the mud.

"Do something," she said.

Dean shook his head. "There's no help for her."

The horse stood and fell again, her eyes rolling into her head, her nose frothing as she lay prostrate in the wet grass. Unable to stand it any longer, Sadie ran down the ridge toward the horse, bramble slashing her legs, the hem of her dress soaking up watery mud. She reached the horse, ran her hand down the curve of the horse's shoulders, patting her neck. The horse's sweat lingering on her hand, she slipped her fingers beneath the wire and pulled. The barbs bit her palms, tearing the flesh from them, pinning her knuckles into the sticky fur above the frail pulse beneath the horse's neck. She kept pulling, numb to her own pain, until she felt Dean's hands unclasping her fingers from the wire, turning her away from the horse and toward him, his face boyish, frightened.

"You'll shred yourself to ribbons." He knelt in the mud and pressed two fingers against the side of the horse's foot, the left side of her chest, beneath her jaw, searching for the pulse. The horse lay her head upon his leg, her large eye open. "She's gone," he said softly.

Sadie's insides ached so fiercely that she placed her bloodied hands over her abdomen. Dean looked at her stomach. He took her hand, leading her back through the cemetery and churchyard, not stopping at the stranger room. When they reached the spring house below his mother's farm, he stopped. The creek had begun flowing again, its low water trickling around smooth yellow rocks in the bed. Dean motioned for her to sit beside a soapstone bowl cradled in a bed of limestone, washing her torn hands, bandaging them with strips of his shirt.

"Some old Indian must have ground his corn in this hundreds of years ago," he said, nodding at the bowl.

"I thought you said they were just passing through—"

"I'll bet it's worth something," he continued, kneeling beside her, circling a finger around the rim. "I can't offer you much, but I think you and I could give this old bowl a run for its money."

Sadie looked down at the bowl that was so clearly the end of an ancient water trough, broken and heavy, wild columbine climbing through its cracks, but as she looked down at him, she could not muster the heart to tell him this. His knees bent, Dean gazed up at her so shyly that she needed a moment to understand what he was offering. Above them, the open windows of his mother's house were filled with yellow light, and she could hear "Rhapsody in Blue" playing. Sadie imagined Emma rising from her long, melancholy slumber, peddling the piano, watching its keys move as if played by swift, invisible fingers. She imagined her own child's ghostly hands soon reaching around her, but not the death grip her mother had warned against. She breathed easier with this child inside of her, feeling her great emptiness filled for the first time, each part of her body making sense in ways she felt sure Dean already recognized.

"This should be a happy time," he said.

She nodded, yes, and followed him up to the house, toward the promise of music.

PART THREE

❀ Hannah, 1957

Leaving War

IN EARLY JUNE, Hannah's father, Dean, said it was time to bring his Aunt Maria back from War. It had been nearly twenty years since Dean had lived in the West Virginia coal camp, where his favorite aunt had run a boarding house for single miners. Now that the coal company had pulled out, and the single miners had scattered, Maria sat all day long in the kitchen of the empty frame house, chain-smoking slender cigars at an empty picnic table. Seventy-three and nearly blinded by diabetes, this aunt was becoming a danger to herself. Dean thought she shouldn't be living alone any longer. When he asked Hannah to come along with him to bring his aunt back to Virginia to live on their land, she didn't want to go. The last time Hannah had gone down to War with her father, Aunt Maria had burned her arm with the white hot tip of her cigar. She never noticed, or apologized.

"That woman took care of me the year my father died, and my mother took sick," Dean said, opening the deep freeze on the back porch. "She's the reason I'm still in this world. Now that she's sick, it's my turn to help ease her on out."

"I think I'm sick too," Hannah said. "My stomach hurts."

Her father reached into the freezer and took out a package wrapped in white butcher's paper. "We'll take her some of this wild boar sausage I just made," he said. "If we can't get her to leave, at least we can keep her in meat for a while longer."

Hannah followed her father out to his truck, carrying the package. As he opened the door for her, she smelled his sweat and the Lucky Strikes his cardiologist had forbidden him to smoke after his heart attack. He'd put on cologne to camouflage the tobacco smell. It didn't help. The package of sausage sat like a folded white flag in her lap. A peace offering, Hannah thought, surrendering to her father, feeling dimly chastened by his rough gesture of kindness.

Hannah wanted to help her father, but she dreaded what he called his favorite aunt's "little mean streak." The last time Hannah was in War, after the cigar-burning incident, Maria made her go out before dinner to drive home the goats she grazed on the wooded hills behind her house. When Hannah returned to the house, Maria said she could not eat supper at the kitchen table because she smelled like goat. Since then, Hannah had been terrified of her aunt, wary of getting in her way. As she and her father drove through town, the truck's cabin filled with the smell of her father's cigarettes and bitter cologne. Hannah sat in the smelly truck cab, imagining a whole day spent in the company of her aunt, feeling trapped and nauseous. She opened her window.

"Whew, it's hot," her father said. "Looks like the bank's serving free lemonade. You want to stop?"

She looked at the card table set out on the sidewalk, the clear pitcher half full of water, ice and wilted lemon slices. She shook her head, "I'm too old for that."

He laughed. "Not hardly."

"I'm going into the eighth grade next fall."

"Old," he said, his face as impassive as ever. He looked along the ridges kettling the town. "I guess these mountains look more like dark, strangling arms to you. I'll bet you're studying on leaving. You've already got your escape plans perfected."

"I'm studying journalism," she said. "When I graduate college, I'm going to be a reporter."

They passed the bank and the pharmacy, and for a moment Hannah wished that she'd told the truth. She wasn't too old for lemonade. She wouldn't have minded a cool, sweet drink, especially if it meant putting off the trip down to her aunt's house. Her father gripped the wheel, his hands scarred by frostbite, the lines of his face deepened by the truck's stark light. Suddenly, Hannah fell mute with the familiar panic and dread of losing him to illness. Before his heart attack, he'd worked double shifts at the train station, and she'd hardly ever seen him. Now, he was prone to taking her for long drives in the mountains, staring beyond some timbered-out ridge or tumbled-down barn, beginning most of his sentences with the words "Used to be."

Her father's work-roughened hands made her self-conscious about her own stillness. Passing the Masonic lodge, she took out the reporter's notebook her teacher had given her in journalism class that year. She fell into the comfort of questions and note-taking.

"You ever join the Masons?" she asked.

Her father looked down at her notebook, his eyes amused. "A man asked me to once, but I turned him down. Now why would anyone join a group of men who keep secrets they won't even tell their own wives and children?"

Outside of town, the road narrowed, twisting. Dark and light leaves wove together, casting nets of shadows over the pavement. Chicory and orange lilies sprouted from the roadside ditches. Her father turned right, and complete shadow fell over the truck even though it was only midday. Hannah wasn't afraid of getting lost. Her father knew every road in the mountains. Even though he'd taken a medical leave from the railroad, he still rose at four every morning, staying out late most nights driving the mountain and valley roads in his pickup.

Her father pulled off into a crumbling parking lot beside an old roadhouse converted into a church. "This was on my route when I ran moonshine." He looked back at the bed of the truck, as if remembering moonshine. "I used to load them right here. Now that's the straight truth."

All year in her journalism class, Hannah had been learning how to report the truth, in words clear as water. Along with these skills came the knowledge that her father's stories about his past life were as shadowy and changeable as the mountain road before them. When she'd told her mother, who hated a lie above all other things, that her father had begun telling stories about his past that didn't seem straight, her mother, Sadie, had replied, "Do those stories harm anyone?"

"No ma'am."

"Then why don't you let him tell them?" she'd said.

Now, Hannah listened, though she still wanted the straight truth about her father's past, especially from the time he spent in War. According to her mother, the things that happened to her father in the coal camp were so bad they could not be repeated. These terrible things her mother left unspoken seemed worse than if she'd said them out loud. As they drove deeper into the mountain, the truck began the last stomach-flipping descent into the valley. Her father eased around the switchbacks until they reached the railroad tracks at the bottom. There, he followed the creek. The water ran low, trickling feebly around white stones. Tall, flaky pines were painted dark green, then white, marking how high the flood water had risen the spring before, washing away whole houses, leaving piles of torn clothing and ripped linens heaped along the roadside. Two men, one young and one very old, hunched over the linen heaps, torn bed sheets hanging ghost-like from the limbs above their heads.

Crossing the border from Virginia into West Virginia, they passed the old coal breaker, its sides bleeding with rust. The cemetery rose before the entrance of the town, its blackened tombstones sliding down the slope, half hidden by weeds, shadowed by dripping limbs of hemlock. Her father drove up to a stretch of green field where the drift mouth gaped behind a warped, chain-linked fence, a sign hanging to its right reading, "In Living Memory of Our Fallow Mines."

"They used to call this area Paradise because it was where the miners came up from underground and saw the sky after working all day in darkness," he said.

"Did you ever work in the mine?"

"I went under one time," he said. "But the mine was so dark I couldn't tell if my head was up or down. I figured out real quick that I could find better ways to make a living than being buried alive. My grandmother put me out for not wanting to go back under, said I wasn't earning my keep. That's when Maria started watching out for me. She always wanted me around."

"How does anyone live down here?" Hannah asked.

"Your Aunt Maria owns her house straight out," her father said. "She still lives by old-country rules, from when she was a girl in Sicily."

According to her father, Maria still lived by the rules of Campanilismo, the faith that all necessary goods lay within earshot of the village bell. Maria tended her garden and orchard, picked wild asparagus and strawberries from the fields. She traded with the trainmen who still came through town, or picked up household items from the flood heaps along the road. She trapped rabbits in the cages Hannah's father made for her. She never threw anything away.

"Campanilismo's just a pretty Italian word for poverty

economics," he said. "Now that the workers are all gone, I suspect the church bell rings less often down here, if it rings at all. That's why I've come to take her home."

Her father chiseled a piece of coal from the drift mouth with his fingernail and offered it to Hannah. "Pour some vinegar on it, and you'll make a coal flower."

She accepted the coal, dropping it in her pocket as they got back in and drove the rest of the way to her aunt's house.

The town was a valley wide enough for a row of main buildings, a railroad track, and a couple of back streets that sloped up and away from the colliery. They drove to the end of the last street, past houses with only their facades left standing, their backs and sides crumbled down, their front awnings shredded by wind and rain. Ferns and Queen Anne's lace spilled out of every doorless doorway. Aunt Maria's double-frame house squatted at the very top. Its yellow paint peeled, and its torn screens curled from the windows, but it looked miraculously whole among the other gutted houses. Trumpet vine crawled across its porch rail, its deep orange flowers flashing like bright birds against the dark green leaves.

"House looks good," Dean said. "I think she's got a few more plants on the porch."

He parked on the street, securing the emergency break so the truck wouldn't roll backward. "She lives over the mine, and the kitchen's caved in twice, but she always saves the stove. She'll want me to move that stove outside to her summer kitchen so she can cook without heating up the house. I'll have to tell her I can't do it this year. She's got diabetes so bad she could lose her legs. She's about to go blind. One of these days, she's going to set fire to the house, burn herself alive. She can't be left alone any more. She won't like me telling her this."

"If she could hurt herself in that house, then she needs to hear it," Hannah said. "She should listen."

"She's proud. She still sees things, but she sees them in the past. We're going to have a battle, so you'll have to promise me that you'll be a good lieutenant."

"How am I going to do that?"

"If she tries to feed you, don't eat anything," he said.

That would be easy enough, Hannah thought, remembering the goat incident. Hard to eat when the woman won't let you sit at her table.

They didn't knock on the front door. They entered by way of the kitchen, the largest room in the house, its white walls adorned with dark oil paintings of Henry Ford and Christ's crucifixion, palm fronds curling behind the corners of each one. Dried mushrooms, herbs, and peppers hung to the left of the open kitchen window, and a rabbit hung to the right, its soft fur ruffling in the summer breeze. The four-legged cookstove crouched in the corner, the wall behind it blackened by years of flames.

Hannah's father had not called ahead, but Aunt Maria sat waiting at the picnic table, looking toward the white light of the open window, smoking. She looked a little like her coal stove—short, dusky, and combustible. Her thin, bobbed hair was hennaed bright red, parted far to the left side. Her skin was still smooth and brown, and she wore a clean apron over a yellow dress, red lipstick, and gold hoop earrings. Hannah's father touched Maria's shoulder and placed the sausage on the table before her. Maria looked up, her eyes lingering just above his head, and Hannah knew that she was seeing her father in the past, as a boy.

"You hungry?" she said.

To Hannah's surprise, her father's craggy face softened, becoming boyish. "I'm so hungry I could eat grass."

Hannah tried to catch his eye, but he avoided her glance. His aunt stood, barely taller than the sink. Hannah and her father sat at the kitchen table while Maria produced a big Folgers can filled with biscotti—buttery cupboard sweets topped with tiny green and yellow flowers, hazelnut cookies she called "brutti ma buoni," ugly but good. She set two water glasses before Hannah and her father, filling the glasses with pink wine, adding a little water to each glass, like communion wine.

"So how is Father Edward?" Hannah's father asked.

"He died last month," Maria said, her voice triumphant. "I outlasted him."

"Who was Father Edward?" Hannah asked.

Nobody answered. Maria placed more cookies before them on the table. Hannah's father dunked his cookie into his wine and ate, urging Hannah to do the same, casting a warning glance that told her to eat and drink as he did. "It's vino cotto, dessert wine. She made it from her own grapes. A little bit won't hurt you." Hannah dunked her cookie into the wine. The wine softened the cookies made of cloves, nuts, and honey. They all tasted faintly of coffee from the Folger's can, melting across the tongue. Maria leaned forward, watching Hannah's father eat, replacing the first cookie with a second, the second with a third. Hannah watched her father eat, studying the lost little-boy look on his face. Filled with the dim feeling that she wasn't being a good lieutenant, she stopped eating her cookie, but her father asked for a fourth. His aunt smiled, put another biscotti before him. "Better than your plain American biscuits, eh?"

Her father nodded, though the cookies weren't like any biscuits Hannah had ever eaten. "They taste all right," he said.

The aunt turned toward Hannah, noticing her for the first time, glaring at the uneaten biscuit on her plate. "That one's skinny like a chicken."

"This is my daughter. You remember Hannah."

"She looks like Stella Flora. She has the ginger hair."

Hannah looked toward her father.

"Stella Flora was Maria's older sister," he said. "She had red hair, just like yours."

Maria pulled out a sterling locket from her apron pocket. She placed the open locket in Hannah's hands, revealing a hand-tinted photograph of a girl with red hair and blue eyes that matched the cornflowers on her dress.

"That was when she was a ripe, young peach," Maria said. "She kept her looks a lot longer than the girls who married down here."

"Why didn't she marry?" Hannah asked.

Maria snapped the locket shut. "She ran away before they could get her." She turned to Hannah's father. "It's too hot to cook inside anymore. When you gonna move my oven out to my summer kitchen?"

"That's what I came to talk to you about," he said. "That stove just keeps getting heavier and heavier. I don't think I can lift it this year."

"Then the girl and I will carry it."

"Wouldn't you like a brand new stove, maybe a gas one that wouldn't be quite so hot?" He looked down at the burn scars along Maria's forearms. "You won't burn yourself anymore."

"When you burn yourself, it means the food is good," she said, rubbing a scar on her wrist. "How am I gonna fit a gas stove in here?"

"You wouldn't. You'd be fitting it into a new house up on my land."

Her father explained to Maria that if she came back with him she would have her own house and garden on his land. He'd help her tend the vegetables and mow her lawn.

"You'd be free to do what you want."

"I do not like this idea," Maria said firmly, looking out the window, toward the flowers and vegetable plot, the woods beyond. "This place is my freedom."

"You'd be a lot freer up on my land."

"I'll believe that when the chicken pisses," she said.

"You don't need to be ugly in front of the girl." Her father glanced over at Hannah. "You look like you need a walk. Go pick some zucchini to take home to your mother."

Hannah nodded and walked through the airy back porch filled with blue light, where Maria slept on a single, iron cot. Out in the summer kitchen, lemon, and pomegranate trees grew in washtubs around a stone table. In the garden beyond, white iris drifted up to the arbor entwined with Confederate jasmine, wild roses, and muscadine, their mingled scents thickening the air, tasting faintly like Maria's dessert wine. As Hannah walked through the arbor and into the vegetable garden, she could hear a torrent of Maria's Italian streaming out the window, her father talking back in the same language. Less certain of his words, he spoke slowly, his voice rising to meet her high, trilling one, their voices curling so beautifully that, in the distance, Hannah wondered if they'd stopped fighting and had begun to sing. Hannah reached the zucchini patch and the stool where her aunt kept a knife and basket for cuttings.

She cut the zucchini with the bright yellow flowers still on them, the way her father had taught her, laying them side by side in the basket like a bouquet, recalling the wildflowers he brought home to her mother after they quarreled, usually over money, her father's insistence on not selling off any of his family's land, even if his stubbornness meant eating only beans and potted meat all winter to make do while he was on medical leave. Her parents never raised their voices in argument. Her mother said her piece and grew quiet, wearing her father down with her silence, a battle strategy he called "stubborn, red-headed attrition." Then, her father walked out, ending all possibility of resolution, staying away for hours, sometimes days, always returning with some small peace offering, a wild rose he'd dug out of the woods, a jar of honey. Once, he brought home an old Victrola that he'd bought at the auction in the old dairy and repaired it himself, using a manual he'd borrowed from the public library.

Hannah walked beyond her aunt's and father's voices, through the orchard filled with fruit trees, toward the hill where the goats grazed. The sun shone on the next hill, beside the dark drift mouth, lighting up the field her father had called Paradise. The goats came running, propping their hooves up on the split rail fence, like friendly dogs. Hannah wanted to pet them, then thought better of it. She was getting hungry, and she didn't want to get put out before dinner again. Still, Hannah felt mixed about hating her aunt. Maria had told Hannah she smelled like a goat and burned her with a cigarette, but these wrongs seemed small when she compared them to Maria's mean and lonely life. Hannah wondered about her aunt's older sister, the pretty runaway lost in some scandal, another untold chapter of her father's history, surely something her mother would say was too terrible to talk about. Hannah's mother had lost a sister when she was a girl, but she never spoke of her or visited her grave. Though Hannah had never had a sibling at all, she sometimes felt a longing for a sister that approached grief. She wondered what it must have been like when Maria and Stella Flora had both lived here as girls, if they'd shared secrets, if they'd fought with and defended each other fiercely.

Hannah knew her father would not answer these questions, even if he knew the answers. Down here in War, he'd grown more secretive and confusing. He'd eaten Maria's food after he'd told Hannah that she shouldn't. He'd asked Hannah to be a good lieutenant to him while he battled with his aunt about leaving War, and then he sent Hannah out for a long walk so that he could argue with Maria alone. Now, here she was, pleasantly dazed by a belly full of sweet cookies and even-sweeter wine, gazing at a field that did resemble Paradise a little, with its blue chicory and bright orange lilies blooming around the dark drift mouth. Removed from the battle waging in her great aunt's kitchen, Hannah knew only that she was failing her father. She turned and headed back to the house, determined to be a better lieutenant.

When she got back, the house was quiet, but the cookstove was not out in the kitchen garden. Inside, her father sat at the table, his face red and sweating, his shoulders stooped by defeat though the stove was still inside the kitchen, as he'd wanted it. The rabbit was missing from the wall, and her aunt's apron was stained with fresh blood. She was thumping around the stove, her eyes flashing as she loaded coal into the firebox, opening all the dampers and lighting the fire, testing the oven's heat by sticking her hand inside. She adjusted the dampers, opening and closing the stove doors without looking, needing only touch.

Her aunt's face flushed with the heat, and as she pushed back the damp strands of hair that fell across her face, Hannah saw her as she must have looked young, powerful, and earthy, her brown hands moving expertly over the dampers, redirecting heat and smoke, readying herself to feed a whole room full of men. She wondered why her aunt had never married, why she'd chosen to live in service to her father, then to the single miners she'd boarded, then alone with this stove as her only companion. Maria shook her head, placed her hand back in the oven, proclaiming, "molto caldo."

"She wants to make us a little snack before we go, says it'll keep her blood sugar from bouncing all over the place." Her father shook his head and walked toward the backdoor. "I've got to get some air. Try to hold her down to one kind of dish while I'm gone. We don't need all that food she usually makes. We need to get going."

Maria took the zucchini from Hannah, plucking the blossoms off each one. "Now I can make you zucchini fiore. You like seafood?"

"I guess," Hannah said, remembering the time her father brought home cocktail shrimp from the grocery market in Bluefield. They'd tasted good, conjuring the sea air and ocean her family once visited before her father was too sick to travel long distances. Hannah had eaten a whole pound of them by herself, dipped in cocktail sauce.

Maria opened up a can of slender brown fish stacked in oily brine. "A trainman brought me these anchovies at Christmas," she said. "I been saving them for a special time."

Maria began to boss Hannah softly around the kitchen, relating unwritten recipes, saying, "È molto facile. Is very easy," before every step. She called Hannah "Bella" and gave her a soft hug after she learned each new task, making her feel pretty and proud of herself. In this way, Hannah learned to stuff zucchini flowers with anchovies and the ricotta Maria made from goats' milk. She learned to roll each flower in egg batter, delicately frying them one by one in sizzling oil. After the zucchini flowers were done, Maria took out a flour sack filled with large, brown mushroom caps that smelled of the earth after a long, autumn rain.

"The good food never made it over to here from Sicily," Maria said. "I have a lean kitchen now, so I make little arrangements so that I can live. Maybe I find what I want in the forest, maybe I grow the rest."

Hannah was given a knife and told to shave the mushrooms into the wild boar sausage as it sizzled, cooking the mushrooms and sausage into a cream to spread over thick slices of toasted bread while Maria cut carrots into the cast iron skillet, braising them in another sweet wine from an old dusty bottle she kept out under the back porch. Maria tossed the remaining wild boar into the pot of rabbit simmering in tomatoes and garlic and wiped her hands on her apron.

"Time to set the table," she announced.

The parlor was sparely furnished with a red velvet sofa flanked by two Queen Anne chairs donated by church workers, worn but good. Hannah followed her aunt to a steamer trunk below the window. Maria unlocked the trunk and opened it, and the lid unfolded into shelves as it rose. The shelves were filled with linens, silver, and dishes, all covered with gritty coal dust.

She ran her hands over the dishes and linens. "We will have to wash these."

Maria reached into the bottom of the trunk, pulling out an aged, lace tablecloth. They carried the tablecloth outside, shaking out the dust. Hanging it over the garden wall to purify in the sun, Maria stared out toward the pretty sloping pasture where the goats grazed around outcroppings of field stones, the sunny slope called Paradise. She gently straightened a corner of the lace tablecloth.

"When we first came here, we had no money to buy the cloth at the company store, so Stella Flora and I made our underpants from flour bags and put lace on them. We thought they were so pretty."

Hannah flushed, embarrassed and pleased that her aunt had confided a secret that surely her father didn't know. She wondered where her father had gone off to. Most likely, he was sneaking a cigarette out in the woods, or gathering some wildflowers for the dinner table. The smell of the food simmering in the kitchen filled Hannah with satisfaction and a dim dread. Already, she knew that more than leaving and coming back with flowers would be necessary to win an argument with this aunt. In the parlor, Maria handed Hannah a dry cloth and started pulling out plates and bowls and serving dishes so fancy that Hannah couldn't name the uses for them. Maria began wiping down the plates and bowls with a damp cloth while Hannah dried them.

As they worked, Maria told of her girlhood when she still lived in Cefalù, her village in Sicily. Hannah thought the name of the village sounded like something you'd eat, delicious as the cooking smells wafting from the kitchen.

"The day before we left Sicily, my father took me and Stella Flora on a walk around town. Stella was thirteen, and I was twelve."

Behind the town's bank, Maria said, the girls followed their father along an aloe-lined path that rose to cliff top ruins. They sat with their legs dangling over the temple wall, looking out over the red rooftops, the turquoise sea hedging in the island. The father peeled an Indian fig, letting the green casings from the fruit fall on the rocks below, handing them the sweet flesh. He complimented their French, and spoke of the ease with which they'd soon pick up English in America.

"He told us of wonders," Maria said. "He said to us that Henry Ford gave a free car to all mothers of twins born in America. He said men were waiting to marry us when we got here."

Hannah wanted to ask about the husbands waiting for Maria and her sister, but she worried that Maria would stop talking if she asked that question.

"What's an Indian fig?" Hannah asked.

"A prickly pear," Maria said. "I believe you would call it a cactus. In the convent, the nuns taught me to make Indian figs and oranges with marzipan for All Saints Day," she said, proudly. "The nuns taught me how to do the cleaning and cooking. Cleaning is nun's work, the work of God."

Hannah marveled at her aunt's love of housework. She always tried to get out of cleaning and cooking at home, where all meals consisted of beans boiled with fatback, potatoes, sometimes a little sausage. For dessert, her mother sprinkled sugar over buttered biscuits to satisfy her sweet tooth. Once a week, Sadie took Hannah to her grandmother's house on Wilderness Road to clean. Her grandmother, Emma, sat alone in the front parlor, her head bowed, staring through ladylike fists, as if trying to remember her own body. Every day, her mother brought the grandmother custards made from her freshest eggs, trying to coax the birdlike woman into eating, but the grandmother always shook her head, replying, "I used to be, but now these hips." When they cleaned, they plodded around the birdlike grandmother, dusting and polishing her heavy furniture, covering each piece with a bed sheet, scrubbing the pine floors beneath everything. In those crowded rooms, her mother's face closed like a flower in the darkness. Hannah always felt betrayed by her mother's long-suffering ways, her grandmother's staunch silence.

Here, in her aunt's white-paneled room, early afternoon sun backlit the half-drawn window shades, and a wood-scented breeze blew through the open windows. Her aunt's furniture was uncovered, arranged around a marble coffee table with slender legs, adorned only with bleached feed sack doilies. Standing side by side, their shoulders nearly touching, Hannah fell into a calming rhythm of cleaning with her aunt, whose face was open, neither happy nor unhappy, as if lost in prayer.

This *is* nun's work, Hannah thought. "Were you studying to become a nun in that convent?" she asked.

"I was the youngest daughter in the family," Maria said. "So many children wanted my mother's attention that I did not say any words until I was four years old. When I did speak, I spoke in full sentences. My father saw this as a sign from heaven and took me to the convent when I was ten."

"Did you ever try to leave?"

"I tried to run away once, but the convent was so high in the mountains. I walked all night to get to the next village. By morning I did not reach any place, so I turned around and went back."

"And then your father came for you and took you to America?"

Maria set the final, cleaned plate down with a thump. "It's too hot to eat inside. I think we should eat out in the kitchen garden."

Outside, they smoothed the lace tablecloth over the concrete table. Maria told Hannah to set the dishes and silver, but she didn't tell her how, so Hannah set the table the way her mother had taught her, pretending each plate was a clock, setting the fork at nine o'clock, the knife and spoon at three. She'd lost track of time, but she knew by the shadows cutting across the next mountain that her father had been gone for several hours. Just as she began to wonder if she should go looking for him, he came out of the woods, carrying a bouquet of chicory. Hannah wondered if she should try to warn him about his aunt's feast. As her father walked toward the house, she felt a little sorry for him. His bouquet of chicory, set against her aunt's lace tablecloth, would look exactly like what it was—a bundle of ditch weeds.

When her father took in the tablecloth, Hannah's stomach flipped. His eyes fell upon her hand holding the remaining silverware. His face kept falling as he saw the table laden with impossibly elegant dishes set out for a meal that would last all afternoon, maybe part of the night.

"I asked you to hold her down to one kind of dish," he said.

"It was all very easy," Hannah said, though somehow her aunt's favorite phrase, è molto facile, had sounded better in Italian.

"We need to get going."

Maria stood in the doorway, her apron removed, carrying the first course. "Andiamo alla tavola tutti," she said sweetly as she moved around the table, her hair and dress swirling into a blur of blush and yellow. Hannah's father sat at the table, looking helpless as Maria set the first course before him, slices of toasted bread topped with the wild mushroom crème. Hannah took a bite, tasting the earthy mushrooms and salty meat, the grilled bread beneath it. Just as she thought she couldn't eat another bite, her aunt took the plate and came back with the pasta course, linguine with wild boar sausage. When Hannah paused, her aunt took a slice of bread from the basket, mopped up the sauce in her bowl with it, handing it back.

"This is how you eat," she said.

Her aunt went back inside. Her father was still working on his pasta, his face unreadable, when Maria came out with the hunter's stew. As she arranged it on their plates, her hands were expert and quick, her face full of the pleasure of feeding. Hannah stared down at the rabbit, unsure if she would survive another course.

"Are you not hungry?" Maria asked.

Hannah nodded, and suddenly she was hungry again. She ate the stewed rabbit with her fingers, scozzo ditto, as her aunt instructed. She was washing the hunter's stew down with a gulp of wine when Maria came out with a bowl of fruit—peaches, grapes, oranges, and plums. It was the most beautiful fruit Hannah had ever seen, perfectly shaped and shiny, and she wondered how her aunt had made it grow all in the same season. Her father took a cluster of grapes. Hannah took a green prickly pear, eager to taste it. She took a bite, and it crumbled into dust on her tongue, the rest crumbling in her hands and falling into her lap.

Her father stood so abruptly his chair fell over. "You eat when you are hungry," he said to Maria.

"That which gives pleasure does not do harm," she said, tilting her chin up defiantly.

"Does it look like she's pleased with that marzipan all over her?"

"It was only a joke," Maria said. "She is a soft and expensive girl. I think maybe she is a little bit simple. She needs to toughen up."

Hannah flushed at her aunt's tonic comment. I am not soft and simple, she wanted to say, but the marzipan had dried the words inside her throat. Hannah looked down at the false fruit, already a sticky mess in her hands and lap. She thought of the long afternoon spent cooking and cleaning with Maria, listening to her confidences, believing that Maria thought of her as a lost sister. She thought of all the hours she'd spent on her knees beside her mother, scrubbing the floors beneath her grandmother's furniture, how she'd mistaken her mother's loyalty to her father and grandmother as punishment instead of devotion. She felt embarrassed, fooled by her aunt's disloyalty. Maria had simply needed an ally in her battle against Hannah's father. Hannah was just another little arrangement her aunt made so that she could go on living in War.

Her father had walked into the house. Hannah heard a clanging, as if he were inside the thin walls, pounding so hard she half-expected the house to collapse into a heap. Hannah rose and went into the kitchen, found him kneeling beside the cookstove. He'd already removed the stove's legs, and they were lying sideways on the floor among a scattering of nuts and bolts. He pummeled the chimney, as if he meant to destroy it. Hannah wanted to take a hammer to her aunt's beloved stove too. She could be tough. She would show her aunt what a mean streak really was.

As she walked over to her father, he stopped hammering and looked up. His eyes were reddened, nearly blinded by ashes and dust. He looked bewildered, as when he'd first brought home the Victrola for Hannah's mother and dismantled it. With the Victrola, he'd had no idea what he was doing, just the single desire to put something back together, to take pleasure in making something once-beautiful whole again. Now, the stove's nuts and bolts looked impossibly small in her father's ravaged hands. He stared down at them, utterly confused.

"She's never going to leave," he said, sitting back on his heels before the heap of cast iron and black dust.

Hannah knelt beside him. "You can come back to visit before winter comes," she said quietly. "I'll come with you, help you carry it back inside."

Outside, Maria sat at the table, looking plump and dull as a flightless bird. She'd taken off her sandals and propped her feet up on a wobbly chair. The toes on both her feet were split and bleeding. Hannah remembered her aunt's diabetes, saw that she must have bumped her feet against the table leg while serving and hadn't even felt her own toes splitting open. Hannah tried to pretend that she didn't notice her aunt's bloody feet, just as she tried pretending not to notice how mean the back of the house looked, the thin pieces of wood nailed over gaping seams that would let in wind and snow when winter came. Already, coal dust had settled on the lemon and pomegranate trees, dulling the leaves. Some of the fruit lay in the dirt, shriveled and moldy. Hannah's anger deflated, her own hurt feelings softening into pity. Maria had put all of the meat they'd brought her into the winter stew that lay heavy in Hannah's stomach. Her aunt's kitchen would be truly lean by All Saints Day. Now that the priest was dead, the church bell would no longer ring. Hannah wondered how long it would take before her aunt stopped believing in the rules of Campanilismo. Soon, she would have to face the meanness of her own poverty.

When he finished reassembling the stove in the kitchen garden, Hannah's father looked down at his aunt's feet. "You should get a doctor to look at those," he said.

"You go to a doctor when you are sick," Maria said, though she no longer looked defiant, just tired, her dark skin ashen. She limped into the kitchen and came back with a big coffee can, heavy with cupboard sweets. She handed it to Hannah.

"Prendete questi, per il viaggio," she said. Take these, for the journey.

Hannah carried the can under her arm, placing it on the floor before the passenger seat. Sitting in the dim light of the cabin, with the can between her feet, Hannah felt relieved to be getting away as her father released the truck's emergency break.

"It's a lonely place," her father said, as if knowing what she was thinking.

"Why doesn't she want to leave?" she asked.

Her father took a sharp left and drove straight up into the cemetery, parking beneath a maple grown into a hemlock, beside a Mass grave of 114 miners killed in a mine fire in 1884. Blank slate grave markers slid down the hill, some hidden by grass.

"They show up better beneath a good skiff of snow," he said.

They wandered toward the shady graves, the tombstones etched in Italian. A sarcophagus reclined uphill, its bottom washed out. It belonged to her great-grandfather Palmisano, his wife and sons lying beside him beneath smaller gravestones, each one caved in, chunks of coal scattered around them. Hannah's father picked up a deadfall, rattling it inside the foot of the emptied grave, checking for snakes. Beyond the family plot, where the cemetery path met an old lumber road, they found a small stone with wildflowers growing around it, a single word chiseled into it as if by a crude blade, *Sorella*.

Even without the marker, Hannah would have known by the wildflowers—orange lilies with red stars in their centers—who the grave belonged to. "What happened to her?" she asked.

"When Stella Flora and Maria got to War, their father tried to marry them off to miners three times their age. The night before the planned wedding, Maria hung a nightgown from their laundry line, calling two young miners' apprentices to their window. The four of them caught a train heading north, first to Kentucky, then on to Detroit to get jobs at the Ford plant.

"They had a double wedding on a Tuesday, in the middle of August," her father said. "It was bad luck all around."

Hannah had heard her father tell many tall tales, but she'd never known him to be superstitious. "Why is it bad luck to marry on a Tuesday in August?" she asked.

"Tuesday is the day of Mars, the god of war," he said. "August is the month of the dead. No Sicilian woman in her right mind ever marries on a day like that."

"So things didn't go so well with them?"

"Neither marriage lasted through the winter," he said. "The sisters tried to get back together, but Stella Flora was killed while jumping off a train. Maria had to ride the train home with her sister's body next to her. When she reached War, both her intended husband and her father wouldn't let her back into their houses. They claimed that she was no longer decent.

"The coal company priest ruled Stella Flora's death as a suicide, had her buried out here at this crossroad. I guess he wanted to be sure her spirit wouldn't go off anywhere again," he said.

"What did the priest do to Maria?"

"Maria was put out for a while. I think she lived in the woods all winter and spring. After her mother died, her father let her back into his house to cook and care for the younger children."

Hannah looked down at the crude little grave. "So Maria stays because Stella Flora is still here."

Her father swept his eyes over the crossroad and back to the family plot. "They are all still here."

They sat for a while until they heard a rush of invisible wings, a high twitter fading into the steady pulse of birdcall.

"Is that an owl?"

"Mourning doves," her father said.

"They sound so sad."

"Ah, but they do sing," her father said.

Neither father nor daughter moved to leave. Surrounded by birdcall and soft wildflowers, the grave no longer seemed lonely or outcast. It seemed almost beautiful, a forgiving place. When the doves flew away, Hannah's father stood. "I think they're telling us we should go too."

In the growing darkness, Hannah and her father retraced their steps through the cemetery and found the truck. Sitting behind the driver's wheel, her father nodded at Hannah's reporting notebook lying up on the dashboard. "What you saw and heard back there," he paused. "None of it is newsworthy." Hannah nodded, and put the notebook away. As they drove out of the valley, Hannah could feel the bluffs on both sides of the road pressing in on her, making it hard to breathe. She opened her window. A train sped alongside the road, heading out of the valley under cover of leaves. She heard the screaming of steel against the tracks, the rhythmic rocking of empty coal cars. The whistle blew again, its sound growing lower and softer as the train moved away until all she heard was mountain air whispering around her.

🌸 Sadie, 1962

Cherokee

Sᴀᴅɪᴇ ᴘʟᴀɪᴛᴇᴅ ᴛʜᴇ ʟᴀsᴛ of her mother-in-law's hair, winding the long, white braid around the back of Emma's head, pinning it in place with a rhinestone clip. She sifted through the dresses in the wardrobe, choosing a white tea gown. Emma sat still while Sadie pulled the dress over her head and fastened the tiny hooks all the way up the back. Sliding the wheels beneath Emma's rocker, Sadie rolled her to the window to look out over the wild roses that Sadie's husband, Dean, was planting for his mother on the high, sunny ridge beside the house. It was early spring. The whole hillside flamed with orange azaleas and yellow daffodils, and the old pond stream that Dean had rebuilt gurgled cleanly, fiddlehead ferns tucked between its stones. Emma would not look out at the garden. She stared into her lap, gazing inward, a piece of white paper clasped like a handkerchief in her knotted, ladylike fists.

"What have you got there, Mother?" Sadie asked.

Emma's fingers tightened around the paper, and Sadie guessed it must be one of the love letters Emma's husband, Caleb, had written to her on his lunch breaks at the Norfolk and Western station in Bluefield thirty years ago, before he was shot down by a tramp beside the tracks. The shock of his death had quickened her rheumatism, hardening her spine, legs, and feet until, finally, she never stood or walked again. A few years ago, when it became too difficult to minister to Emma on her own, Sadie had persuaded Dean to put Emma in a nursing home, but after a month Dean had brought his mother back to live at the homeplace, claiming she could only be cared for properly by Sadie, in her own home. Emma spoke very little now, spent most of her time reading the love letters she kept locked in the heart pine chest in her bedroom, where Dean had placed a hospital bed beneath the oil painting of a sad-eyed Jesus sitting on a high and rocky precipice at midnight, overlooking Gethsemane.

"Is that one of them old love letters?" Sadie teased.

Sadie knelt beside her mother-in-law's rocker, and the old woman's fingers unclenched, releasing the note into Sadie's hands. The paper felt warm, soft as flannel from all the unfolding and folding. *I saw Dean kill that little girl,* Sadie read. *Go tell him to turn himself in.*

"Mother, where did you get this?" Sadie asked.

Emma stared through her empty hands into her lap, her eyes filled with long distance. The woodstove sighed. Sadie thought of tossing the note into the flames, but its words had rekindled a question in her mind. *What little girl?*

Sadie folded the note, slipped on her worn flats and cardigan. She stepped out onto the front porch, looked down the gravel drive, toward the blue cedar guesthouse where Dean had been spending most of his time since his last heart attack.

The spring before, a week after he was released from the hospital, he'd driven to Cherokee to walk the medicinal trails and learn the healing properties of wild herbs. He'd come home late the next day, spilling a bag of coins across the foot of the bed, showing Sadie the buffalo nickels, Mercury dimes, and trade silver dollars dating back to 1885. He said he'd gone into a local grocery and seen the cashier giving a young woman trouble about trying to buy food with her dead grandfather's coin collection. He started pulling out his money and bought all the coins from her.

"She was just a little girl," he'd said. "I thought I was helping her. I didn't know what I would find." He'd put the coins back in the pouch, slipped the pouch beneath the folded handkerchiefs in his top dresser drawer. Then he mentioned that he'd brought the girl home to live in the guesthouse, that maybe she could help Sadie out with his mother while their daughter, Hannah, was at school. He closed the dresser drawer and shook his head. "You have to wonder what happens to people like her that don't get help," he said. "Hard times."

The Cherokee girl never helped out with Dean's mother. She stayed inside the guesthouse all day long with the curtains shut, smoking cigarettes and eating the butter lettuce, tomatoes, and snap beans Dean had picked from Sadie's garden. He worked on the guesthouse every day, claiming its shower kept backing up. When her commode overflowed, he brought in a backhoe and began digging up the leech bed, cleaning out the septic tank. He became so distracted with fixing the girl's plumbing that he began neglecting his own house and garden. The wild roses mildewed. Fallen leaves clogged the bottom drains of the pond stream. The goldfish overpopulated themselves, caught bacterial infections, and turned belly up in the basin.

In late August, after she'd scooped the last dead fish from the pond stream, Sadie went looking for Dean. As she knocked on the guesthouse door, the lace curtains mingled with a figure wearing a white dress Sadie recognized as one of Emma's trousseau gowns, sewn by an immigrant aunt, impossibly elegant for farm life. Emma had kept them all in the pine chest with the old love letters from her late husband. As the girl backed slowly into a pair of shadowy arms, Sadie backed away from the house, not wanting to see whose arms were holding her in the darkness. Her heart chilled and fisted as she walked back up the hill. Her whole body filled with a frozen wakefulness, she stayed up all night waiting for Dean to come home, sitting straight-backed on the bench beside the piano, unplayed since Emma had begun failing. She was still waiting for Dean at dawn. When he finally came walking out of the woods and into the house, Sadie could not bring herself to ask if he'd been in the guesthouse with the girl. She knew the answer to that. She couldn't bear to hear him say it. Instead, she asked about the dress.

"It suited her," Dean had said. "I thought someone should get some use out of it."

"Your family is your charity," Sadie said, crossing her arms across her chest to end the argument.

Dean had taken the girl back to Cherokee, but he'd never apologized, and they never spoke of the girl he'd kept for a whole spring and summer in the guesthouse. He stayed outside, hauling rocks down from a secret place at the top of East River Mountain, repairing the old pond stream, planting more fiddlehead fern between the stones. He slept alone in the guesthouse. The next spring, Sadie went out into the woods and dug up a wild rose bush to give him, a peace offering he could plant beside his pond stream. Dean stopped when he saw her, his face falling softly with disappointment.

"Oh, it's you," he'd said, already turning his back to her, heading inside the guesthouse. "I thought you were—"

Her, she thought, dropping the rose bush, running back up the hill. After that, Sadie stayed inside the big house, careful not to cross him on any path, nursing her mother-in-law's body until she felt more dull and spectral than this tiny, birdlike woman he'd brought to live with them now that she no longer could live alone in the big house up on Wilderness Road. Sadie began dressing Emma every morning in a different trousseau gown, as if to justify her demand to get rid of the Cherokee girl. The women of this family get plenty of use out of those dresses, Sadie thought, each time she buttoned or hooked her mother-in-law into one of the dresses. She bathed and dressed and coiffed Dean's mother every day, as if repeating a charm that might bring her husband back to her one day, though it never did.

Dean was inside the guesthouse now, Sadie was sure of it, but she could not go down there. She couldn't bear another falling look of disappointment in his eyes, his turned back, his shoulders stiffened by the sound of her voice. Sadie dipped her hands into the pocket of her cardigan, fingering the sharp corners of Emma's strangely cruel note, feeling the mixed urge to punish and defend him. She began to question her husband's random act of devotion to a stranger. What if that girl really was only a charity case? She had to wonder what had happened to her since she'd been sent away. Sadie had wanted her gone, not killed. Surely her husband, who took such pleasure coaxing plants into life, gathering and stacking stones into a beautiful stream, did not have it in his nature to murder anyone, especially a young woman having a hard time. As she thought of the unfortunate girl, Sadie's chest ached, and a chill dread settled over her skin, sinking slowly into her veins, draining her arms and legs of all strength. The only way to fight this leaden feeling was to flee this house that had never felt like her own, the woods that hedged and silenced it.

SHE WENT INTO THE BEDROOM and ran her hand across the bed, her husband's side neatly made up, her side unmade. She tried to recall when he'd stopped wanting her, when he'd first turned away. Had this happened before or after his heart attacks started? She called her mother, Jane, who'd gone gaming in the back rooms of Cherokee with her first husband, Sadie's father. Sadie asked Jane if she remembered the way to Cherokee.

"You planning on doing some gambling on the reservation?" Jane asked.

Sadie pictured her mother standing beside the single barber chair in the beauty shop she'd been running from her cabin on Dump Hill since Sadie's father had left.

"Do you remember the way you took to get there?" Sadie asked.

"Well, if Bluefield, Virginia, is the gates of hell, you go three levels down, and turn west," Jane said.

"Mom."

"Oh, girl," Jane said. "That was so long ago. I can't remember my own name sometimes. How do you expect me to figure all this out?"

"I just thought you might remember something from before—"

"Why do you want to go all the way back there?"

Sadie knew better than to confide her marriage troubles to her mother. Sadie's father had left the year her older sister, Grace, died of cancer. Jane had married three more times, but none of the other marriages took. When Sadie was seventeen, unmarried and pregnant by Dean, Jane urged her to get rid of the unborn child, warning her against marrying a man whose mother was still alive and in charge. Sadie went through with it all, the pregnancy and the marriage. It was the bravest thing she'd ever done, marrying against her mother's wishes, her one rebellion against her outlaw mother.

Waiting out Jane's silence on the other end of the line, Sadie's heart banged inside her rib cage, and her throat fluttered. How easy it would be for Jane to point out that she'd been right about Dean, that Sadie's marriage to him had been a risk taken, and lost.

Sadie braced herself for Jane's long-awaited chastening, feeling vaguely that she deserved it.

"You still take the old road, number 441," Jane said, quietly. "I don't know what you hope to find when you get there, but that road can get lonely in the level places."

After hanging up the phone, Sadie went over to Emma's room and shifted through the wardrobe where she'd hung the trousseau gowns. In a playful moment, she'd named each one, calling the nightgown "A Gap in the Hedge," the going-away dress Emma wore after her wedding "I Missed the Boat Upon Which I Should Have Sailed." Sadie put on the going-away dress. The tea-length skirt crumbled as she hooked the waist, and a few of the pearl buttons popped off the blouse as she fastened them. She walked over to the vanity mirror.

She hadn't thought of her own body for a long time. She'd lost weight from the physical labor of nursing her mother-in-law, and for the first time in her life she had cheekbones. Tired of fooling with her hair, she'd cut it all off, and it curled around her face in an old-fashioned bob, making her eyes look large and startled in her pale, thin face. She'd never been a great beauty, but the big eyes and high cheekbones might have made her look younger under different circumstances. Standing in the beautiful antique dress, she appeared faded, used-up. She backed away from the mirror, walking through room after still room of the house, many of them closed off, bed sheets covering the heavy furniture. Dean had painted the house that spring, forgetting to prop the windows open so that they wouldn't stick. This is marriage, Sadie thought. A silent house full of unused rooms whose windows were all painted shut.

She wandered back into her bedroom and opened Dean's dresser, found the bag of coins he'd bought off the Cherokee girl. The pouch was a child's suede marble bag, dyed purple, stamped with a yellow caricature of an Indian wearing a tall headdress like those worn by the Western prairie tribes. Dean had told Sadie that he'd dropped the girl off at her father's house on the reservation, that she was waitressing at one of the tourist restaurants. Though Sadie had never gone anywhere beyond these mountains, she suddenly wanted to get away, go anywhere, be anonymous in a tourist town. She placed the coins in her other dress pocket, the one that did not hold Emma's note. She weighed out what had been taken, and what must be returned.

Sadie went outside and looked at Dean's Model B Ford parked beside the house, the key always in the ignition. It had belonged to Dean's father, and Dean still washed and waxed it every week, calling it his "moonshine coupe." Climbing behind the steering wheel, she hoped the car would make it to the Smokies.

I'll take my chances, she thought as she turned over the engine. She bounced the car down the rutted gravel drive and onto the paved road that wound beneath East River Mountain until she reached the tunnel. On the other side, the high land unfolded, smoothing into rolling pastures dotted by solitary black barns. Chestnut horses walked slowly along the split rail fences, grazing around still farm equipment bowing in the center of pastures starting to green in late-May sun.

As Jane had predicted, the road's level places were lonesome. Dean's cigarette scent rose up from the car's upholstery, bitter but familiar. Sadie considered turning the car around, heading back through the mountain, telling Dean that she was having one of her migraines and had gone to the pharmacy for her headache powders. Maybe he'd take her down to the guesthouse and lay her across the brass bed, rub lavender oil into her temples, as he'd once done to ease her headaches. She longed to feel his rough, frostbitten fingers on her face, even if that touch felt like charity.

But the time to turn around had passed. As she crossed the

North Carolina border and neared Asheville, the Smokies looked dark blue, distant, the paler ridges swelling behind them like memories of mountains. She drove until the rain hit the windshield, two big drops, then a blinding cascade. Sadie closed her window. The hard rain sealed and silenced the car, and the tobacco began to smell stale, illicit, one of her own family's secrets. Her mother had been a nurse during the World War I and had kept the uniform. Sometimes, after Sadie's father left, Jane had put on her nurse's dress, claiming she liked the way she could still turn a man's head in that dress. She unbraided her hair so that it would sway softly at her waist as she walked downtown and into the nearest bar, where she would drink and play cards with the trainmen, sometimes bringing home one of the men who'd lost to her in a game of stud poker. Sadie often heard them fumbling in the next room, but the men were always gone by morning, as if they never existed.

Fog rolled over the mountains and across the road, softening the panic that had sent her speeding away from her house. The downpour dredged up a new and different doubt. What would Dean say when she got back? Would he be angry? Worse yet, would he even notice she'd been gone? She thought again about turning around, but all the road signs—MAGGIE VALLEY, GHOST TOWN—urged her forward. On the exit road for Cherokee, she turned left at the brick reservation school, its windows fingerpainted with yellow flowers and a blue river. To the right on Main Street, a strip of weather-beaten motels called Newfound Lodge and The River's Edge flanked the Luftee River, their cedar balconies jutting out over the cascades.

Beside the last motel on the strip, a young and an old man danced on a tented stage in front of a diner with a light-up sign out front boasting, "Authentic Native American Cooking."

Sadie pulled into the parking lot and walked over to sit behind an elderly couple on a wooden bench. The younger man wore a cut-off tank shirt and a high prairie headdress made of bright red and white feathers. An eagle tattoo was burned into his bare, muscular arm. The older man was thin, short, and wiry, his still-black hair cropped close to his head. He stood at the back of the stage, his arms crossed, wearing deerskin leggings and a delicate, beaded vest. Sadie thought he looked more authentic than the drummer, more dignified, his slate eyes looking beyond the dwindling crowd of off-season tourists.

"I'm Lone Wolf, and this here is Chief Graybeard," the drummer said into a microphone. "He's going to show you the warrior dance."

The older man crouched, stepping with the slow drumbeat, shaking a gourd rattle over imaginary prey. He stalked across the stage, turning toward the audience, staring in mock menace. When the music ended, he ducked into a teepee guarded by a mangy, stuffed buffalo.

"And now Chief Graybeard will show you the most difficult dance," Lone Wolf said. "It's called the hoop dance. His great-grandfather taught it to him when he was a boy. He's the only one left who remembers the steps."

Graybeard came out of the teepee, carrying five plastic hula hoops that he set out on the stage in a row. The hula hoops disappointed Sadie more than the drummer's prairie headdress. She looked back at the sign in front of the restaurant, feeling unaccountably betrayed by the sign's promise to be authentic. She stood to go, but the drummer looked right at her.

"Of course, Graybeard and his great-grandfather would have gone down to the river for willow branches and made them into hoops. But the Chief draws his energy from a source even more mystical than the willows."

Sadie sat again, wondering, What could be more mystical

than a willow? The rain came down harder, but she could hear the river's rush above it, the drumbeat pounding beneath. Graybeard picked up each hoop, stringing it along his arm like a giant bracelet. He turned slowly, moving the hoops over his body, until the circles formed an eagle's wings spanning his shoulders. He crouched, forming a turtle shell across his back. He continued spinning and moving the hoops across his body, the drumbeat pounding in Sadie's stomach, frightening, thrilling, until she forgot all about the hula hoops being plastic, and she imagined Graybeard dancing down by the unseen river, beside willow limbs that arched and swirled like long hair across the water, their cut wisps bending easily with his body as he shape-shifted into a hummingbird, a butterfly, a spider's web.

When the music stopped, the dancer bowed to the crowd and went back into the teepee. The drummer spoke into the microphone. "Let's give a hand for Chief Graybeard, the hardest working guy in America, the most photographed man from North Carolina besides the Reverend Billy Graham."

Graybeard came back out of the teepee and passed around a woven basket. "The Chief just got out of the county correctional facility," the drummer said. "He and his family would appreciate your tens or twenties."

In her rush to leave that morning, Sadie had left her purse at home. She reached into her sweater pocket and felt Emma's note. She considered putting it into the basket, dashing back to her car, driving back home. She reached into her other pocket, found the coin pouch, and dropped two of the trade silver dollars in the basket. The chief nodded, "Thank you, pretty lady." She blushed, relieved by how he'd accepted the coins as gracefully as if they were a ten or twenty. She ran back to her car.

It was dark now, sprinkling, the wet air so black she could no longer see the mountain looming across the street. The long drive through the rain had made her sleepy. She considered renting a room in one of the motels, sleeping until the sun rose and she felt rested enough to drive home, but she had only the coins left in her pocket. The roadside chief had accepted those coins. Maybe someone in the restaurant would take a silver dollar for a cup of coffee.

Inside the diner, the walls were bright blue, adorned with dream catchers and wooden masks. Cactuses in southwestern-themed pots lined the windowsill above the cash register. Sadie sat at the counter, and a waitress walked over. "What can I get you, Sweetie?"

"Will you take these coins for a coffee?"

The waitress nodded. "The money police don't live here anymore. You can pay with what you've got."

Sadie ordered a cup of coffee with cream, a basket of fry bread. The waitress brought the coffee, and Sadie wrapped her cold hands around the warm cup, studying the three waitresses to see if one of them could be the owner of the coins. One girl filled salt-shakers, the second wiped down tables, and the third dried water glasses. Any of these girls could have been the one Dean had brought home with him, but none looked as if she'd ever been a runaway or a charity case. Their black hair tied back, they moved like sure-footed dancers, their dark eyes pleasantly absorbed in closing tasks. Sadie felt a soft pang of loneliness for her daughter, for her lost sister, for the company of any woman who hadn't grown too old for a conversation free of grief and bitterness.

When the waitress brought the basket of fry bread, a man slid onto the stool beside her. He offered his hand. She recognized him as the older man who'd performed the hoop dance. "The name's Graybeard."

Sadie shook his hand. "I'm Sadie. I saw your dancing."

"Sadie, Sadie, pretty lady." Graybeard said. He lifted up a jar of honey, poured it over her fry bread. "If you're going to eat that, you may as well eat it right."

Sadie unwrapped her fork from its napkin, took a bite. The warm honey burst across her tongue, spilling out one side of her mouth. She ate quickly, swabbing the plate with the last bite of bread. The man handed her the napkin. Sadie put down her fork and dabbed at the corners of her mouth as daintily as she could.

"I must have been hungry," she said.

Graybeard laughed. "It's all right. I liked watching you eat."

He took out a pipe with a bowl carved like a bird, its stem strung with two tiny feathers. He tamped down the bowl, lit it. Sadie breathed in the smoke, recalling her mother smoking wild, sweet tobacco in a dainty pipe at her kitchen table.

"My mother is part Cherokee," Sadie said. "She used to smoke a pipe like that."

"I thought we were from the same tribe."

"What do you put in your pipe?"

Graybeard smiled, nodded toward the cactus plants lining the windowsill. "Some of my relatives go out West every summer to live with the Old Settlers. When they come back, they bring stuff with them."

He signaled the waitress, and she brought a kettle of hot water, a clean blue cup.

"Here, try some of this." He poured hot water into the cup, sprinkling green buds from an unlabeled tin can. The buds unfurled, darkening the water. Graybeard stirred sugar and honey into it. She sipped, wincing from the bitterness beneath all the sweeteners.

"You didn't like my dancing, did you?"

Sadie took out the coin pouch. "All I had on me are these coins—"

"I don't want to talk about your money. Tell me why you didn't like my dancing."

IN THE GARDEN OF STONE

"I liked your dancing." Sadie paused. "I just didn't like your hula hoops. They weren't...authentic."

Graybeard looked down at the Indian head on the bag of coins, but he continued to speak in his rough, good-natured voice. "My family has been here since the white settlers thought up Manifest Destiny and kicked most of us out of these hills. My great-grandfather hid in the cliffs above Deep Creek and fought the government during the Removal so that we could stay. My family signed the civilization treaties, but we never promised to be authentic," he said. "If you want authentic, go to the museum down the street."

"I'm sorry.," Sadie said, pouring more sugar and honey into the tea, trying it again, wincing at the bitterness that no amount of honey could disguise.

"Don't be. I come from a long line of people who never did anything they didn't want to do. Besides, kids love seeing an Indian. I'll bet you always wanted to be Pocahontas when you were a little girl."

Sadie smiled. As a girl, she'd wanted to be anyone but Sadie May Musick, the good daughter of a lawless woman who styled hair for railroad wives who praised her clever hands and high cheekbones, but never befriended her. On days the trainmen came for haircuts, Jane sent Sadie outside, telling her not to come back until it was dark. She'd spent long hours roaming the woods and rivers with her little brother, Michael, pretending to be an Indian princess, guiding him along all the trails.

The tea eased her shyness. She began enjoying Graybeard's company. After so many months of her husband's silence, she liked this man's easygoing conversation. She tried to keep him talking. "You ever want to be somebody else?" she asked.

"I used to be a policeman," he said. "I started chiefing by accident. A gift shop owner asked me to fill in when the regular roadside chief didn't show. I made more money that weekend from chiefing than I did on the police force in a month. I kept doing it because I could take care of my family no matter what the government did," he said. "I've always found ways to get around the federal government."

"If you've always gotten around the government, why were you in prison?"

"I lost this restaurant in a poker game to Lone Wolf on my forty-fifth birthday. I tried to stake my wife to get it back. She got mad about that and divorced me. Then she had me put in jail for failure to pay child support," Graybeard nodded toward the waitresses. "Those are my daughters. Lone Wolf lets them work here to pay off some of my other debts. He's got a little room in back where he lets me sleep."

"That's terrible," Sadie said.

"What's terrible? Another man would have taken my wife."

"Well," Sadie said. "I don't think it was very nice of him to take advantage of your ... sickness."

"Gambling isn't a sickness," he said. "It's more like a resurrection. Every time you lose, you die. Every time you win, you get to be reborn." Sadie frowned, still unconvinced. "Let me explain it another way." He took out a leather pouch, loosened the drawstring and poured two dried butter beans across the counter. The beans were painted blue on one side, white on the other. "Here, let me teach you a traditional Cherokee game."

"Is it older than your hula hoop dance?"

"It's as old as these hills," he said. "Each person takes a turn flipping a bean. The light sides are worth six points. The dark sides are worth four. The first person to reach twenty-four points wins."

Graybeard scooped up the beans, side-arming them across the counter. When both beans landed dark side up, he slapped his hand on the counter. "Eight points."

Sadie took a turn, rolling out one light and one dark bean. "Ten points," she said.

He took his time now, and she grew impatient, eager for him to tip his hand open and cast the beans so that she could take her turn. She rolled two blue, and he rolled two light. The tea had eased her worries, blurring the memories of Dean's retreat into the guesthouse, softening the words in his mother's note. Sadie felt the thrill of losing, the giddy hope of winning something back.

"Twenty-four," Graybeard announced, sweeping the beans back into the pouch.

He picked up his pipe, tamped down the bowl, and lit it, watching her face.

"So what have you won from me?" Sadie whispered.

Graybeard leaned closer. "A kiss."

"Right here?"

"Meet me in the back."

She laughed, but he stood abruptly and headed toward the back of the restaurant. Sadie sat at the counter, feeling too old for a stranger's kiss, especially one that might take place in the back room of a diner on an Indian reservation, possibly over a reeking toilet. Her mind felt cloudy, unfurled by the mysterious tea, still capable of asking the most obvious questions: Why didn't a man called Graybeard have a beard? What kind of husband stakes his wife in a poker game? She wanted to run back to her car, lock the door, and sleep beside the river until it was light enough to drive home. She left some coins on the counter for the fry bread and coffee. The pouch felt lighter as she walked to the back of the restaurant.

Graybeard's room was made of rough-hewn wood, furnished with a single cot pushed up against the far wall, a framed print of a Cherokee rose hanging above it. Near the back, a glass patio door opened out onto a balcony that overlooked the river. Sadie stepped onto the balcony and stood beside Graybeard. The moon reflected and split like two sides of the same white coin on the water's black surface. The cool air and river water cleared her senses a bit, but the tea had begun working on her like a truth serum. She thought of wheeling Emma down to the Catholic church in Bluefield once a week so that she could make a confession. Sadie had always wondered what kind of sins could have been committed by a woman who'd stayed inside her own house for thirty years after her husband had died. Now, she understood her mother-in-law's urge to confess without sin or shame, her need for someone who would listen, unsurprised by anything she could tell. Sadie took the coin pouch out of her pocket and showed Graybeard the buffalo nickels, the bust half dimes, the trade silver dollars.

"My husband came here last spring," she said. "He bought these off a Cherokee girl who was having a hard time. He didn't know they were worth anything until he got them home." Graybeard looked down at the phony Indian head on the pouch, his face unreadable. "He brought the girl home, too, and kept her out in our guesthouse." She told him about her husband's obsession with the guesthouse plumbing, her own untended garden, how she made Dean send the girl away. She stopped, pulling her mother-in-law's note from her pocket. "His mother gave this to me this morning," she said. "It made me worry about what happened to that girl. I came up here to find her, to make sure she was all right, and give her back the coins. I suppose it was a foolish notion."

Graybeard took the note. He read it, letting the frail paper flutter over the water, and for a moment Sadie hoped he might release it into the wind, let it tumble down the river, let it sink into one of the dark, trout-filled places.

"Maybe this note bothers you because it's partly true," he said.

Sadie waited to hear which part was true. Above her, the moon was as bright as it had been on the nights Dean had courted her, when he'd taken her out riding on his quarter horse in the woods. At the time, he'd seemed so much older than twenty, a grown man walking ahead on the trails, expertly naming the wild herbs in the undergrowth—mint, wild ginger, watercress. She'd believed everything he'd told her back then. Now, she understood that she'd been just a little girl, taken in.

Graybeard folded the note and gave it back to Sadie.

"What should I do with it?" Sadie asked.

"If it was me, I'd take it out into the woods and bury it," Graybeard said, moving toward her. "Now. Come over here and let me fix your plumbing."

His kiss was soft, but not tender. He tasted of smoke and honey and the bitter tea they'd both been drinking. She startled as his sharp tongue twisted slowly against her own. He kept his eyes open. When she looked into them, they were flinty and dead.

She pulled away from him. "It's getting light out here."

He shrugged. "I like the light, you like the dark." He led her into the room, sat her on the cot, and knelt before her.

"When I saw you standing in that white dress in the rain, I thought you were a vision," he said. "I nearly had a heart attack."

Sadie's heart flipped as she recalled Dean's weak heart, those first twilight days of mourning his lost health, how he'd turned away from her in his grief and how, eventually, she'd turned away from him. Her husband hadn't murdered anyone, but his shadow life in the guesthouse was killing. She flushed, her skin itching inside her mother-in-law's ill-fitting dress. Whatever had possessed her to wear it?

Graybeard put a cool hand on her face. "You're burning up."

"It's this dress," she said. "I can hardly breathe in it."

"Take it off."

She paused, deciding. "I will if you don't look at me."

He pulled the blanket off the bed, making a pallet on the floor. He lay down and closed his eyes. As she began unbuttoning the dress, he laughed, "If you had the courage to cut your losses and leave your husband, I'd fight to win you. I'd keep you here with me."

She stopped unbuttoning herself and looked up. "I don't want to be fought for," she said. "I don't need to be won or kept. I've been feeling…dispossessed lately, but I don't think I should be here. I think I should be talking to a preacher, or a priest."

Graybeard leaned forward. "I can be your priest."

He reached for her, but she put a hand firmly on his chest. "I don't think that would help either of us."

"Can you do one thing for me before you go?"

She nodded, and as he started to unbutton her blouse, her hand flew up to block his hand.

"I promise," he said, gently stilling her hand with his own. "You need this."

She dropped her hand. As the dress fell around her waist, she felt free of its weight. He ran his finger along her collarbone. "This is pretty," he said. He cupped her face in his palm. "Good bone structure." He continued touching and naming the pleasing features that most people overlooked when they saw her. He unhooked her bra and held his face against her chest. His head soft against her skin reminded Sadie of her daughter at age two, when Hannah had liked to press her head against Sadie's chest, continually amazed by the discovery of her mother's heartbeat. Sadie closed her eyes and heard him murmur, *I'll bet myself against yourself. I'll bet my feet against your feet. I'll bet my legs against your legs.* His smoky voice sent a wave of heat through her, fevering her whole body. She desired him. She broke out sweating, thick rivulets of water pouring between her breasts, pooling at her waist. The river rushed outside the open backdoor, loud as a waterfall, its noise filling the room. She closed her eyes, feeling pleasantly soaked, relieved. It had been a long time since she'd wanted anyone, but she did not move beyond this strange embrace. It was enough to simply want again.

When he let go of her, Sadie buttoned her dress and stood. At the door, she looked back one last time. Lying back on the pallet again, Graybeard had set the two silver dollars she'd given him upon his eyes. Already, he was cutting his losses, fading. She had the idea that if she stayed with him in this dim room, she'd disappear too. Sadie held the coin pouch in her pocket. Judas coins, she thought. Already, with the silver missing, the pouch felt lighter.

"You still want to know what I put in my pipe?" Graybeard asked.

"Yes."

"It's the breath of gods," he said. "Maybe tomorrow, maybe next week, I'll rise up and live again. We're going to have an uprising."

Outside the restaurant, she sat in her car before the stone overlook, beside a sign that read "Swim at Your Own Risk." The moon's reflection had disappeared from the river. Watching the brown water run high beneath the white sky, Sadie allowed herself to hope for her own uprising. She imagined her husband kneeling above the pond stream behind their house, planting another wild rose she'd bring to him, his head bent, as if he were atoning. She could see herself burning his mother's note, offering the ashes to him with the morning's tea leaves, telling him it was all compost. As the two stood side by side, trellising the vines along the garden wall, he'd offer back, "If this rose gets its legs, it should stand on its own and bloom again in a year, maybe two."

On the other side of the river, ravens bounced on the branches of spruce growing from the muddy bank, preening their shiny black wings. She started driving. Ahead, clouds draped around the dark mountain like torn and faded batting.

Vines

HANNAH'S MOTHER, SADIE, came into her bedroom before dawn and woke her so that she could go down the hill to help Luther Boyd with his tomatoes. Hannah reached for her jeans and t-shirt on the chair beside the bed, pulling them on under her quilt. Down in the kitchen, she sat beside the picnic table mounded with tomatoes—beefsteak, Roma—three baskets for each week she'd already worked for Luther that June. Glass jars rattled inside the pressure cooker on the stove. Her mother stood beside them at the counter, peeling tomatoes for canning.

Sadie walked over from the range and finger-combed Hannah's hair into a tight ponytail, securing it with a rubber band. She took a beefsteak from the top of the pile, sliced it onto a piece of white bread, and pushed it toward her daughter on a paper plate. Hannah's stomach lurched at the sight of the tomato slice; the tight tracery of flesh around seeds reminded her of the X-ray she'd seen of her father's weak heart. For a moment, she wished that Luther Boyd grew peaches, some sweeter fruit that normal families sliced over breakfast cereal.

"How are you planning on using all these tomatoes?" Hannah asked.

"Your father and I are trying to eat better now, lots of fresh vegetables," Sadie said.

"Maybe you could give some of those tomatoes away, or trade them down at the produce market for some cucumbers and snap peas. Luther wouldn't have to know about it. Even if he did, he wouldn't mind."

"Luther's tomatoes are a gift, and you don't give away something that somebody gives you." Her mother frowned, her voice trembling softly as it did these days. "It's a sad change what's happened to tomatoes. Most people don't even know what one tastes like anymore. They just eat the grocery store ones with thick skins and no smell at all."

We could use a little change, Hannah thought but couldn't say. She looked at her mother's face, swollen from canning steam, the skin beneath her eyes bruised by worry over Hannah's father, Dean. That year, her father had given up the construction company he'd started after retiring from the railroad. His disability benefits wouldn't cover all his hospital bills, so he'd sold the bottomland between East River Mountain and a tributary of Cove Creek to Luther Boyd, an ex-English professor who'd been renting the land from her father for ten years. While Luther grew tomatoes in the Virginia dirt that had once belonged to her family, Hannah's father sold off his backhoes and loaders piece by piece. He refused to sell any more land. He kept the family's old homeplace across the valley, on top of Wilderness Road, though nobody had lived there since they'd moved her grandmother into the nursing home.

Hannah wrapped her tomato sandwich in an empty bread bag and thanked her mother for breakfast. Outside, the dark mountain loomed behind the house, the red sun burning through the hazy sky above it. She walked down the gravel drive to the black apple tree and stepped onto the pass that sloped down to Luther's cabin, slipping through pitch pine and brambles, landing on the road bordering the stream. Above the bend where irrigation pipes slaked water into the tomato field, she stopped, unwrapped her sandwich and threw the tomato slices along the ditch speckled red by tomatoes that had fallen off Luther's market truck. She picked up a few whole tomatoes lying on the ground, spun around, splattered tomatoes against tree trunks. She felt good, smashing something. The spinning eased the queasy restlessness she'd felt in her mother's kitchen.

Hannah knew she should have been grateful for the job and the tomatoes Luther gave her, a welcome relief from the beans and potted meat that sustained her family all winter. She should have felt sorrow for this man whose grown son had fallen off a nearby waterfall last winter, and died. Luther's young wife, Ruth, had put out word that their son was doing a handstand at the top of the waterfall when he fell. By spring planting time, unable to face the merciless whispers and questioning eyes of her neighbors, she'd run off to California and joined a religious community. Now that summer had come, the never-dwindling pile of tomatoes on the trundle table made Hannah feel uneasy, as if she'd increased her mother's worries. Still, Hannah kept working for Luther. She was fourteen. She wanted a job, a car, and a driver's license. Luther paid a dollar an hour, and the bushel of tomatoes he gave her once a week pleased her mother, who said the tomatoes helped her stretch her grocery allowance.

Hannah walked on to Luther's cabin beside the river. In the open doorway, Hannah let her eyes adjust to the dimness of the single room furnished with a sink, a woodstove, and a table that wobbled on the stone floor. Luther was lying on a bed tick in the corner, beneath a stopped clock.

"What time is it?" Luther asked.

"Seven o'clock," Hannah said.

"Now why did you let me sleep all day?"

"It's seven o'clock in the morning."

Luther rose and shuffled to the sink, filling the bottom of the coffee percolator with water, the middle with coffee, screwing the top down and placing it on the woodstove. Water gushed to the top, steaming. He poured a cup for Hannah, another for himself, pushed an unmarked bottle across the table toward her.

"I can't have this anymore, but you're welcome to have some in your coffee."

"I'm fourteen," Hannah said.

"You sure? I thought you were in college."

"Most people think I'm older," she said. "I spend a lot of time with my mother."

Luther's eyes softened. He put the bottle away. "Your mother has a voice that sounds like the King James Bible. I could sit at her feet and listen to her all day."

Luther wasn't religious, but he believed Hannah's mother had saved him. Sadie had been the one to find him last spring, on the Good Friday after his wife ran away. A storm had knocked down the power lines all over the mountain, blowing the gardening tarps off Luther's field. When the storm had ended, Sadie noticed the hail-beaten seedlings. She'd taken Hannah with her to Luther's cabin, where they'd found him lying face down on the floor, a grocery sack filled with empty Old Crow bottles on either side of him. Sadie had told Hannah to turn away and go home, but Hannah stayed on the porch, watching through the window as her mother threw away the bottles and headed out into the field, telling Hannah to make herself useful by ripping strips of Luther's old t-shirts so that she could tie back the surviving plants. After rescuing the tomato plants, as they'd walked the logging road home, her mother had kept her own counsel, saying only, "Are you all right?"

Sober since last April, Luther seemed always to be moving. A wiry man, barely taller than Hannah, he paced his cabin, lighting the stubs of cigarettes from burned-down cigarettes. He smelled of tobacco, dirt, and tomato leaves, comforting scents that reminded Hannah of her father, who still smoked Marlboros on the back porch, a habit he thought nobody noticed.

Luther's hands shook as he drank his black coffee in two gulps. "We need to get going," he said. "We'll do some pruning first. We need to groom them while the earth is still turgid."

Hannah followed him out into the field, studying the hitch in his step, the deep wrinkles crosshatched into the back of his neck, wondering if *turgid* meant "dry and dirty." Luther stopped at the first row and held a vine, teaching her how to groom it.

"You need to learn how to do this." His face solemn, he snapped off all the bottom leaves and suckers, leaving the skinny stems bare.

"Now they look like they're going to die," she said.

He laughed. "Just like you breathe heavier when you're running, the tomato plant needs to breathe more when it's producing fruit. If you don't prune them right, all the sweetness goes into the leaves."

When the dew dried, they began picking, Luther bringing in eight pairs of baskets for every one pair Hannah brought in. The red sun yellowed, firing up the valley. The cicadas revved up in the tops of distant pines, rattling as Hannah worked her way along the row on her knees, picking tomatoes that were fuzzy with dust. As she worked, every inch of her bare skin itched. The heat and sweat turned her mind to thoughts of Luther's son, David. She wondered why he'd come back from college to such dirty work.

Last fall, David Boyd surprised everyone by returning with a degree from Virginia Tech and taking a job teaching English at the local high school, helping out on his father's farm. A month into the school year, a girl from over on Dump Hill got pregnant and filed a complaint against David, accusing him of seducing her during an after-school help session on *Arabian Nights*. The grievance turned out to be untrue, but the school principal fired David anyway, and David spent all fall and winter roaming the ridges and valleys off Wilderness Road. Some said he sped his father's Buick up and down the switchbacks on East River Mountain. Many believed David was the one who graffitied the sides of the abandoned rest stop on the summit, breaking all of its windows. He disappeared in January. When his body washed up in the plunge pool beneath the falls, his mother, Ruth, put out word that he'd been doing a handstand at the top and fell by accident.

Hannah had known David Boyd shyly and from a distance, but she knew that he would never have done a handstand on top of a waterfall, especially a frozen one. The fall before he'd died, she'd gone down to Luther's place to practice gymnastics on the river grasses. She'd decided to try out for the cheerleading squad, but she didn't want to risk practicing in front of the town girls who'd taken gymnastics since they were toddlers. She was perfecting a handstand by the river when David walked out of the tomato field. Much taller than Luther, he was dusky and doe-eyed, and he wore a Virginia Tech sweatshirt with the sleeves ripped out.

"You need to keep those arms straight." He smiled rakishly, but his eyes were kind. "You look like you're trying to stand two pieces of cooked spaghetti on end." When Hannah fell into a heap, he said, "Please. Stop pile driving your head into the ground."

He showed her how to place her hands on the ground, fingers spread and facing forward. When she kicked up, he spotted her, his hands wavering closely behind the small of her back, never touching her. The absence of his hands felt like a cruel hunger that made her almost angry. Even as she rolled forward out of the handstand, his arms stayed at a safe distance, and she ached to fall into them. Now, she wondered if the girl from Dump Hill had felt the same way around David, if the absence of his touch had made the girl angry enough to accuse him of seducing her.

Luther stood behind her. Hannah startled, embarrassed by her thoughts of David, trying to think up something casual to say. "You ever think about growing peaches?" she asked, too quickly.

Luther studied her, his gray eyes hardening to slate. He picked a tomato, holding it up to the sun, admiring its hue and heft. "*Lycopersicon esculentum,*" he said. "That's Latin for 'wolf peach.' In the old days, people believed they were poisonous, and they put them outside in the woods to kill the wolves that came too close to their houses. Then a man by the name of Colonel Robert Gibbon Johnson of Salem, New Jersey, brought home a whole basket of tomatoes and ate them all on the courthouse steps without keeling over. The firemen band played a mournful dirge as he ate. They thought he was committing suicide. They thought him an object of pity."

Hannah heard a tugging beneath the leaves of the next plant, a rattling softer and slower than the cicadas. She saw what looked like the edge of a dead, brown vine coiled just beyond her reach on a field stone. Slowly, a heart-shaped head lifted and swayed off the ground, the eyes watching her, as if deciding. Hannah stared back at the rattlesnake, her heart quickening inside her chest.

She'd seen plenty of dead rattlers along the trails, their sides slit, hung from high branches by the old time mountain men, but she'd never been so close to a living one. She stared down at the swaying snake, unmoving, until two hands clamped upon her shoulders, pulling her gently to her feet and away, leading her down to the stream, easing her beneath the shade of a maple beside the bank. She closed her eyes, waiting for her heartbeat to slow. Luther went away, and when he came back Hannah opened her eyes, and saw the rattlesnake's skin spread on the rock beside her.

"That old girl was just giving herself a beauty treatment on that field stone," he said. "You won't see her again."

Hannah stared at the empty snake skin, a cold pain freezing the base of her spine, spreading through her arms and legs. Luther went down to the creek, soaked his shirt in the water, folding it across the back of her neck. She shivered, though it was the hottest part of the day. Luther urged her to stay out of the sun, setting out two lawn chairs on the riverbank beneath a golf umbrella, settling a bucket of ice between them, saying, "You're so pale. You look positively diaphanous." The sun seared the pale blue sky, its light creeping toward her like a saw blade on the grass. Luther's wet shirt rested on her neck like a warm, heavy hand. Her skin prickling from heat and sunburn, she wanted to go home and lie on her bed beneath her open window, let her mother rub witch hazel over her shoulders and arms.

If she went home early, her mother would worry. She might make Hannah stay home for the rest of summer, or worse. After her sunburn healed, she might send Hannah to the municipal pool, where the town girls swam. Hannah felt shy around these girls, envying their tanned legs and tapered waists. They sat on the edge of the pool in bikinis, flutter-kicking water into the faces of boys who grabbed them from the edge and dunked them under water as they laughed. Hannah wished to be as beautiful and carefree, but her skin nearly glowed beneath the sun, burning unevenly, and she had to sit in the far corner of the deck beneath an umbrella, sometimes with a towel wrapped around her back, stomach and feet. Once, she'd overheard one of the girls making fun of her, "What's wrong with her? Does she even know how to talk? She looks just like a birthday candle with that pink-and-white-striped body of hers."

Hannah felt the cool water spray off the stream's surface. She let her mind swirl pleasantly with the river oats in the current.

Luther never called her a birthday candle. When he'd called her "diaphanous," she'd imagined he meant lean and willowy, her skin delicately pretty. Luther sat on the lawn chair beside her, pulling iced Cokes from the bucket of ice for Hannah, plying her with cold boiled shrimp and cocktail sauce on saltines, though he didn't eat anything. She liked how he talked to her as if she were another adult. She felt both young and old listening to him tell her about driving his old Buick out West that spring to visit his runaway wife, who'd moved into a shanty she rented from the religious community.

"The house was a wreck," he said. "Just a room with no water, no electricity. It had a hole in the wall."

He stayed for a week, he said, installing indoor plumbing, patching the hole in the wall. Outside, he'd planted a little kitchen garden with snap beans, cucumbers, and squash, hedging it with daisies and coneflowers to attract the bees. Every day, Luther's wife practiced her breathing exercises beside the bee garden, explaining the teachings of her new religion, which involved learning how to breathe correctly and how to avoid the Forbidden. Ruth said she was not hiding or defending her mistakes; she accepted Luther's weaknesses and offered to heal him with breathing exercises and herbal remedies, allowing him to sleep on the floor beside her every night. Still, at the end of the week, she said she could not go home with Luther. She was grieving differently, moving far ahead of him in the process. She'd already been through a healing ceremony, a ritual that involved chanting, athletic dances, and drinking a glass of blessed milk.

"She's got a man living with her," Luther said. "He calls himself 'The Teacher.' She believes him to be transmitting the divine light from his heart to her heart. He's really just a dog breeder. He's got her taking care of his dogs. He's told her she needs to devote herself to the humility of caring for canines before she can be truly purified of her lower self."

Hannah knew how low it felt to care for dogs. Her father had decided to raise German Shepherds after his first heart attack, when Hannah was twelve, and she was told to feed and water them while he was out working. The dogs were always catching rats that wandered up from the old dairy. Hannah shuddered, remembering the last rat she'd found, all its feet chewed off, lying belly up in a dog bowl sinking in the muddy backyard.

"She's practicing an ancient religion called Sufism," Luther said. "The word *Sufi* means 'companions of the porch' in Arabic." He passed Hannah a saltine topped with a cocktail shrimp. "Hey, now there's an idea. You can be my companion of the porch."

Hannah shook her head at the shrimp, unsure if she should be taking food from this man or sitting beside him all afternoon instead of working. She felt uneasy with being his "companion of the porch." She said, "You don't have a porch."

"The Muslim Sufis don't have porches either," Luther said. "They're too poor, so they travel to the prophet's mosque to pray beneath his veranda." Luther continued, "Ruthie's always been a bit of a seeker. Right now she believes she's searching for the presence of the Divine. But she'll get tired of looking. When she does, I'll be here waiting for her."

Late afternoon sun crawled under the golf umbrella, its heat trapped in the air around Hannah's head. Luther moved the umbrella, standing behind her, his odor of cigarettes and tomato leaves suddenly nauseating. Her head throbbed, and her stomach clenched. If she didn't start moving again, she would throw up.

She stood quickly. "I've got to go now."

When she reached the tomato-splattered place on the road, she picked up a tomato and spun, but the sight of Luther's field stopped her from throwing. The pruned plants stood bare and skinny in their straight rows. Winter seemed to have come back early and taken everything away.

❧

HER FATHER'S BLACK TRUCK was parked on the grass beside the driveway. He'd been out driving all night, prowling the back roads, checking on his land, sometimes sleeping out at the family homeplace. He drove quickly along the narrow switchbacks, sometimes swerving too close to the limestone bluffs that bordered the roads. Hannah knew about his reckless, late-night drives because she'd run into him one morning on her way to Luther's field and found him re-attaching the mirror to the passenger side of his truck with duct tape. He'd looked up sheepishly. "Don't tell your mother," he'd said.

The sound of metal clanking against glass chimed through the kitchen window. The smell of corn syrup and vinegar wafted all the way down the drive. Hannah's stomach clenched, knowing her mother was making ketchup, her father ladling it into the canning jars. On the back porch she paused, recalling a long-ago afternoon when she was nine or ten, before her father got sick. He used to plan Sunday dinner right after he and her mother washed the breakfast dishes. His hands still moist with dishwater, he peeled potatoes and carrots for the roast while her mother poured hard candy into the center of a pound cake. He gently touched the small of her mother's back as he reached for the salt; she arched her spine absentmindedly to let his arm pass. Their cooking was a graceful dance between two people who kept all domestic grievances out of the kitchen.

Hannah opened the screen door and saw her father holding his ladle mid-air, the vein in his forehead pulsing as it did when he was really mad. Her mother was still stirring, looking deep into the vat of ketchup. They were fighting over Hannah's job picking tomatoes, and their heated voices made her thirsty. She walked over to the water cooler her father kept on the sink, left over from his contracting days. She pulled a paper cone from the side dispenser and pushed the spigot, watching the water swirl inside the blue tank.

"He's not drinking anymore," Sadie said.

"He may not be drinking, but he's still a drunk," her father said. "I heard about the things that went on in that house during Luther's drinking days. He used to beat that boy every morning, said he was bound to do something to earn it at some point in the day."

"And the boy came back and forgave him. He did the right thing."

"Look where that got him."

"There's no need to be ugly about another man's afflictions."

"Luther's not afflicted. He did all this to himself."

"We need to do the right thing now. All those tomatoes will rot in the field if we don't help him."

"I always thought selling that land to him was a bad idea. I wouldn't trust him working one of my horses, but now you've gone and turned our daughter into his field hand."

"You don't have a horse anymore," Sadie said. "And a child needs to see people who aren't at their best."

"She's not a child," Hannah's father said. "I've heard Luther talk about women. I don't much like what he has to say."

"If she's not a child, you should stop treating her like one," her mother said. "She wants a car and a driver's license. If you'd allow her these things, she could find a better job and drive to it. She'd have options."

"She'll have options all right. I've seen the options girls her age have after they get their own cars. Before you know it, she'll have her choice of any boy with a pair of lips and Levis. She'll learn how to park a car faster than she'll learn how to drive it."

Hannah flushed, embarrassed by her father's low-rent comment. She'd liked a boy, it was true, though not just any boy with lips and Levis. She thought of David Boyd's hands wavering behind her back as she practiced handstands by the river, her urge to fall into his arms. She picked up a long-handled spoon, stepped beside her mother. Steamed vinegar rose from the ketchup, burning her sinuses, but she kept stirring until her father threw his ladle into the sink.

"I won't have this conspiracy in my own house," he said, moving swiftly toward the front door, looking more beaten than angry. "We need more salt."

After his truck pulled away, Hannah sat at the table piled higher than ever with tomatoes. Her mother stood at the sink, motionless, staring out the window.

"Why does he act that way about Luther?" Hannah asked.

"Because he's ashamed."

"He didn't do anything to him."

"It's what he *can't* do for Luther that shames him."

Her mother raised the window above the sink higher, and the dishtowel curtains blew in with the evening breeze. She buttered some bread, sprinkled sugar over it to curb Hannah's hunger. She would not start supper until her father came home. She never ate without him.

After an hour of stirring ketchup and waiting for her father to come home, the ketchup curdled inside the canning pots, and the whole kitchen smelled overripe, like the produce stands Luther delivered to. Her mother turned off the fire beneath the pots.

"How long do you suppose it takes to buy a box of salt?"

"Maybe he's out mining it," Hannah said flatly.

Sadie frowned. "During the depths of the Depression, my father sifted the dirt from the smokehouse floor, where they had cured ham and bacon," she said. "He did this just so the family would have salt."

Her mother's voice trembled, her large brown eyes knowing, as if she could not be surprised by any hard-luck story. Hannah wanted her mother to stop talking about the Depression. She wanted to tell her about the rattlesnake in the field, but then she thought better of talking about the dangers of tomato farming. She decided it would be safest to describe Ruth Boyd's new life in the religious community.

"Luther went out West last spring to visit her," Hannah said. "He helped her fix up her house and hang curtains for her. Now why do you think a man would hang curtains for a woman who's left him?"

"Sometimes, you can't stop loving someone, even if that person hurts you," Sadie said. "Sometimes, it feels good just to be doing something."

"Luther's wife is trying *not* to do anything. She's working on avoiding the Forbidden."

"She's just frozen," Sadie said. "All of her decisions—marrying a drinking man, having his child—have ended so badly that she's afraid to make any more choices."

"Do you think that's why David Boyd jumped off the waterfall last winter, because he was trying not to make any more bad choices, like coming back here to teach school and help Luther with his tomatoes?"

Her mother frowned. "Girls your age are prone to great thoughts during these moody hours," she said. "You need to keep busy."

Hannah braced herself for another Depression story, but her mother stood, slipped on her worn flats. "I think the time has come for your first driving lesson," she said.

"Right now?"

"Just on the back roads. No highways."

Sadie let Hannah drive the old Ford that had belonged to her grandfather. Keeping her right hand on the wheel, Hannah propped her left elbow on the open window frame as she'd seen her father drive. In the dark, the roads narrow, she eased the car around switchbacks and beneath roadside bluffs, feeling sure of herself, happier than she'd felt all summer. Her mother looked mildly out the window, her hair blowing softly across her forehead, her face no longer swollen, almost pretty again. Rounding the last hill at the edge of town, they passed the limestone quarry, its stripping shovels and railroad cars sitting beside overburden heaps that glistened, petrified by moonlight.

When they reached the state highway that ran beside the mountain, her mother looked up at the Buick dealership perched on the ridge to their right, then over to the Holiday Inn beside it. Her mother frowned, as if remembering some unfinished task she'd left back at the house. Suddenly the straight road became confusing, more dangerous than the switchbacks. Hannah asked her mother to take over the wheel, but Sadie insisted she circle the hotel parking lot, turn around, and take the interstate back home.

"This is highway driving—" Hannah said.

"You need to learn this," her mother said.

On the way home, they passed a black pickup driving the other way, but Hannah couldn't see in the darkness if her father was inside of it. When they reached the house, chill air drifted down the stairs, meeting them as they stepped inside. Hannah followed it up to her bedroom, found an air conditioning unit blocking her open window. Her father had brought two back from the barn up at his mother's homeplace, leaving one in each bedroom, where they sat in the windows like big, black, peace offerings. The one in Hannah's room blocked her beloved view of the mountains, its frigid clanging knocking the soft grassy breeze out of the room. My window, Hannah thought, turning the air conditioner off. She thought of the cool breeze coming off the river beside Luther's cabin. She pulled her Webster's dictionary off her bookshelf and looked up the new words she'd learned that day from Luther, *turgid* and *diaphanous*.

She felt her mother sitting downstairs in the dark kitchen

beside the picnic table mounded with tomatoes, staring through hands swollen from eating too much salt and bread, her body shapeless beneath a white nightgown. Hannah wondered why her mother hadn't taken up quilting to pass all the time she spent alone. Nights like this, the only craft her mother seemed to have mastered was the art of waiting, of listening for the crunch of tires over gravel, the backdoor swinging open, slamming shut. When Hannah asked why she put up with her father's roaming, Sadie explained that men were hard work, and that she always counted to ten before speaking to her husband so that she wouldn't stir up their oldest arguments. Hannah knew a terrible truth: her mother was at once turgid and diaphanous, an earthy woman slowly vanishing.

THE NEXT MORNING, the sky was antifreeze blue, the air cool enough to wear a jacket. As Hannah stood on the road above Luther's place, the tomatoes looked too red, suspicious as forest berries. Luther wasn't in his cabin, and he'd already been out to his field, picking roughly, dropping most of the fruit on the ground. Hannah found the culled tomatoes stacked too closely to the plants, his half-filled picking baskets out in the middle of the field, the ripe tomatoes bursting beneath the sun. Without a word, she began carrying all the full baskets of tomatoes into the shade. When she finished, she walked down to the river to find Luther.

She found him sitting on a high rock in the middle of the stream, sipping from the unmarked bottle, watching sunlight scale the surface of the green water. She wasn't surprised by Luther's drinking; she'd felt it coming. She was almost relieved now that it had begun. More irritated than afraid, she reminded herself that men were hard work. She counted to ten before walking over to him.

When he saw her, Luther stood and began demonstrating his wife's breathing exercises. Shirtless, he hopped from one foot to the other on the high stone in the middle of the river, spinning around with his arms outstretched, teetering back and forth on the edges of the rock. Afraid he might fall, Hannah told Luther to get down.

"You could break your neck—" she stopped herself too late.

Luther laughed and climbed down, sitting in the chair beside her. "Now wouldn't that be provident," he said. "Ruthie called last night. She's going to marry the dog breeder. She says they want to get pregnant on their wedding night."

"Maybe she's confused."

"She may be a little mixed-up about religion, but she's always been clear-headed about me," he said. "You know, things had been difficult with Ruth before David left us. Nobody had a worse temper than I did when I was drinking. She didn't much like who she was when she was with me. She never could stand any kind of cage."

Hannah pondered Luther's use of the word *left* to describe his son's death. Did he expect David to come back? She spoke carefully. "It was an accident. You didn't make anyone leave."

Luther shook his head. "Ruth's always had a little bit of gypsy in her. Making this baby with that man is her way of saying that she wants to tie herself to him and stay put."

Hannah closed her eyes, angry with Ruth Boyd. She thought about her mother sitting in the kitchen the night before, surrounded by piles of rotting tomatoes, waiting faithfully for her father to bring home a box of salt. She felt unaccountably jealous of Ruth's flight from Luther and this farm, of how she'd skipped town on their shared and heavy grief. "You don't have to love the people that hurt you," she said.

"Her pity wasn't love," Luther said quietly. "Our sadness wasn't an aphrodisiac."

Hannah knew dimly that he was about to speak of something Forbidden. She didn't want to hear about it, at least not from him. "It's getting late," she said. "We've got to get those tomatoes to the market."

Some of the baskets were dry-rotted, with weak handles. Hannah was careful to place her hand on the bottoms as she carried them to the truck, but Luther used the handles, carried too many at a time until one of the handles broke, spilling tomatoes over the ground.

"Get down," Luther snapped. "Get down or we'll never finish."

Hannah ducked away from his sharp voice and began crawling on hands and knees, collecting the rest of the tomatoes that had rolled beneath the truck, suddenly afraid of him. Would he beat her too, as he'd beaten his son? She felt him kneeling beside her, gently lifting her off the ground, brushing the dirt from her hands and knees. He opened the truck door for her. He slid into the driver's seat, but he sat perfectly still in front of the steering wheel, staring through the windshield.

"I don't think I should drive," he said.

"Where's the key?" Hannah asked.

"I once thought it was at the bottom of this bottle," Luther said. "Now I'm not so sure." He took his keys from his pocket, handed them to Hannah. He got out and walked around the car as she slid into the driver's seat.

When they reached the place in the road where Hannah threw tomatoes every day, Luther gazed out the window, his face filled with wonderment. "Look. The roads of America are paved with tomatoes." Hannah flushed, feeling guilty for smashing the fruit, ashamed of her own childish ritual.

Driving with Luther was different from driving with her mother. Luther put a fatherly arm across the back of her seat and placed the unmarked bottle between his knees, smoking his cigarettes with the windows closed, filling the cab with the scent of tobacco, calling to mind her father's illicit smoking on the back porch. They took the market route, stopping at the produce stands along the road, until they both lost interest in stopping, and they were simply driving. They began following the creek, Luther pointing to scrub oaks skidding down the sides of timbered-out mountains, to black barns and singed houses.

"Turn right," he said.

She turned, and the road narrowed, twisting upward. Dead pines had fallen beneath the spring rains, their trunks lying smooth and white on the roadside. The truck was rising, but she felt like they were moving into the center of the earth. They drove on until they reached the summit of East River Mountain.

The abandoned rest stop served as a lover's lane at night, but in the late afternoon, plenty of light was left to see all its broken windows, its fallen roof. Broom and chicory grew up around the crumbling base, camouflaging the words "I love Helen" spray-painted red along its front. Hannah wondered aloud if David Boyd had ever been in love or desperate enough to spray-paint a girl's name over a ruined building, breaking out all its windows.

"In my experience, a person will sometimes get frustrated by an unrequited moment," Luther said. "The only way to relieve this combustible feeling is to break something."

They sat quietly, looking over the valley—the train station, the white church steeples, the car dealership and Holiday Inn—all kettled between the two mountains on either side of the town. Puffs of mist rose from the sides of the mountain, as if ancient fires smoldered beneath the green canopy. Then Hannah saw the black pickup parked outside the motel, its side view mirror bandaged by unmistakable duct tape. Shame washed over her like a swift sunburn, burning and chilling her skin at once.

She felt a sudden, inconsolable loss of David Boyd, as if she'd loved him all her life instead of that one brief moment by the river.

She got out of the truck. Reaching down to a scattering of rocks, she threw them down the hill toward her father's truck parked outside the motel room, but the rocks fell short, clattering at the edge of the parking lot. The motel curtain startled, mingling with the figure of a woman in a white nightgown, a man standing closely behind. As the two figures backed slowly into the room's darkness, and the curtain fell shut, Hannah felt a calloused hand closing around her throwing hand, turning her toward the ruined rest stop. She heard a whiskey-cured voice speaking softly beside her, "Aim this way instead."

The rocks flew through the empty windows of the rest stop, falling silently into the weeds growing up through the floor, but she kept throwing until her whole body ached with unrequited love and grief. Her legs buckled, and she felt the arms of a man she knew, and didn't know, around her shoulders and behind her back. He lowered her slowly to the ground, his touch forbidden, yet safe. She curled up on her side and turned, saw Luther Boyd lying on his back beside her, his arms folded across his chest. Mist rolled in, so low that she could see each water particle softening the air until she realized they were both lying in the middle of a cloud.

SADIE WAS HANGING WET BED SHEETS along the porch rail when Hannah got home. When she saw Hannah, she lifted her free hand from the pile of wet sheets and gave a tired wave. "Dryer's broken," she said. "Your father went up to the homeplace to see if he had an extra one at the barn." Hannah moved toward her mother, muted by melancholy and dread. When she reached the porch steps, Sadie's knowing eyes forbade her to speak. Hannah could not tell her mother about her father's truck parked too long beside the anonymous motel room. The secret was one her mother already knew, one that must always remain unspoken between them, the only real conspiracy Sadie would allow into the house.

Hannah went upstairs to her room and stared at the black air conditioner that blocked her view from the window. She raised the sash high and pushed the unit out, watching it crash down through the maple beside the house and shatter on the grass. Down the stairs and back outside, Hannah found her mother standing over the smashed air conditioner, her hands on her hips. She silently took stock of Hannah, who stood shivering in her own dried sweat.

"I don't want this," Hannah said. "I don't want to go down to Luther's farm anymore either."

Her mother nodded. "It's a hard place. I worried that you weren't ready for it."

Her mother had run out of line to hang laundry on the porch railings, so she'd strung a rope between the maple and a hemlock.

"Can we go for another drive tomorrow?" Hannah asked.

Sadie nodded. "I'd like to find a jar of honey."

Hannah heard her mother's unspoken promise beneath her words. *It won't be much longer until you'll be old enough to leave. I won't keep you. I know how much you hate a cage.* Her mother pinned a nightgown on the makeshift laundry line. A wind blew in, filling the gown, kicking up its hem. It twisted, evening sun the color of honey pulsing through its middle. When the breeze died, the dress hung empty and still as ever.

Sadie, 1964

Ostriches

THE DARK HOURS. Dreaming, Sadie stood on her front porch in a hurricane, her bra flying out of her hands, rising into the dark arms of hemlock that shredded its lace and batting. She woke, reached into her cotton nightgown, touched the cyst curled above the jagged scar across her chest. In the mirror at the foot of her bed, her face was haloed by fine, white hair, her skin clear as lilies from all the radiation treatments. Outside the window, telephone wires twisted into the hemlock, and the blue mountain ridge hulked against the red-streaked November sky. She glanced back to the telephone on the bed stand, thinking, I cannot tell this over the phone.

Down in the kitchen, Dean slept on the picnic bench beside the table, one frostbitten hand resting across his chest. The stove's eyes were covered with dirty pots and pans, the counters lined with jars of apple butter, squares of brown sugar fudge, a whole chess pie he made for her yesterday. Above the china-filled hutch, his rifle rested. His long, silver hair unwashed, his square chin unshaved, he looked like one of the old-time mountain men who sometimes wandered through the cemetery beside the house, cursing at the cats napping on the tombstones. Later, he'd take the gun into the wooded ridges above their house to hunt wild boar, squirrels, elk, stock the freezer full of wild game. After months spent in still hospital waiting rooms, he needed this walking. He'd wander for hours on his land, up leaf-covered ridges that kettled their red brick house, his flintlock rifle on his back.

Sadie pulled Dean's red and black flannel hunting jacket over her nightgown, slipped his boots over two pairs of wool socks. When the screen door creaked, Dean startled, grabbed the edge of the table, pulled himself up.

"Sis?"

"I've got to go tell her," she said.

"I'll take you."

She placed one hand upon his chest, softly pushing him back down on the bench. "Lie down awhile, get some rest."

On the crumbling brick porch, Sadie considered Dean's black pickup, decided the drive up the mountain road would take her to her mother's farm too quickly. Instead, she grabbed the tamarack cane propped against the porch rail. Her daughter had bought it for her on her way down from Ohio last spring, when the cancer filled her right femur, snapping it. The cane was unlike anything Sadie had ever seen. Its polished handle was hollowed out, filled with pieces of jade that slid inside like beads along an abacus. She thought it too pretty to use but knew the ridges were too steep for her to climb without it. Slowly, she began walking down the gravel drive toward the guesthouse that hunched beneath the first ridge.

Outside the guesthouse, the last winter apples hung from bare branches. Wizened and yellowed, their vinegar scent followed her as she passed the abandoned trailer sinking into red maple leaves. The scent called forth an unbidden memory of a girl, the charity case from Cherokee, North Carolina, whom Dean once brought home to live in the guesthouse. The girl stood at the kitchen window of the guesthouse, plump and raven-haired, peeling apples by the stove, boiling them with cinnamon into dark, sweet butter while Dean stood close behind, holding empty jars in his hands. Sadie's chest tightened, and her lungs burned.

"Oxygen thief," she hissed at the dark-haired girl. Picking a soft apple from a low branch, she threw it at the guesthouse window, but it skidded beneath, waking a milk snake that crawled languidly out from the tomato bed Dean kept beside the house.

She looked back into the guesthouse, but the vision of the girl had vanished, and the real Dean now stood grizzled and shirtless up on the front porch of their house on the hill, looking out over her. Watching her husband, who was alone and worried and waiting for her in the distance, she forgave his long-ago roaming. He's with me now, she thought. Now it's me who's got to leave.

Inside the woods, tombstones from the last pandemic leaned into the mountain, blanketed by soft drifts of fallen leaves. Others squatted among thick, green outcroppings of rock lilies, their faces worn smooth since 1918. Sadie made out an epitaph, *Gone but not forgotten*, but she didn't recognize the name. Leaves had fallen into two exhumed graves, softening their sharp edges into ovals, as though two giant cameos had been dug out of the earth. Above the empty graves, the trunks of two towering pine trees were slashed with white paint.

She climbed the first ridge. At the top, she turned back to look down at the graves. The tombstones were brown and dull as tree stumps, a playground where she and her brother, Michael, had once played Civil War. Thinking the flags scattered in the leaves belonged to fallen soldiers, they'd used deadfall branches for muskets, dodging invisible gunshot among the graves. Michael had always wanted to play a Confederate of the 32nd Virginia because Jane once told him that his father had hailed from Tidewater country but had moved to Bluefield to work as a lumberman.

Rolling in the weeds and dead leaves, her brother often caught poison ivy, and they had to go home so that their mother could bathe him in bleach. On the other side of the ridge, the sloping path led to Cold Stone Creek. She and Michael had ridden their bikes down this path, Michael always ahead, always turning at the last minute before the high, rocky drop into the creek. Now, as Sadie edged carefully down the leaf-slippery path, she wondered how she'd never caught poison ivy in the graveyard or taken a neck-breaking fall into the creek. Lowering herself into the embankment, Sadie slowly crossed over the fallen maple that stretched across the creek. The water was low and clear, filled with black rocks and brown sand, glistening with dusty shafts of sunlight that drifted down through the forest's canopy high above her head. Sunning turtles rolled off the log, thumping into the water before she reached them.

On the other side of the creek, morning sun warmed the thicket, lighting the red, swollen berries that hung from bare, gray branches. When Sadie's hair had begun falling out, Dean had brought home a wig and two guns he'd bought at the auction held every weekend in the old dairy down in Bluefield. He taught her the names of guns—Saturday Night Special, Cowboy Sidearm—claiming he was once able to hit a pie pan swinging in the wind at fifty yards. He took Sadie out to this same thicket, hung a pie pan on a locust branch, slipped a ladylike 22-magnum in her hand, and taught her to aim through its sights. She aimed too high, missing the pie pan, but the gun's report, ringing through the thicket, thrilled her anyway. The wig itched her scalp terribly. Dean told her to take it off. As she pulled the wig from her head, patches of her own hair came with it. Dean put down his gun, motioned for her to sit beside him. Cross-legged in the grass, she nodded and leaned toward her husband, and together they pulled the last strands of hair from her head, letting them fly across the thicket. She'd kept the bullet casings in her purse for weeks. She never wore the wig again.

Now, she parted the sawbriar, followed a deer path through thickets that tore the hem of her nightgown, clawing her bare calves. Half a mile from the tree line, she stopped to rest in a thorn-free place, examining the stripped bark, brown droppings, matted-down weeds. So tired, she felt much older than thirty-six. She imagined how lovely it would be to sleep and sleep in the deer bed. Warmed by mid-morning sun, protected by a wall of thorns, she gave in to her fatigue, lay down on a clean bed of matted grass, folded the hunting jacket beneath her head. She tried to remember a time before constant ache and weariness coursed through her body.

Sis? SADIE WAS THIRTEEN, holding an empty tin measuring cup. In the dim cabin's kitchen, her mother's face was gaunt, her eyes strangely bright and unfocused. She couldn't stop the foundling child from crying, though she swayed around the cabin, holding him in her arms. Sadie had named the boy Michael on her own, and she was taking the cup up to Miss Emma's place to fetch some milk for him. Then she was running with the empty cup down Dump Hill, along the street past the dairy, up through the pandemic cemetery. It was late fall, galax poking up waxy green through the dried leaves tumbling between the graves. Crossing the turtle log above Cold Stone Creek, she followed the deer path through the thicket. Free of thorn scratch and leg ache, she was barely winded as she climbed the steepest ridge and looked down into the valley called God's Thumbprint. The ridges did look as if a god had squeezed the soft, old mountains through his giant fists, pressing and molding them with his blunt thumbs. She loved the lone, white farmhouse in the middle of the thumbprint, its wide painted porch steps guarded on each side by purple rose of Sharon, its sides lined with straight, narrow beds of rhubarb.

Beyond the house, she saw Dean, Miss Emma's son, polishing a Model B Ford beside the barn, his shoulders bare and broad. A brown quarter horse stuck her head out through the barn window, as though waiting for Dean to notice.

"Don't you scratch my moonshine coupe with that tin cup of yours," Dean teased. "This'll be worth something someday."

Because the run through the familiar woods eased her shyness, and because she'd already decided to marry him, she sassed back, "What's a car like that worth without its tires?"

She ran to the front door before he could answer, waited for Miss Emma to finish playing "Adore and Be Still" on the piano before knocking. A young widow, Dean's mother never left the house. She was known through the valley for playing the piano and cooking exotic meals with the wild animals her son hunted—wild boar stew, game pie, pan-fried venison with chestnut sauce. She called eggplants "aubergines" and could make a dish called "paella" out of two pigeons, one pheasant and a single rabbit. Some said she could have been a master chef. Others said she never left her property because she was afraid of running into the man who'd shot her husband dead on the Norfolk and Western tracks five years before, widowing her.

Sadie believed that if she could live among such elegant wonders—a walnut piano, pure white doilies crocheted from feed sack string, a bay window overlooking a broad, pretty hollow molded by God's thumbs—she might not be inclined to leave either. Dean's mother answered the door. A tiny woman with brown Victorian braids piled on top of her head, she took the tin cup to the kitchen, returned with the milk and a wild boar shank tied up in a flour sack. "Tell your mother to put some molasses in the milk. It'll sweeten it." Then Sadie was running down the mountain so that the milk would stay fresh.

BEFORE REACHING HER BROTHER, Sadie startled to the sound of footsteps shuffling through leaves, coming toward her at a repentant pace, two steps, a pause, then three more steps. At first, she thought it must be Dean coming to carry her back to their house, wrap her in warm quilts, feed her slices of baked sweet potatoes smothered with brown sugar and butter. Then she saw a white tail flash in the sun and knew she was the only human in the thicket, the unseen eyes of a deer upon her.

She wanted to turn back. She recalled Dean's worried face, could almost smell his tobacco as he wrapped her in that quilt. She was almost hungry for the sweet potatoes he'd feed her for breakfast. The ridge before God's Thumbprint was the steepest, stabbed with bare sycamore trunks that rose like gray prison bars, buttery morning light drizzling down their trunks. Her bad leg ached and she was tired, but she couldn't turn away from what she needed to tell her mother. She tied the cane to a hook on the hunting jacket and pulled herself from trunk to trunk until she reached the top and sat on a fallen oak, looking down.

The white farmhouse was a used-to-be place that Dean had given to Sadie's mother, Jane, after Miss Emma died. Deep green ferns sprang from the pond stream where the water used to be, its stones tumbled by wind and rain. The farmhouse's tin roof had gone missing, and trillium and trumpet vine slowly churned the stone porch steps to dust. The two rose of Sharon still bloomed mysteriously on either side of the front door, which swung off its hinge, and Miss Emma's rock lilies and rhubarb still poked through leaves in the overgrown flowerbeds. Inside the house, dried wisteria vines tangled in fallen electrical wires down the blackened and crumbled brick chimney. Empty paint cans and Skoal lids littered the floor, left over from when Dean had tried to rebuild the house, before Sadie finally told him about the new round of cysts, and he'd lost interest in restoring anything but his wife's body. Standing where the bay window used to be, Sadie looked out over the valley, searching for God's thumbprint, but she saw only gold, sloping pastures, the tall tombstone, light gray and clean, shaded by a maple entwined with the trunk of a hemlock.

Though Sadie couldn't see the words chiseled by hand on the marker, she knew they read, *my darling son, Michael.* Looking at the quiet grave, she recalled Michael. He didn't speak at all when her mother had first brought him home, but Sadie had taught him to read the family Bible, the only book in the house. When he turned six or seven, the words came out of him in beautiful and whole sentences, with the cadence of psalms. What else could he become but a missionary? The summer Sadie met Dean, Michael had decided to apprentice himself to a missionary, travel to the tiny coal towns in West Virginia to preach and work side by side with the miners. With wild, coppery hair flaming around his fiercely beautiful face, he'd looked a little like an archangel, ready to smite any kind of sin wriggling into this world. Sadie had been glad Michael had left home before she'd had to explain about her unwed pregnancy. She had only to tell Jane about Dean's plan to marry her in secret so that she could finish high school. Jane told her to get rid of the baby, that it was a bad idea to marry any man whose mother was still alive.

Sadie had gone against her mother's admonition, never regretting the baby, Hannah, or marrying Dean, though she and her mother had quietly broken after she made this decision. Now an unseen hammer rang in the distance. Most likely, the hammer belonged to Luther Boyd, the tomato farmer to whom Dean had sold some of his land. A trailer sat behind the remains of Miss Emma's farmhouse, the side door opening to a tiny kitchen crowded with metal filing cabinets, a writing desk stacked with rare-bird breeding magazines. The trailer had appeared right after the farmhouse burned down, and Dean gave Jane the insurance money to rebuild it. After the trailer appeared, six giant white eggs arrived at Sadie and Dean's post-office box in town. Before Dean delivered the eggs to Jane, Sadie reminded him of how Jane had ordered a still from a catalogue right after her husband left. She'd put the still right on her marble coffee table, where she'd once kept her broad, white Bible open to the picture of Samson in the treadmill. Jane had planned to supplement her hairdressing income by making and delivering moonshine from the trunk of her Buick in Dickenson County. But too many of the roadhouses had been turned into churches by the Primitive Baptists, and Jane eventually began using her first failed investment as a novelty planter for her geraniums. When Sadie pointed out the similarities between the moonshine and the ostrich schemes, Dean only shook his head, frowning. "She's your mother," he said. "The land is hers as long as she lives."

Sadie knocked on the screen door. When nobody answered, she walked around to the old black barn, saw right through its wide, warped slats out to the mountain grass rustling on the foothills behind it. Guinea fowls poured out of the barn, swirling around her feet. A woman stepped out of the barn, leaned in the dark doorway. Coatless, her bare arms were muscular, still deeply tanned against a white T-shirt. Her long, black hair was streaked with silver, caught into a thick braid that hung down to the waist of her faded blue jeans. Once, Sadie offered to make her mother a dress, but when she asked Jane what her favorite color was, her mother shook her head, saying, "I'm done with all that."

Facing her mother, Sadie hesitated, recalling the shame and

happiness she'd felt as she told her mother she was pregnant. She wished she were young and unwed and pregnant again, and that all she needed to explain to her mother was, "Dean and I celebrated too much one night after we helped a cow give birth. He's going to marry me." She strained to find the words spoken and understood so easily in the surgeon's white office, *metastasizing quickly, no more chemo or radiation, maybe before Christmas.* Always more comfortable outside than indoors, Sadie was surprised by how much harder it was to say these final words to her mother in this graceful, open valley.

"I've got to go," she said, finally.

Jane glanced knowingly over her daughter's chick-fluff hair, her frail and winded body, the polished cane hanging useless from her jacket. She nodded, her face as impassive as ever, her eyes wary. "Will Dean take his land back?"

Sadie counted to ten, reminding herself of Dean's unaccountable devotion to Jane, repeating his admonishment, *She's your mother.* "You don't know anything about me or Dean," Sadie said. "If you did, you'd know that he wouldn't take away this land after I'm gone."

Jane nodded. Then she motioned for Sadie to follow her into the barn. "I was just about to feed them," she said.

In the first pen, blue and pink pastel eggs glowed in the straw as though sapphires and rubies stoked from within. Jane cradled a red, araucana hen in the crook of her arm. "Foxes got into the barn last summer. They got her left eye, but she lived. She has trouble seeing, so I have to help her eat." Sprinkling corn and mountain grass on the lid of an upturned coffee can, Jane guided the hen's beak until the bird found the feed, stroking her craw until she ate. Satisfied, Jane unrolled a garden hose, pulling it outside. "You must see this."

Out behind the barn the black dots in the pasture turned out to be emus, squatting on the hillside. Her mother turned on the garden hose, spraying the one nearest the old, faded Ford. The emu rose, spreading his black, flightless wings, twirling, panting, and snapping up the water. Jane laughed and sprayed the emu while a trio of ostriches sauntered to the edge of their muddy pen, black necks straining, thick-lashed eyes wary. Their dirty eggs sank like footballs stripped of pigskin in the mud along the fence.

Only one male joined the eight females. Jane had rigged up a pulley so that she could open the feeding trough door without entering the ostrich pen. The ostriches clambered in, pecking and hissing. Jane poured feed into the trough, swatting away their fierce beaks distractedly, explaining how only darkness calmed them. "They could kill a man," she said, turning over her arms, revealing the pale, upraised scars trailing the inside of her arms down to her wrists. She explained how she approached them only at night, slipping a soft, white pillowcase over their eyes and ears, becalming them enough to gather the eggs.

Sadie traced her mother's sorrowful career path from nursing to hairdressing to moonshine to ostriches, wondering aloud, "Why ostriches? Why not soft-muzzled cows, or horses?"

Without answering, Jane led her to the back of the barn and into a small, whitewashed incubation room, but she didn't let Sadie enter it. The eggs were too fragile, the hatchlings too susceptible to air-born bird diseases. Even the slightest change in body temperature could kill an unborn ostrich. Jane made Sadie stand behind a plate glass window to look at the unhatched eggs, but Sadie studied her mother's face instead. In stillness, Jane's frown lines looked like deep hinges around her mouth, but her faded brown eyes gazed placidly through the glass, and Sadie realized, suddenly, that her lawless mother had found peace in one of the most graceless creatures on earth.

Behind them, the shelves were lined with items for sale: emu plumes and ostrich jerky, giant white and smaller black polished eggs, spiral-bound books filled with ostrich meat recipes. In autumn, Jane gave tours of her farm to schoolchildren from Bluefield and Princeton, dreaming of a time when tourists would drive from Charlotte and Roanoke to see her exotic birds. Sadie knew that the local schoolchildren called her mother "Jane the Insane Bird Lady." She knew how the children repeated the grim tale of how Jane traded her young, unfaithful husband off to an old Indian woman high in the mountains for two hunting dogs, then took the dogs out behind the barn and shot them. Sadie had always been too embarrassed to mention this cruel story, and Jane had always seemed oblivious. Jane finally made a good living selling the full-grown ostriches to an abattoir from France who stunned and carved them into the low fat fillets. She stacked the fillets into a deep freeze by the door, shipping out orders to expensive restaurants that served the same dishes that Dean's mother once cooked, long before they were in fashion.

Jane and Sadie faced each other above the deep freeze.

"Ostrich is supposed to be better for you than red meat," Jane said, offering to let Sadie take as much as she wanted home with her. "It tastes like chicken, of course."

Sadie recalled her dream in the deer bed, remembering the immaculate farmhouse when it still belonged to Dean's mother. She wanted to slap her mother for burning down the farmhouse, for thinking she could make it all up to her by giving her some ostrich meat. She shook her head. "Dean's already stocked us up for the winter."

Jane turned, walked back to the whitewashed room, and Sadie stood at the door of the barn looking out over her brother's grave. Though Michael was never in the military, Jane had staked two American flags beside the marker, placing a heavy drift of fresh white lilies around the marker's base. When Michael was seventeen, Dean found him lying on the side of the road and brought him back to the farmhouse, where they were living with Dean's mother, who was failing. Sadie put cold washcloths on her brother's forehead while he slept, thinking he looked much older than seventeen. His coppery hair receded, his shoulders stooped, and his wrists and joints stiffened with arthritis. While he slept, Sadie washed all the tin ware in the house, clanking it, hoping to wake him. While she was drying the final cookie sheet, Michael appeared in the kitchen doorway. Backlit by evening sun, his long hair hung loose and dull, his dark eyes focusing on something beyond her face.

"I was working for the Lord, but I got tired," he said. "He wore me out."

The next morning, he fixed the rusted chain on his old bicycle and took it out for a ride. Sadie imagined her brother, worn out by mining and Jesus, hunched over the handlebars of his childhood bike, riding up through the pandemic graves and down the slippery, root-crossed path. Perhaps the extra weight, his slow, adult reflexes made him miss the curve before Cold Stone Creek. They found his body down in the low water, his neck broken against a sharp rock in the creek bed.

Jane came out of the barn with a giant alabaster egg and offered it to her daughter. "I've been making these to sell to the tourists, but you can have this one," Jane said. "I have all kinds if you want more."

At first Sadie wondered if this gift was her mother's idea of a cruel joke. Then Jane turned it over, urging Sadie to look inside the hollowed-out shell at the tiny angels and shepherds, the holy mother leaning over her child. Sadie pictured Dean alone next winter, his calloused and frostbitten hands fumbling over the ceramic camels and sheep of the old nativity she always set up beneath a newly cut scotch pine. She knew her husband would roast a turkey, sauce cranberries, and bake a sweet potato pie, wrap it all up in aluminum foil to take to Jane's farm on Christmas day. She knew he would accept her mother's gift of ostrich meat with a simple nod. Finally, she understood that her mother's gift would save Dean from facing the sadness of old family ornaments, the complicated decision of whether to put them up or leave them buried beneath tissue paper in attic boxes. Startled by her mother's uncommon grace, Sadie reached for the egg.

Encouraged, Jane handed Sadie a bouquet of blue, iridescent emu plumes, *for the grandchild*, nodding back toward the barn. "They're going to hatch next week. Come back and see them."

"All right." Sadie nodded, though she knew she wouldn't be back.

She wrapped the egg in her jacket, tucked the plumes inside her pocket, picked up her cane. Turning to leave she paused, looking over the valley. She recalled the first time she took Michael to see it, how he'd been confused about its name, calling it God's Eye, creating in Sadie's mind an absurd and painful image of a giant god lying across the mountain valley with cows trampling over its open eye. She let her own eyes linger over the valley, its old hills smoothed and creased. The farmer's hammer had stopped ringing, and a red tail hawk hung in the silent blue air. Her eyes filled with what she needed, Sadie turned away from her mother, heading down toward the foothills sinking like flightless birds into the dusk.

🌺 Dean, 1966

The Lilies of Wolf Creek

AT FIRST LIGHT, DEAN SYPHER stood on his back porch, watching his daughter run down the sloping lawn toward the game trail leading from his house to Wolf Creek. She was wearing a flowered summer dress, her red hair flaming behind her. Dean set his coffee on the porch step and followed her, keeping a distance as she twisted through pitch pine and briar, dropping down a clay steep, reaching the bank. As Hannah slid the canoe into the creek, Dean stood on the bottomland above the bank, scouting downstream. It was late July. Oaks and poplars towered over the water, bending beneath a summer's weight of ivy and moss. Mist rose from the eddies, brimming above laurel overhanging the limestone bluffs on both sides of the stream. Beneath the mist, a black otter worked the sand bank, pulling the debris of two week's rain from the water, dragging it beneath a tree toppled by an outer current. The wind played rough above the squirrelly rapids. Dean waved his arms, pointing toward the water, calling out, "It's not the same as you remember it."

Hannah paused but did not look back. She stepped into the craft, pushed off, and knelt in the center. The boat rocked and settled beneath her delicate weight. Dean scrambled over two boulders as she pried her paddle's blade through mist and water. Along the left bank, a wave chain unfurled, spilling over gold and copper stones. To the right, eddies chopped and hissed across broken rocks. As Hannah steered smoothly through the chute between wave and eddy, her body disappeared into the mist, but her hair remained in sight. The red hue of it looked unearthly, like a tropical flower circling along the Amazon, and for a moment Dean stopped worrying about her safety, remembering that he'd taught his daughter how to read water before she learned her letters. She knew how each rock moved a current, and how to let the current work for her. Her fight was not with the water. It was with him. He needed to get to the source of it. As he walked down the bank, the mist passed through him like a cold and weary hand.

Hannah's whole body reappeared at the bottom of the rapid. She dug in, allowing the eddy line to turn the boat, pulling it into shore. She stood with her feet against the bilge, perfectly balanced, and looked him directly in the eye.

"It's never been the same as you remember it," she said.

He studied her thin dress, blooming with yellow and orange poppies, her bright hair tumbling wildly around her pale face and neck. Her mother's skin, Dean thought, knowing his late wife, Sadie, would have reached their daughter sooner than this. She'd already have told Hannah that she should be wearing bug spray, sunscreen, and a life jacket. Though Hannah never said so, Dean knew she believed he hadn't protected her mother enough. He should have forced Sadie to go to the hospital sooner, but he'd promised her that she could stay in her own bed as long as she wanted, beneath a window that overlooked the mountain, her mountains.

How tough his wife had been, enduring more pain than anyone he'd ever known. Even when the cancer moved from her breasts into her spine, flaking bones that spiked her spinal cord with her every movement, she would not go into the hospital, claiming she didn't want to die drugged in an anonymous gray room. When the cancer spread into her pelvis, snapping it in two, she still would not go. He took the snowplow off his truck, readying it for the drive over the mountain to the hospital, but she'd simply shaken her head, "Not yet."

Hannah settled her hands on her hips, another Sadie gesture that tightened his chest and knocked the air from his lungs. As she stood before him, twenty-one and motherless, his daughter seemed the hardest kind of woman to keep safe.

"The river's changing," he said.

"You mean it's dying," she said.

"It's impaired. You can't paddle all of it."

"Well," she said, moving into the bow seat, waiting for him to climb in. "You'll just have to show me how to get through the rough parts."

Dean tucked his matches and cigarettes inside his hat, stepped into the stern. A wave splashed over the left gunwale, shooting water into his left ear, deafening him.

"Water's cold," he yelled, flipping his head to shake the water out, rocking the canoe.

Hannah grasped the gunwales, steadying herself. "Don't make me a swimmer today."

"Since when did you get so girly?"

"Since you started smoking and going around to Rosie's Island again."

"That old dive? I call that The Toothless Bar. Ain't a woman in it that's got all the teeth in her head."

Hannah turned on him. "I didn't say anything about the women." She glanced sharply over his chest. His ribs and breastbone tightened again, as if she could see the white scar running through his sternum. "I was talking about the smoke and the bar, and how going there might not be such a good idea with your bad heart," she said.

"It was a good bypass," he said, weakly, suddenly tired of her knowing comments. How much could she really know about him? She'd been away at college. She'd come home that summer with a degree in English and Foreign Languages, without a job or money. She needed a place to stay before she went on to graduate school in Italy that fall, where she would live off a scholarship. He didn't want to charge her for board, but she insisted on paying him for her food, though she hardly ate anything. As payment, she offered to clean out her mother's belongings from the spare bedroom where Sadie lived the last year of her illness. The room had been closed off, untouched since his wife died in the cancer wing of the hospital on Good Friday. All spring, Dean had stayed far away from the room, often the whole house. Most of the time, he slept in the garage or wandered over to his family's land on the next ridge to sleep in the cedar guesthouse beneath the burned-out ruins of the old, empty farmhouse where he'd grown up.

Dean pushed off and sat in the stern seat. He steered past a friendly stone sleeping above the surface, a soft pillow of water pouring over it. Ahead, water circled and crossed a broad limb that had fallen into the channel. He had no idea what the water around it was doing. He couldn't see the whole river stretching beyond it.

"You can't go downstream blind," he said.

"I can see the next eddy," she said. "We can catch it and hop to the next one."

"You want to know what the water is doing. You need to put yourself in a position to see."

"I can see far enough. We can read the rest of it on the fly."

"If it's easy enough," he said.

"Is there ever an easy thing?"

Dean wondered when his daughter had become so unpredictable, her moods changing swiftly from calm to hostile to quietly knowing. While Hannah cleaned out her mother's sick room, Dean had brought lamp after lamp to the room whose window remained half-lit by sun filtered through pine. "You got enough light?" he asked every time he brought another lamp, lingering in the doorway, amazed and almost angered by the ease with which his daughter packed up her mother's belongings. Hannah's face softened, but she never once cried as she folded Sadie's cotton housedresses into grocery bags, topping the dresses with bars of herbal soap carved into shapes of flowers, still wrapped in cellophane. Dean had bought the loose dresses after Sadie's skin began burning from all the radiation, when she couldn't stand the touch of her own clothes. She'd thought the flowered soaps too pretty to open. Hannah couldn't have known these details. She'd come home on weekends to help him take care of her mother, but she didn't live through the day and night rituals of her mother's illness. Dean guessed she must have seen the dresses and soaps as small, impersonal gifts given to comfort the sick. Nothing in the room had belonged to her mother when she was healthy, nothing that would dredge up hazardous memories. Dean had left his daughter alone to finish packing the room, dimly shamed, wondering what he'd been so afraid of finding in it.

"Which way? Hannah asked. They'd come up on an island that forked the river into two waterways. To the right, the currents poured around a souse hole, waves curling back under it. To the left, a bridge hung above the channel, thin as fishing filament, its pilings glinting silver with paint from other aluminum canoes that had been drawn to it.

"Right," he said, noticing too late the faded skull and crossbones flag on the right bank of the island. The flag was Rosie's joke, a secret signal she hung out on the island whenever her liquor license expired and she still wanted to stay open. The bar was an old homestead patched by salvaged lumber and tires, hidden just inside the trees. When the rangers came around, fining fishermen and campers to make up for state revenue cuts, Rosie took down her flag, moved her establishment to a different island, another abandoned homestead. Wherever the bar floated to, you could only row or swim to it.

The sun flickered through spikes of skinny black pines on the bank of the island, and Dean felt guilty for telling Hannah that all the women at the bar were toothless. He wanted to holler out for Rosie, the bar's proprietor, to catch their rope and haul them the rest of the way in. Rosie had a good set of teeth. She kept a jar of Dean's favorite mustard in the bar's fridge and named a country ham sandwich after him, the Sypher Special. Widowed ten years before, she'd been set up with ninety-six acres, two vacation homes in Gatlinburg, a red Dodge truck, and a John Deere tractor by her lawyer husband, though he'd left her childless. She ran the bar to ease her loneliness, claiming that her patrons were better than any of the bereavement groups offered by local churches. Dean agreed with her. Who wanted to sit around talking about his dead spouse in a church basement? He and Rosie had discussed Hannah's drifty behavior since she'd come back, Rosie smoking philosophically over a glass of Old Crow.

"It's only the grief," she said. "When a child loses a parent, she'll usually start acting like one or the other. If Hannah acts all ornery, like you, she won't have to think of Sadie, the sweet one. She won't have to let go of her mother."

"You don't think I'm sweet?" Dean joked.

"You have your kind moments, but sweetness isn't your nature. Sadie was the nice one." She tapped the ash of her cigarette into his empty glass, adding absentmindedly, "Saint Sadie. You know I saw her once in church, when I was still going. I turned around, and she was right behind me, and I thought, 'Now that's the saddest-faced woman I ever saw.'"

Rosie's comments had stung. At the time she'd said this, Dean had hoped her teeth would rot out of her head for telling him that he wasn't the nice one, for implying that he'd made his wife into a sad-faced woman pitied by strangers in church. He hadn't been back to see Rosie since that conversation. Now, he guessed her words hurt because they were partly true. Sadie *was* the nice one. His shy, easy-going wife would not have wished for a friend to lose all her teeth, no matter how angry or hurt the friend made her feel.

The water became easy for a while, so they worked harder paddling. The mist evaporated in open sunlight, and Dean began to look forward to the rapids, the cooling buffer of water and wind between himself and his daughter. He felt glad to be in the guiding seat, where he could see what the rocks were forcing the water into, the patterns on the river, and what the patterns on the top meant about the bottom of the river and what they were coming up on. In the calm places, Hannah swirled her hands in the icy current, as she had when she was younger. Her wrists were still thin as a child's, so tiny he could wrap his thumb and forefinger around them. She held her head just over the side, letting the tips of her hair trail in the water, leading him to ponder why she'd dyed her hair such an unnatural shade of red.

The week Hannah came home and started cleaning her mother's room, Dean had found a red stain around the bathtub drain. Panic shot through him as he rummaged the medicine cabinet, searching for razor blades, suspecting a sad and messy business. When he confronted Hannah about the stain, she'd shown him a box of henna powder she'd used to dye her hair. He thought of his daughter's daily shots of Jack Daniel's, which she drank from tiny bottles she kept in her purse, the way she stayed up all night reading Dante's *Inferno* in Italian. Once, he'd asked her to read aloud to him from the book, and she'd read, "nulla speranza li conforta mai,/non che posa, ma di minor pena." Then, she translated what she'd just read, "There is no hope that ever comforts them—no hope for rest and none for lesser pain."

Dean had learned to speak some Italian from his Aunt Maria, but he'd never learned the Northern, written dialect. The words coming from his daughter sounded so beautiful that he asked if he could tape-record her, but she laughed, saying that she'd just read from the fifth canto, where the lustful were forever buffeted by violent storms. Dean guessed she needed to be out here on this water for the same reason she needed to henna her hair and study Italian, drink those whiskey miniatures. He would stay here with his benumbed daughter, try to buffer her from the violent currents of her unspoken grief.

Near the end of his wife's life, Dean had acquired his own numbing habits. Crazed by Sadie's pain, he'd run down the game trail in the middle of a snowfall and break the skin of ice over the creek. Wading in, he'd stand among rocks crusted by five inches of snow, letting the freezing water pierce his ankles, imagining himself under snowy quilts, making love to all the women he'd known, each one younger than Sadie, bewitching him on the brass bed of the little guesthouse where he often took them. As his wife lay in the house on the hill above him, quietly enduring a pain he could not imagine, all the women he remembered became faceless but with healthy bodies, both their breasts intact, their pelvises unbroken. He hadn't strayed from his wife during the last two years of her life; he'd nursed her himself until the very end of her illness, but as he recalled himself standing in the winter creek, calming himself with thoughts of other women, he felt completely faithless.

The canoe approached a calm pool. A steel beam bridge hung

288

over a line of quiet water running across the entire width of the creek. Beyond the line, he knew, was a blasted mill dam. What used to be an eight-foot, solid wall was now a one-hundred-yard stretch of broken concrete, jagged rocks shredding the scrolling water until it was unreadable. He steered the boat to the shore, searching for a take out.

"We need to scout this one," he said.

They walked the scouting trail and looked out over the rapids. The rocks bit at the water, forming waves upon waves devouring each other, pouring into foaming holes that could hold a boat under and keep it there. He saw a whole fallen chestnut leaning against the top of the ruined dam, its roots reaching skyward, as if it had grown upside down in the middle of the falls. He nodded toward the uprooted tree, the dry boulder garden at the end of the rapid. "We'll have to portage this part," he said.

Dean shouldered the canoe, tucking his head inside, keeping the boat high enough to see the trail. Hannah walked ahead, carrying the paddles. They climbed up stone stairs that ended before they reached the burned-down grist mill. They stepped carefully over the petrified tree roots that veined the dirt around the long flat limestones that once formed the mill's foundation. Somebody had built a bonfire on top of the limestone, using the spokes of the old overshot wheel. The charred remains crawled with soiled condoms, empty beer bottles.

"Wasn't this the mill village?"

"It's past," Dean said, urging her forward.

The locusts droned, and the canoe trapped heat beneath it, and Dean had to set the canoe down gently every few yards. He glanced back over their difficult run, already longing for chill mist and rapids. A white heron stood in the shallows, still as an ice sculpture, hunting the low current that trickled around the dry stones. Dean willed Hannah to look back with him, to take comfort in the beauty of the heron, the patterns of water falling over the mill dam. Hannah turned away, staring down at the sordid condoms scattered over the charred gristmill. She pulled her hair into a loose ponytail. Dean noticed a black mark shaped like an 'S' on the back of her neck. Believing it was a wet leaf, he reached out to wipe it off, but it would not come off. He wiped again and looked closer, saw a tiny, black dollar sign burned into her skin.

"What have you done to yourself?"

"It's a dollar sign."

"I can see that. Why a dollar sign?" he asked. "How could you do this to your pretty skin?" Your mother's skin.

"It's so I'll always remember to name my own price."

"You're too young to have one," he said, meaning the tattoo.

"Everybody's got a price. What's yours?"

"I never had a price."

"Yours was expensive, but she always paid it."

Dean felt as he had when she'd read to him about hell in Italian. Her talk of human currency seemed as mystifying as any foreign language, though the drift of her meaning seemed far from beautiful. He felt tired and unschooled, bewildered by her anger at him, her refusal to find hope or any comfort in the water and woods.

"Is this how they taught you to talk at college?" he said. "Because if it is, you just wasted a whole lot of time and money. I don't understand a word of what you just said. I wish you would talk straight and tell me why you've been giving me hell all day."

He sat on the overturned canoe, letting his heel bang against its side more violently than he intended. The trash-can echo startled the white heron. It flapped its lanky wings, its flight ungainly as it rose slowly and bounced on a cypress limb. Hannah didn't flinch. She sat down on the canoe and pulled a bottle out of her dress pocket, setting it between them. At first, he mistook it for one of the whiskey miniatures she kept in her purse. Then he saw that the glass was filled with a strong pink liquid that changed color as she held it up in the light, its pink deepening into orange, then red.

"Who did this nail polish belong to?" she asked.

"It was your mother's."

"She never wore color."

"She usually didn't."

"Then why was it in her bedroom? Why was it in the drawer of her bed stand?"

"She thought her feet looked ugly," Dean said. "That's the reason she gave for not wanting to go into the hospital sooner. She didn't want the doctors to see her ugly feet. When it got so bad, I bought that polish for her so that she could paint her toenails. It was the only way I could get her to go."

Hannah stared at him, disbelieving. "You owed her," she said. "You could have waited at least until after she was gone to start up again."

He tried to explain why Sadie, his shy wife who wore no makeup and refused to dye her hair, was struck by a sudden case of vanity at the very end of her life. He tried to explain his trip to the New Graham Pharmacy, how he'd left the safety of aisles stocked with eyeglasses and heating pads, turning into the treacherous cosmetic section, passing picture after picture of women with their heads tilted back, lips parted, as if waiting to be kissed, above the shelves of bottles filled with jade, red, and copper polish, their names more head-spinning than their bright colors—Ocean Love Potion, Cherish, Autumn Promise. He'd put a bottle of each kind of polish into his basket and taken them all home, spilling the bottles on the bed beside Sadie. She'd picked out the deepest pink, Caliente Coral. As she leaned forward to paint her toes, she winced, and he took the bottle from her hands. "Let me." His hands shook, but she spoke to him until his hand steadied

and he could finish the first coat, blowing gently over it, starting on the second. Kneeling at his wife's feet, painting slowly and
carefully, he felt like he was repeating a powerful prayer or chant.
"It helped her," Dean said.

But Hannah had already turned and walked away from him,
toward the end of the creek. She slipped through a marshy patch
of cattails that thickened and arched over the shoal. On the other
side of the marsh, a mountain formed at the confluence of Wolf
Creek and a newer river, the first slope unfolding from the shoals,
rising into green waves of grass dotted by outcroppings of red
picnic tables. Above the picnic tables, orange lilies ran across the
hillside, clinging to the bluffs. Silver canoes crowded the new
river, sending safe, uniform ripples across its surface. Hannah
had no interest in paddling it. Dean found her sitting on the bank.
When he reached her, she bummed a cigarette from him, and he
shook one from the pack he'd hidden beneath his hat.

"It's a strong color," she said. "I can see how it would have
helped her."

Encouraged, Dean nodded toward the bright lilies on the slope.
"The old-timers used to make a wine from them that had an odd
effect," he said. "After two or three glasses, a man saw dreams that
had a great power and beauty, but in the morning he always felt
like he'd committed a terrible crime."

He lit a match, and Hannah cupped her hand around the flame
he offered. She lay back on the bank, looking like something
beautiful and expensive dredged from the water's silted depths.
Her bright dress blended with the dark grass and white clover.
Her red hair glowed, sun-streaked and deepening as it swirled
wildly around her face and throat. The threat of blush or sunburn
lingered just beneath the delicate surface of her white skin. She
crossed her forearm over her chest and closed her eyes, balancing
the cigarette expertly between her fingers. Her smile remained a

secret. He'd never know what she remembered about his marriage to her mother, or if she believed there'd been any kind moments between them. That was her price, and he'd keep paying it. He sat beside her, reaching to take the burning cigarette from her fingers before its ashes could drop, but he put down his hand, afraid of waking her. A black shadow slipped down the mountain, exposing the soft green summit. The hazy summer sky billowed like a starched sheet, chafing all that lay bare and devoted beneath it.

✿ Dean, 1967

Wilderness Road

LUTHER BOYD'S EX-WIFE, Ruth, came back when the great rhododendrons budded and the Dogwoods bloomed, their white
petals snowing over the Boyds' homestead down in the valley.
Dean first spotted her walking the pine pass that led from Luther's tomato farm up to his own house at the end of Wilderness
Road. Ruth had been gone since her and Luther's son jumped
off a nearby waterfall, and she'd run away to live in a religious
community in California. Now that she was back, Dean knew
her, and he didn't. Tall and willowy, she still dressed in the blue
jeans she'd worn at thirty-nine, before leaving, but ten years had
streaked her long brown hair with fine, silver strands. Dean stood
unseen beside the faded trailhead sign with the horse head on it
as she slipped through pitch pine and thicket, oblivious to him.
Surprised by her young and sure-footed movements, he thought,
That old path's inside of her.

Dean stepped off the road and onto the pass, the brown fallen
needles soft beneath his boots. He walked beside a limestone
bluff dripping with beaded veils of ice, looking down the ridge
spiked with bare sourwood. It was late March. In the valley below,

irrigation pipes snaked from the river into Luther's tomato field—long rows of dirt, covered with black gardening tarps. Dean's weak heart ached from the chill air, and his eyes watered from the sun shimmering off the tarps. He walked down the ridge toward Luther's cabin.

Dean had been walking the ridges and valleys off Wilderness Road since his wife died of cancer. The day after her funeral, a land developer with a nasal accent drove his silver Ford Bronco right up to the house to tell Dean that the county was building an industrial complex on the hill beside his family's old homeplace, and that they'd pay a good price for his land.

"It's hard to be alone on this mountain," the developer had said. "A man could get lost up here and never come back. You could sell, make enough to buy a place outright in town, never have to worry about land taxes again."

Dean had not liked how the man parked his shiny new Bronco behind his old Ford pickup, blocking him in. He'd wanted to gut punch the man for knowing why he was alone, for hinting that his mind was turning, for assuming he could not pay the rising taxes on his family's land. Dean couldn't pay the taxes. He'd already sold off part of his land to pay off Sadie's hospital bills, but all of this was nobody's business.

The day after the developer's visit, Dean started walking, following Wilderness Road until he reached all that remained of his mother and father's burned-down farmhouse—three concrete footers filled with fallen leaves and a crumbling stone chimney woven with ivy. He began clearing stones from the pasture that sloped beside the house, working his grief and anger into his muscles until the soft aches dulled his restless mind. That night, too tired to walk home, he'd slept on the floor of the blue cedar guesthouse that sat beneath the ruins of the big house. He'd been going back to clear the land every day since, as if this were his job, though he still wasn't sure if he would sell it. It was a place to go. A retired railroad man, he still needed to go places.

I am not lost, he told himself as he stepped off the path, tangled in some locust briars, climbed down a jutted bluff of limestone. He slid down a steep cleft, landing at the brambled riverbank. The river ran high and swift, its green surface mottled with golden scales of sunlight. Above the one-hundred-year flood line, Luther Boyd's chinked cabin was held up by stones at the corners, joined to concrete footers and blond sawmill boards warped by years of rain. Out on the lawn, an orange painted sign demanding "No Annex" was nailed to a snowy dogwood.

Dean walked beside the house, startling a blue heron stalking fish in a still pool of water. The heron rose slowly as mist, faded into feathery hemlock. In the open doorway, Dean adjusted his eyes to the darkness inside the house. Dusty sunlight filtered through the planked walls, and he could make out a coal stove topped with a coffeepot and cast-iron skillet, a washtub beneath a crude spigot. A small, wiry man lay upon a straw bed tick shoved against the wall.

Dean spoke into the cabin's darkness. "Luther Boyd."

The man sat up. "What time is it?"

"Six a.m."

Luther stood, shuffled to the spigot, filled the coffeepot, and set it to heat. He motioned for Dean to sit at the table while the coffee brewed, and when it was ready his hands shook as he filled two cups. The chicory coffee was bitter, black as the earth below the gapped floor planks. Dean refused Luther's offer to lace his coffee with Old Crow, looked around the bare kitchen for some sugar. He didn't see any. If a woman had been living here, he knew, he'd find sugar in the kitchen. He wondered where Ruth Boyd was staying.

"I saw Ruth on the pass this morning," he said.

Luther nodded, his face impassive. "She got rid of her second husband, and she needed a place to stay."

"Having someone around to do for you again must be nice."

Luther shook his head. "We try to be patient with each other, but this old bachelor's pad's not fit for a woman anymore."

Luther looked toward the next ridge, toward the blue, cedar guesthouse still standing beneath the remains of Dean's family's big house.

"Sometimes I see lights in that old potato bin up on your land," he said. "Can a person still live in it?"

"It's called the Cold Potato," Dean said. "I've been up there working. I'm thinking of selling it."

"Ruthie was too young for me, but she was a good wife and mother," Luther said. "She always cooked. She worked at one of those fancy bed-and-breakfasts out in California. She stayed independent. She could pay you rent."

Dean recalled the spring Luther's schoolteacher son fell off the top of Looking Glass Falls. According to Sadie, a pregnant female student had accused David Boyd of seducing her, and angry parents encouraged the girl to file a complaint. Though the accusations turned out to be untrue, the school's principal fired David anyway, and David wouldn't press charges against the girl or sue the school district. He claimed that his reputation as a teacher was still ruined even though he'd been found innocent.

When David Boyd was fired, Luther had found a guard job for him down at the Buchanan county prison, but the son had seemed unable to hold a job where no school bell measured out his time. He'd roamed the ridges and valleys all winter. In early spring, after a heavy rain, two workers from the Conservation found his broken body beneath the falls, tangled on a fallen tree that stretched out over the spillway rocks. After the accident, Ruth told everyone in town that her son was doing a handstand on top of the falls, and slipped. But everybody down at the Coffee Shop in town agreed that David Boyd was a hillbilly boy, practically part goat. Everybody wondered, but did not ask, what David Boyd had been doing on top of Looking Glass Falls in the middle of winter, when icicles hung from the top, the plunge pool froze over, and the old stepping-stones leading up from the base cracked open from the cold, the fissures so wide that a whole child could slip into them.

Their coffee finished, the men walked out of Luther's cabin and over to the river. Though he was only five years older than Dean, Luther's white whiskers glistened on his gaunt cheeks. He wore a Virginia Tech sweatshirt with its sleeves torn off, tucked into a pair of faded twill trousers. Dean recognized the clothes as David's cast-offs, remembering how Sadie had told him about finding Luther a week after his wife had run away. A spring storm had knocked down the power lines all over the mountain and blown the gardening tarps off Luther's tomato seedlings. When the storm ended, Sadie had been the first to notice the dead plants in Luther's field and his darkened porch light, which he usually kept on all night so the neighbors could see their way up their winding drives. She'd found him lying face down in the middle of his bare, wide-planked floor, two grocery sacks filled with empty Old Crow bottles on either side of him.

Sadie also found Luther's electrical bill, and paid it. She'd looked in on him once a month, bringing him a can of pinto beans or freshly baked banana bread, until she was too sick to walk the ridge. Remembering his wife's kindness toward their neighbor, Dean felt deeply shamed by his own reluctance to help him.

"Do you know how much people are charging for rent up here these days?" Luther said. "Old man McCullan put a pool table and an air conditioner in his shed and started calling it a 'gaming cabin.' He says businessmen from Ohio will pay $300 a week to stay there while they hunt and fish."

"I never thought about it," Dean said. "I don't stand with charging such high prices, but I guess a little rent money would help me get back in good with the IRS."

Luther nodded. "Your land is your ace in the hole. You'd be better off keeping it, timbering off the weak trees. If you did that, at least you could keep it."

"They're paying good money," Dean said. "I've got to get it ready."

Both men looked at the fallen sourwoods that criss-crossed down the ridge, the irrigation pipe connecting the river to Luther's tomato field. The green river curled back and forth across Dean and Luther's property.

"Looks like the river is deciding who it will belong to this spring," Luther said.

"I don't guess it ever really belongs to anyone," Dean said.

Before leaving, Dean agreed with Luther that Ruth would pay one hundred dollars a month, plus her share of the utilities. As Dean walked the riverbank toward the homeplace, a hawk quarreled with him from the limb of a walnut. Dean argued with himself, wishing he'd written out the rental contract for Luther's ex-wife. He wondered why Ruth had gotten rid of her second husband, if that husband wanted to be gotten rid of, and why she'd returned to these mountains.

She was too young, Luther had said by way of explaining Ruth's leaving, but Dean knew you were never old enough to face your life's greatest losses. After Sadie died, he'd been tempted to buy up a bunch of tickets with his railroad discount, ride the trains across the country until he reached high, open prairie, maybe going all the way to California, but now that she was gone, he'd become protective of his land, as if it were sacred and must be guarded. He walked along the riverbank, his legs weak and heavy. When he reached the fenceless pasture, a white horse ran by him, stopping beside a pile of black fence posts stacked in the center.

Dean approached, and reached out toward her knotted mane, but she shied away.

Wishing for some sugar to give her, he thought of Luther Boyd's chicory coffee and tried to guess at how many years of solitude a man needed before he planted himself in a dark cabin, drinking bitter coffee laced with Old Crow, still believing in the sweetness of a woman returning. The horse backed away, heading toward the forest.

THE WEEK RUTH BOYD MOVED into Dean's guesthouse, the black bear woke. Thin and hungry from hibernation, she stumbled down the ridge and ripped the lid off Dean's trash can, sipping the sweet dregs from his tossed-out Coke cans, scattering the refuse around the base of his great rhododendron. After cleaning up his trash, Dean put the can in his truck and drove over to the homeplace to clear the thicket beside the guesthouse.

Ruth had not found steady work as a pastry chef in downtown Bluefield, but the owner of the General Francis Marion Hotel across the mountain had told her to bake something different for him every day for a month. If he liked everything she made, the resort owner would hire her at the beginning of tourist season. Beneath the kitchen window of the guesthouse, Ruth's trash can overflowed with apple cores and empty sugar sacks, a broken mason jar with a dollop of dark molasses rimming its bottom. The smell of baked apples floated out the open kitchen window, filling Dean with loneliness, desire, and the fear that Ruth was summoning every waking bear on the mountain onto his property.

Dean piled three rocks on the lid of the trash can and headed up the hill to chop and clear the pasture beside the old farmhouse. On the east ridge, above the pasture, developers had girdled the windbreak trees until they fell like jackstraws, leaving Dean's hardwoods defenseless against the winter winds. A white oak had fallen beside the Cold Potato. Sinking into curling, brown leaves, its thick trunk was bearded with ivy, camouflaged by bent saplings and briars. Its unearthed root ball reached up like a dirty, arthritic hand.

All morning, Dean worked the scythe on the thicket around the deadfall, swinging it through high grass and briars, ignoring the thorns that planted themselves in his calloused hands. He made easy, rhythmic sweeps, breathing in the smell of earth and grass, fantasizing about keeping the land, planting a winter garden of squash and potatoes. He chanted the song his daughter, Hannah, had sung when she was small and used the Cold Potato as her playhouse. "Irish potatoes, jacket potatoes," he sang under his breath, swinging the scythe harder. "Sweet potatoes. French fries." When he stopped to rest, the white horse came out of the forest, her footsteps sounding dainty, almost human. He enjoyed her quiet company and didn't try to touch her.

By noon, he wearied, and his chest tightened, as though a large hand rested upon his sternum, pushing him down until he lay across the giant, fallen tree trunk.

Closing his eyes, he imagined following Wilderness Road all the way to Paradise, California, but when he reached its end, he found Saint Peter standing at the pearly gates. He tried to cut a deal with St. Peter to let him bring Sadie back down with him. The saint shook his head, so Dean just turned around and walked back down the road, empty-handed.

He woke to the sound of a rattlesnake twitching drowsily from the thicket. In the distance, the mountain wrapped around the valley like a burly, sunburned arm, late afternoon shadows spreading slowly across it. Ruth Boyd knelt over him, her face so close he could see the age on her that he hadn't noticed before—the deep lines gouged beside her pretty mouth, the finer ones scratched across her forehead. She put his arm around her shoulder and helped him walk to the guesthouse. She smelled of baked apples, and as they walked into the guesthouse, she talked slowly, asking simple questions, steadying him with her voice.

"Doesn't this house have a name?" She urged him to lie on the old brass bed, took off his shoes, brought him a glass of water and a thick slice of apple cake. "Didn't you used to call it the sweet potato or the French fry?"

"It's called the Cold Potato," he said. "My mother named it after an old song. She and my father lived here while they built the big house."

As far as Dean knew, his mother never had stored potatoes here. He'd furnished it with some of his mother's furniture and set out a little garden, hoping his daughter, Hannah, might use it when she came home to visit. Now, Ruth was using his mother's vanity as a bed stand, topping it with a stack of Sadie's books— *The Last of the Mohicans, Jane Eyre, Wuthering Heights.* She'd set a guide to the gardens of Italy beside the stack of books on the bed stand, folding over the pages to mark her place. Annoyed by the dog-eared pages of his wife's book, Dean stood quickly. He lost his balance, sat again.

"I think a black bear's been coming around," he said, his voice too loud.

"I saw one running through the ridge when I was sitting on Luther's porch last night," Ruth said. "Luther said the bears don't come down this far, that I must have seen a dog, but it didn't have the rump or tail of a dog."

"It's a female, maybe pregnant—the most dangerous kind. I could build a humane trap for her."

Ruth frowned. "Now what would you do if you ever caught a bear?"

"I'd drive her back to the other side of the mountain and

release her on conservation land so that she could have her cubs in peace."

"So you're going to put a live, pregnant bear in the back of your truck and take her over the mountain like you're on a Sunday drive?"

"I tell you what," he said. "If I catch her on a Sunday, I'll take her out for a drive before I let her go."

Dean told Ruth how a bear's musk smelled worse than rotten garbage. He described a bear's deep warning huff. If faced with a charging bear, he said, she should stand her ground and raise her hands in the air, give it the impression that she was bigger than she really was.

Ruth laughed, shaking her head. "You're a real Daniel Boone."

Dean stood, unsure if he liked the way Ruth teased him. Though he had told her to make herself at home, he felt uneasy with her use of Sadie's belongings. He looked at the piece of apple cake she'd placed on the bed stand. Dark brown and thickly sliced, it smelled rich with cloves and cinnamon. Ruth wrapped it up in a napkin and handed it to him.

"Control your food," he said. "If you don't, that bear's gonna see your trash like one big candy shop." He turned to leave. "I go on a dump run every Thursday. I can take your trash with me when I take my own."

Outside, the pale moon held itself above the loblollies, its round melancholy face upturned, reminding Dean of a word he'd heard one of the few times he'd gone with Sadie to her church, *supplication*. Below the canopy, the air was so black Dean could not see his truck. He walked slowly, letting instinct and memory guide him down the gravel drive. Inside the cab, he thought of Ruth alone, her trash can overflowing with sugar and molasses, and he decided to stay up here and keep an eye out for bears. He put the piece of apple cake on the dashboard and leaned against the door handle. He propped his feet on the passenger seat, scattering a stack of medical bills that kept coming after Sadie died. He sent in payments when he could, but the balance was so high that he knew he'd never pay it off, even if he sold every last acre of his land.

The bills settled like drifts of melted snow on the floor, reminding him of that final winter, when the disease took Sadie swiftly, piece by piece. Dean had brought her home from the hospital so that she could celebrate the holidays in her own house. On Christmas morning, he'd found her sitting in the kitchen with the lights off, watching snow clouds pour over the mountain. She seemed too young for the tamarack cane leaning against the hutch, much younger than thirty-six. Her skin flawless from all the radiation treatments, her round face glowed against her white robe. Her perfect stillness terrified him.

He'd bundled her in his hunting jacket and carried her outside, placing her in the cab of his truck. He took the plow off his front fender, and they drove down Wilderness Road, bumping over the deep, frozen ravines and high piles of frozen snow. When they neared the hospital, Sadie shook her head, "No, not there." They crossed the railroad tracks and wound slowly up Dump Hill, where Sadie was raised. Near the top, Sadie pointed to the side of the road, saying softly, "That's where my mother found my first mattress. She saw it lying on the side of the road and we carried it home. That was my first real bed." Then she'd made Dean promise to take her home; she didn't want to die in an anonymous hospital bed. Dozing, Dean felt the medical bills and tax forms knitting themselves into a white, spidery afghan. He tried to pull the ragged coverlet over himself, but couldn't.

He woke at three o'clock, stepped out of the truck into the coldest part of the night, and walked up to the ruined old farmhouse, his mind still full of Sadie. He imagined her at eighteen, newly married and pregnant, keeping the winter fire going all day, heaping ashes over the coals to keep them hot at night. Every morning at four a.m., she'd stoked the sleeping fire, adding fresh wood to make his biscuits and gravy before he left for the railroad.

Just below the house, Dean halted when he saw the bear. She sat on a stone in the corner of the crumbling footers, her hands folded over her swelling stomach, her head bent and eyes closed, her posture so human that when she looked up at Dean, he stood unafraid, unsure if he were awake.

Dean looked down at the guesthouse. The lights were still on, and the smell of cooked apples wafting up the ridge brought an unbidden vision of himself standing inside the guesthouse kitchen. His middle-aged stomach swelling over the waist of the Levis he'd worn in high school, he'd peeled green apples into a pot as the raven-haired Cherokee girl sauced them with cinnamon and sugar. He'd told Sadie that he was letting the girl live in their guesthouse until she got back on her feet. He'd kept this girl in the guesthouse the spring and summer after his last heart attack, almost believing his own stories of his charity toward the young woman having hard times. Then, one evening he came home and found his wife sitting in the dim living room on the bench before the piano his mother used to play. Her hands folded ladylike in her lap, Sadie said, "Your family is your charity."

The bear stood, looked straight at him, her brown eyes patient, and he recalled the danger beneath his wife's words, the panic of being caught. The bear dropped on all fours and rambled out of the house, across the field. Dean walked the other way, pausing at the window of the guesthouse to watch Ruth stirring more apples in a pot on the range. How good it would feel to lie in that old brass bed, watching a pretty woman cook and stack apples between cake sweetened with dark molasses. He thought of the bear's great, still eyes that reminded him of Sadie's, and how the bear had forgiven his intrusion, walking away instead of attacking. Dean imagined the bear must have been telling him that he should be alone for a while longer. I still owe her, he thought, stepping out of the window's soft light and across the shifting gravel. He got into his truck and drove home.

WHEN SHE WASN'T BAKING, Ruth hiked the ridges and paths off Wilderness Road. She stepped over logs without checking to see what lay on the other side, stuck her hands in limestone crevices as she climbed the outcroppings instead of walking around them. Ruth seemed so fearless when she hiked that Dean felt afraid for her. At least, that's what he told himself while he followed her. Walking at a distance, he carried a rifle and told himself he was out hunting. But he always found himself tracking Ruth, telling her in his mind the truth about his Wilderness Road. It was not the famous route carved by Daniel Boone in 1775. Now paved, the historic road led safely to Roanoke, and you could rent out its fort for family reunions. Named by some long-ago relative for some forgotten reason, Dean's Wilderness Road was a winding ten-mile swatch of rutted gravel that began at a funeral home and ended at the remains of his family's two-story farmhouse. In his mind, he also reminded Ruth that the overgrown paths branching through these ridges and valleys were much more dangerous in early spring than they were in winter. Bears clambered down the timbered-out ridge; rattlesnakes coiled beneath the soft green ferns and toad trillium. Though Dean hated admitting it, the land developer had been right about one thing: you could get lost up here and never come back.

Most days, Ruth let him follow her. They hiked off the pine path, straight down the ridge, winding along the river that divided the tomato field and the old horse pasture. By the time they climbed to the next summit, Dean was so close behind that Ruth could have turned around to whisper a secret to him, and he would have heard.

One morning, while Dean was clearing stones from the back pasture, he saw Ruth carrying a hatbox to her truck. He went up to help her and saw the rows of French custards in glass dishes, chiming together as she rushed past him, saying, "I've got to get these to Marion in an hour, or I'm out of work for the summer." That afternoon, he saw her truck parked beside the guesthouse, its passenger door still open. He knocked on the screen door of the guesthouse to ask if everything was all right, but she dodged past him, onto the trail, slipping away through laurel and rhododendron until Dean lost sight of her. He walked alone until he saw two wild turkeys running beneath an overhang of limestone, moving like two swirls of brown leaves against the real fallen leaves. He shot one, brought it home, smoked it over hickory chips, boiled its frame and strained it, added carrots and noodles to the soup.

The next morning, he found his trash can overturned, the wild turkey carcass crushed and scattered across his back porch. A strong musk remained in the air. Though it was only Tuesday, he went over to the farm to check on Ruth and offer to take her trash with his own to the dump. The door to the Cold Potato was open, and he could hear the agitated clanking of pots and pans in the tiny kitchen.

"I'm going on a dump run," he called through the screen. Ruth appeared, her hair falling from its loose ponytail, a smudge of flour on her forehead. The counter was lined with the custards he'd seen her load into her truck the day before, their tops the color of lightly toasted marshmallows.

"You hear anything walking around your house last night?" he asked.

"I've got worse things to worry about than little black bears rummaging through my garbage," Ruth said. "The man over in Marion wants three hundred sweet rolls by noon or he won't hire me. He says that people don't come to these mountains for crème brûlée. It's apple stack cakes and sweet rolls, or I'm out of a job. Then, yesterday, some conservationists came out to Luther's place with their lawyer, asking Luther to sign over his land. Those conservationists may look and act all nice, but they are just as aggressive as the developers. What kind of people would bring a lawyer up here to talk a feebleminded old man into signing over his land?"

"Luther's been on his own for some time now," Dean said. "He's not as feebleminded as people might think."

"They called him a 'human intrusion,'" Ruth said. "They should go over to the falls and see the pesticides they spray over the ivy on the power lines," she said. "They should take a look at that awful new bridge the Forest Service built on top of the falls."

Dean caught his breath as Ruth pulled the rubber band from her ponytail, and her lank brown hair poured around her narrow shoulders. Dean wondered again why Ruth had gotten rid of her second husband. He wondered why her second marriage hadn't stuck, even though the wedding license had been signed in a place called Paradise.

"What was it like living in California?" he asked.

"I cooked," she said. "I grew up. Some of my friends bought land in the foothills, sold it for thousands ten years later. I forgot to do that. When the divorce happened, I decided to come back. I shouldn't have called Luther feebleminded. He's been waiting on me. That house of his is a fixer-upper, but he's done small things to get it ready. He put crystal knobs on all the doors."

Dean didn't recall seeing doors on Luther's cabin, let alone crystal knobs.

"It's not his land I've come back for, if that's what you're thinking," Ruth said. "I could have gone to a culinary school in Italy. I've got an offer to go to Alaska to cook in one of those fish camps this summer. I could have gotten away from here, but then who would take care of him? No one's left. He's been waiting on me, and now I've come home."

BEFORE DAWN THE NEXT MORNING, Dean awoke to the sound of something thumping over the roof of his house on all fours. Dean lay in bed, wondering if it was the black bear or just a raccoon ransacking his trash. He recalled Ruth's sudden fury at the conservationists, and he wondered why she'd lied about Luther putting crystal knobs on a cabin without doors. He'd heard stories of prodigal family members coming back to reclaim the old houses of sick or dead relatives, selling off the antique crystal doorknobs, fireplace mantels, pine flooring, and all the colored glass windows until, finally, they auctioned off the entire stripped-down house. Sometimes, they came back to sell off the graves bought for them in their family's plot. Luther Boyd was very much alive, and Dean wondered why Ruth wasn't living with him yet, caring for him. Finally, Dean wondered why he'd allowed a woman as displaced and dangerous as Ruth Boyd into the still safety of his own family's guesthouse.

Dean dressed and drove over to the farm to tell Ruth that he needed to sell the land sooner than he'd planned, and that she'd need to find another place to stay for the summer. But when he arrived at the farm, he found Ruth's truck gone, the windows to the Cold Potato shut, the door locked. Certain that Ruth had gotten fired by the resort owner for not baking enough sweet rolls, Dean thought that she'd gone off to Alaska to cook in a fish camp.

He was not as relieved by her abrupt disappearance as he thought he'd be. He recalled her anger over the pesticides and the new bridge on top of Looking Glass Falls and decided to drive over to the falls to see if she'd been telling the truth about them. At the pullout for the access trail, he spotted Ruth's truck. He parked beside it and walked through the old apple orchard, down to the river. At the horse ford, he saw her boots in the sand beneath a flat stone, the broken zip line hanging from a tree on the other side. His stomach sinking with dread, he sat on the stone beside her boots and took off his own, rolling his socks into the toes. He tied the strings of Ruth's boots together, slung them over his shoulder, carrying his boots in each hand as he stepped into the water. He waded through screaming cold water, toward the orange trail sign on the other side. Climbing onto the bank, he sat on a fallen log, drying and rubbing the sand from his frozen feet with a sock, slipping his damp, gritty feet back into his boots.

He followed the blazed trail until he reached the swath cut out of the trees, saw the power line crossing over his head, a thick tendril of brown ivy hanging from it. He reached for the dead ivy, but his hand froze in mid grasp when he saw the heart-shaped head and diamond back. The dead snake's rattle hung at eye level, its entrails spilling out of its slit side.

It had been a dry winter. Through the cleared swatch of trees, Dean viewed Looking Glass Rock, the monolith that towered above the falls. When wet or frozen, its face resembled a mirror. But it had been a dry winter, and the rock reflected nothing. Thin water spread over only the right half of the falls, the new black bridge spanning the top. Below the bridge, Ruth stood on a high, dry rock at the edge, looking down, wavering, and Dean saw what Ruth must have known for the last ten years: David Boyd would have known to rock-hop the strongest and swiftest currents. He would have hiked the steep sidehill up the cliff, trusting the footholds of damp earth over the crumbling stepping-stones and wet ledges. He would have known better than to stand on the edge of a half-frozen waterfall. He never would have done a handstand.

The wind shifted, and Dean heard Ruth's voice above the water's white noise. She was still standing on the precipice, looking down, but not at him. She was fussing directly at a young family climbing the dry boulders below her, telling them to get down off the rocks before they killed themselves. The father stood shirtless on a high rock, holding his toddler son against his shins, while his wife stood below, looking nervous, swearing, "I'll not go up there. I'm staying right here." The man looked up at Ruth, his face puzzled. She was waving, the water's white noise washing away most of what she was saying.

Dean took the side trail up the cliff, moved under the covered bridge, determining how he should approach Ruth without startling her. He stepped toward her slowly, walking between the ankle-twisting basins. As he approached the edge, the air turned briny, as though the water were coming from the sea. Before Dean reached Ruth, she turned to him and sat cross-legged on the high, bald rock beside a dry tidal basin filled with brown, empty beer bottles. Dean walked the rest of the way and sat on the other side of the basin.

"You always come up here to yell at the tourists?"

"Only the foolish ones."

Dean nodded toward the empty beer bottles. "That right there is how people get killed up here. They drink too much and climb on the falls and slip. Sometimes, they bring their dogs with them, and when their dogs fall over, they get killed trying to save their dogs."

"My son wasn't a drinker," Ruth said flatly. "We never had a dog."

Dean looked down at the tourists. The father had climbed another rock, pulling the child up with him. As the child teetered against his shins, the father held up his son's pudgy arm and waved down to his wife.

"I knew it before it happened," Ruth said. "I was the first one to see him. It was like you see in the movies, all that yellow police tape."

"This is a private story," Dean warned. "You don't have to tell it."

Ruth nodded, as though deciding. Dean looked away, watched the family on the high rocks below, the young father climbing higher, more foolhardy than brave, playfully taunting his terrified wife. Dean felt like an imposter, like Ruth had mistaken him for a kinder man, a good listener, when the truth was that he remained quiet because he didn't know what to say.

"After I left here, I was crazy for a while," Ruth said. "I drank too much wine. I checked myself into a rehab center, but they sent me home. They said I didn't have a drinking problem, but that I probably could use a psychiatrist. Then I got married again. I guess I thought if I married a religious man I'd be closer to heaven, to my son, but you already know how that turned out," Ruth said. "Sometimes, when I'm up here, I'll see a rhododendron budding, and I'll feel as raw as if it happened last week. Sometimes I come up here hoping I might find him and that things might go differently." She stopped. "Tell me, do you think that's crazy?"

Dean shook his head. Grief was neither sane nor insane; it was a natural force that could drive a person to the edge, sometimes over it. He longed for his wife to be with him now, answering Ruth's hard question with her own harder ones: *Why do you keep returning to the source of your greatest sorrow? What truth will you find if you ever come upon it?*

He looked down at the family on the rocks below. "Wait here," he said.

Quickly, Dean walked back across the rocks and into the woods. The steep, downward path was criss-crossed with fossilized roots and smelled of fermenting vines. He stepped across the roots, as though walking a web of unburied bones. At the bank, he stopped beside a fallen tree that arched out over the shallows, watching a crawfish scuttling beneath a limb. Then he crossed out onto the rocks and stood beside the woman, who was weeping now. He called up to the man.

"See that lady up there?" He pointed to Ruth. "She's got something she's been trying to tell you. Would you let the lady speak?" The man looked at Dean, then up at Ruth. She was standing again, her hands on her hips. Dean called up to her, "I've got his attention now. He's listening. You can tell him what you need to say."

The wind had died a little, and Ruth's hair had stopped thrashing. She scaled down one of the rocks so that she could talk to the man in an almost-regular voice. "Even somebody who knew what he was doing wouldn't be climbing where you're taking your son," she said. "It's not the waterfall that's dangerous. They don't reach out and kill people. Death happens when people get too close, too caught up in the moment. The next thing you know, you're falling over."

The husband looked back at Dean, and Dean nodded at him. The man looked at his wife's frantic face, her empty arms reaching out to him. He handed the child down to her. After the man sidled down to safety, Dean went back to Ruth. She had climbed back up to the top of the falls, but whatever force had driven her barefoot up to this precipice had left her, and she sat quietly, her shoulders so stooped and weary that for the first time he saw how she belonged with Luther. Dean took her boots from his shoulder, unknotted the strings, and kneeled at her feet. Her toes were long, the nails crushed and unpolished, the callused soles raw from walking barefoot. He started to guide her feet into her boots. She shook her head, but her pretty and haggard face remained unguarded. Dean shouldered her boots and took her hand, led her across the dry stones toward the black bridge, away from the falls. They took the dusty logging road that switchbacked down the other side of the mountain, moving slowly down the longer, gentler incline until they reached the pullout. Dean helped Ruth into his truck.

Dean drove past the turnoff for his house and stopped his truck beside Luther's tomato field. Green seedlings had grown out of the rows of black gardening tarps. Luther was out in a middle row, bending on one knee, stringing the tender seedlings. All around him, the mountain ridge became a blur of pink and green. When the sun sank behind the mountain, a solid, black dome of sky covered the valley, flaking into stars that filled the pasture with a soft, clear light. When Luther went inside, Dean led Ruth into the pasture and stood behind her, pulling her toward him until her back rested against his chest.

They looked up and found Ursa Major and Ursa Minor, viewing the celestial bears the ancient way, finding the big dipper in the she-bear's rump and tail. Locating the North Star in Ursa Minor, he talked of how the earth sometimes wobbled and celestial poles shifted, but that you could stand in this inviolate meadow, in any season, and find your way by looking up at the North Star. Lifting Ruth's arms out to each side, he held them up with his own, and their bodies became one sturdy compass, the North in front of them, the South behind. "Rest easy," he whispered, "The closer we remain to this place, the more we know who we are."

Ruth was softer than he'd expected. Her hair and skin smelled of apples and limestone water. His chest ached, as though he were thawing into her womanly warmth, and he couldn't help comparing her tall, thin body to Sadie's short, sturdier one. He wanted to wrap his arms completely around Ruth's waist and fall into the soft grass with her. They were still touching, but she seemed distant, unreachable, and the whole valley had filled with the smell of her husband's tomato vines. He saw the river furling and unfurling across his and Luther's property lines in the dark distance and knew that he could not take what had never belonged to him.

He let Ruth's arms drop gently and stepped away, urging her toward Luther's place, "He's waiting on you. Go on."

Ruth nodded, heading toward Luther's homestead. Across the pasture, the white horse grazed, beautiful and unshy in the snowy moonlight, and Dean felt that if he walked toward her she would let him pet her, and she would be his. But even after Ruth walked into the dark doorway of Luther's cabin, Dean continued to stand in the pasture, content to admire the horse from a distance. A soft wind blew across the wild oats, tousling her mane. The horse looked up, catching his scent. She walked toward pines at the edge of the pasture. She kept moving, climbing slowly up the first ridge.

🌼 Hannah, 1973

Rooms People Live In

HANNAH'S FATHER HAD LEFT most of the heavier tasks unfinished, but he insisted on filling a washtub with the fallen green apples that covered the ground in the old orchard. She watched him from the back porch as he lifted the tub to his shoulder, carried it down to the back of his two-acre lawn, and dumped the fruit over the stone boundary wall. His arms and legs were tanned and muscular, but his stomach puffed from the blood-thinning medicine. As he turned to make a second trip, she walked down the hill to stop him.

"You should be resting, or fishing," she said. "You shouldn't be out here working."

She'd just driven from Ohio to Virginia against her husband's warnings, ignoring all the childbirth books that said her baby should have moved by now, the sixteenth week of pregnancy. She was more worried about her father. A blood clot hung from one of his bypasses, ready to shoot into his weak heart. The week before, Rosie, her father's sometime girlfriend, had called Hannah to report that he still spent his days cultivating the plot of land behind his house. At night, Rosie said, he slept wrapped in a serape on the living room floor, sometimes wandering deep into the woods while smoking unfiltered cigarettes. He refused to write a will. Then Dean had called Hannah himself, asking her to come home for her own baptism, though neither of them had entered a church since her mother's funeral seven years before. When Hannah had lived at home, while Sadie had been alive, Dean had always taken an extra shift at the railroad or gone out to work on his family's land, during the Sunday service; as a widower, he'd grown nostalgic for his wife's religion.

"It's your afterlife," Dean had said over the phone. "But if I were you, I'd let the deacon throw me into the deepest part of Wolf Creek."

It was late August now. Deer and cattle grazed the foothills beyond the yard of his stone house. Wild Shetland ponies roamed out of the woods toward the fence, to eat the dumped apples, backing into the canopy when Hannah reached out to pet them. Father and daughter walked up through the yard, past the Sheltie that ran the length of its chain and snarled at Hannah. Behind the house, her father had built a pond stream down the sloping lawn. Hauling five truckloads of stone from a ridge pocket up on the East River lookout, he'd built it the old-timey way, stacking stone upon stone, mortaring them with sand and mud, tucking fiddlehead ferns between them.

"I built this in only one day." Dean smiled proudly at the pond stream. "Makes this yard feel like the old homeplace."

Hannah frowned at her father as he rubbed his left shoulder, knowing that telling him to rest was useless. Her father had never rested, not even in sickness. When she was a child, Dean had been a shifter and then a railroad officer, grading tidewater coal shipped out to Norfolk. After the first heart attack, he'd retired from the railroad to become a contractor, a plumber, and an electrician. He'd built houses all over the county and took out loans against those houses to build more. He'd taken a trailer as payment for a one-bedroom house; he'd financed the mortgage loans for several others. After his last heart attack, he'd been forced to sell his building business. The frames of his unfinished houses remained on lots all over town, emerging from mountains of hard mud, sometimes coal. Bored and restless in retirement, he'd built the pond stream in one day, sending himself back into the hospital with chest pains. Hannah reasoned that the long-distance driving would cause less risk to her unborn child than all the time she spent worrying about her father.

Inside, the house smelled like woods and river water. A dark mahogany dining room table with nine chairs, a highboy, and a giant walnut hutch were crammed into the tiny living room. Dean had brought out his wife's Bible, opening it on the marble coffee table, displaying a color picture of the River Jordan.

"Jesus came up from Nazareth of Galilee and was baptized by John in the Jordan," Dean said. Hannah nodded, thinking he needed encouragement. He closed the Bible.

"You look pretty, Hannah." He looked at her stomach. "You'll gain all your baby weight in your belly like your mother did. When she was expecting, she looked like she was hiding a melon under her dress." He grabbed Hannah's wrist, placing another book in her hand. "I want you to have this," he said. "It belonged to your grandmother. I have no use for it."

Hannah opened the 1920s medical counselor to pages filled with advice on childbirth and venereal disease. She found pictures of small children with tumors on their lips and between their fingers, a portrait of a woman with an engorged breast swaddled in a cotton sling.

"The book says that children can be born with water on the brain," he said. "Their heads are so large they must be delivered feet first."

Hannah shut the book. "I can't listen to this kind of talk right now."

"I'm to blame for my sickness," Dean said. "I'm being punished because I have not lived a Godly life. The church would cave in on my head if I walked through its doors."

"You have heart disease," she said. "You're not sick because you skipped church."

Dean's eyes flashed with a familiar rage, but Hannah didn't regret her admonition. Instead, she remembered why she'd avoided a homecoming for so long. She put the book by the kitchen sink and followed him out the back door.

Outside, Dean climbed onto the roof. As he pulled up rusty, ragged shingles, Hannah caught her breath. Her father's blood was so thin he could not risk shaving every day. She imagined him falling, the blood from his broken ribs filling up until he burst.

"Why don't you fry up some chicken," he called down to her. "We'll go to Wolf Creek for a picnic."

"You keep eating like that, and they'll have to put you back in the hospital."

Dean wiped his hands on his jeans. "Go on and get yourself something to eat." He turned back to his work, and she walked back into the house.

THAT NIGHT, HANNAH WAITED FOR DEAN to come home from the grocery. She felt she'd spent her whole childhood waiting for her father, who often disappeared at dusk, saying simply, "I'm going to check on some land." He always returned in a few days with an armload of winter apples or October beans, or, once, an antique banjo with its back removed.

"For resonance," he'd said, leaning the instrument against the stove and placing a miniature tape recorder that played the sounds of "Dueling Banjos" before her mother's folded hands. "That's me playing," he'd said. "I learned how by listening, without any notes."

As she waited for her father to return that night, she sat in the kitchen, where the tables and sink counters were stacked with grocery sacks filled with snap beans, potatoes, sweet onions, and corn. Her mother had canned and preserved, but even though she was gone, Dean still brought home the produce. The produce sat for weeks, eventually turning to foul liquid that seeped through the corners of the bags.

Hannah threw away sprouting potatoes and softening onions. She was just about to sterilize some canning jars when Dean came into the kitchen with his tackle box.

"Let me see your wedding ring." He tied fishing line around her ring and let it dangle over her stomach. "If it twirls in a circle, the baby will be a girl. If it swings back and forth, it's a boy." They took turns with the ring. Hannah swung it back and forth because, though she had no medical proof, she knew that the baby would be a boy. But as she watched her father twirling the ring, she doubted herself. She began to dread the end of her pregnancy. She wanted this child to live safely inside her forever, bouncing against soft bags of fluid in the red darkness.

"You can baptize your infant," Dean said. "You can even baptize yourself if you need to."

Hannah could not stand anymore. Her lower back ached and her feet were swollen. She went to the bathroom and drew a bath, swirling the sweet apple tree bark that Dean had given her into the lukewarm water. She opened her own childbirth manual near the section on the end of pregnancy, the thirty-sixth week, and the pages threatened her with symptoms of perinatal death. While reading the section on spina bifida, she couldn't stop thinking of her father spinning her wedding ring over her unborn child, reciting the ritual prayers for baptism.

She rose slowly, feeling weak and heavy with water as she stepped out of the tub. She pulled her husband's T-shirt over her head and stomach and crawled into the bed. She stuffed pillows between her knees and behind her back, though she didn't need them yet. She set the phone next to her, pulling the quilt over her head, and dialing her own phone number. By the time Joseph answered, she was nearly crying.

"I'm getting baptized in a creek tomorrow," she said.

"Is that safe?" he asked.

"It's more like a small river," she said. "But it's perfectly safe."

"Then why are you crying? Where are you? You sound like you're in a cave."

"What if our baby is born with a spinal cord outside his vertebrae, or a heart outside his chest?"

"Please stop reading that childbirth book," Joseph said. "They put those illnesses in there to spice the chapters up."

"What should we do with this baby?"

"What?"

"It needs to be baptized."

"I thought you weren't religious."

"I'm not," she said. "But what if the baby grows up and resents us because we didn't take it to church?"

"I'm coming down there in the morning," he said.

"No. Stay where you are. You won't have anything to do here."

"Please, try to sleep," he said.

"I'll be home in a few days."

While waiting for sleep, Hannah regretted not booking a hotel room. In her cramped childhood bed, she grew uneasy with memories of her mother. When Hannah was a sophomore in college, Sadie found a tumor in her breast but didn't tell anyone until the cancer had spread into her bones. The final winter of her mother's life, Hannah had come home for Christmas break, rising early to sit with her mother in the dim kitchen beneath the Norfolk and Southern clock that had stopped keeping time. With hopes of tempting Sadie to eat, Dean stayed up one night, making every one of Sadie's candy recipes. Then he'd taken off somewhere in his truck, leaving behind a mess in the kitchen. Sadie had surveyed the marzipan foaming over the sides of pots, the peanut butter balls dripping on wax paper between the oven burners, and looked weary.

"Where does he go when he leaves this house?" she'd said. "What have we lost him to?"

Neither Sadie nor Hannah turned on the lights or cleaned up Dean's cooking mess. Instead, they sat together in the darkness, eating the candy. Sadie tested out the penuche on her chemo-cracked tongue while Hannah ate a row of peanut butter balls, eying the polished tamarack cane leaning against the hutch. Hannah had given it to her mother when her femur had broken, but Sadie refused to use it. She looked younger than thirty-six, her round face glowing against the silky tufts of pure white hair that had grown back since she stopped all the chemo treatments.

Watching her mother, Hannah felt her chest and lungs ache with grief and terror. She could not speak for fear of weeping. Sadie kept talking in her soft mountain voice, telling the old family story of how, when she was only twelve, she'd saved her younger brother's life by walking up the mountain to Dean's mother's house every day for a cup of milk.

"I did this every morning and every evening, just so the milk would be fresh," Sadie said.

Hannah knew her mother retold this story to buoy her up, to assure her that Hannah would have the same quiet strength after Sadie was gone, when the time came to save what was left of the family. But after Sadie's funeral, when Dean asked Hannah to stay on "to keep the family together," Hannah had turned on him, accusing him of wearing her mother out.

"She *was* this family," she'd said. "Now that she's gone, I don't see the point in staying."

Now, she regretted her own cruelty, but she didn't regret leaving. As she waited for sleep, Hannah longed for the early weeks of pregnancy, when the manual was concerned only with the size of the fetus. *Your baby is the size of a green pea, an olive, a small, ripe peach.* She saw herself anointing the wet forehead of her own child with trembling fingers, giving a mother's blessing, stronger than any preacher's. She missed her husband, wanted to move her stomach against his back so that he would wake in the night, as she did, unnerved, wondering if she would ever feel the baby's elbows and feet kicking. She dozed, dreaming of her young mother running up the mountain with an empty tin cup in her hand, clouds pouring over the ridge. A summer storm began, and the rain began clattering on her father's roof. Hannah imagined it flooding the yard, the kitchen, the bedrooms, and the cellar. Growing up here, she always had plenty of water, and plenty of milk.

HANNAH WOKE AT SEVEN the next morning, when Dean's pickup crunched over the gravel driveway. She went downstairs to the kitchen. He wore the same muddy jeans she'd seen him in the day before, and he smelled of tobacco. He scooped shortening into a measuring cup filled with water so that it wouldn't stick, then mixed it into powdered sugar for the baptismal cake's icing.

"Are you hungry?" Dean asked.

"Always," she said.

He pulled a plate down from the cupboard and filled it with ham and biscuits, poured some buttermilk into a glass and told her to sit. He began to hum "Shall We Gather At the River." Watching him beat the cake icing, Hannah remembered why she loved her father. He took such pleasure in making things with his hands.

Every time Dean visited Hannah in Ohio, he brought hand-carved bookcases that he'd built in his barn at the old homeplace up on Wilderness Road, spending weeks crafting the furniture, polishing the wood with twenty coats of varnish. When Hannah and Joseph bought their first house, Dean had slept on the floor of the still-empty living room the night before they moved in. He seemed to hear the crackle of faulty wiring, feel the foundation sinking into the ground. The next morning, he'd met them at the door, saying that houses took on the spirits of those who lived in them, and that the rooms of their new house were filled with good ones.

"I'm going to sell this place," Dean said, looking around the kitchen. "Build a bigger house up on Wilderness Road, where the old farmhouse used to be."

"How will you pay for it?" Hannah asked.

"I've got some land I could sell," he said.

Her father's land. All her life, she'd heard stories about his family's forty-seven acres of land, the money that would come in when natural gas and thirty-foot coal seams were discovered upon it, the lawyer that would help him make a fortune from thirty percent of the gas and coal money when it came in. Nobody in the family had ever seen all the land, the lawyer, or the money.

"Baptism's in twenty minutes," Hannah said.

Nervous about the ceremony, Hannah left her food and hurried upstairs to change. She stepped into a yellow maternity swimsuit, and the empty front panel of cloth sagged against her softly swelling abdomen. She pulled a white choir robe over her head and brushed her auburn hair into a loose bun. In the mirror, her body looked like a candle flame muted beneath the filmy gown, and she felt even more anxious. She wanted to be heavy with this child, feel its kicks, and hear its strong heartbeat.

Dean wanted to take the scenic route to Wolf Creek. He helped Hannah into his pickup and pulled the seat belt over her, watching as she adjusted the belt beneath her stomach before he closed the door. As she waited for her father to start the car, she counted fifteen paper coffee cups on the floor below the passenger seat. She smelled the pine air freshener meant to camouflage his stale cigarette smoke. As a small child, she'd felt privileged to sit in the passenger seat of his truck, listening to him tell stories on himself, blowing smoke. He'd flip his two false front teeth out with his tongue, claiming to be just like James Moore, the captive of Abbs Valley who was kidnapped by Shawnee Indians. To escape, he'd knocked out his own front teeth and used them to sever the ropes that bound his wrists. Hannah knew that parts of her father's story were as unlikely as the forty-seven acres of hidden coal and gas on his family's land, but she longed for a time when she still believed her father's mythology.

Dean drove slowly. He seemed to be on his own schedule, oblivious to those who waited for them at the creek. He raced the muddy water that ran beside the truck, slowing beneath the swing bridges. Dean stopped the car under a railroad bridge and unrolled his window to hear the hum of the Norfolk and Southern over their heads.

"Listen," he said. "We're being run over by a train." When the train passed, her father started the car. He lectured Hannah on the hardships of parenting and childbirth.

"I'm not gonna lie," he said. "I was there when you were born, and I have seen how the act of birth will shake a woman body and soul."

"Dad, I don't want to hear this," she said.

He continued, "During my last heart attack, when I was unconscious, I dreamed I went all the way up to the pearly gates. I tried to make a deal with St. Peter to let me bring your mother back down with me. He wouldn't, so I just turned around and came back empty-handed."

Hannah wanted to change the subject. "Were you baptized in Wolf Creek?"

Dean nodded. "Your mother wouldn't marry me until I got baptized. After the ceremony was over and everybody went home, we snuck back to fish below the baptizing place. We figured all that blessing and baptizing would make the fish around here bigger."

As they headed down the mountain, coal seams formed jagged black walls on either side of the road. The sky was a dull sepia, and a soft warm rain fell. Dean pointed to a two-story pine home nearly hidden by evergreens and giant ferns. "That's one of mine," he said. "If you move back here, I can build you a house like that." He always said this, and they both knew that she would never move back. This time, his words seemed more like a polite wish than a hostile reproach. The front of the house was all glass, and she wondered where the owners dressed or made love in a place with so many windows.

Concrete trucks were parked alongside a creek lined by pitch pine and fallen timber. The drivers had cleaned their trucks out in this stretch of water, and after years of dumping, a sheet of pale concrete had hardened like a layer of melting snow around the rim of the baptismal pool. Elderly women in bright church dresses with lace collars walked unsteadily on the concrete, so close to the edge that from a distance they appeared to be tottering on water. The preacher stood at the shore. A barrel-chested man whose burned scalp showed through his thin white hair, he greeted every church member, clasping each single outstretched hand with both of his beefy hands.

Dean and Hannah stood in awkward silence, looking eagerly into the brown and silted pond, as though the water could tell them what to do next. Hannah picked jewelweed, its yellow pods bursting in her hands. Dean spat absentmindedly into the pool.

A single bream rose, rippling the water, the tiny waves widening until the pond's surface resembled the top of a rusted tin can. The preacher walked over to greet them. He shook her father's hand and waved the other towards the sky. He smiled at Hannah, though his eyes looked beyond her. He spoke jovially, impersonally, as if to an entire congregation. "We're having good Baptist weather today."

Hannah tried to joke with the pastor to ease her own nerves. "Don't you mean Baptism weather?"

Her father hushed her with a glance, but the pastor looked away, toward the creek and the arriving church members, as if he hadn't heard her at all.

Downstream, the water quickened, splashing against sharp boulders, sucking and swallowing itself. Two fishermen drank beer from Styrofoam coolers and cast lines out into the churning water. At the center, the deacon stood on a sandbar, calling for her. Standing at the water's edge, Hannah stuck her toe in the chill water, and a piece of silt stuck to it. She shivered as the wind cut through her bathing suit and thin robe. She began to regret coming here. She'd been so careful throughout her early weeks of pregnancy, trying to keep her baby weight at twenty pounds, steering clear of sugar so the baby wouldn't grow too big. She'd thrown out her morning sickness pills, chewing on peppermint and anise seeds to get through the worst days of nausea. Now, she wondered if the shock of this icy water would harm the baby. Would the baby ingest parasites hidden within the silted water she swallowed when the deacon held her under? Her mother would have known the answers to these questions. Perhaps, if Sadie were still alive, Dean wouldn't have had this late-life conversion to her church. Maybe he wouldn't have needed to call his daughter home to this confounding baptism. Hannah knew for certain that she wouldn't have found herself standing, pregnant and terrified, at the edge of a creek surrounded by concrete and dwindling wilderness.

Hannah longed for her mother's comfort, but when she turned back from the water she saw only her father. He nodded, urging her forward, "Go on." She waded out to the deacon.

A frail man with chest-high fishing waders on beneath his robe, the deacon steadied her against the current, saying, "Do you accept Christ as your savior?"

"Yes," she said, unsure if she would be saved. She knew only that agreeing with him would ensure that the ceremony would end more quickly.

He touched the small of her back and placed his other hand across her mouth and nose. "In the name of the Father." He dipped her backwards into the water, holding her in a clumsy embrace. While she gasped for air, he said, "In the name of the Son," and pushed her head under a second time.

She closed her eyes against the black water that filled her ears and seeped into her mouth. She pushed against the deacon's thin arms, but he held her down.

"In the name of the Holy Ghost and Amen." When the deacon pushed her under a third time, she slipped from his hands. She sank away from him, feeling free and weightless, almost holy. She remembered a life-saving course she'd taken in college, when she'd jumped into the ten-foot end of a pool fully clothed. She'd kicked off her water-heavy shoes and let them sink to the bottom. She'd removed her jeans and tied the legs together, tossing them over her head, blowing into them until they ballooned. She'd felt saved, her bare feet suddenly light as fins, her own breath-filled pants keeping her afloat. The deacon's bony fingers clamped down hard on her shoulders and pulled her up to air and light. River silt clung to her skin, and her sinuses stung. She didn't feel blessed. She felt soggy and unclean.

Then it was over. The church crowd thinned as the deacon escorted her out of the water, her arm draped over his shoulder. He handed her over to her father. Dean pulled a beach towel around her, forming a tent with the towel so that she could put on dry clothes. Smiling proudly, he walked over to his truck. He pulled two fishing rods out of the truck bed and handed one to her.

"It's family tradition," he said.

Hannah didn't recall sharing this tradition with her mother or father, but she shrugged and accepted the pole. She knew how to fish but had never liked it. She'd always read on an open, sunny bank while her parents picked their way through stinging nettles and clouds of mosquitoes to cast their lines. Now, fishing alone with her father, she cast between two logs and pulled a bluegill out. The fish was dull, bluish-green, prehistoric.

"Don't touch it," Dean said. "They're prickly. Here, use my gloves."

She put the gloves on and handled the fish, releasing it. As she cast her line under a limb two feet off the stream, Dean explained how Confucius was one of the early fishermen, and that he'd tied feathers to a string, casting the string into rivers, imitating the movements of a fly on water. Hannah developed a gentle rhythm of her own, tossing her line out with hopes of pulling a fighting trout back in.

"I found a sawmill in Hurley," Dean said. "Why pay a lumber company when I can cut my own pine and avoid the middleman? After I rebuild the old farmhouse, I'm going to make you some furniture. What kind of furniture do you want? How about a cherry wood cradle?"

"Dad, I need to know how you want me to settle your affairs."

"After I finish this new house—"

"There won't be another house," she said, then, softly. "I don't care about your money."

Her father turned sharply away from her. She held the first trout delicately, careful not to wipe the protective slime from its body, daintily working the hook out of its mouth. The next trout struck so fiercely that she had to use the pliers to twist the hook out of its stomach. It fought and bled in her hands as she wrestled with the deep-set hook, and when it died she spread it on the bank grass, sitting beside it.

"Is there someone else taking care of everything for you?" she said. "A woman?"

"Your mother may not have been the only woman, but she was my only love," he said. He took both fishing poles and threw them into the bed of the truck. "Come on. I want to show you something."

He didn't look back as they climbed the game trail leading to Wilderness Road. They reached the ruins of the old, burned-down farmhouse. Its brick porch steps rose to a few scattered footers and a crumbling chimney overgrown with ivy. Behind the ruins of the house, the pond stream had become a swollen tear in the earth, stitched together by chunks of gray limestone that tumbled down the slope. A wave of goldenrod spilled into what must have been the kitchen garden, ebbing and flowing over a bed of rosemary and lavender bushes that were as large as prehistoric plants. Hannah followed her father along the pebbled path lined by pear, apple, and plum trees; they walked through an arbor trellised with Scottish roses that tangled with wild muscadine. Beyond the arbor, where the understory began, Hannah saw the head of a stone woman resting in the shade among the high weeds and deep green ferns. Her features worn down by wind and rain, her large eyes looked half-closed, and her wild hair swirled softly around her round face. Hannah thought she looked like a savage goddess who'd emerged from the deepest part of the woods. She sat sentinel and sleepy, watching over the ruins of the house and its gardens.

Hannah had never seen the unearthly woman before. She wondered if her father had brought her home from one of the auctions he haunted, or if he'd carved her from one of the stones lying on the property. Before she could ask, Dean walked past the sculpture, heading toward the black barn at the top of the hill. A metal "Keep Out" sign made from an expired license plate hung on the door of the barn. As they moved closer, Hannah noticed the new shingles on the roof, shiny white gutters, and a rainspout. Her father gripped the rusty padlock on the door, pulled a key from his pocket, and unlocked it.

"I always thought this property could have been the next Gatlinburg," he said.

It began to rain again. Her father's breathing strained in the wet air as he forced the heavy, warped door open with his shoulder. He switched on the single bare light bulb hanging above their heads. "I know a man who's an architect. He said he would draft up blueprints for a theme park to build on this land if I ever wanted him to."

Inside, the barn was filled with antique oak, walnut, and cherry furniture. Leaning against the walls were double ovens, red oak trim, a mahogany door, a stained glass window. It looked as though an entire mansion had been broken into pieces and crammed into this one, cavernous room.

"Your grandmother was the one who gave me this barn and all the property around it before she died," he said. "I saw in *House Beautiful* that you can fix these barns up real nice and live in them. You're the only one who knows about this place now. When I'm gone, you'll be the one to divvy this stuff up to the rest of the family."

What family? Hannah thought. "Where did you get all this?" she said.

"When the mining was gone, people just left their homes with what they could carry. They left all these fine antiques for the fire department to burn. I bought it all, a little at a time. I meant to have the house ready for your mother, but I never got to it."

Hannah recalled her mother's favorite saying about her father: "My Prince Charming won't just knock on my door. He'll build it." Hannah knew that, like her mother, she'd never see her father complete this house. She remembered a time when she was in college, when her father had asked her to read to him from her Italian primer. She'd read the phrase, "When an American woman is hungry, she is angry."

"Say it again." He'd clapped his hands, his face filled with awe and pleasure. Now, she wanted more than anything to see her father this way again. She lifted the small stained glass window.

"Where will you put this?" she asked.

"I'll put it over the front door," he said.

She propped the window against the door. She carried a quilt rack over to the foot of the four-poster bed and placed marble lamps on the end tables, pushing them to either side of the bed. When she finished with the bedroom, she created a small sitting room, arranging yellowed *Time* magazines in the slots of the magazine rack. She left the big pieces of furniture alone, building imaginary rooms around them, careful not to lift more than twenty pounds or risk the baby's safety. Then she stopped, feeling the first, soft trembling, like tiny moth wings quivering inside her abdomen, a thrill so brief she caught her breath when it ended. Her father took the small woven rug from her arms.

"It's okay," she said. "The baby moved."

Her father smiled, taking his shirt off to work. He unrolled the rug in front of a lounge chair, carried the heavy wingbacks to the corners she pointed to, pushing a walnut player piano to the center of the floor.

After an hour, Hannah stood back to examine their work. The makeshift rooms were tiny, cramped, but strangely comforting.

"How do you like it?" she asked, finally.

Her father stood in the center of it all, running his thumbs over the dusty surfaces of his hoarded legacy. He seemed like the proprietor of a carefully organized yard sale, nodding, assuring himself that each piece of furniture had been arranged to resemble those rooms people lived in. He placed a hand to his chest, which had been shaved, the skin pale compared to his rugged face. When he reached for her, she drew back, repulsed by the upraised scar running through his sternum like a shiny jagged crack. Then she leaned into him, stunned by this sudden closeness. She shut her eyes and listened to the relentless sound of rain.

Parts of this book first appeared in *Shenandoah* (Fall 2007 & Fall 2009), *New Letters*, *Crab Orchard Review*, *Best New Writing 2007*, *Expecting Goodness*, "World Voices International Chapbook Series" by Webdelsol.com, *Contemporary World Literature*, *Serving House Journal*, and *The Girl With Red Hair*.

Acknowledgments

Thank you to all members of Hub City Press for their devoted attention to getting this book made. Special thanks to Betsy Teter for expertly shepherding this book all the way through the production process, to the talented artist Emily Smith for designing the book, and to proofreaders Jill McBurney, Megan DeMoss, Lyn Riddle, and Emily Harbin.

Thank you to Josephine Humphreys for selecting this book as winner of the 2012 South Carolina First Novel Prize; thanks to the South Carolina Arts Commission for supporting this contest and for providing so many opportunities to artists and writers.

Thank you to C. Michael Curtis, who believed in this book and offered virtuoso editing and writing advice about matters large and small.

Thank you to Walter Cummins, Tom Kennedy, Bob Stewart, R.T. Smith and all the other people who edited and published portions of this book in journals and anthologies.

Thank you to Rachel Hall and Melinda Defrain, good friends and writing partners who read first, middle and last drafts of each chapter, offering vital insights and steadfast encouragement over the years. Special thanks to Rachel Hall and Bob Olmstead, who read the entire book manuscript once it was finished, and then reassured me that I was done.

Thank you to my colleagues at Converse College, especially Melissa Walker, Anita Rose and Rick Mulkey, for answering my abundant questions about Appalachian history and culture.

Thank you to my colleagues and students in the Converse College MFA in Creative Writing program, who listened to me read portions of this book during our summer and winter residencies over the last few years, and cheered me on.

Thank you to my mother-in-law, Mary Mulkey, for telling me her family's stories at her kitchen table; thanks to Grace Gosheff for tape recording my own family's stories and mailing those invaluable tapes to me. Both of these women passed away while I completed this novel, but their voices linger on in its pages.

Thank you to my mom and dad, Nancy and Paul Tekulve.

And finally, my deepest thanks to my husband, Rick, and my son, Hunter, always.

HUB CITY PRESS

HUB CITY PRESS is an independent press in Spartanburg, South Carolina, that publishes well-crafted, high-quality works by new and established authors, with an emphasis on the Southern experience. We are committed to high-caliber novels, short stories, poetry, plays, memoir, and works emphasizing regional culture and history. We are particularly interested in books with a strong sense of place.

Hub City Press is an imprint of the non-profit Hub City Writers Project, founded in 1995 to foster a sense of community through the literary arts. Our metaphor of organization purposely looks backward to the nineteenth century when Spartanburg was known as the "hub city," a place where railroads converged and departed.

RECENT HUB CITY PRESS FICTION

The Iguana Tree • Michel Stone

Mercy Creek • Matt Matthews

My Only Sunshine • Lou Dischler

Expecting Goodness & Other Stories • C. Michael Curtis, editor

Through the Pale Door • Brian Ray

TEXT   Monotype Bulmer 11.7 / 15.5
DISPLAY   Monotype Bulmer Italic 20